Shadows of Eternity

J.M. MULLER

Shadows of Eternity
Book 3 of the Colors of Immortality series

Print ISBN: 979-8-9895815-2-8

This story was derived from a mind that enjoys fantasy a little too much, and is completely fictitious. Any similarities to living people (or dead, for that matter) is entirely coincidental and should be deduced as pure happenstance. The opinions expressed by the protagonist (who isn't real) or the villains (who REALLY aren't real)—and every character in between—belong to those characters and not the author. This work is fiction and should be treated as such.

For JD. Because you wouldn't let me quit. Because you cared. Because you're you, and I think that's pretty damn great.

A MESSAGE FROM THE AUTHOR

Dear Reader,

Chances are you're already familiar with my style. With how I write, and the dark twists I like to take. You most likely know how I arrange a story—both at the start and the back. But just in case you're not, allow me to touch on a few things.

For starters, please don't skip "The Legend" following the epilogue. It is, without fail, my favorite part. It gives insight. Perhaps a little clarity. It may even soften a villain.

Secondly, the *Colors of Immortality* series is dark, and often deals with heavy topics and tragic situations. I'd like to remind readers to read with care (because it never hurts to bring up this sort of thing).

And, lastly, thank you. (I can never NOT mention this.)

Thank you for taking a chance on this story and for taking a chance on me.

I appreciate you. For your support. For picking up these pages. For giving these words a go.

My gratitude is ever present.

Sincerely,
J.M. Muller

CONTENTS

CHAPTER 1
REBIRTH

It was odd being away from the trees and seeing the clouds, the sky, feeling the falling rays on my shoulders. The sun was slipping beyond the horizon and it shifted the meadow to a shade of gold, warming me in ways a fire never could. I'd taken the openness for granted and longed to push back time, to relive freedom that only endless sky could provide.

I realized something about myself, if I could've picked any place to live, I would've selected the desert.

Where trees didn't exist.

Where Thorn's power wasn't that powerful.

Where away from her, away from Narivous, there was still much to live for—even for a wretched, undead soul such as myself.

Sun was hope.

I wanted infinite sun. Let it cover me. Scald me. Burn me. Anything other than the shadows.

I kept my eyes closed and inhaled, breathing in the disarrayed smells of fading summer with its warm soil and rotting mulch.

A delighted squeal punctuated the tranquility, adding to the quality of the moment.

Her sound was the most welcomed sound. Especially in its joyous stage.

It beat the natural hum of nature.

I opened my eyes to see Lacey pounce after a butterfly, her red hair cascading back like a kite tail, her entire frame moving in a blur.

"I got another one," she shouted—albeit, in a Narivous level shout—so it was more like a soft exclaim. We naturally spoke in gentler tones, our hearing detected even the subtlest of sounds.

A leaf falling.

An axe slicing through the air.

"What does that make?" I asked, sitting up and draping my forearms over my knees. The light bloomed in my eyes as it haloed around her. Vision was another heightened sense and out in the open like this it brightened in remarkable ways. "Six?"

"No." Lacey bounded toward me with the Animal grace her clan was known for, and swept up the jar next to me. She made careful work placing the butterfly inside and sealing the top. "This makes eight."

"I think you're lying."

"Here, look." She thrust the glass at me and gave it a gentle shake. I took it and made a show of inspecting it.

"Ah, you must've not told me about that second white one."

"Then that would make seven."

"When did you get so smart?"

She shrugged, and pointed to a small blue one about the

size of a harebell. “I think that one’s the prettiest. His name’s Gerald.”

“Gerald?”

“Yeah, Gerald.”

“How do you know it’s a boy?”

“Because he told me.” She beamed. Her bottom teeth had finally come in; they appeared too large for her small mouth—the way adult teeth often do. They flashed big and white.

I smiled and handed the jar back. She put it to her ear as their papery wings batted against the glass.

“Well then, Gerald it is. I think it’s a distinguished name.”

"Dis-ting-uished," she sounded it out, uncertain but still interested, and then she did what little kids are known to do—switch topics rapidly.

She began to rock on the balls of her feet. “Isn’t he the prettiest?”

“I think the word you’re looking for is handsome.”

“Boys can be pretty too.” She cradled her collection to her chest. Her eyes pivoted to a spot behind me where the city rested deep inside the forest. Her smile faltered. “Everyone is pretty in this place.” She leaned in and breathed into my ear, “And kinda scary.”

I cleared my throat and looked down.

She was right.

Everyone was beautiful here, boys included, no matter the features or physical alterations. Even Plague, with half his face missing, still had a mystical look to him.

Rotting flesh and all.

A trick of the mind? We all knew that was possible. Humans were susceptible to it. Who’s to say we weren’t as well?

Undead didn't mean unfeeling or incapable.

In our case it just meant different, for we experienced the world through a different lens.

And that lens shadowed Lacey's view of the world—a travesty considering she was killed and resurrected at a tender age.

She'd just turned six.

Life had only started for her.

And then Narivous took dastardly control of it.

"Gerald is both pretty and handsome, and not scary at all—like me and Dolly," I said. "I'm lucky to have you here to correct me when I'm wrong." I gave her a wink, only she met it with a leery glance.

I was scary no matter how much I tried to convince her otherwise.

And boy did I try to convince her otherwise.

When that didn't work, I angled toward diversion.

"I think I spotted a newcomer—one that's even prettier than Gerald," I said. I nudged my head toward the open meadow. "You better go get him before he flies away."

It worked; the spell shattered and Lacey bounded away. Someday I would run out of distractions and we'd have to have a hard conversation.

Until then, I chose the moment.

And in this moment, I watched her with a sort of unfamiliar contentment. I nearly smiled.

But then she froze and stared toward the forest. It was sudden and jerky.

The sort of action that spoke volumes beyond words.

I didn't hear her speak, but more or less saw her mouth form the words, "More are coming."

I followed her gaze. Behind me, two Velores emerged from the trees, they wore bags on their backs and moved without animation. It had been a constant trickle since Thorn had shut down her Army's home-base on the Southside.

She wanted them closer.

Narivous was swelling by the day, and with it the tension that came when a population distended beyond its capacity.

The duo kept along the path edging the forest, staying in the bounds of Narivous territory. They shot a quick look our way, and then did a double-take in my direction.

I knew what that look meant.

Before the suppression, I was a marvel. After the suppression, I was exalted. I had done something no other Poison had ever hoped to achieve.

I had pulled back my powers. I had made my aura go obsolete.

It gave Thorn hope she could find a cure to my toxic touch.

It filled me with resentment.

The taller of the two hesitated as if he were tempted to bridge the gap and introduce himself, the other tugged on his sleeve and shook his head no.

A wise decision.

Technically, we were in a forbidden spot. Hence why it was open. But with my rank—I was able to pull off the insubordination and get away with it.

Them—not so much.

The Velores quickly slid into the forest, disappearing like shadows. Lacey bounded up to me like a graceful fawn.

Her freckled cheeks lifted with a sheepish grin, and I knew what was coming. She placed her hands behind her back and rocked on her heels, distorting her sinewy frame like a sapling reaching for the sun.

"Can we go there again?" she asked. "To the special place?" She pulled her hands out and pointed in the opposite direction of Narivous.

I shook my head.

"Only for a second," she whispered.

"You and I both know it won't be only for a second."

"But I want to go."

"I told you before we came here that it wasn't an option and not to ask. And what are you doing?"

A pregnant pause stretched between us.

"I'm asking," she muttered.

"That's right." I sighed, being firm with her was never my strong suit, this took effort. "Look, Squirt, I need you to hold up your end of the bargain. You promised me, and I took you at your word. And you know what they say about someone's word?"

"We are only as good," she said.

"That's right. Now I want to go back too, but we can't."

"Why can't we?"

"It's a rule."

"It's a dumb rule."

I laughed and nodded. "That it is." Lacey nestled in beside me and crossed her legs, holding her jar in her lap.

"If I promise to be good and to listen?" she asked.

She bit her lip as if her words had betrayed her. She gripped the glass, and her claws poked out. I winced and looked away. They were nearly as long as her fingers with a lethal arc, made of gray material akin to bone.

"You're always good, it's just the listening part you need to work on. And you know we can't," I murmured. "You weren't supposed to go in there the last time, but you did it anyway. And then I nearly nicked my skin going in after you. And you know how dangerous that can be."

The poison particles running through my blood were swift and severe. There was a reason I wore gloves, and why I was careful to avoid cutting my flesh.

They wanted out.

I needed to keep them in.

"Yeah. Scary bad," Lacey said.

"Scary bad is right. So no, we can't go back. It's not safe."

"Nothing is safe anymore ..." she replied bitterly.

She had a point.

"C'mon, Squirt. If I could, I'd take you, honest, but we really can't."

"But—"

"No. And that's final."

She threw out her lip.

"Have I told you that stopped working about two years ago?" I indicated her pout. "When you went through this adorable, but terribly destructive four-year-old stage? And you tossed some of Gram's cat litter in my fish tank? Yeah, you lost your powers that day."

Lacey held her ground. She crossed her arms and if anything, exaggerated her objection.

"Do we need to go back home?" I asked, albeit not unkindly.

I could never be unkind to her.

She was my soft spot.

She turned, hiding her disappointment, and lifted herself from the ground. It was like floating, her bones nothing but air. She resumed her task of butterfly hunting, bolting down the soft hill toward a briar patch.

I shouldn't have told her about the house. Scream warned me it was off limits—that she shouldn't have even shown me. But she did. And I, in turn, took Lacey. I couldn't handle the sorrow that had settled on her; I wanted to detach it, even if only for a moment.

It was the distraction method.

To stop the hemorrhage of pain.

The house had the same effect on Lacey as it did on me. Scream said it was magic.

More powerful than any pull of the supernatural—it was history, time, and a story with hidden chapters begging to be discovered.

I fell back against the grass and closed my eyes. Maybe I didn't want endless sunshine. The light was beginning to hurt. My eyes had gotten accustomed to muted colors; brightness acted as an assault.

The desert at night.

Dark and open. Yeah. That felt more right. Closer to who I was.

I wasn't sure if I fell asleep, but by the time I opened my eyes Lacey was gone.

Dammit.

I knew where she went.

Perhaps I wanted her to go and subconsciously gave her an opportunity to do so.

The place really was magic.

I got to my feet and ran full-tilt into the forest, weaving around loosely placed trees, beyond the creek that cut through an old path, past the boulder angrily hunched over and sitting off to the side.

The poison beneath my skin didn't like this area. It hummed a warning that I didn't understand, but respected nonetheless.

I shuddered every time I passed through and kicked up speed.

In no time, I was upon it.

Where she wasn't supposed to go.

You could barely make it out through the thick skin of brambles, the stonework merely a glimpse in spots of weakness. This is the only place where Thorn's magic touched beyond Narivous' boundaries.

It meant this place was special.

And significant.

She had fenced it in, with briars so thick you couldn't make much sense of what rested behind it. I was certain, however, she only started the barrier. The newest growth was natural, the invasive nature of blackberries resuming the task of concealment.

I quickly located the small gap amidst the thorns that Lacey had managed to burrow her slender frame through. Same as last time.

The kid was predictable.

I kneeled and let my eyes hover over the soil, looking for disturbances other than those that were fresh. One was best to stay alert. If others had been here, it could be problematic. Narivous was a city full of snitches, opportunists looking to gain favor.

I silently cursed myself for showing this to Lacey. I knew better.

But I did it anyway.

It was three or four weeks after her transformation. Time didn't make much sense in the throes of grief, so I couldn't say for sure. It either lapsed quickly or refused to tick along at all.

However long it was, I couldn't stand her sorrow.

Or the hauntings of what caused that sorrow.

My hand instinctively went to my pocket, to the small weight I carried there. A token of pain. I didn't need to pull it out to gather strength from it.

Having it close was enough.

I was flooded with gratitude toward Dolly. She'd given it to me.

Dolly.

My unexpected savior. A refuge of contradictions. She used soft words to lash out cruel insults, but I think it was all a cover. She was warm but didn't like too many people to know.

With the exception of kids.

She was the source of love in the chilly castle. The beating heart Velores thought resonated from Thorn's quarters really came from Dolly's.

She took Lacey under her wing—as she did with all child recruits—and was the one to stop the tears.

To hold her when she was racked by violent nightmares.

To sing when Amelia's abrasive shouts had fractured her already fractured spirit.

To ease the transition.

Dolly made it better.

I found the patch of vines I broke through before and took a deep breath and inhaled my surroundings, feeling the energy and checking the wind.

Confident we hadn't been followed, I began calling on my translucent phase—where my poison powers surfaced—and deployed my newest trick.

This is the part of me that I liked. The part no one knew of.

I took off my gloves as the breath in my lungs started to mist.

Thorn's vines began to weep from the hover of my touch, not melting entirely, but singeing around the edges, turning into themselves to give my own flesh a wider breach. The green new growth turned brown and the brown old-growth went black. The fibers creaked as they bent, moving to make room for me and me alone.

I ducked my head and entered the tunnel of my power, letting my magic collapse behind me. The color change, the hold I had used to shift the thin branches, evaporated. Green went back to green. Brown to brown. The thorns lost their dull edge and found their points.

They sealed in, like the curtains on closing night, shutting me out and obscuring my presence.

I stood up and swiped at my pants, knocking the dirt off. And then I took in the sight before me.

The cabin. Or maybe it was a shack.

Who's to say?

It was dilapidated and abused, with a roof precariously close to collapsing on one side. Traces of a fire had left part of the home black and papery. The rest was aged by neglect and time.

What was left of the lawn was overgrown and uneven. It flowed into an overgrown orchard, with its rotting fruit spoiling on the ground.

It smelled sweetly sour and made the air sticky.

I stepped onto the rickety porch, with its broken baseboards and shattered railing, and allowed my powers to rest. There was no need for magic. The door, left ajar on broken hinges, swayed as I stepped inside.

It groaned on my arrival.

Lacey was sitting in a rocking chair—the only piece of furniture worth sitting on in the living room—holding that ugly doll, with the name Sally sewn on its foot. Aside from its decrepit state, poor stitching, button eyes—one of which was missing—and lopsided limbs, it was the ratty mane I found most peculiar.

Borderline disturbing, nearly.

Someone had used red yarn and tried to blacken it with dye. It had bled onto the fabric, leaving bruises on one side of her plush body.

Lacey held it close and was humming to it. A tune Dolly often sang.

"I see you don't care about the rules," I said.

She shrugged and looked at the doll. She was picking absentmindedly at her one button eye.

"Squirt, I told you that—"

“Why do you always call me Squirt?” she asked. She started to rock, her feet kicking out from under her. When she looked up, there was an accusation in her stare.

As if she knew I spoke around the truth.

That her human identity was lost when her life was first stolen.

“I’ve always called you Squirt.”

She shrugged again.

"Do you not like it when I call you Squirt?"

“It’s different here,” she said. “No one ever calls me by my name. They just say Kitten.”

She twisted her lips, and then kicked a leg out, steadying her chair. She placed Sally beside her and gripped the arm rails, leaning forward. “I told The Lady that Kitten wasn’t my name, and that I was ... that I—” She blinked, almost blankly, as if she’d already forgotten who she once was. She found it, but not without effort. “That I was Lacey and she said no. I was Kitten. She said she’s my mom now. But she’s not my mom. Won’t ever be my mom, either.”

‘The Lady’ was Amelia. Lacey never called her anything but ‘The Lady.’ Wise beyond her years, Lacey skirted around any direct addressing of Amelia. Mostly through avoidance.

Amelia's bouts of violence left most skittering.

But soon Lacey would run out of skirting room, and she'd have to call her mother.

I feared that day.

I feared the day she'd come to believe it even more.

That Amelia would have influence over her. Shaping her actions and beliefs.

“Squirt, you’ll always be Lacey, no matter what. And your mom will always be your mom.” I managed to keep my face still and free from cracking. Aunt Marie’s death wasn’t something we’d confronted. She was a memory no one talked about.

Same as all the innocent deaths before her.

"The Lady likes to lie, doesn't she?" she whispered.

"Yeah."

"She said my old mommy won't be coming back for me and that I should just forget her."

Rage curdled my insides, although I did my damnedest not to show it. I steadied my breath and took a moment before answering.

"Well that's a whole lot of impossible. Your mom is special, and I know she loves you a lot."

Present tense.

That always took effort.

At least Amelia hadn't told her the truth, that Marie was not only dead but her skull was on a mantel in Thorn's corridor, placed next to her father—who'd been flayed alive to send a message.

A message to me.

At least Amelia hadn't gone into detail.

So far.

Lacey sighed, and glanced down at Sally. She went to pick her up, when she suddenly snapped her head upwards. There was a moment of stillness and then she bounded from the chair. She flew past me, bolting across the room, her outline blurring as her feet barely touched the ground.

She leapt over the small dining table, beyond the broken, dust-covered chair, and landed as softly as a phantom.

And then a horrifying sound followed.

Too quick to properly register, she lifted her right foot and sent it crashing down. It sent a tremor through the cabin, causing doors to rattle and shattered panes to splinter. A mucky, sickening sound of bones and flesh collapsing accompanied it.

She'd obliterated a mouse.

Only a mouse.

But it was the sequence that disturbed me.

One moment she was in the chair, reminiscent of her mom, and the next she was a rodent slayer.

A pooling of red stain seeped beneath Lacey's tennis shoe; the splatter reaching halfway across the room.

She scraped off her foot using the edge of the chair, the small gray corpse landing with a wet splat.

Lacey grinned, and I felt it then.

That urgency I'd felt for some time.

"I got it," she whispered, a purr making her voice rusty. She flashed her teeth in a smile frighteningly like Amelia's. "I got it so fast."

Growl and bite.

Her transformation wouldn't stop with her physical body —it would go beyond that. They wanted to create a predator. To shatter the innocent.

To make her one of them.

I kept my face steady. "It's getting late, Kiddo. We should go." I held out my gloved hand, and she eyed it suspiciously.

"Did I do something wrong?" she asked. "It was only a mouse."

"Nah, Squirt. You didn't do anything wrong. It's just getting late and people might start to miss us." I waved my hand, and she finally took it. She tugged and looked up at me with big eyes.

"Mice spread germs," she said.

"You're right. That's one less thing to worry about now, isn't it? How about we get back? Dolly probably has a treat waiting and is anxious to let you have it."

That was the trick.

We left, Lacey exiting the briar patch first. I followed, concealing my magic behind me. Lacey walked with a skip to the meadow, every motion pulling on my muscles since she wouldn't relinquish my gloved hand.

Lacey let go only to collect her jar of butterflies, before returning it back to mine, fingers settling deep in my palm. I gave it a squeeze and expected to receive a smile for it, only she angled her head as her eyes darkened, the pupils swallowing all traces of color. Tiny sharp points began to pinch my palm, and I reluctantly let go—lest her claws pierce through my glove.

She wasn't looking at me, but squinting into the distance. I kneeled down and tugged on her shirt sleeve. She turned her head and her eyes filled with black tears.

I put both my hands on an arm, and gave them a squeeze, while keeping her eyes on mine. "What's up, Squirt? Is everything okay?"

She shook her head and bit her lip.

"You can tell me," I urged. "You know that."

"The drums," she whispered. "The drums are beating again."

Again.

I couldn't hear it, but I had no doubt she could. "It's going to be okay," I said.

She swallowed hard and tried to look away. I wouldn't let her. "I promise you, Lacey. It will be okay. You have me, and I have you, and as long as we're together, things are going to be okay."

"You won't go anywhere?"

"Not without you." A black tear fell from its place, and streaked down her cheek. I wiped it away. She didn't flinch. "I can't fix everything, but I can make things better. And I promise you, I will do everything that I can to make things better. Do you believe me?"

She moved her weight from foot to foot. "I'm scared."

"I know. But you won't always be." I tucked a strand of hair behind her ear. She didn't smile, but she wanted to—I could tell by the cut in her jaw. "You're gonna be okay. We are both going to be okay. I promise you. I will do whatever it takes to keep you safe. To make you happy again. No. Matter. What."

She believed me, I think, because I believed it too. I had a possible plan, one that I'd been considering for a few weeks. I just had to figure out the details.

It was lack of planning that usually got someone killed.

Especially here.

I gave Lacey's palm a squeeze and she managed to lift her cheek into a halfhearted grin.

"Now let's go see Dolly. I bet you can con her into two scoops of ice-cream tonight."

"With extra toppings?"

"Of course."

We walked into the forest, her hand in mine, the sun falling on our shoulders. My free hand drifted to my pocket, where the two rings, tied together by a piece of frayed ribbon from the gown Lacey wore the day she died, sat heavy. I let my grip snare them, and made a vow.

An oath.

To make it better.

Or die trying.

The promise held hope, even as we walked toward the drums and the beating sound of death.

CHAPTER 2
PUBLIC NOTICE

It'd been over a month since Lacey and I visited the cabin. That visit became my metric.

Before I started to plan and after.

Before I started to act and after.

Before, when there were butterflies and after, when there were rats.

How quickly things could change. How drastically too.

Case in point, the event I was attending. They turned it into a party—unlike the last one, which was so achingly quiet you could hear your heartbeat boom.

Velores of all stations and clans mingled and laughed, edging close to the empty scaffold, built on a platform high enough to give everyone a good view, but not so high as to take away from the grandness of the royal gardens or the hedgerow maze that boxed us all in.

The smell of caramel-corn and cotton-candy drifted through the trees, sliding between the tightly packed bodies and overpowering other smells.

Mainly the stench of blood. Perhaps fear too.

The sweet aromas didn't fully mask, but it muddled the senses enough to entice genuine laughter from a few eager onlookers.

A waft of cinnamon broke the barrier, and it brought me back to a memory, a girl, Fantasia. So close, yet so far.

I shook her image away.

Or tried to.

It didn't always work.

A clown on stilts handed out balloon animals to sticky, small hands. I recognized an inflated crocodile, a poodle, and a purple t-rex.

Not many children were in attendance—Narivous didn't have a lot to begin with—but those that were wore eager expressions and a frenetic excitement.

I was grateful Lacey wasn't among them. The last execution she witnessed gave her night terrors.

She was right to be afraid of the drums.

That's how they gathered us to the killing block.

I looked to the left, where the castle, gray and foreboding, stretched tall, its pitched roofline grazing overhead branches. Ivy clambered up the sides, concealing stone, framing diamond-hatch windows. Blooming roses and flowers were everywhere.

Tropical, native, rare, all varieties growing in harmony. It didn't matter that we were technically in the early stages of autumn.

Everything was vibrant.

As flowers drew my attention, a pretty girl—part of the Fire Clan, if I had to guess—crossed in front of me. She smiled flirtatiously when our eyes incidentally locked. I shot her a wink and her face brightened.

It didn't matter my toxic touch.

I was still a catch.

She hesitated and contemplated approaching—I could tell by her shift and the way she handled the trim of her cloak—when a cardinal, a bird not native to our area, swooped in front of her and started beating its wings against her head.

It caught us both by surprise.

She squawked.

The bird squawked.

A few spectators laughed.

And as she went to swat it away, the quick little dive-bomber flew upwards like a demented arrow, a strand of her hair lodged in its beak.

It chittered on an overhead branch. The girl huffed but stood her ground, glaring at it.

I would've too, but I was too busy looking for the source.

There was always a source.

Dreams.

Sure enough, I found her, along with Torti, standing behind me. The pair looked similar and different. Stunning, but with polarized coloring and attire.

They also wore matching glares.

Dreams' blonde hair was shaved on one side, the other cut to an angle, tips dyed turquoise—making the blue of her eyes pop. Her blue cloak no doubt covered up some sort of eccentric costume.

She was gifted at making a statement.

Torti, meanwhile, was more conservative. Her clothing always matched her arrogant visage. She managed to make sneering an art form. She traced her hand over her long, brown hair and tutted softly.

The cardinal landed on Dreams' shoulder and deposited the ember strands into her palm. Dreams held them out toward me—never breaking eye contact—and let them flutter to the ground.

I shrugged and offered up a sheepish smile, but both of their beautiful faces refused to crack.

Instead, they shook their heads in reproach and turned away, slipping into the crowd.

The Fire girl was long gone too.

Terribly disappointing.

I found an evergreen on the fringe and leaned against it. A chill cloaked me and Polar was soon at my side. He always knew how to make his presence known long before he actually presented himself.

"How does Dreams do that?" I asked in lieu of a greeting. "With the birds?"

"Is she here?" he asked. "I don't see her."

"She left. So how does she do it? There's gotta be a catch."

Polar gave a tight smile and raked his fingers through his white hair. "Ah, Fred," he clarified. "The little cardinal I gave her? Is he creating a ruckus?"

"Yeah. Fred the eighth, right?"

"I think this one's nine," he said. "She's the bird whisperer. What can I say? The girl has a gift." He glanced at the scaffold. "So they're making you watch?"

"Again."

"At least Thorn's trying to break up the mood this go around."

"Yeah, it feels like a party," I replied dryly.

Polar grunted.

He must've been the token witness. The authority figure required to report back.

This crowd was larger than the last one. The festivities and promise of food lured in greater numbers.

Technically, I think it still classified as a private execution. And it wasn't without notice that none of the Seven were there.

Polar didn't quite count since he was a husband—but he'd have to do.

A few eyed him and some, even from a distance, bowed their heads.

My eyes went to the stained scaffold.

"They're trying to send a message," Polar replied carefully, "while keeping morale up for the innocent bystanders."

I snorted. Polar pretended not to hear it.

"Dismiss it all you want, but messages act as a warning. Especially if they're ugly. Perhaps even more so." He hesitated. "They're not always a bad thing. If done right, they could prevent further loss of life." Polar waited a second and followed with, "I'm sorry you have to witness it, though."

"Me too."

"Let's hope this is the last."

"Doubt it."

He remained quiet.

An execution entertainer leapt onto the stage—he was the jester in charge of the magic show. He immediately took command of the audience, using sleight of hand to amaze.

The chatter became organized oohs and aahs.

"So, what's the story with this one?" I murmured.

Polar cleared his throat and narrowed his gaze, not entirely cooperative. "He was caught with contraband."

"What kind of contraband?"

He gave me a toothless smile. "The kind you're not supposed to have."

"Don't do that."

"Don't do what?"

"Play the word game. You know how much I hate it."

He shrugged.

"So are you gonna tell me?" I pressed.

"I gave you the Crown's official statement and that's where I'll leave it."

Frustrated, I kicked a rock and glanced down. Something in Polar thawed, because he gave me a crumb.

"The murmurings are gathering weight," he said in hushed tones.

"So there's really a rebellion building?" I asked, my words falling below a whisper too.

"Looks like it."

"And this guy? Is he really guilty?"

He breathed in through his nostrils and the temperature dropped. "Of course he's guilty. Why else would he be here?"

Ah, now we were on to the listening game. One recreational hop to the next. Polar was ever aware of the supernatural hearing surrounding us. To say they weren't guilty would be treasonous.

I leaned in close; so near, I think a flinch would've had us bumping heads. I barely formed the words, making the movements of my lips practically indecipherable. "C'mon, Polar. Level with me. That's all I'm asking. It's not like I can ask just anyone." I glanced away for a second. Execution after execution, and so far, I believed none of it. They were all innocents, guilty of nothing except stumbling across the path of a paranoid, tyrannical ruler. I was almost certain.

Almost.

He breathed ice into my ear. "Between you and me," he did a quick look around, "this guy *is* guilty."

Meaning: *the others weren't.* I clenched my jaw.

"But we think he's a pawn," Polar added. "He wouldn't talk, but we have reason to believe there's a mastermind in our midst. We don't know who it is, but it's someone of value. A larger player."

"Someone in a position of power?"

He nodded and surveyed the crowd. I did too; it was a habitual action.

Paranoia breeds paranoia.

But the entertainer was good—a master of his trade. And as the jester gained ground, no one paid us any attention. He'd recently added puppets and was acting out a one-man play.

And we were far enough on the crowd's edges to fade.

"And this guy gave no answers as to who was leading the fray?" I asked.

Polar shook his head as a shadow crossed over him. "Not a word, no matter which tactic they tried to get a confession: coercion, threats, and...." He let his message drift.

I knew the third strategy was torture.

"And what is it this rebellion is said to have done?"

"That's where our moment of candor ends, I'm afraid."

The set of his mouth told me he wouldn't budge.

"They're gonna do to this guy what they did to the other," I muttered.

"Botched it pretty bad, eh?" Polar raked his fingers through his hair. His volume rose to normal.

"It was awful, much worse than all the others." I indicated my shoulder. "First hit was across the blades, another directly on the shoulder. Seems odd someone so well trained would make such a ... *mistake*."

Polar's eyes blackened. "Indeed."

Today would be another such showing.

I wished I'd taken a second cup of balm tea this morning.

"Is our Queen going to come down for this? Or is she just going to destroy him from her window?" I asked.

Polar shot me a disapproving look.

"Well, that's what she did," I argued. "She stood at her window"—I pointed to the back section, where Thorn's quarters existed—"and sicced her vines on him. When they were done rummaging, the executioner came up and botched the kill shot."

"There are better ways to say it," he said.

I shrugged and moved on. "Will you be giving the royal statement?" I asked.

"No. I managed to get out of it."

"How'd you do that?"

"Charisma, my dear boy. You really should work on yours."

"So not a lost cause?"

"If my brothers can learn charm, surely you can too. If I were you, I'd start with not talking so much...."

Somehow, I managed a real smile.

"Tell me I didn't hear what I think I just heard," Ferno said. He approached from the deep wave of onlookers, wearing a stocking cap of black, instead of gray.

Funeral garb.

He wedged in between me and Polar.

"What do you think you heard?" Polar asked.

"That I was taught how to charm."

"You were."

"You're remembering wrong." Ferno nudged me and shot me a half-lopped grin. "*I*-stress on 'I'-was born with all the charm. It's this ice-stick that had to learn it. You can't fake this level of magnanimity."

Ferno then pointed to my face. "Where's your mask?"

"It broke."

"That's the third one," Polar said.

"Yeah, I know. I can count that high."

Ferno snickered.

"I hate your sarcasm," Polar said.

"Me too."

Polar shook his head. "How are you possibly breaking them?" he asked.

"Probably has your grace, Polar," Ferno shot out. He scratched near his ear where a prominent burn scar rested.

"I don't need your input."

Ferno stashed his hands in his pockets, unabashed.

"They want me to wear it during guard training," I started, "and the thing gets knocked off while I'm on perimeter runs." True. But I omitted the part about breaking them on purpose.

Which I did.

They drew too much damn attention.

"I doubt they're going to keep replacing them," Polar said.

"I think that's the point," Ferno added.

Right.

The crowd shifted and a clamor broke out as the executioner climbed the steps and took his place.

He wore the same uniform as he always did: a cloak of raven feathers and a bird's mask. The beak, carved from bone, stole all his features. Even his eyes were lost. No one knew who the executioner was. It was a mystery practically furled in folklore.

He wore a cologne designed to conceal his scent—an invention created by our own boy genius Chanticlaim.

Nothing was left to chance.

Polar said it was a kindness. The anonymity. To be the bearer of such ugly deeds. Destroying your own kind was no simple task.

He must've been paid handsomely for it.

In his gloved hand he held the axe—its ancient head eroded by rust.

They called it Lucky.

Narivous named their important weapons.

The back door of the castle swung open and three people emerged. Two guards and the condemned. A knapsack had been placed over the prisoner's head; it pulled in with every ragged breath he took. Short stabs, indicating fear, contrasted with the strength of his gait and the squaring of his shoulders.

He didn't hang his head like the others.

The crowd shushed, a few hissed, and a lone sob ricocheted. Everyone craned to get a better look.

The clown on stilts was nowhere to be seen. Even the scent of popcorn had dissolved. It was replaced by iron and trepidation. The party had been usurped by a funeral.

The difference in aura color between the two royal guards and the one set to die was shocking. Guards were beacons, while the prisoner was a flickering light. Narivous had a name for those lacking in brightness; they called them Pastels. In a land that covets power, this Velore nearing his end, was a nobody.

Same as the others.

Perhaps that's why they didn't bother with a more public display. It was a waste of resources.

'Quietly and discreetly, but enough to send ripples of warning.' That's the mantra of the Seven.

They had to balance the art of justice with the art of discretion—scare, but not feed.

A tricky tightrope.

But this one, he wanted to live. His name was Ether, and I wasn't entirely sure what powers he possessed. Employed as a servant, I'd only seen him on occasion in the castle.

He wrestled against the bodies urging him forward. A scream, muffled from the cloth sack, spoke of injustice.

My blood took to fire. And not entirely at Ether's condemned state—but at the two guards holding him.

Two of the cruelest men in all of Narivous: Locus and Crusher. They were Thorn's most beloved guards, willing to do her dirty work without the slightest hesitation.

I knew from experience.

Heathens.

I wished it were their necks about to be severed and heads placed on pikes.

I flexed my hands and Polar edged next to me, placing his palm on my shoulder.

To anyone looking at us, they would've thought he was offering comfort.

Only he wasn't.

"Easy," he breathed into my ear. "Do you need Dexitrol?"

Dexitrol, our power-numbing powder. This would've been a good time to nod. My translucency should've been surfacing, but I had a strong grip on my powers, a control I often lied about.

I was under no obligation to share my knowledge and capabilities.

So I didn't.

Polar cocked his head, curious, and I finally found my fib.

"I made sure to take some before I came out."

He nodded, satisfied. I placed my hand in my pocket, and grabbed the rings, a memento of strength.

They forced Ether to his knees and a moan broke from the crowd. Someone shouted his name, a bold move in this tumultuous climate.

They'd already stripped him of his identity.

Technically he wasn't Ether anymore.

A new ploy for the markings of a traitor. His headstone would have his Velore title with a line drawn through it.

Salt on the wound.

A ray of sunshine—something wholly unnatural in our city — broke through the overhead barrier. It pulled the focus from the condemned to Thorn's window. She stood behind the pane and held up her hand in greeting.

The crowd roared with approval.

She made the foliage bend even more, spotlighting herself and the stage. Her hold on plants was nothing short of miraculous.

Witnesses moved like a tidal wave as they all bowed with respect.

Thorn smiled.

I fought back a hiss and Polar jabbed me in the ribs. I made sure to buckle at the waist.

Thorn locked eyes with Locus and gave a subtle nod. He bowed and stepped forward, directly behind the kneeling Ether. His uniform didn't quite cover all his tattoos. The golden "G" blazed on the front of his vest.

He brushed the brown hair out of his eyes and grabbed the bag from Ether's head, ripping it off.

I think we all stopped breathing.

Ether had a strap of leather shielding his lower face, buckled and cinched tight beneath his jaw and across the back of his hair.

Same as all the others. To stop them from shouting in defiance.

Ether's expression was surprisingly flat—despite the signs of translucency cracking around his skin.

Many of the other condemned had at least flashed their eyes while kneeling on the scaffold. Actually, they all had. It was the first indicator of emerging powers—where the whites light up and the pupils swallow all signs of color. To flash your eyes at anyone was a sign of defiance.

Or desperation.

And yet he was dim.

Something was off. I couldn't quite make out what.

Was he drugged?

"As instructed by her most Gracious Highness," Locus lifted his palm to indicate Thorn, "let this serve as a warning.

All traitors to the Crown will receive no mercy. We have a duty, an obligation, to our most magnanimous sovereign to represent her reign in nothing but steadfast loyalty. To go against the Crown, is to go against all that is right. For she has chosen us to receive the greatest gift. A gift well beyond our worth. Disobedience, traitorous behavior, will first be met with disgrace ..." pause for dramatic effect, "then death."

"Bless Queen Thorn!" someone shouted.

The crowd parroted the expression, lifting their arms and roaring with cheer.

Locus smiled and gave another bow—acknowledging the good will—then beamed at Thorn.

She beamed right back.

Polar fidgeted and looked down. Ferno lifted his chin.

I couldn't pull my eyes away.

Crusher, his face soft in comparison to the rest of his body, stepped forward.

I knew he had a spiel coming. His voice rankled me more than Locus' did. My heart flashed in temper. I practically imprinted the rings into my palm; it didn't matter that the gloves acted as a thinly veiled shield—they were no match for my rage. I could feel the metal bite into my flesh.

"It is an honor to see this traitor sent to his second and final death." I kept my heart steady and stared beyond him. Blocking him out.

In his hands he held seeds. In a moment, he would toss them around Ether, where Thorn would force their growth to begin the execution process.

But he still wasn't done. He needed to keep talking, to garner more attention for his inflated ego.

He should be a bobble-head with all that air filling the space around that minuscule brain of his.

He opened his mouth to speak but froze, his lips agape,

eyes wide, a sweep of confusion blowing the smugness from his features.

We all settled on that same expression. Or close to it.

Something had shifted.

The scene was different.

It started with a wind.

The autumn air, cold, crisp and lively, rattled along the trees, sending leaves fluttering. That in itself wasn't unusual—it was how they pulled away that was strange. Organized and deliberate.

It was no September wind that'd dislodged them.

And as time notched by in slow increments, it became clearer how deliberate it was.

The leaves never met the ground—but swirled in a spiral, tight, coiled and precise. They gathered in height. The cluster forming a shape, no different than a banner fluttering in the wind.

The other component, perhaps the most shocking of all, was that, Ether, the condemned on his knees, was no longer dim. His aura reared in a blast of color. He went neon. Cracks of translucency spread from his eyes, bleeding over every spare inch of flesh.

His dullness, his whitewashed aura, was a lie. It had always been a lie.

Because this type of magnificence, what we were all witnessing, was too grand to be a one-time incident. It was power on display.

He'd kept his strength hidden.

And now, he'd ripped away the falsehood.

The leaves continued to gather in masses, pulling from the trees, taking Thorn's gifts to use for his own.

His aerial message was rapidly growing.

Everyone was lost to stillness. Crusher's knuckles were white where he gripped the seeds.

Next to me, Ferno's breathing labored. It had such force, it reminded me of the time Mom hyperventilated. How she'd attempted to hide it—the strain of taking in oxygen that the body wanted to reject. Her smile, fake and full of effort, turned more grotesque than she could've realized. We shouldn't have to think of how to breathe.

It's pre-programmed.

Only that's not always the case.

One thing. Just one thing needs to go wrong and our reflexes go defunct. Our bodies forget how to operate.

I was stuck between heat and ice.

Polar wasn't looking at his feet anymore. He was as captivated by the performance as everyone else.

Watching. Witnessing.

Ether was a Telekinetic. High above him, as he kneeled on the scaffold, was an image erected from leaves. A banner.

A protest.

A spade.

I'd seen the image before, carved into the bark of a tree. I thought it was art, a token of creativity.

But now I realized what it was.

This was their sign.

There was a rebellion.

The crowd's murmurs traveled like a current.

The executioner acted quickly, not even allowing the seeds in Crusher's palm to bloom. He lifted the axe and swung fast, severing Ether's neck, extinguishing his flaring aura in one stroke. There was no time for botched shots.

And as Ether's head landed with a dull thud, I kept my hand tight around the rings.

I looked toward the castle—as if seeing beyond the stone and walls.

I thought of two things, and only two things. It wasn't of the rebellion, or the screaming, or the angst flooding the garden.

My thoughts were louder than any scream.

My plan.

Lacey.

I was running out of time.

CHAPTER 3

PLOTTING ON THE RUN

"Who's been in my room?" I asked.

Scream and Plague looked up in unison from the meal they shared in complete silence. I went to stand between them—they were on opposite ends of an absurdly long dining table. A servant held quiet in the far corner of the room.

Scream was beautifully pieced together, as per usual.

Plague was not, also as per usual.

Scream's black hair was pulled back, knotted elegantly at the base of her neck. She opted for a simple pair of onyx earrings to match her dark eyes. They made her alabaster skin even more luminous.

She was dressed for a meeting with Thorn, and looked every part presentable, even in the early morning hours.

Plague appeared as if he'd just rolled out of bed.

He wasn't even wearing his mask, the rot ever-present on one side of his face.

I wondered if that's why Scream lacked an appetite.

She placed her spoon down and carefully folded her hands, giving me her full attention.

"What is this with you? You've been on this kick lately, thinking someone's been snooping through your things. I can assure you, no one has been in our apartment aside from the few servants who serve our needs—and they all follow the strictest of orders not to disturb that disaster of a room, even if it needs a proper tidying. So tell me, darling, what makes you think someone has defied our orders?"

Behind her, the Pastel girl pulled her shoulders in, trying to dissipate into the corner. Threats of any measure—especially in this new climate—the one Ether created with his defiant death, left everyone insecure, on edge. *Afraid.*

"I don't think it was a servant," I replied hastily. The girl softened. "It just feels ... off. Like someone's been in there."

"Has something been moved?" Scream asked.

"No."

"Taken?"

"No."

"Well then, I think your paranoia is getting the best of you."

How could I tell her? That ever since Ether's death, my room had been frequented often, my poison telling me so. They left a code behind. It wasn't a scent trail, but something less—if such a thing truly existed—almost like a soft-footed impression stamped on the passage of time, unnoticeable by most everyone, unless you had a peculiar power with the ability to hone in on such subtle alterations.

My poison was a rarity indeed.

Not even Plague and Scream possessed this ability—of this, I was sure. And it wasn't something I was prepared to share with them. Or anyone, for that matter.

"Besides," Scream gave a serene smile, "you yourself

haven't left so if someone slipped into your room, they would've had to have been invisible. We may have many gifts, but the ability to vanish is not one of them." She turned to Plague. "He was here the whole time, isn't that right, dear?"

Plague sat a little straighter at the address—lapping up her slight kindness with a lighted look.

"Right. I haven't seen you leave the apartment either," he said to me.

Scream's sweet smile went mean.

"Because, Death darling, Plague never leaves the apartment. He would know—since he's long adopted being a pathetic shut-in." She took a bite of oatmeal and made a show of savoring it.

Plague looked equally vexed and wounded.

This was, unfortunately, their new normal.

Their marriage wasn't a happy one. More often than not, it was as toxic as their clan.

They hid it well—or at least tried to—but behind closed doors it was up for unraveling. Scream more so than Plague.

He loved her.

She resented him.

The best course of action was to ignore it.

"I was in the screaming room for the past two hours. That's when the snooping happened."

At this, Scream beamed. Her beauty expanded tenfold.

"Two hours? Oh, my darling!" She slapped her hands together. "I love that you were practicing that long and this early—right before guard practice of all things. Have you gotten any closer? You must've made progress to stay that focused. Oh, do tell. It would be delightful to share such positive news with Thorn; she's been so cross lately. You would be her absolute bright spot."

I shook my head and watched her face fall. Even Plague

looked disappointed.

"I'm not there yet ... but I'm trying."

Scream nodded, not unkindly. "I know you've been working at it. You're in there a lot nowadays—for longer durations too—for which we're grateful. And don't think I've been shy on bragging about your efforts." She looked at the clock above the doorway and rose. "Here, let me walk you to the Skull Corridor. You have a perimeter run today, yes? We know how Laquet feels about tardiness."

She took my arm and led me out. Resting her head softly on my shoulder as we made our way into the Poison Throne Room. She stopped and held my hands, glancing at me with motherly pride.

"I know you're getting close," she said. "I trust it." She placed her forehead against my own and looked directly into my eyes. "I trust you."

It broke me a little—to see so much love and validation shining back. "I'm making progress." Not a lie, but not the truth. I *was* making progress—on so many things.

The suppression was mastered a long time ago.

Only I wasn't telling anyone.

Nor did they know I had new tasks to tackle.

She smiled and stepped back, reaching out to straighten my vest.

"I've been talking to Thorn, trying to convince her to bring Fantasia back. I told her it might inspire you to find your abilities again. I think she's considering it. And ... if you manage to regain the suppression, you two can be together for all of eternity. Not even Amelia will be able to challenge it. Think, Death. Think of what that would mean to Fantasia. To you. Love, my darling. There is nothing quite like it. We all deserve that happiness." She paused and grew grim, looking away, facing an internal thought that hardened her jaw.

Was she thinking of her loveless marriage to Plague?

How sour it had become?

But it wasn't just her vows that locked her into marriage.

It was her toxic touch, too.

"They made a mistake sending Fantasia away to the Southside," she said. "I think it's love that will break the block—not absence."

If only they knew.

I was grateful they had sent her away.

Because the farther she was away from me, the farther away from any implications if I were caught.

My plans were dangerous.

I wanted her safe.

My fake smile was passable.

"I'm gonna keep doing my best," I said.

She kissed me on the cheek. "You're a good boy. Do well on your run today. Laquet said your numbers are shameful."

Spark was running a step behind me, our movements in tandem. "I don't understand why they wanna complicate it," he said. It had rained earlier in the day and our footsteps sent mud splatter everywhere.

As always, he let me set the pace.

We ducked under a branch simultaneously, water droplets still clinging to pine needles.

"I don't get it. No matter which way I look at it, it doesn't make sense. Labels, man, they're no good. We should enjoy each other and not make it messy. The moment a label slips in, bam," Spark slapped his hands, never breaking his gait, "all the good gets sucked out of it. It's a curse, I'm telling you. Every. Single. Time."

I jumped over an overgrown root, the sound of Spark's practiced feet right behind me.

Perimeter runs meant very few trails to follow. We had to keep to the fringe of Narivous' territory yet we were still close enough to the city that Thorn's magic was strong. It was an obstacle course of foliage, fallen logs and boulders. Nature on steroids.

I passed a Tucking Point, a birch tree with yellow roses climbing along the trunk, and forced my eyes not to linger.

I needed to ditch Spark ... and that's when it dawned on me: his one-man monologue had silenced.

Our footsteps and the slushy slapping of mud were the only sounds to be heard, until Spark—perhaps wanting to stave off the suffocating silence—cleared his throat.

"Hey, uh, can I ask you something?" he asked.

Magic words. Did anything good ever come from them?

I slowed and he kept pace with me. We downgraded to a lowly jog.

"Depends," I said. "But you can give it a shot."

He smiled—or at least tried to. His face was in opposition with whatever thoughts he had whirling inside his bald head.

"Do you ever think about the what-ifs? The people ..." his words trailed off in a very un-Spark way. For a man who knew his own voice, to lose it spoke mounds—perhaps more so than the actual words themselves.

He put his head down and the line of his shoulders bowed. His fingers—wrapped in a set of black rubber gloves to offset the constant electrical current flowing through his body—clenched.

When he looked back up, the moment had passed and so had his question.

"I was just thinking of all the things that have happened lately." He threw out a smile that was almost passable. "And I was wondering if it were true. Can you really not do it anymore? Your ability to suppress?"

"Is that really what you were going to ask?"

"In my roundabout way, yes."

I narrowed my gaze.

"So?" he pressed. "Can you or can't you?"

I swallowed and slowed even more. We went to a walk.

"I can't."

"What do you think the holdup is?"

I shrugged, choosing not to say. It was easier.

Spark nodded, as if he expected as much.

He grabbed my sleeve and pulled me to a stop.

"I don't know if you know this, Death, but the rumors are growing, and it's not only about the rebellion." His voice dropped to a breath at the last word. It was an ominous talisman when spoken aloud. "There are suspicions you're holding back, and that you're doing it intentionally. And what with ... *everything* ... you need to be careful. What if they start to think you're one of them, that your unwillingness to cooperate is part of the sabotage? It's not a far leap between the two, and it isn't just your life you have to be worried about if you, uh, catch my drift...."

He swallowed, taking slow care on selecting his words.

"I've been meaning to bring it up for a while, but I didn't want to add any pressure. And this is my own thoughts working here. I haven't heard anything, if that's what you're wondering." He held his hands up, palms forward.

It wasn't what I was wondering.

But he had pointed out a glaring piece of obviousness that I was embarrassed to have overlooked. I would've never thought it possible to be roped into a rebellion I had nothing to do with.

Yet, that's not how things worked here.

The countless others that had died—most of them were

innocent.

Why couldn't the same happen to me?

Was that why the pressure on me to perform the suppression was growing? It was coming from those closest to home. From those who loved me.

And while I was worried my current undertakings would be considered part of the insurrection, I never stopped to consider that withholding my abilities could be considered part of it too.

The thought hammered in my chest. It made me want to work harder, quicker.

Spark was studying me closely. "Look, Death. I'm sorry. I didn't mean to dump this shit on you. I was just thinking out loud, ya know?"

"No. No, it's okay." I spoke with precision. "I'm glad you brought it up, that thought hadn't crossed my mind."

Why hadn't it?

"Well, that means this place hasn't ruined you yet, otherwise you'd be edging near paranoia on any given day." He gave a crooked smile, a bit on the guilty side if I had to label it. "I kind of feel like an asshole even nudging you in that direction. No one needs any help in this place. It's where madness is made. That, and *if* you're doing your best ..."

His words trailed off.

"I am doing my best—it's just ... hard." I almost said complicated, but that would've been the wrong word.

He shot me a concerned glance.

"Death, sorry. Honest." He held up his hands. "I'm making this a helluva lot worse than it needs to be. I shouldn't have even brought it up. But you gotta admit, it looks suspicious, right? I mean, you did it twice before—once even on command —and that's more than they've ever seen in all the years Scream and Plague have existed *together*. For it to just go away like that," he snapped his fingers, "seems peculiar, even to me. And I trust you."

"And no one has said anything, this isn't outsourced?"

"No, like I said."

"You're sure?"

"Dude, yeah. This is my own workings. I haven't heard a peep."

It felt like a lie. It was how he moved.

"And you would tell me?" I pressed.

"Of course. We're friends."

"Friends." I snorted. "Not to be a dick, but friends don't count for much around here. Survival is the trump card."

"Fair enough." He nodded and cleared his throat. "Survival is the trump card—but some things are bigger than our own mortality. Death isn't the worst. Not here anyway."

When did Spark start crafting riddles? I looked at him and he shook his head.

"Gotta keep the spirit alive," he said sheepishly.

And the thing was, he was right. Completely and entirely. No matter how I tried to play it off, to be still in a time that required action would make one complicit.

A part of the bigger problem.

For me, doing nothing meant damaging Lacey. She was the life beyond myself.

Someone had the same effect on him.

But I didn't know who it was.

We continued our run, only this time in our own silent bubbles.

WE'D GONE another four miles, maybe five, when I decided to make my move.

I think that's when I noticed it.

Wondering, again, how I'd missed such an obvious sign—it's like not seeing neon at night.

"Hey, Spark, I gotta take a piss. You go on without me."

I stopped—Spark did too. That was my first signal. It's like he'd become an extension of me.

I jumped, he jumped.

I ran, he ran.

I stopped, he stopped.

My veins tingled, the sensation flowing through my heart, telling me things I tried to drown out. Friends were a rarity. I wouldn't—no, couldn't—challenge Spark's motives.

I moved off the path and tossed my hand in dismissal.

Still he stayed.

We were farther from the city and the trees were less dense. Natural light filtered in, flickering across him, slashing him into ribbons of dark and bright.

It reminded me of the split between good and evil, between honesty and lies.

Spark's eyes went hard; and he shifted as he looked beyond me.

"Why is it you always have to piss on these runs?" he asked.

There was either suspicion or curiosity there. I couldn't tell which.

"I don't always have to—"

"Yes you do." He finally moved, only it was toward me. "Every run you break off and ditch me. Is there a reason? Because it seems ..."

He drifted. And that's when I recognized what I'd been too oblivious to recognize earlier.

Spark was my shadow.

For a reason.

He was keeping tabs.

I don't know if it was embarrassment or anger that made me bristle, painting over every positive attribute he possessed.

But in that moment I was lost to his duplicity.

Incited by it nearly.

"How does it seem?" I asked, my voice blending to a hiss.

Spark rubbed the back of his neck. He shook his head, refusing the question. "You know you can trust me," he said.

"Can I?"

Spark offered up a smile. "Of course, I'm your friend."

"That word again." My matching smile was full of venom. There was nothing kind about it. "Friends don't follow friends. I can't believe I missed it. What is this? Are you making a report for Laquet? For Thorn? Pretending to be my friend to get inside dirt?"

"I'm not pretending and I'd never—"

"What? Betray me? Lie to me? I don't need false friends, Spark. Shit." I felt my body smoldering. All this time. All this time I thought he was true. "Who put you up to it? I want to know."

"It's not what you're thinking."

"Then what is it?"

He shifted on his feet.

"Finish your run, Spark, I don't need a babysitter."

I pivoted on my heel, and darted into the forest, shutting him out before he could give me a reply. He called out after me.

I didn't miss a step.

And all the while, as I pushed past the brush and ferns, clipped through the firs surrounded in briars and violent nature, a solitary thought rotated in my head: maybe I didn't know Spark at all.

He was Thorn's guard, after all.

And we were in the middle of a rebellion.

Still, you'd think that would be enough to stop me.

But it wasn't.

Not. Even. Close.

Not when it came to Lacey.

IT WAS DIRECTLY in my line of sight: The birch tree.

Number 21 according to the record books.

This one was properly spaced out—three down from the last one. I knew better than to hit up the same one two times in a row.

I was careful to avoid the statues with their camera eyes, strategically placed to keep a watchful gaze on anyone who passed.

I also had their locations memorized.

Thirty feet away I stopped and took in my surroundings, the details sharpening.

I could smell the others before me, the guards who'd already completed their run.

What was once used against me, I now used to my advantage. Their scent helped hide my own.

I steadied my breath. Same as the time before.

And the time before that.

I let my toxin reach beyond me, to feel for others, and when I was sure I was alone, I removed my glove.

The poison was such a peculiar beast. It was a chameleon.

I walked with great practice to the birch.

A spider, lost on the tree's flesh, crawled toward me. A second followed. The only living creatures not repulsed by me—and were actually drawn to my energy—were arachnids. It was such a strange gift.

Had it not been for the uptick in executions and the unraveling of my psyche, I would've spent more time honing that ability.

Beckoning spiders.

Having found myself liking them all of a sudden.

I lifted the birch door, its flap made of bark paper, revealing a keypad with an eye scanner.

With one code and a subsequent unblinking shot, the door revealed a small pharmacy of miracle medications.

Medications I desperately needed. My hoard wasn't grand enough yet, not for what I hoped to achieve.

And I was thankful the trees were still unmonitored.

That's what I told myself. Truth is, I had no way of knowing. But I'd been taking from them on a regular basis—during each perimeter run, to be exact.

Surely if they were monitoring them they would've come for me?

Silence here was proof.

It was the only proof I had.

There was a measure of risk. There was a measure of reward. The latter overshadowed the former.

I grabbed the tin lodged deep inside and rummaged quickly, grabbing pills—all wrapped in protective plastic—like a desperate junkie on a painful detox.

Normally I'd only take one or two, but today felt different. Maybe it was Spark. Maybe it was the whisper in my veins. Either way, I went bold. I doubled my grab and carefully replaced the tin.

I transferred the pills to a plastic bag wrapped in velvet and stowed them at the back of my waistband, concealed by my cloak.

And even though I was playing a dangerous game, I couldn't help but smile to myself.

I think that smile held as I moved through the forest,

cutting through the center, abandoning the perimeter run altogether to try and make up for time.

I wasn't even considering Spark.

Only my next step.

And how I would move forward with my plans.

Lost in thought, I somehow missed Jaguar, with his massive frame barreling in like a stampeding bull. He cut through the trees, the way a predator glides over terrain, and slammed into me—sending my body flying and my mind reeling.

I landed with a hard thud against a massive fir, the bark busting on impact. My shoulder screamed and my skin threatened to split, but it stayed knitted together.

Barely.

Jaguar stood over me, his expression hard to read. Where he was towering before, what with his exaggerated height, he now loomed into a great eclipse.

Deep within the forest, his black hair and tan coloring turned him into a shadow.

He was breathing heavily, his lungs lifting with every hefty draw. That should've been a tipoff, but it wasn't. The Animal clan didn't strain while utilizing their athleticism. It was in their code not to; they were built for agility.

For sprinting.

I gripped my shoulder, convinced it had slipped from its socket, and glowered at him from the ground. "What the hell, Jagu—"

"I've been looking for you everywhere," he said. "Why the hell are you not on the perimeter?" He glanced around and sniffed, sensing the air. "Hurry," he said. "It's your cousin. They have him."

Eric.

I ran.

CHAPTER 4
COUSIN

They. Such an ambiguous term.

I wasn't even sure who *they* entailed. I knew, however, that it wasn't good. Anyone within the forest was a potential villain.

Myself included.

I wasn't foolish, nor arrogant enough, to exclude myself from that toxic lineup. Falling into the realm of corrupt morals was par for the course.

I shouldn't have been able to match Jaguar's speed. His stride was equivalent to two of my own, yet I remained on his heels. That's how badly I wanted to clear the distance. Adrenaline gave me force.

We flew through the trees, jumping briars, working off the path—a pair of bending arrows searching for their target.

I was relieved when we angled away from the city and toward the entrance to the forest where the oak trees with their yellow roses marked our gateway.

I analyzed Jaguar's mannerisms, even at a full tilt. Checking everything on him. He would occasionally throw his head back and sniff, and subtly adjust his direction. Eventually, as the forest opened and expanded, he softened and slowed, his shoulders releasing. His unwinding was a positive sign.

Jaguar turned toward me, still at a fast clip and said, "They haven't taken him far. That's good."

"Unless he's dead?"

He shook his head. "I can tell the difference. He's alive. We made it in time but ... don't lose your cool, we have to play this steady. Get him out before anyone knows."

"Who're they?"

"Your archenemies."

Locus. Crusher.

I flashed in a spot of righteous anger. Jaguar shook his head, barely paying me much notice as he pressed along at an urgent speed. "Don't lose your head," he admonished. "You'll put us all in a state of hurt if you do that."

I couldn't. No. I wouldn't. I forced my rage deep, my rattling toxin to a low hum. The light in my eyes was aglow, but there was no help for that.

Not in that moment, anyhow.

We slowed and Jaguar held out his hand to still me.

"He's a Protector, for damn sake," I hissed. "It's illegal to capture him."

He shook his head, and said softly, "Not now, man. Not now. We'll manage the details later. But, above all else. Remember. Keep. Your. Head."

Figuratively and literally.

I stifled my temper along with a groan.

A quick set of footsteps approached behind us and I turned with bared teeth. Spark held up his hands and stopped mere feet away. The golden G on his vest was vivid in the fading autumn light. Jaguar tipped his head in Spark's direction.

"Spark's the one who found 'em with him. He found me since he couldn't find you."

All the suspicions of earlier vanished in a puff of gratitude. Relief sang in me too.

He was my friend.

On my side.

And his reasons for keeping tabs on me were most likely a source of kindness and watchful guardianship.

I cursed myself for doubting him. But he was right; this place created chaos.

We all lived amongst it. It touched everything. Ruined everything. It was insidious and far reaching.

Jaguar waved us forward and held his finger to his lips to indicate total silence. We moved without presence, as if our footsteps never reached the ground.

We edged near briars that swallowed half of a towering tree, and that's when we found them.

Locus, Crusher, and Romeo.

And they were all standing in front of Eric, who was down on his knees. Eric was a stocky guy, usually arrogant and cocky, but none of that was evident as he wallowed in a state of vulnerability.

Eric's head pivoted between the trio, only to whip back in the direction he'd come from, to the Field of Entry and the location of his truck.

Trees threw shadows over Eric's face, but even the drapery of darkness couldn't hide his fear. Or regret.

You could smell both.

Fear had a distinct odor.

Regret was almost as unpleasant.

They often intermingled in this forest.

Eric ran his hands through his brown hair. He'd been

reduced to fragments. He looked like he'd been hit. At least once. Most likely more.

It brought back a flood of memories. Jester among them. He had been a Stronghold like Crusher, only less vibrant.

These were the heathens Jester spoke of.

The pair who lured me out of my rooms the day Jester used me as his vessel for his own suicide. Locus, I learned later, was the one who wore the mask and cloak, to fool me into thinking Fantasia had come for me. Crusher was the one who threw the dust in my face before I found myself in the graveyard.

It wasn't a group—only a pairing—and when the plan backfired, Thorn sent them to the Southside, lest I recognize them and lash out with my deadly powers and newbie inability to control them.

But then she brought them back.

She brought them *both* back.

And it was for more dirty work. Far more severe than Jester's loss. She used them to take a chunk of my soul.

Aunt Marie.

Uncle Dean.

The hell I was going to let what happened to them happen to my cousin.

Crusher would always resonate as Babyface and Locus as Tattoo. That's how I knew them before I learned their names.

I went to step forward and Jaguar stopped me, his massive hand grappling my shoulder. His fingers dug in a little too forcefully. I brushed him off and he shook his head, not looking at me, but staring at them—much the way a predator would assess his prey. He was considering, planning, plotting.

Spark, too, was calculating how to move forward.

Weighing what would best suit us.

And if I had any wits about me, I'd best follow their lead.

Only rage had made me reckless. I couldn't hear Eric's

voice as he pleaded with them, begging them for his release. The blood was rushing in my ears and muffling his message. I was underwater above ground.

I told myself to breathe.

Again. And again. And again.

That's when I recognized the tilt of Spark's stance. I forced myself to focus.

They were planning an attack. If success were to be had, I needed to join them in their methodic tactics.

I started to remove my gloves, and Spark nodded his approval. Jaguar shifted a step away, in clear agreement.

"I'm a Protector, and I have a right to request to see him. You're not supposed to treat me like this," Eric said.

"You sound like a broken record," Crusher said. He spoke in a low growl. "I feel like I'm gonna have to keep smacking you to change your tune."

"But ... it's the truth. I swear it."

"Well, see, we'd know that if he could read your mind." Crusher motioned to Romeo—a Doppelgänger.

A shifting occurred, and Locus stepped behind Crusher. We could only capture incomplete pieces as they spoke softly amongst themselves.

"Why can't he?" Crusher asked.

"I can't explain it, man. I really can't. I want to see Daniel —"

"Death. His name is Death. And it's not like knowing him is going to save you. I don't know if you've heard, but he's not really as great a Velore as they were hoping. I dare say, he's a disappointment, and a Velore without worth is a Velore worth losing."

That had a ring of truth to it.

With my gloves fully removed—carefully, excruciating inch by inch—I reached for the clasp of my cloak, only to stall when I recalled the contraband I had tucked into my waistband. Spark recognized the hesitation, and nudged me in the ribs to keep going. But that was impossible—to discreetly remove both and not be detected. Especially with Jaguar right beside me.

I lipped, "I got this." Spark narrowed his eyes.

And I did have this.

Unbeknownst to Crusher, he'd given me an idea. I knew what I had to do and how to do it.

It was terribly unfortunate—the secret I was going to reveal. It was my ace card.

Eric was worth playing it.

"Do you know what the punishment is for trespassing on our land?" Crusher continued.

"But I'm a Protector! It's not trespassing if I'm a Protector. My grandfather, Charlie, he, uh ... he knows that ... uh, Polar guy—and I can assure you—"

"Assure us of what?" Crusher interrupted. "That you're breaking Narivous law with an unreadable mind?"

"A mind I've been able to read in the past," Romeo clarified.

I don't know who was more pissed at that moment—Romeo for his inability to properly read Eric, or Eric, recalling the last time he'd encountered Romeo from what seemed like ages ago.

Eric kept glancing toward the path leading from Narivous. I knew what was flitting through his thoughts. What must've been flitting through Romeo's as well.

Someone had given Eric something. To block his mind.

And now Eric needed a rescuer.

He needed me.

"I need your mouth to work since your mind is shut off, and I'm sick of this story you keep regurgitating," Crusher said. "It's old. Used up. I want a different one." Crusher stuck his finger on Eric's forehead and pushed him back. Eric had to catch himself, his hand shot out behind him, fingers flaying, his nails biting into the dirt. "Or else I'll be forced to beat the story out of you." He lifted a fist to indicate he was serious, and that's when I made my entrance.

It was a perfect cue.

The growl I emitted crawled from somewhere deep and lethal and riveted into the space between Crusher's poised fist and Eric's fearful face.

It locked Crusher's arm midair and stilled some of Eric's tremble.

They all turned toward me. Romeo blanched, but there wasn't time to relish his regret. Eric, so small on his knees, instinctively reached out his hand in my direction as if I could transcend the distance and guide him back to his feet.

Spark and Jaguar were on my heels.

Free of gloves—and with contraband on my person—I moved with careful precision. Crusher slowly lowered his fist and threw me a mean smile.

I wanted to rip it away. Ruin his face so he couldn't ever manage it again.

"Well, lookie who just showed up."

"Step back from him, Crusher," I said. My voice had gone rusty. The particles dancing in my lungs making everything thicker.

Crusher only grinned, but his eyes betrayed him. They scanned my bare arms. My bare hands. And inadvertently—or perhaps intentionally—they skipped over to Locus.

They exchanged a glance and I understood the conveyed message. He was going to lift me with his mind.

"Don't you think, for even a fraction of a second, of doing it, Locus. So help me. I have nothing to lose and I'll let you all have it."

Romeo took a step back, surveying the scars between Crusher and Locus, and ran his hand through his perfect hair. His concern was etched on his face. My temper and its poisonous ramifications had a tendency of destroying good looks; he didn't want to join that fold.

"Let's be easy about this," Romeo said, flashing a shock of white teeth. "We're all friends here. No need to toss out threats."

"That's all they are," Crusher said. "Threats. Don't worry, pretty boy, he's not gonna unleash because if he did, his little friend here'd be gone."

I moved closer to Crusher, and matched his smile with one of my own. Behind me, Locus' translucency stalled; it held at a point of light.

Ready—but not beyond repeal.

"Your confidence will be your undoing," I said. "Tell your buddy there that he better not lift me, because I will unleash —"

"The hell you will—"

"The hell I won't," I shot back. "I know you, Crusher. I know how you operate. And I know you have no intention of letting Eric go without having a bit of torturous fun. And if that's the case, I might as well return the favor on my own terms." My voice grew throatier, my energy more static. Cracks fissured around my eyes. "And my torturous fun will have greater effect than yours." I turned my head in Locus' direction, while keeping my eyes trained on Crusher. "Let's not do anything stupid."

They believed. All of them.

The scene changed as some of the upper hand shifted to me.

It was a powerful, intoxicating sensation: gaining ground with only the promise of my magic.

"Get up, Eric," I demanded. He stumbled to his feet and stepped back. I held up my hand to stop him from running. "This illegal interrogation is over."

"There's nothing illegal about it," Crusher spat. "He's a trespasser—"

"He's a Protector."

"With a blocked-off mind," he ground out. "There's only one way for that to happen. He's taken something."

I smirked. "Just because you chose a subpar Velore to read his mind doesn't make him guilty of any crime."

"I've read him before," Romeo bristled. "He took something."

"Says you. I think you're just a shitty Doppelgänger. You couldn't read my mind back when I was human—and I'd taken nothing. Don't you remember?"

Which was a lie, of course. I had taken something. Romeo didn't know that; his ignorance played into my favor.

Now he was in a bind. Either call me a liar or accept he failed.

Neither option was pleasant.

Only one promised to keep his face pretty without my poison scars.

I knew he'd concede.

I continued, "Seems your sight is blotchy. It happens, my friend." I laughed. "There is nothing nefarious about this. Just you having a power hiccup. Let's not make a bigger deal out of your shortcomings."

"Don't try and twist this," Crusher said. "You're not one to talk about shortcomings."

"Is that so?"

"Yeah. You're a dud."

"Why is that? Because I'm performing in the exact same way as Scream and Plague? Are they duds too?"

He blanched.

"I didn't say that."

"You implied it. They can't suppress—so if I'm a dud, you're calling our betters duds. And last I checked, that's a rather serious offense."

"You're twisting my words."

I moved so close he backed away. The heat building around my core radiated. I could feel my eyes burning—the whites of my eyes no doubt glowing from my burgeoning translucency. It zapped some of the darkness in the heavily shrouded forest.

Crusher and I were nearly touching. "Did you hit him?" I asked—knowing the answer, seeing his response reflected in the flash in his face. The forest swelled. A haze of red flooded my vision.

Eric moved a few feet away. I could feel the space between us grow.

Good for him.

At least his instincts were working.

"I hit him for good cause."

And that was my opening. Before Crusher could react, before he could see it coming, I closed my fist—my bare fist—and sent it flying at his face. The impact had a gratifying thud to it.

The shock of it, and the rage propelling it, made him reel back. He nearly lost his footing. He clawed at his cheek as panic scrawled across his face, waiting for the poison to infiltrate.

Everyone—even Jaguar and Spark, who had faded to background—held their breath. Suspended in this strange moment of violence.

And that's when it occurred to Crusher.

He didn't scream or wilt. The Poison wasn't blooming.

And the trick I had mastered made my face break into a smile that wasn't mean or taunting.

It was purely authentic.

"Don't worry, Crusher. I hit you for good cause, too. Seems maybe I'm not such a dud, which is something you should well remember."

"You've been lying this whole time—"

"No, not lying. Just waiting for it to come back with consistency. This was a gamble—so consider yourself lucky." I smirked. "Besides, if I failed, the worst to happen is that you'd be in agonizing pain. Not much of a risk in my eyes. However —" I looked at everyone—friend and foe—I had their rapt attention. "No one had better take this surprise away from me. I've been working too hard, for far too long. When my abilities are revealed, I expect to be the one to reveal them. Do we understand each other?"

Romeo, Locus, Jaguar and Spark—for different designs—held the same look: awe and fear blended in unison. Everyone nodded.

"You're a fraud, just like that traitor Ether," Crusher said. "Lying about your abilities. Keeping secrets."

"Those are loaded words. You best shut your mouth or I'll have your head on a pike."

"How do you figure? I'm a favorite—"

I laughed. Hard. "You and I both know the promise of my ability is better than the full-fledged talent of yours. I could slip into your spot as favorite before nightfall. And this *was* an illegal interrogation—so yeah. Head. On. A. Pike."

The silence, heavier than a thick blanket of snow, fell on us.

Crusher experienced fear.

I enjoyed every moment of it.

"So why don't you do me a favor and get the hell out of my sight—before you really piss me off and I decide to fuck up your face even more." I turned toward Eric. "I'm going to take our *Protector*—"emphasis on Protector, "back to his truck and send him home where he belongs." I leaned in close and spoke in a gravelly tone. "And you know what? Because I'm in a forgiving mood, I'm not going to report what you did to Thorn. Perhaps it's in everyone's best interests if we forget this whole damn incident took place. Otherwise ... who knows what direction the wind will blow."

There was an undertone. One everyone in the circle understood.

I won't tell.

You don't tell.

Perhaps we'll all live.

Crusher, wrapped in fury, couldn't stop his mouth from moving. "Are you threatening me, Death?"

I smiled, slow and deliberate. Showing weakness was not an option. "Of course I am, Crusher." And to punctuate my point, I whipped my hand out and grabbed his face. Again, bare skin to bare skin. He went ghostlike and still, afraid to break the spell. "If you know what's best for you, you'll shut your mouth, tuck your tail between your legs, and leave." I let him go with a thrust, and he teetered back.

The pride in him held—we challenged each other with incinerating stares.

But he obeyed.

Because in the span of a breath—in the time it took to reach out my hand—not once, but twice, I had become untouchable.

One by one, they turned, and in an obedient single file line, marched into the trees, letting the forest absolve them. Jaguar and Spark were last, Jaguar handing me my gloves and lingering as if he wanted to speak—only he failed to find words.

Spark looked as if he'd never seen me before. Our lies resting between us.

I grabbed his sleeve to still him, and both he and Jaguar paused. "It's a long story," I said, in lieu of an explanation. "And I don't really want to get into it right now." They nodded in tandem and slipped away.

I turned my full attention toward Eric.

"You've seen better days," I said.

"You too," Eric replied. I wasn't sure if he even registered the movement, but he took an incremental step back. I tried not to let it pain me—but it reverberated.

I wondered why he was here.

"So, um ..." I nudged my head toward the exit trail. He nodded, and looked down—shoulders slumped, doing his damnedest to find a place to set his sights that wasn't on me.

Had I changed that much?

Become horrific?

I wondered how I appeared: same and different, I suppose. Daniel but not Daniel. I'd been swapped out with something more frightening. Perhaps bigger. Definitely more unstable.

It was easy to understand the physical wince. I would've done it too.

As Eric and I walked side by side to the clearing, I managed to keep my distance. Steps away. Worlds apart.

He failed to speak until he was safely in the cab, key primed in the ignition—with me in the passenger seat.

He dropped his head on the steering wheel, his whole body crumbled on a sob.

He was holding on to something heavy.

When he finally spoke, it came out muffled and broken. "Mom and Bill are on a cruise to Hawaii. Gramp, Grandma Grace and me ... we're gonna meet them there. Our plane takes off tonight and we have no intention of coming back. But I need your help before we go."

"You're leaving?" Fantastic news. Amazing news.

Eric's parents will be gone.
Grand Uncle Charlie, Grace and Eric will be gone.
It made my planning easier.
I smiled, only Eric's expression wiped it away.
"I need a favor," he started.
It felt bad.

CHAPTER 5
PLOTS AND PLANS

I made Eric drop me off beyond Narivous borders.

Mainly because I wanted to make sure he was out of bounds.

And then I made the long, lowly trek back to the city, murmuring to myself—even if only in my head—about the favor he needed.

I wasn't sure which was heavier, the slip of paper in my pocket from Eric, or the contraband in my waistband. The former I held onto for courage, the latter, I stashed in the one place no one would look.

With all my other contraband.

And then I went in search of Polar. Time, even with eternity laid out before us, was narrowing by the minute.

Eric's request was lofty.

It was dinnertime for the servants, so the Skull Corridor was devoid of life, and considering the quiet hum, I took relief that the mangey three from the forest hadn't spilled my secret.

To share wasn't in their favor.

I glanced up at the shelves lined with skulls—a habit I struggled to break—and made sure to skirt where Dean and Marie's now sat. The empty sockets had a way of trailing the living.

Or in our case, the undead.

I entered the Ice Apartment. They were still and equable as they always were.

I walked past the thrones that held a layer of dust and noted the coating on the drapes. Of all the Seven, Polar was the only one to deny room service.

His space, his sanctuary.

His dirt.

I made my way down the familiar hallway, passing the family photos lining the walls, entering the living room just as Polar emerged from the master bedroom. He held tightly to the knob, his upper body bent like a willow sapling as the door clicked closed.

The chill was stronger today. Frosted air billowed from under their door. On any given occasion their master bedroom was an icebox and on the rare times of unthawing, mold wanted to grow.

The musty smell never left.

I wondered if he and Frigid had a fight. Or if, more likely, Frigid was locked in some dark memory that was spurring her translucency.

"She's not having a good day?" I asked.

Polar glanced off to the side, refusing my stare. He went to his favorite chair, an eclectic gray recliner that had seen better days, and fell into it, his nails digging into the fabric with stuffing spilling from the seams.

"No. Today is not a good day," he said. He took a breath and let his head fall back. "I'm afraid if you're wanting a proper visit, now is not the time."

"Well, what about time for a thank you?"

"I always have time for a thank you." He gave a soft smile. "But I'm not sure for what."

"Lots of stuff."

"That's true. I'm pretty helpful."

"Extremely so."

"One of the best."

"Yeah." I sat down on the couch across from him, and leaned forward, my hands tapered together, forearms resting on knees. "You really are. But this time you outdid yourself."

He paused, waiting.

"What did I do?" he asked slowly.

"Got Eric, Charlie, and Grace out of here."

His spine stiffened against the soft padding of his overstuffed chair. The clock kept time with a soft tick behind him. It had a transposing ability of making the silence stronger.

"How would you know such a thing...?"

"Eric came here."

Polar's eyes popped and he went ashen—which was impressive considering he was pale to begin with. "What do you mean, he came here? When?"

"To the forest, near the entrance. A little over an hour ago."

Polar stood with his mouth agape. He looked toward the hallway as if expecting an insurgence of guards to come flooding toward him at any given moment.

"He came here today?" he asked again. His head operated on a swivel, from the hallway to me and back again. "Was it just you?"

"No, unfortunately not. But don't worry, I handled it."

Polar stilled, his white t-shirt lifting with every practiced breath.

"Details," he ground out.

"Locus, Crusher and Romeo found him; Jaguar and Spark

found me. They've all agreed to forget the situation even played out. As of right now," I made a point of glancing over his shoulder at the clock, "they should be leaving for the airport—safe, human, and hopefully never to be seen here again."

He groaned and fell back into his chair, rubbing his hands vigorously against his face, trying to eradicate the information I gave him.

"Dammit." He pulled his head up and glanced again at the hallway. "What the hell was that boy thinking?"

He wasn't really asking, simply wondering out loud. The implications were pretty clear.

In a time of rebellion, raising any sort of suspicion would require extreme bravery.

I'd like to think my stand-in counted as a form of courageous action, but truth be told—I was surpassed. Polar had taken the first step.

He had behaved heroically.

Eric erred by casting light on it.

As always, I was indebted to Polar.

He'd done the right thing, even though the risk was great. That's how heroism happens. Times of trials and tests, not in times of calm and peace.

"I'm grateful for it, Polar."

He shook his head. "I didn't want you involved. I purposefully kept you out of it to keep you safe. And what does that little shit do? Shows up. And now you're wrapped up in it."

"Not really. I escorted him out is all."

"That's still involvement."

"Minor involvement."

"Minor involvement in this climate is still extraordinarily dangerous."

"Another reason why I'm grateful. It took balls to do what you did."

"Did he at least have a good reason for being here? What was his purpose?"

"To tell me goodbye," I lied.

Polar squinted. That answer didn't sit well.

"He came here, risked his life, simply to tell you goodbye? Do you really expect me to believe that?"

I pressed my lips into a thin line, indicating he wasn't going to get more of an answer.

He moved on.

"The others—how did you manage to silence them?" he asked.

"I threatened them."

"Threatened them how?"

I held up my hands. "With my powers, what else?"

"No. I want you to tell me what you did. Work with me here."

"I am working with you."

"The hell you are. Look, I'm letting your lie on why Eric was here slide by. I don't know why he showed up, and as long as it doesn't create more problems, I don't care. That's nice of me, right? Not asking you to elaborate?" He lifted a brow. "But this isn't something I can ignore. How did you threaten them?"

"Maybe threaten isn't the right word. I gave them incentive not to say anything."

"I want specifics."

When I didn't reply, he leaned forward, tapering his fingers, scrutinizing me with his chilly stare.

"I think you're forgetting your place and, in turn, I think you're forgetting mine. I have a more solid foundation here. I know how things work and I know secrets aren't kept when there are others privy to the information. That's why you knew nothing about Eric and Charlie. Why no one here knew anything. The more players, the greater the risk."

I swallowed and looked down.

"I'm not your enemy, but Locus and Crusher are. Romeo is your wild card. Tell me what they know, so I know how to shield you when it's revealed."

"Can't you have a little faith in me?"

"I have little faith in them and I need you to have faith in me."

Why was I holding this from him? Especially now that five other witnesses knew at least some of my abilities? Polar had been nothing but my ally.

He would be on my side. Risking it all for those who meant everything.

I was part of that everything.

He was right.

He was always right.

I wondered what that felt like.

I took a breath. "I punched Crusher."

"And what does that have to do with—"

"With my bare fist." It took a second. He cocked his head and his eyes flashed over. Suddenly he was staring at me as if I were some unkempt stranger.

"You suppressed?"

I shrugged, attempting to make it look innocent.

"You little shit," he spat.

"I'm not good at it, Polar. It was a gamble, and considering it was a gamble against Crusher, I wasn't too worried if I failed. Worst case, I would've caused him more pain than the actual hit. And since they now know I've at least held onto some of the abilities, they're going to try and stay on my good side—because my value surpasses their own."

He gave a noncommittal "humph."

"I told them not to ruin my surprise reveal, either."

"You're playing a dangerous game."

"So are you."

"I'm willing to sacrifice everything for those that I love."

The smile I gave didn't touch my eyes. "Me too. Speaking of, thank you for shrinking my human pool. With them gone it gives Narivous less collateral."

"And what about your Velore pool?"

"Dolly wouldn't allow them to touch Lacey."

"And Fantasia? Or is she no longer relevant?"

I twisted.

"That's not fair. I care about her more than words can say. But she's invaluable. She's the only cure to the toxin."

The air settled around us, it was heavier than before. All the things that were said. The things that were unsaid.

Truth and lies.

"I need to ask you something," I said. I looked to the coffee table where the daily newspaper sat folded and waiting along with a kettle and a pair of tea packets.

Both luxuries in Narivous.

Some of that tea was meant for Camille.

"So Romeo, he's in charge of Trestle, right?"

Polar leaned back and gave me his full attention. "He is."

"Are there any others in charge of this area?"

"Everything is split into sections and grids. As long as he manages to stay on top of things, I don't see another individual being assigned to the area."

"Because they don't like to do reassignments, correct?"

"Correct." Polar's eyes were slits. "Reassignments leave room for error. And too many Velores within the human population leads to loose ends." He spoke slowly, with weight.

Checking every syllable before releasing it. "Why are you asking?"

"No reason really ..."

"Try again."

"Well, it got me thinking about Grace."

"What about Grace? She's on a plane, soon to land on an island, separated from us by a vast ocean. I don't think there's anything to discuss here."

"She could come back."

"She won't."

"But if she did, how do you think you could combat that?" I pretended to mull on my thoughts while feigning contemplation. "What about allergies? Something to give her if they do return."

"Allergies?"

"Yeah, allergies, something to make Romeo's mind-reading capabilities falter."

Polar let out a brisk laugh. "There's no such thing. We don't have allergies, that would go against the very nature of our being."

"Of course we do. That's why Gram kept lavender around, so Camille couldn't get into her mind—"

"That was a lie." He shook his head. "I thought you knew. We made that up as a cover, so that if Lillian were ever discovered with forbidden information, the axe wouldn't fall on Camille's head for not having turned her in for her knowledge."

"So Camille wasn't allergic?"

"Of course not."

"But then how would that have worked?" How could they possibly have passed off that lie, if such a thing never existed? It wasn't falling into place. The logic scattered.

It boiled me a little.

All these pieces I was overlooking. No. Not overlooking. Hidden from me. Feeling sluggish and dumb, I was being left out of explanations and forced to feel my way through this wretched existence blind.

When Polar, and those who claimed to care for me, could just turn on the damn light.

"Because, Daniel, in Narivous someone is always the first. Besides," he brushed his hand to ward off the topic, "it never came up, so it wasn't challenged—*thankfully*. Don't worry about it. Grace won't be coming back. Charlie will see to it."

He paused as a thought occurred to him. "We are talking about Grace, right?" Polar asked.

Deep and center, I was utterly lost, but managed to hold onto my performance. "Yeah, Grace. Of course. Just planning for the worst."

He only greeted my answer with stony silence. Perhaps his energy was depleted, or maybe he didn't care. Either way, he chose not to challenge me on it.

"Thank you for all your help, Polar. I mean that."

"Thank you for thanking me." He grabbed the paper and snapped it open. He let out an exhausted sigh. "Try not to do anything stupid," he said.

I left the apartment via the back and slipped into the crisp air. I stalled, my hand reaching for the treasures kept in my pocket, when the door behind me cracked open.

The chill following it was unmistakable.

I turned, expecting to see Polar, only to encounter the delicate frame of Frigid.

Today clearly had not been a good one, her pale hair was knotted down the middle of her back, and the scar across her throat stuck out with a vengeance, red and angry, as if she'd spent the better part of the day tracing it.

Her robe of white was askew, one boney shoulder visible.

She was angular like an Animal, but less sharp in a way akin to kindness.

And even though her entire presence spoke of madness, her eyes—her clear, blue eyes—were vibrant like a winter fire. Alert and alive.

She scanned our surroundings, checking for breathing bodies and leaned in, speaking in muted tones.

"Allergies may not work," she said, her face softening in the falling light. "But dreams do. There's no way to prove a dream. It could work. Maybe." She touched my hair and let her fingertips trace my jaw. "Just do something to dispute any challenges —change your hair, for example. Or wear a fake tattoo. Or do both. Make it real and unreal at the same time, so if a Doppelgänger sees it, they won't be certain what they're reading is correct."

She nipped her lip and dropped her hand. "Good luck," she said. "I'll be cheering for you. For her."

"Wait." I grabbed her hand, squeezed it. "I don't understand. How? How did you know it was about a girl?"

She laughed. It sounded like a chime. "A woman always knows when it's a girl." She blinded me with her smile and slipped into her apartment as quickly as she'd appeared.

How was it the mind most lost to madness was also the one rooted in clever cunning?

My love for Frigid grew tenfold.

And Eric's mission just became more plausible.

I CHOSE to walk it out. The planning required movement. Steady paces to steady the mind. I traversed through Dolly's park with the weeping willows and the clear pond. It was one of the more beautiful places in the entire city—and, perhaps, the most tragic.

It was wildly avoided.

Dolly's statue had a way of cutting the vision and paining the eyes, and due to her beloved nature, most didn't like to be reminded of her troubled past.

I found a bench and let the shadows shift from crisp lines to blurred inkiness as I sat and mulled, the sun falling to my back.

Frigid was right. I could make it a dream, an impossible dream. I had the supplies tucked away—I'd grabbed amnesia pills in one of my many Tucking Point raids.

I could do it.

It wasn't foolproof, but it was an option.

Perhaps my only one.

And then, with Eric's task complete, I'd tell Fantasia. Everything. Every single detail.

I'd explain why I pulled away. Why I chose not to visit her on the Southside. Why I flirted with other women.

All the whys.

And hope that her wicked temper wouldn't make her deaf to my explanations.

And if she chose to stay behind, she'd at least be safe. By refusing to suppress, I refused them their cure to the Poison touch. Since she was the only salve, they would have to keep her.

It was the best I could do.

And then I'd run. Grab Lacey, my stash, and run.

Teach Lacey how to act human and hide in plain sight. The pharmaceuticals I stole would aid us while we blended.

And I had enough practice—thanks to all my time spent in the screaming room—that not only could I suppress on command, but manage my poison in ways I never thought possible.

If they came after me, I would show them.

Now it was down to timing.

Precision. I needed precision.

The city was soft by the time I exited the gardens; Narivous was a different beast after sunset. It was infinitely more beautiful, calmer, non-anxiety riddled. Since the moon and stars couldn't breach our quarantine, the only glow to be seen was from the lampposts stationed between cobblestone homes. The amount of light emitted was barely measurable, yet it made no difference. Our eyes captured all of it. The glittering rocks, the various shades of gray, the soft edges of darkness.

It was peace in tangible form.

I walked to the far back and paused at the newest creation. So much strangeness as of late. The rebellion. The executions.

This.

A greenhouse.

Something greatly bizarre considering our queen was the master of Mother Nature.

It was nearly half a block long. The walls, made of frosted glass, revealed very little. Inside, the plants grew under artificial light—since they couldn't release the tree cover overhead.

The entire structure was secured with locks. All entrances had at least three. Aside from Tipper—Chanticlaim's mother—no one else was seen going in.

Tipper was almost as crazy as Thorn, as evil as Amelia, and perhaps the most clever of all the Brilliants.

A horrible concoction.

There were cameras surrounding every corner, keeping a careful watch.

The greenhouse garnered nearly as much talk as the rebellion.

"They say it's for educational purposes," Jaguar had said as we made our way to the coliseum, passing the opaque glass walls two weeks before Ether's execution which had, without effort, became a metric of the before and after in the Narivous timeline. "But that's bull. We don't need to study plants when we have Thorn—she's the master of everything."

The next day he had another theory, one he hissed much more quietly. "You don't think Thorn is sick, do you? Is that why they're studying plants?"

And after that, other whispers, other sources.

"It wasn't plants—but bombs—camouflaged in starter pots—"

"They're hybrids—"

"Trying to create new vegetation—"

Panic made the vibrations unavoidable. The greenhouse became a thrum of energy.

As I passed, the silhouette of a woman with wild hair piled on the top of her head started towards the door.

Seconds later Tipper emerged.

She was quick to secure the entrance, latching all three locks while cradling a small plant to her chest. She was murmuring under her breath, and it took a moment before I realized she was talking to the plant. Cooing nearly.

There was something sinister to it.

She spotted me and gave me a smile that was close to madness.

"There's the boy with no skills." She laughed which contaminated the divide between us. She shifted the parcel in her hands and approached. "You're quickly losing your value. If I were you, I'd get it back. Because bad things happen to objects of no value."

So I was an object?

Not shocking.

Chanticlaim said his mother saw the world in clinical terms—a large laboratory of objective components to be analyzed and placed into categories. Everything was to be measured, weighed, itemized, and broken down into worth and value. Our emotions were not a subset of our living experience, but a reaction based off our environment. They were open to critique.

His words. Not mine.

I suppose we were all objects in her world.

Her lack of nurturing spirit made me cringe for Chanticlaim.

"What do you think of this?" she asked, holding it up for my appraisal. "It looks good, yes? Perfect formation, lush green foliage with flowering that meets benchmark criteria. I dare say, it appears correct, wouldn't you agree?"

"It looks like a strawberry plant," I replied dryly.

"Strawberry?" She cackled—actually cackled, there was no way to define it as a laugh—and brought it back to her chest, curling her frame around it. "You said strawberry—without prompt from me." She leaned forward and spoke in a lower, conspiratorial tone. "I'll make sure to mention it in my notes. Thank you for your assistance." She sighed and cut through the grass, directly in line to the castle.

"Hey," I called out. She stopped and turned, only a partial twist, however. "If it's not a strawberry plant, what is it?"

She arched a brow.

"Oh, pet, you'll know soon enough." She gave me a wink and vanished into the night.

I gave one last look at the greenhouse and wondered what bigger events were at play. The toxin in my blood rattled.

I forced it to quiet.

My rooms were different. I knew it straightaway. Everything had shifted and I didn't like it.

I knew every empty nook and cranny, from the cup left on the nightstand to the pile of books on the shelf.

The intruder wasn't all over, unlike every other time. It was more concentrated. Heavier. My poison called me to the bed. I grabbed the edge of the quilt and pulled it back, holding my breath along the way.

There, sure enough, I had proof.

Physical proof.

On top of my sheets was a note. It was the size of a playing card, small enough to slip into a pocket and leave no bulk. My name was written on it.

My real name.

My old name.

The name I missed.

Daniel.

And next to my name, was a spade.

The paper was unlike anything I'd ever seen or felt, the texture both soft and coarse. I flipped it over and my lungs seized. The message was simple, but enough to strike fear.

The branch trees are being monitored. Stop harvesting.

8/27 14:38

9/1 18:53

9/7 11:35

9/9 6:02

9/15 23:36

9/16 10:30

9/23 14:26

10/2 7:03

10/7 13:33

Run under water to destroy.

Sincerely,

The Unrests

CHAPTER 6

TURNING OF THE GUARD

"Last week's numbers were pitiful. I was embarrassed to report them, and I have no intentions of doing so again." Laquet paced in front of us, his onyx hair slicked back, eyes dark as obsidian.

We stood with our hands clasped behind our backs, chins up—as was the usual during a training lecture.

This type of berating wasn't uncommon. Laquet, Guard Master, was getting sorer by the day.

I tried to pay attention, but my eyes kept drifting toward the doors, imagining them being thrown open at any moment as an authoritative second string of guards—perhaps hidden on the Southside—stormed in with an arrest warrant held tight in their grasp.

My execution wouldn't be public. There was no way to take off my head in the middle of a crowd and not have the toxin spread through the air and take out the spectators.

I would've fled last night, except it was too soon. I needed time. To tell Fantasia. To collect Lacey. To go on Eric's mission.

I theorized that the rebellion wouldn't have tipped me off if they meant to sink me. What would be the purpose of that? You don't spook the lamb before slaughter, fear ruins the meat.

That, and they would've said in the note to run. Not stop harvesting.

Two very different messages.

Still, last night had been hell. I watched shadows.

And listened to silence.

Paying attention to nothing and everything at the same time. The only thing I didn't do was sleep, and I felt it in my bones.

Laquet surveyed us for imperfections as he moved up the line. We were in the arena, the arched walls and dirt floor ideal for training. Earth to soak up spilled blood, no corners for retreating.

A cage for combat.

"For all of you who think your position is safe, simply because you were elected during trials, think again. Things are different. Narivous is changing. *Evolving*." He pointed to the far wall of the coliseum, as if we could see the city beyond its concrete barriers. "There are countless Velores waiting in the wings, salivating for your spots. What was once sacred positioning is now a task of merit. Prove your placement. Show us this is where you belong. Show us the right decision was made."

Laquet's footsteps were light despite his massive frame. He was the epitome of Animal finesse. "We are predators," he reiterated. "We are the best. I expect nothing short of perfection."

I chanced a glance to my side, and saw Spark flash a smirk.

Laquet rocked on his heels, placing his hands behind his back and honed in on a person standing out of my line of sight.

He cleared his throat, and rolled his shoulders, as his voice took on a rusty pitch. It was strained.

"So, unfortunately, there's something else I need to discuss with all of you ... and it's not going to be pleasant."

Jaguar, a little farther down the line, laughed. It was a short, brisk jaunt of a thing, quick as a sneeze and reactive as a knee jerk.

"And what is it you find so funny?" Laquet asked.

I let myself glance sideways. Jaguar was easy to spot; he shrugged, a grin still playing on his face, "You said it's not gonna be pleasant—that's a kick. Nothing's ever pleasant in guard training."

"Jaguar, for once, I need you to be serious—"

"I am being serious," he elbowed Splint next to him, the stocky bulldog of a man barely moved. "It's funny, right? Don't tell me I'm the only one."

Splint remained stoic, refusing to yield.

Jaguar's good mirth faded too. It was the look on Laquet's face that wiped him of his humor.

"I was trying to lighten the mood," he muttered.

Laquet twisted his mouth and remained stationary. He was trying to keep his emotions in check—a feat he was failing at.

That's what unraveled me. He wasn't somber, he was sad. And sad brought different connotations.

"I wish this were a laughing matter," Laquet replied. "I wish today didn't have to happen, that we could go back in time, and one of us would have made better decisions. Not just for himself, but for the morale of all of us."

Was this the prelude? Was this how I fell? I forced every muscle in my face flat.

Only, Laquet's gaze kept wandering down the line to the same spot, and it was nowhere near me. Despite holding our positions, many of us were watching where he was watching.

I did too.

I craned my neck and felt a tingle of pleasure when I realized he was looking at Crusher—who had his brow turned in, confusion knitted deep.

He'd done something.

What was it?

Laquet turned and walked toward a table at the back. He grabbed a clipboard with a paper attached to it and returned to his original position.

I could see the shadow of print underneath. He turned over the sheet and held it up high.

"This," he said, shaking the board, "is a problem." I squinted; we all did, trying to make out the lettering.

It was a bunch of numbers.

"We are living in a different climate." Laquet dropped the board, turning the codes away from view. "And an unfortunate one at that. I have troubling news to share with you." He cleared his throat and angled himself away, closing himself up.

Jaguar's smile was long gone.

Laquet chose to stare off, toward one of the exit doors. Speaking to us from an angle, without having to look at any of us directly.

"For the past two months, surveillance has increased. Areas are being monitored, areas that were once a trusted source are now scrutinized. No one is above the law, and every action is suspect until proven otherwise...." He cleared his throat for a second time, pausing, as if he didn't know how to proceed. He looked down, and turned back, so he was facing us. "So I suppose there is an explanation for this ... at least there better be. If not ..." His words trailed, the implication apparent.

Heads will roll.

He flipped the clipboard and started reading off numbers.

They made no sense, until the pieces fell into alignment.

He was reading off dates and times.

My dates.

My times.

The same ones I'd been warned of.

Each one impaled.

I should've run. Why didn't I run?

Why? Why? Why?

Laquet's voice boomed as he ran down the list. They were all mine. Every. Single. One.

Stupid. So stupid.

He didn't say what the numbers meant. He didn't say what was taken. But I knew. I knew.

I started to call on my powers, imploring the translucency to grow like a toxic bloom. The thrumming beneath my skin rattled. The room was growing into acute focus.

I would fight.

I knew that much. I clenched my hands, flexing them, my gloves a minimal barrier as my nails bit into my flesh. I would rip them off too, an atomic bomb of poisonous proportions.

I needed touch and air.

I needed it all.

My lungs rasped with a growing frenzy. Somehow, perhaps it was shock, my face flattened further. I felt it go without emotion. Blank and bored almost.

Good.

I looked to the back door, expecting the hinges to swing open and for guards to emerge fully clothed in body armor, packing bags laced with Dexitrol, perhaps wearing gas masks to prevent any inhalation.

The knob didn't twitch. The door showed no life behind it. There was a tug on my sleeve. Spark was looking at me, bringing me back, and he nudged his head down the row. Laquet had stopped talking and was staring with a look so hard, it could cut.

But, again, it wasn't at me.

He had his gaze on Crusher, who was shifting under the weight of his stare.

I paused my power, capping it without a blink. Impressed with my level of hold.

"You need to explain this," Laquet spat. He grew with wrath and tossed the clipboard at Crusher's feet.

"I-I ... I don't understand—" Crusher stammered.

"What don't you understand?" He pointed to the paper, dislodged from its clip, laying like a philanderer's cheating photo captured outside a seedy hotel, harlot at his side. "It's your eye code. You've been getting into the birch trees for months. Stealing supplies."

"I've done no such thing—"

"You can't fake an eye reading! Your denial only adds to your guilt. Tell me, are you feeding the resistance?"

Crusher held up his hands, as if to ward off the allegations.

I stopped breathing.

Jaguar stepped back, distancing himself from his uncle's wrath, unwittingly giving me a better view.

"No. No. No ... it's wrong. I, I, I don't know how, but it's wrong, I swear it. It wasn't me."

"There's no mistake!" Laquet took two strides and reached him. Grabbing him by the collar and shaking him with such force, had he not been a Stronghold, he would've knocked his joints loose. "ANSWER ME! Are you a traitor?"

Crusher had no ground to stand on. Airborne and in the paws of an angry lion, he clutched Laquet's hands, trying to provide stability. It only added fuel. Laquet dropped him, and the tips of Laquet's claws peeked out.

He pointed one at Crusher, using it in place of a finger. The lineup lost its formation; we all gravitated to stand around Crusher, building a mosh pit of lethal potential.

Only Locus stepped back, distancing himself from the allegations and the undoing that was likely to follow.

"You are to go to the tower, to answer to the Queen for your dealings." Laquet's voice was smooth, authoritative. "And may your answers be enough to save your head."

"It wasn't me.... This is wrong. It wasn't me. It wasn't me." Crusher continued to lament and stammer. It's like he didn't know any other words.

Laquet sadly shook his head. "If that's the best you have, I'm afraid I'll be seeing your head on Thorn's mantel." He looked in my direction and hesitated, before turning to Spark and barking orders, "Spark, JC, Splint, please escort Crusher to cell 33."

He placed a key into JC's hand, who closed his fingers over it with mindful precision.

Spark and Splint helped Crusher to his feet. Not only had he lost his words, but he'd lost his ability to function. He barely knew how to walk. Despair stole every ounce of arrogance.

"It wasn't me," he said, weaker, broken and locked on repeat. "It wasn't me."

They started toward the door, and I had to step out of their way. Spark locked eyes on me, lasting for only a fraction of a second; and I saw the glee in them.

They left a pall-like silence in their wake. No one even moved.

Laquet, in an attempt to either prove a point—or to distract us—ordered us on a perimeter run three times over.

For once, I was allowed to run on my own.

And I didn't pillage.

Scream was pacing the Poison Throne Room when I finally made my way back after guard practice.

I was exhausted, both physically and mentally.

She wore a gown of tightly-fitted silk, the black fabric moving in waves behind her as the train swayed with every step.

Strangely, she was biting a tapered fingernail, a habit I'd never seen her perform before. She looked completely upended.

"There you are." She came to me and placed her hands on my shoulders, pulling me into an embrace that radiated from her core. The scent of jasmine infiltrated my nostrils. "I've been waiting on you all day. Tell me all of it," she whispered. "Every sordid detail." She grabbed my hand and pulled me farther into the apartment, to the back where the living space sat empty and waiting.

She took a seat on the black leather couch, tugging me down next to her, keeping my hand tightly in her palm.

On the table was tea.

Cold from the looks of it.

"So?" she prompted.

"There's not a lot to say. It happened so fast." I responded honestly. "One second we were lined up and the next Laquet has Crusher tight in his fists, screaming that he's a traitor. Spark, Splint and JC hauled him up to the towers."

"You should've heard how he screamed," Scream purred, releasing my hand to take a sip of tea. She scowled at its lack of warmth and placed it on the table. "It was the most beautiful music—there is no better sound than that of agony coming from the depths of your enemy." She stroked my cheek, her face softening. "It wasn't fair that I was the one to hear it though, it should've been you. Why weren't you here?"

"Laquet made us run laps ..."

"Today? After all that happened this morning?"

"I think he wanted to distract us. Crusher isn't a favorite, but he's still a guard."

Scream let out a disapproving, "Hmmm."

"So how did it happen? Are there more details?"

Her smile stretched; it filled her whole face. "Oh, very much—"

There was a throat clearing behind us, and we turned to Plague standing in the doorway.

He hesitated in the threshold and fidgeted with his shirt cuff.

"Why are you here?" Scream snapped.

"Oh, I'm sorry, I thought I lived here," Plague replied.

"Must you remind me?"

"Must you forget?"

"Trust me, darling, I try to forget every day." Plague worked his jaw and Scream surprised us by putting on a smile. "You know? I take that back. I'm glad you're here."

"No, you're not."

"Oh, yes, I am."

He narrowed his eyes. "What's the catch?"

"You think there's a catch?" She asked it all sweet and sing-songy. There was most certainly a catch.

Plague wisely waited.

"Seems our servants have been lacking in their duties lately. Why don't you be a dear and get us some tea? This," she waved to the kettle and cups, "has gone cold."

"I'm not a servant, Scream," Plague said, annoyance twisting the half of his face into one of disgust. "Last I checked, I was your husband."

"As my husband," she practically spat the word, "you should serve me better. I am a Seven and you bend to me."

I wasn't sure where to look and chose to stare at my lap.

The interaction reminded me of Mom and Dad. How they acted when they had to share breathing space, making everyone else in the room, primarily me, shrink.

"There are better ways to ask for it," he said. "I thought you had manners."

"I don't have to ask for it any other way, nor have manners. Now, do as I say."

He hesitated. I could feel what he was trying to do.

He was trying to hold on.

To Scream. To their marriage. To her light.

When Plague didn't move, Scream lashed out. "Why are you still standing there?" She snapped. "Go. Get. Me. Some. Tea."

Plague gave a sardonic bow and disappeared.

Her shoulders slumped and she rubbed her eyes, letting the haughtiness go. "What's happening to me?" she said, so intimately, she seemed unaware of her words. "This is what happens. With time. Fissures become caverns. I'm sorry. I'm so sorry you had to see that."

"I think you're apologizing to the wrong person," I muttered.

She whipped her head up, and her dark eyes went completely obsidian.

"Excuse me?" she challenged, and even though I knew it would serve me poorly to talk back, I chose to anyhow.

"He was trying to be nice, Scream, and you unleashed on him."

"I unleashed on him because he's always around."

"Well where else is he supposed to go?"

"He has an entire forest to explore, a city that bows to him—he doesn't need to be underfoot every minute of every day."

"He's around because he cares about you."

She pinched the bridge of her nose and took a collecting

breath. "Don't pretend to know what's going on between the two of us. You have no idea what I deal with, what I contend with, what I go through—so it's best you keep your nose out of it. Understood?"

The cut of her jaw was rigid. She would not yield, and I wasn't in it for a fight. I, like Plague, selected silence.

"I'm sorry you had to see that though," she said, softer.

"Can you rebuild?"

The look she shot me lost its edge; it fragmented to sadness. "I don't want to," she replied honestly.

And because I didn't know how to move with that, I chose to circle the conversation back to a distraction.

"So what were you saying about Crusher? Did they find more evidence against him?"

She perked up. "Oh, yes. The investigation was very thorough. This morning as he was being hauled into the tower his rooms were raided. The contraband was staggering."

I leaned in, eager, despite the pang of guilt blooming.

Screw him. He deserved this. Karma had come knocking.

"What type of contraband?"

"All the pills he stole from the birch trees for starters."

I kept my face flat, unfeeling, even though I wanted to dart from the room. To check my stash. Air was suddenly in short supply.

I found a question in the haze of panic.

"And what else?"

"Papers, small card sized papers with spades marked on them—the symbol of the rebellion. And who knows? Perhaps he was the mastermind all along. They're trying to get names, but so far he's holding out."

I was still unraveling the knots. Something was screeching within me.

"They named off a lot of dates...." Think. Think. Think.

"Why did the investigation run so long? Why did they wait to report him?" I asked.

And who the hell were *they*? The question danced on the edge of my tongue.

But it would be too suspicious.

"Oh, that's simple ... to make such harsh allegations against a favorite needs evidence to back it up. We have it now. We gave him just enough rope to hang himself."

A chill crept. Someone had held onto my indiscretions, kept them buried away as they accumulated, only to transfer them to Crusher.

"Will he die?"

"Yes."

"Are you sure?" She had to be sure. I needed to know. Certainty helped with compartmentalization.

"Absolutely. He's guilty as sin. They will strip him of his title and then they will strip him of his head, and it will be the most public display yet. Everyone is invited. Even the Southside will be called in."

Fantasia. My heart started.

To see her—all of her—for only a moment, it was like my heart found out how to beat again.

"Do you know when?"

Her face stretched into a vindictive grin. "Tomorrow, my love. At sunset." She reached out and stroked my cheek. "By nightfall, his head will be on the mantel as it should be. As it belongs."

"That fast?"

"Well why not? He's guilty. And if you must know, I was the one who encouraged a speedy execution—as a token of my love for you. That's what family does after all, isn't it? We fight for each other. As you should well remember."

Scream never divulged the details of her hatred for Amelia

—nor did she indicate how she'd planned to take her down, only that it revolved around the suppression, that the pairing would go hand in hand.

It was a curious thing, of course.

I approached it from different angles and came to one steadfast conclusion: she needed me in a position of value. To become indispensable. Because, as the mantra goes, a valuable Velore is more coveted than a favorite one.

And if you happened to be both—the results would be simple: Ineradicable.

Which led to my other suspicion: I would be the weapon to kill Amelia, my toxin could handle it with ease and we could pose it as an accident. Thorn would be upset, of course, but as long as she couldn't prove any malicious intent—heck, maybe even if she could—she'd let the transgression slide as long as I provided her with her greatest wish.

Total and complete power.

Maybe.

"Fight for me the way I fight for you." Scream grabbed the side of my face and forced me to look into her dark, depthless eyes. They were bright with shimmer, the way the night soaks up the stars. "His head will rest next to your aunt's—special placement, at my behest—and once you see it there, your grief will lessen, for your heart will have received a balm it so desperately requires. I'm asking *you* ..." she settled on that last word, "to try, in turn, to show me the same kindness. You have to get it back. Suppress and we hold all the cards."

She let me go then, and stood up. Her smile angled.

"If you love me the way I love you, you will suppress."

I opened my mouth to shoot out a reply—but words failed me. She wasn't going to hear it anyhow, because she'd already turned away.

She paused in the doorway, and kept her face hidden from me. "I'm counting on you, darling. Don't fail me."

She left then, taking the atmosphere with her.

I stood to leave when Plague arrived holding two teacups.

When he saw me alone, he placed them on the table and left—sparing no words.

I took both cups and downed each in a single, scalding gulp.

Then I checked my stash.

It was intact.

Meaning, whoever placed the contraband in Crusher's rooms had to have access to a heavy pharmaceutical load. They had spared me, but for what?

My rooms were heavy again. I went to my bed and pulled back the quilt, knowing all along there would be a message.

There were fewer words this time, but they were infinitely more ominous.

You can trust us, but you can't trust the tea.

What the actual hell?

CHAPTER 7

A DREAM IN THE MAKING

Maybe the Universe was on my side.

It dawned on me, in the dead of night, that this could be, in fact, the perfect synchronized opportunity.

Crusher's execution would make for the ideal distraction.

I could run Eric's errand while Crusher's head was being severed and afterwards make my plea to Fantasia, all wrapped up in a matter of hours. Her proximity would make it simpler —cleaner.

Everyone would be feeling their way through the aftershocks, too absorbed in their own internal conflicts to pay me much attention.

And since I could no longer harvest from the birch trees, I had no reason to stay.

Come early evening, I'd be gone, Lacey would be gone and, hopefully, Fantasia as well.

The Universe wasn't so bad after all. This felt serendipitous, like driving through town and making all the lights, or having exact change at the cash register.

The little things that always made you feel a bit better.

I held Eric's note in one hand and the phone in the other. It was early morning and the sun was barely up. That new day energy bled through my palm; I wanted it to translate to success.

I needed it to.

I longed for the balm tea, but after reading the Unrests message last night, I knew better. I trusted them. Not to say it didn't leave a void.

It was a small luxury I'd grown quite fond of.

The satellite phone was heavy, cumbersome. I experienced a pang of gratitude that Polar showed me where he kept it. When would I ever be done experiencing pangs of gratitude for Polar? At this rate, never. If he kept it up, he'd need to be outfitted with a cape.

This was how he worked around Chanticlaim's cellphone blockers and, fortunately for me, Polar wasn't up when I went to retrieve it.

The Screaming Room's powerful sound blocking walls were ideal; it afforded me privacy and silence. I punched in the number and told myself to breathe. If she didn't answer, I would try again.

And again.

And again.

My private number made it unlikely she'd pick up on the first ring, but hey.

The Universe was being nice.

I was going to ride this luck until it ran out.

The ring ricocheted until it turned to voicemail, and my stomach dropped at the sound of her voice asking me to leave a message. It brought back a host of memories. It hurt. It fed. It clouded.

I hung up.

And repeated.

Over.

And over.

Each attempt made me more leaden, more desperate. Leaving a voicemail was actual proof. I couldn't do that.

Again.

She would eventually pick up. I was certain of it.

Again.

And then finally, there was a click—and this time it wasn't a recorded greeting, it was her.

"Sarah," I breathed.

She sucked in her breath, a sharp, raspy gasp of shock. Followed by a heavy, stagnant pause that carried on for the better part of a decade.

"Daniel?"

I was undone.

I LIKED how the drums sounded and it bothered me that I liked it.

It also bothered me that I wasn't feeling all that bothered.

Apparently, my guilt was a short-lived sensation.

Fine by me. Guilt was an emotion that created weakness, second-guessing, and fractures. I didn't have time to entertain such craven sentiments.

Not with a rebellion brewing.

And an escape plan to deploy.

Crusher was falling for my crimes, but in a sense, it was just. He was a predator—a true creature of his environment. My lack of remorse was eclipsed by a solid truth: his death would save countless future lives.

This was a healthy purge.

That's what I told myself.

Part of me believed it. Part of me didn't. I willfully forced myself to accept the former.

But I was right—no one paid me attention as I left the city.

I realized cameras would pick up my leaving, but the Unrests were obviously being led by someone in a position of power. They covered for me once, they'd do it again.

If they could fake an eye scan, place contraband in Crusher's rooms and somehow sneak into mine, all the while remaining anonymous, something told me the cameras would be of little consequence.

For whatever their reasons were, it seemed I had an ally. A powerful one at that.

Besides, after today, I'd be a memory. Who cares if I started to fall under suspicion, I was soon to be a free man anyhow.

I selected a nondescript silver sedan from the parking garage and pondered, as I made my way down the winding, mountainous road, if this could be my getaway vehicle.

Up until I reached Charlie's, that is, because once there, I would swap it out for Eric's truck. He left the keys in the back of the garden shed—a gift for the favor I was completing for him.

Truth was, I would've done it regardless.

This was important.

I understood why he risked his life. I would've done the same.

I slipped through Trestle like an old memory. The town held only a few unremarkable changes. There was a new vet office and the second-hand thrift store had expanded into the lot next to it. The pawn shop was now buying gold and the dingy motel on Main Street finally closed down.

Other than that, it was exactly as I remembered it.

Mick's Grocery.

The barber shop.

The fast-food joints with their tantalizing scents, only all the better now that my senses were heightened.

I wasn't expecting to miss it so much.

Had it not been for time, I would've pulled in and gorged.

Instead, I found myself on the corner of Fifth and Jefferson, two blocks away from a park, and three away from Eric's newly abandoned house, taking to the sidewalk and doing my best to blend in. I had my hoodie up, my hands stowed in the pockets, and my shoulders slumped forward.

To make myself as small as possible, of course.

From a casual glance, I was nothing more than a misplaced soul walking off discontent.

The toughest part was keeping my stride intact at a human pace and not clipping along too quickly.

It was all about the details.

The park was not only convenient—but strategic. Surrounded by old growth oaks, with a play structure off to the side and a walking trail that harnessed a pair of batting cages, it was obscure and often forgotten.

The feature I looked for, however, was the wetland restoration area riddled with no trespassing signs—wildly ignored, and never enforced, clearly marked by a small walking path beaten into existence by the countless tennis shoes of those with a rebellious streak.

I slipped through the grove, weaving around massive trees and made my way toward the fading spot.

I had a pair of sunglasses stashed in my hoodie pocket and slipped them on as I rounded the final corner. I stopped cold. The ground felt like it was rising up around me, clawing at my feet and stilling me in its grasp as if it wanted to swallow me whole.

Or maybe it was my heart seizing, or my body forgetting how to function.

There was really no way to tell.

Not with her standing in front of me.

Sarah.

Beautiful, perfect Sarah.

She was standing with her hands cupping her elbows, wearing jeans and a white tank top with one of those pleather jackets that fit her frame the way a glove molds to a hand.

She was prettier than I remembered.

Maybe that was a gift of my heightened senses too.

My gaze traced the outline of her body, from the curve of her graceful neck down the length of her torso, to the sway of her hips. I wanted to commit this moment to memory.

No. Correction. I wanted to commit *her* to memory.

With any luck, it would be the last time I saw her.

And she would be safe.

Safe.

That was my mantra. I held that word, repeated it, forced it into reality.

She took a step toward me, full of hesitation, as our eyes locked. Disbelief commandeered her expression, followed by an influx of emotions: happiness, anger, relief.

She must've settled on joy, since she bridged the space between us and jumped into my arms. She wrapped her limbs around me, her face nestled into the crook of my shoulder, legs latched onto my torso.

My hold on the poison was stronger than I gave it credit. I was able to not only pull it back, but the touch of her flesh against mine didn't reflect pain, but deep-seated pleasure.

I held her like that. Just her and me, tied in each other's arms, trying to keep the pieces from falling away.

It lasted for the span of a century, neither one of us ready to let go—neither one of us prepared for the next step. We wanted to extend time and make the inevitable heartache wait.

With great reluctance, she finally unwrapped her legs and I helped her to the ground. She let her hands linger against the length of my sweatshirt, where my heart slowly beat, and looked into my face with a curious scowl. Carefully, she pulled my glasses away and dropped them near my feet.

She searched my new, abnormal eyes.

Eyes I should've hidden from her, but didn't want to, and if there was ever a time when I could come uncloaked and vulnerable, this was it.

They were paler now, and no longer paired her own. That was a joke we had to let go.

We didn't match anymore.

As if she needed to see more, she gently removed my hood, revealing my hair. It was lighter now too, with a streak of black. Sure, it could've been chalked up to hair dye, but it had an authentic quality to it.

Her eyes sifted through the information, darting across my features, trying to make sense of me—but not me. I grabbed her hand, it felt wrong against the shield of my glove, and I aptly removed the fabric so I could experience her flesh the way I used to.

With nothing between us.

"What happened to you?" she breathed, as I closed my fingers around her own.

I shook my head and tried to organize my thoughts.

"It's a story," I said. I cleared my throat. Because of the pain lodged there, not the poison. "But you're gonna have to forgive me, because I can't answer you just yet. I need to know something first ... did you follow my instructions?"

She narrowed her eyes, and her chin flexed in that stubborn way I always admired about her. My steely Sarah.

"I'm here, aren't I?"

"That's not what I asked. Did you tell anyone you were meeting me?"

She held my gaze. "Why does it matter?"

"I'll tell you after you answer."

"And what if I did?" She arched a brow. "I've been sick to my stomach worried for you. You can't just up and disappear, with no explanation. People have the right to know."

"You're right—"

"It's irresponsible. And for someone always preaching responsibility, it makes you a total hypocrite by the way."

"Sarah, I need you to tell me. Don't mince words. Did you tell anyone you were meeting me? Yes or no, it's that simple."

"I didn't tell anyone," she said, albeit a bit bitterly. She gave the front of my sweatshirt a shake. "I wanted to though, the way you left, with no explanation, that wasn't fair. I wanted to tell...."

"It was shitty of me."

"Very shitty."

"And you deserve better."

"A lot better."

I smiled; it was real. I loved this about her. Her resilience, the confidence. The fact she trusted her placement in the world.

"Damn," I whispered, practically awestruck. "I've missed you." I meant it, too.

She still held my sweatshirt in her hand, and something with her grip, her words, it called on me. She felt it too, and pulled me closer, and I followed in step—wanting to be pulled, offering no resistance. We were close, our breath mingling into a solitary unit. She raised her blue eyes to me and exchanged her angry grip for a gentle one, unfolding her fist to lay her palm softly on my chest. My own hand gravitated to the delicate spot at the back of her neck—the poison retracting without much thought.

It knew to pull back. It went into deep hibernation—had it not, I would've never allowed myself to be sucked into her orbit.

But every part of me—both alive and undead—wanted her. Even if it was only for a moment, even if it was only in farewell.

For from this day forward, she would have to exist only as a figment. Someone I would force myself to forget.

Someone I would reluctantly revisit, only in my memory, perhaps with fondness, perhaps regret.

She sighed, and her breath licked my skin, touched my lips, and I was helpless when she leaned up. I naturally leaned down.

The kiss we shared—it brought back the past. We kept it chaste, our mouths closed as if we could keep our emotions at bay by maintaining restraint. Yet it seeped far beyond a pair of lips touching. It pierced something I'd forgotten about: the simplicities of feeling.

It was so dangerous and reckless—not necessarily because of the poison thrumming through my veins—but because of the play on my heart.

It took to a different rhythm.

I was happy for that moment. A moment that was broken down into simple pleasures.

A boy. A girl. What could've been. What never would be. There would be no regret.

Even if there was guilt.

Fantasia was never far from my mind.

But I told myself it was to save Sarah. Because a man of deadly means—with a toxic touch—couldn't kiss a woman without destroying her. It was as Frigid instructed: make all challenges disputable.

It would make Sarah's "dream" more cloud-like and unreal. No one could refute my role.

She stepped away, and shook her head. "I shouldn't have done that," she said.

Eric.

She meant Eric.

Her expression was the same one he wore when he told me what he needed me to do. When he gave me the paper. Spilled the second task.

"We didn't mean for it to happen," Eric had said, looking out the windshield, and then at his lap. Anywhere but at me. "We were both pretty messed up. Sarah thought you didn't care—and I tried to tell her, without telling her, that you didn't want to leave, but it was near impossible to explain away your absence without making it obvious. I mean, I wasn't allowed to say anything." He started to work on a hangnail, his shoulders turned in.

"You were gone. Tony was gone. Everyone was gone, and I was left knowing too much—and not having anyone to turn to." He finally looked at me.

There was earnestness in his face.

"Not even Gramp would talk to me. He kept shutting me out. Sarah was all I had. I was all *she* had. It's like we grew hotter or something simply because there was nothing else left to burn."

He hesitated then, perhaps waiting to be absolved of his choices. For falling for Sarah.

For failing me.

There was no need.

He'd helped her in ways that I couldn't. There wasn't anything to be angry at.

Jealousy, however, was a different beast. That one would take more time.

Maybe forever.

I nodded my head; it was the most I could offer.

He took a big breath and let his head fall back, releasing it in one swift gust of relief.

"She has an opportunity to go to school out of state," he said. "Convince her to go—and I'll do the same. Her aunt's willing to take her in anytime she's ready to go—and she already has enough credits to graduate. Do whatever you can, but don't let her stay here."

It was a task I was willing to take on.

She was worth the risk—for both of us.

And now I stood in front of her, knowing he wasn't coming back. Knowing I couldn't tell her he was gone. Similar to the predicament Eric was placed in when I disappeared.

I grabbed her hand and ran my thumb across it before raising it to my lips and kissing the back of it.

"I'm glad you did. I'm glad we did. There's nothing to feel bad about. Sarah, you're one of the best memories I have—someone who made my life so much better. You know how thankful I am for that?" I squeezed her hand. "I have never once—not even for a moment—regretted you or what we had together. I've only regretted me. And the things I've done. The things I've said. For not believing you. I'm sorry, Sarah. I should've said that a long time ago. I'm so sorry."

I reached into my pocket and pulled out a pill. One of the mercy medicines JC told me about so very long ago. It would erase the memory, turn it into a dream-like recollection.

Thank you, Frigid.

"I would never encourage you to take something that's dangerous," I said.

She nodded.

"Nor would I ever encourage you to take something not knowing what it is—"

"I wouldn't take something if I didn't know what it is," she cut in.

"I know. I know. But this one time. I need you to do it this one time."

"Daniel, no dice. I don't care who's offering me what, I won't swallow anything if I don't know what it is. That's dangerous." She looked at the pill and stepped away. It hurt. To have that distance. But I got it, she was making a point.

And if she needed space, I would respect that.

Although it took all my willpower to remain rooted.

"Sarah, please—"

"No." She crossed her arms to further cement her stance. Part of me was thrilled. It was a good practice to have, and I was proud of her for standing behind her convictions.

"What if I told you what it was?"

"I'm listening." *But still clearly skeptical.*

Damn. Good girl.

"This," I held it between my hands, "is called an amnesia pill. It will turn everything I tell you and show you into a memory. Make it feel like a dream."

She rolled her eyes. "Oh, please—"

"I'm serious, Sarah."

She smirked, clearly not convinced. My heart hammered in my chest. How difficult was this going to be? To make her believe? If something as small as an amnesia pill could be dismissed, by the time we got to the meat of the story, she'd think I'd gone mad.

"But that's impossible, Daniel."

"I have bigger impossibilities to tell you—but we gotta start with this."

"This is weird."

"You're telling me."

"I have questions, lots of them. For starters—"

"Wait," I held up my hand silencing her, "I'm gonna have to show you first; I see that now. Then I can field questions. You'll have a ton no doubt. But will you at least do me a favor?"

She narrowed her eyes.

"Simply hold this. Just hold it. Please."

She sighed and held out her hand. I placed it in her palm and she was quick to wrap her fingers over it.

I paused. There was only one way to make her believe, show her.

I knew I had to go at maximum strength. Let my eyes turn black, my aura darken, my death to radiate. It needed to cover me entirely.

"I want you to pay close attention," I said, and took a step back. "Don't come near me, don't touch me, and hold your breath ... just in case. Do you understand?"

"What—"

"Tell me you understand." I took another step, and then a few more for good measure. "Do you understand?"

She nodded.

"Watch. Stay silent, and when I tell you to, don't breathe."

I found a patch under a low hanging evergreen, the needles prickly and within reach. I pulled on my training in the screaming room and found my center. The poison seemed to understand—it truly did listen—and I began to call on it. I could feel my powers pull, I could feel the heat behind my eyes, knowing the whites were luminescent and the pupils dissolving the pale blue of my irises. And right before it was ready, I said, "hold it," and saw her body stiffen with a preserved breath.

The needles near my flesh pulled back, they wilted on the branch, dying and falling at my feet. The decay continued, crawling, weaving, stripping the bark, moving the way blood transfers through a vein.

No doubt, my face was a hazard to look at.

The translucent phase—especially that of a Poison—was terrifying to witness.

Sarah's expression wore that fear.

And then, I called it back. The strong grip I had on my powers was noteworthy, they collected together and simmered to a low hum.

My practice had paid off. This whole day was a test of confidence.

I felt my flesh return to its normal pallor; Sarah's, in turn, matched it. I scanned the branches. I would have a lot to clean up afterwards to try and remove my presence.

She looked at her hand, the one that held the pill, and nodded. "How?" she whispered.

I went to her then, grabbed her free hand, and did what I should've done a long time ago—I fell to my knees.

Going all the way back to the beginning, when I should've believed her about Alex. About the events of the party that was the catalyst for our breakup.

Orchestrated like so many other things Narivous was good at.

And I started again with the one phrase that would become my mantra, "I'm sorry."

CHAPTER 8
DEN OF WOLVES

I made quick work of changing out of my sweatshirt and jeans, ditching them in a dumpster in Eric's old neighborhood, and back into my uniform.

All I had left was to see Fantasia.

The city still held traces of celebration, the aftermath of losing a Velore that wasn't much liked by anyone. Jeers, no doubt incited by hefty alcohol consumption, could be heard above the din of gossip as it leached out beyond the city's walls. No guards stood watch; I wondered if they surrendered their post to partake in the party.

Most likely.

A flash of color swept overhead as Fred the Eighth—or Ninth—landed on the wrought iron gate and let out a knowing chirp. His greeting seemed like a positive token.

For if Dreams was close, so was Fantasia.

It put a pep in my step, only to lose its buoyancy when Torti emerged, her green eyes sharp, her expression accusatory.

It was hard to say if my imagination detected her look of

disgust—or if it was actually in play—both because Torti was known for her hostile expressions and I was feeling a surge of guilt over what happened with Sarah.

A deed I justified in my head as necessary. It was one of salvation and little of lust.

That's what I told myself.

Because it was the truth.

Certainly, the truth.

I wouldn't allow myself to consider otherwise.

Right. It *was* the truth.

"Well, there you are. The wanted man," she said.

I stopped in my tracks.

"What's that supposed to mean?"

Her smile twisted. "They've been asking for you."

"Who's they?"

"Scream. Thorn. Splint was searching for you a little while ago."

Shit. "Did they say what they wanted?"

She shrugged. "He didn't seem alarmed if that's what you're asking—so from my understanding it wasn't urgent."

I wondered briefly if I still had time to see Fantasia.

Torti took a step forward, sauntering up to me. She had her brunette curls wrapped tight into an over-the-shoulder braid, and now ran her hands along it.

Almost as if she were nervous.

"Well, since you're here ..." I made my voice light and friendly. Not guilty. Even though it felt a little guilty. "Do you know where Fantasia is? I think she and I need to have a little chat. Only for a second, of course. I wouldn't want to keep my betters waiting much longer." And before she could protest, I lifted my hands in innocence. "It will not be out of the eyesight of others." Technically not a lie. It would be in eyesight, but definitely out of earshot.

We could drift to the margins and no one would challenge us. And then I would lay it all out.

Explain. Urge. Plead.

Something dark and heavy shadowed over Torti. Fred flew off and she inched close—so close I could feel her breath breeze along my cheek.

"I think we've had enough ... events for the day, don't you?"

"What are you implying?"

"The execution, you half-wit." Her lips twisted into a smile that would never pass as genial. "And you still have so much more to ... attend to. Why don't we leave the Fantasia visit for another, less eventful, day?"

"I appreciate you looking out for me—"

"I'm not looking out for you. I'm looking out for *her*. The last time she was in your company, she came back less than before. Or need I remind you?"

My face flattened at the verbal slap.

"Besides, just because it isn't urgent, doesn't mean you should leave Thorn waiting. Not today. And—for your information—this token of advice is *me* looking out for *you*." She turned and moved away, calling over her shoulder. "Besides, Fantasia has already left for the Southside. So get a move on, Casanova. Today's not a day to be messing around."

And like that, poof, my good luck was gone.

I TRIED NOT to get too far ahead of myself. This could be for anything, anything at all.

Two guards stood outside Thorn's primary door and admitted me without batting an eye. No one really questioned me in the castle anymore.

I entered Thorn's Throne Room, unique in its grandeur and

sterility. It resurrected painful images. This was the place that saw Tony's last breath. Marble floors polished to a mirror shine led to thrones, all mighty and grand, Thorn's the biggest of all. Plants climbed along the walls, thick ivy and rosebushes with exaggerated points.

The room smelled like disinfectant and petals.

Ahead of me, flanking Thorn's back door, was the place of honor for any guard.

It was where her favorites were stationed.

Locus was there, obviously. Standing heavier than I'd ever seen him, the toll of Crusher's arrest and death dressed him in lead. And opposite, both in spirit and placement, was Spark.

Wearing a smirk.

Clearly pleased.

If something were wrong, he didn't give any indicators.

This was as far as I'd ever come.

As far as most anyone had come.

Spark pressed a button, activating the intercom, and announced my arrival. The door swung open and Scream waved me forward. The doors sealed behind us.

I stepped inside a small, intimate sitting room. It was practically barren.

There was a single door on the other side and I realized this parlor acted as a partition, a move for privacy so anyone within the marble Throne Room couldn't catch a glimpse of Thorn's quarters.

The room was framed with heavy-duty molding, and had only two abstract paintings, a pair of chairs and a small table. It felt intentionally empty.

Nothing else.

Not even a flower.

Scream looped her arm through mine, pulling me close. Even though we were alone, she dropped her voice to bare syllables. "About time," she hissed. "I expect the very best of behavior."

And then, with a practiced flick of her wrist, threw open the door.

Nothing in Thorn's quarters made any particular sense, at least in comparison to the other Six. We stepped inside a huge suite, one massive room, with both furniture and subtle steps acting as dividers to each space—giving them their own identities. Her bed along the farthest wall, was raised three steps, creating a pedestal effect. Her sitting area, two steps up, and on the main floor, straight ahead, was a massive fireplace of river rock swallowing one entire side.

There were paintings of the Sevens adorned in ornate, unique frames. Amelia's and Scream's images seemed grandest, with expensive casings that made their images appear bigger than the others.

Aside from that, there was nothing else. No décor. No knickknacks. Nothing to soften the space. It was a void. With essential furniture and minimal details.

Not even a plant.

There were three chairs, however, and a small round table centered in front of the fireplace.

And even though it wasn't cold out, a fire blazed in the hearth, wrapping the room in warmth and a strange calm.

The space reminded me of a phobia. Someone afraid of tight areas.

Thorn and Serpent occupied two of the seats. The third was, no doubt, for Scream. Each held a hand of cards, with another pile lying face down.

Serpent fanned her set and covered her mouth.

Even though her lips were hidden, a smile was in her eyes. They glittered, and it wasn't from catching the dancing flame.

Thorn sat stone-faced.

I unhooked my arm from Scream and made a show of bowing. I went lower than necessary, but if I'd learned anything, Thorn enjoyed kowtowing. Serpent chuckled.

"Another player?" Serpent asked, her eyes swimming between Thorn and me.

Scream reached out and touched my cheek with a grazing thumb. It was a peculiar move.

Affectionate and out of place.

They were all studying me, and Thorn's brows knitted.

"Death," Scream started, "go grab a seat." She nodded toward a spare chair next to the stone hearth.

I grabbed it and placed it between Serpent and Scream. It was nice having a buffer to Thorn, but it placed me directly in front of her. I wasn't sure which was worse.

"Another player!" Serpent practically clapped her hands, but since she was still holding her cards, she made do with patting them between her palms. She yanked the cards from Thorn's hand and quickly reshuffled.

"I had a winning hand," Thorn spat.

"You'll get another," Serpent replied dismissively. "You win too much, anyhow. I think you cheat."

"I don't have to cheat to win."

"But I wouldn't put you past it." Serpent shot me a wink. This dismissiveness with Thorn took my brain a second to compute. "Be wary, Death." Serpent paused her shuffle to fan Thorn with the deck. "This one is a scoundrel."

"Just because you lose all the time doesn't make me a cheat. It only makes you a loser, and a sore one at that," Thorn said.

Serpent shrugged. "I'm not *that* bad. Plus, I can't help but notice you don't deny the allegation. You're just talking around it." She leaned in close to me and spoke in a mock whisper, "Which is what she does when she's guilty." She sat back up and flashed Thorn a dazzling smile. Thorn shook her head, not in disgust, but exasperation.

This urgency to see me no longer felt ominous.

"You can keep that information in your arsenal for later," Serpent said. "It's valuable ... and useful."

Scream rolled her eyes and propped her elbows on the table. "Would you deal or what? We don't need your endless commentary."

Serpent began dishing out cards.

"Do you play poker?" Serpent asked.

"Maybe once or twice," I said.

"Well, if you ask me, we need four players for a proper game. Lucky for us you decided to finally show up." She gave a playful pat to Thorn. "Especially since Amelia decided to ditch us...."

She let that sentence hang, her emerald irises twinkling with mischief. She glanced at Thorn and said, "I don't see why you enjoy spending time with her. She's a wet blanket. Never laughs at my jokes."

"Maybe you need to be funnier," Thorn replied.

"I'm funny," Serpent said, before giving me a dazzling grin. She had an intoxicating way about her. This was the closest I'd been, and now that I had full access to her features, she appeared the youngest of the Seven.

"She's too serious," Serpent muttered, tucking a strand of long, brown hair behind her ear. "And, quite frankly ... draining. Never laughs. Never cracks a smile. I think she clawed out of the womb with a scowl."

Scream chuckled.

Serpent pitched her voice into a nasally mockery—it sounded nothing like Amelia, but it reminded me of her all the same. "That's not funny, Serpent. You're a child, Serpent. If you call me a pussy one more time, Serpent. And on, and on, and on. It's exhausting."

I snorted a laugh and pressed my hand to my mouth to stifle it.

"See?" Serpent pointed to me. "He thinks I'm funny."

"You're only encouraging her, Death," Thorn added, rapping her knuckles on the table. "Serpent, you shorted us a card."

"Just seeing if you're paying attention…." Serpent handed out another.

"Or maybe you can't count."

"Anyway," she continued, "I'd think I'd much rather play with this dashing brute. He seems a little less *stiff*."

"Enough of the Amelia bashing," Thorn said.

"What? It's not like I said she was anal."

"Serpent."

"Even though she is …"

"Serpent."

Serpent hooked her finger at me and leaned forward. Once again, she spoke in a whisper everyone could hear, "But between you and me," she looked at Thorn and Scream, her eyes wide, "Amelia could sit on a needle and not even a Stronghold could yank it out."

Her and Scream laughed in tandem; it trickled around us. Even Thorn cracked a smile.

"Ah, that's what we've been working for," Serpent said. "I knew I could bring out your good humor."

"Enough, let's play," Thorn said.

The card playing commenced, and I found myself beginning to relax. The chatter was easy, flowing, and without effort. From an outsider looking in, you would've never known a favorite had recently met the axe.

And for the record, I was pretty confident Serpent was the cheat.

"So, Death, darling," Thorn purred, after our sixth round, placing a card on the discard stack and collecting a new one. "Your auntie thinks we should become better friends. Hence why you're here."

"I thought it was because we needed a fourth for poker since Uptight ditched us," Serpent interjected. She picked up a card. "And I must say, he sucks. I vote we keep him around."

"Another person for team Death," Scream said.

"So you're setting up teams now?" I asked. This was the most I had contributed in all the rounds. Everyone was content to talk around me. I was more of an ornament, the little kid sitting at the grown-up table, to be seen and not heard.

"I was merely telling her you would make an excellent favorite. Which you will."

"That's what you keep saying," Thorn replied dryly. "But I've yet to be convinced." At this she narrowed her eyes, and I had a feeling the lightness of our conversation was about to gain some weight. "As it is, I'm hesitant to fill that spot, what with the events of late."

Scream scoffed. "Why? Because Crusher turned out to be a snake?"

"Don't start insulting snakes," Serpent said.

"You know what I mean."

"You make it sound so inconsequential," Thorn said. "He's my second favorite to betray me. First Chugknot, now Crusher."

"Ah, but that's only because you like to pick the strongest for your personal guards. They see your power and they try to take a slice of it for themselves," Scream said.

"How can you be so flippant?"

"Because that's the cost of your position." Scream leaned

forward. She gave a half smile. "It's to be expected, Thorn. It's nothing new. Every king in every kingdom had to contend with the same issue. They'd go through lulls of quiet only to discover the silence wasn't real—that plotters spoke in hushed tones while sharpening their spears. And you know what they did?" She lifted her chin. "They took their heads, and they did it with a wrathful might—the same as you."

"This is different."

"How so?"

"They didn't select their citizens. They were granted by chance. My kingdom has been chosen carefully."

"Not really." Scream arched a brow and looked at me. "You select primarily based on background and auras—both of those can be chalked up to chance. Besides," she placed a card down, "humans are precarious. And gratitude wears off the moment one forgets what it's like to be without. Velores, although better, maintain their human core. Mistakes are still made."

"Mistakes at this level are not to be had."

"But they are, and always will be. It goes with being a mighty ruler with mighty citizens and, speaking of which, it makes sense to keep the strongest around you. Death here—"

"Has turned into a disappointment," Thorn finished for her. "And therefore wouldn't serve me as well as you believe."

"That's a little harsh," Serpent muttered.

"Excuse me?" Thorn challenged.

"Well, look at him," she used her cards to sweep the length of me. "He's got great color. The potential is still there, we just need to draw it back out."

"And how would you suggest that?"

"You should give him something worth fighting for," she breathed. "Or maybe someone."

Thorn tsked. "I need harmony in my kingdom. I prefer not

to madden Amelia. Furthermore, I shouldn't have to *bribe* my citizens to obey me."

"It's not bribery, it's an incentive," Serpent rebutted.

"Fine. I shouldn't have to *incentivize* my citizens either. They should serve me with fealty. I've granted them the greatest gift after all."

"Don't twist our message, Thorn," Scream said. "Death is of the utmost loyal when it comes to you and our goals. He spends hours in the screaming room practicing."

"So you say. I've yet to see any of his efforts come to fruition." Thorn picked up a card and peered at me from over her hand.

"As for the incentive part," Scream continued, "we all know Death does his best work when his heart is invested."

"And it's not invested with me?"

"He hasn't really gotten a chance to know you, now has he? Hence why I suggested this meeting. Our visit. Give him a chance and he'll love you the way we all love you."

"Except you're not really letting him talk, are you?"

"Are you accusing us of commandeering the conversation?" Serpent asked.

"You're always commandeering the conversation," Thorn replied.

Serpent shrugged.

And I realized this was, indeed, their way. They were working off each other.

That's why they were hiding out in Thorn's rooms. It wasn't for comfort—it was to push their own agenda.

And right now, I was top of the list.

"And as for releasing Fantasia," Thorn spoke slowly, "all for a what-if, it would not be worth the wrath—"

"Oh, c'mon," Serpent cut in. "It's not like she's ever *not* mad. And, if I were a betting woman, which I am," she lifted her eyebrows at me to indicate she was, indeed, a gambler, "she'll continue to be mad. It's part of her identity, I think she likes it—creepy little thing that she is. Besides, denying Fantasia freedom hasn't lifted her mood by any measure. I say wait a day or two—since she's bound to find something to be pissed about, and lay it on her then."

Thorn set her cards down and leaned back, crossing her legs and giving Serpent her full attention. "And why is that? Why should I wait for her to already be enraged?"

"Be-cause," Serpent spread out the word, "it's foolproof. They're mad to begin with; they're mad when you're done. Nothing changes. It's like taking a crappy day and confirming it is, indeed, crappy."

Thorn almost smiled.

"I'd be more inclined to accept your argument if you didn't hate her."

"I never said I hated her. I said she's always in a mood. And mad. And anal. And impossible. And creepy. But there was nothing in there about hate."

"How could I have been so misled?"

"You make too many assumptions." Serpent glittered. "So, anyhow, I say let's make this brute a regular card player because I want to win some mon-ey," again, she stretched out the word, "and he's absolutely terrible. Then get him a lady—and poof—everyone capable of happiness shall, indeed, be happy. Myself included."

"So simple," Thorn said.

"Extremely so."

"It'll work, Thorn," Scream said. "Death can do it, I know he can."

"Fantasia, you say," Thorn mused. "You think giving him Fantasia, bringing her back from the Southside, will spur his abilities again?"

"What wouldn't one do for the matters of the heart?"

"Makes us do crazy things," Serpent followed.

"Yes. What wouldn't one do? Crazy, reckless things." Thorn looked at me with narrowed eyes. It's like she knew all along. "You know, I think he could do it without her."

For once, neither Scream nor Serpent swept in.

We all recognized the shift, and none of us wanted to dislodge the storm.

"I think, maybe, Death darling, you've been much more in control of your emotions than you know."

I refused to break eye contact, and asked, with full sincerity, "Why is that?"

She smiled. It was bright and blinding like the sun.

"Crusher's arrest, his execution, all the pressures of being strong and fairly new; why, most newcomers flicker in and out of translucency. But you don't."

"He has the Dexitrol dust," Scream argued.

"That he does. That he does." Thorn stood up and propped her hands on the table. She leaned forward, looming both in physicality and mood. "How much on average, Death, do you use of the Dexitrol?"

"It depends on the situation and day, what's in store," I answered honestly. "Some days I take more than others."

"And when Crusher was arrested, such a spur of the moment event, how much was in your system then?"

This was a trap. I knew it. Scream knew it. Serpent knew it. Thorn knew that we all knew it.

"My regular amount."

"Right. Because you wouldn't have known any different, would you? It was so sudden. For all parties involved—myself included." She clicked her tongue. "But strangely, by all reports, you handled yourself with great aplomb. Bravo, by the way." She gave a pregnant pause. "Why do you suppose that is? Your ability to remain cool under such unexpected circumstances?"

"Maybe the batch was more potent—"

"Maybe you're a liar."

"Why would you think—"

"Because I can see it on your face," she spat. "You can do it. Even now, being in the hot seat, you're mellow. For a person who claims he has little control, you show remarkable translucent stability."

Her smile turned syrupy.

"I used Dexitrol before I got here," I lied.

"Oh, I don't think that's it at all. How much did you take, darling?" Thorn asked. She was shimmery. Her whole being. Even her aura magnified.

The sweat came on, and I thought about pulling parts of my translucency out to prove a point, but right now it would appear staged.

"A full vial or so."

She shook her head and stepped around the table, moving close. Scream and Serpent became background characters.

"Dexitrol burns up quickly for those who have little control over their powers."

"I guess maybe I took more of it than I thought...."

Thorn touched the front of my shirt. I kept stock-still.

"I suppose I have a confession, Death." She gave me an all-knowing smile. "Those vials of Dexitrol you've been using? They have a red topper, don't they?" Her grin grew. "Did you know they come from a select batch? At my behest? Tipper was kind enough to make them for me. You're familiar with Tipper, right? Chanticlaim's mother?"

I was barreling toward a precipice.

This was bad.

I nodded, since I couldn't form a word even if I'd tried.

"I ordered her to make placebo batches. Just for you. Because something told me your inability to suppress was all in your head."

She took a step back and opened her arms wide. "And look at you now! You can control it better than you thought."

She turned to Scream, "And you say I can trust him." She shook her head and flicked her hand. "Leave us, Death. I'm tired of you."

I left with three sets of stares heating my back, practically with my tail tucked between my legs.

I WENT STRAIGHT to the screaming room to find my stash. It was comfort. The moment I stepped inside I knew something was wrong.

Same as all those times in my rooms.

The space had shifted.

When I unlatched the vent and reached inside, my grasp met nothing, it was already gone.

I dug deeper, thick in denial. I needed something. Anything.

That's when I touched paper.

I ripped it out and read so fast the letters blurred.

Forgive us, but running won't work—Caseao and Bronson are proof. Your family will never be safe, for the Art of Famine is upon us.

Help us and we'll help you.

Wait for the boom and travel in the opposite direc-

tion of the smoke. Leave at sunset and find the man with red on his cloak.

Come alone. Tell no one. Destroy note.

Sincerely,
The Unrests

CHAPTER 9

A POISON'S TALE

The next three days were spent in a haze of rage and rampage.

Velores—even those fighting against Narivous—were working against me. So I stopped caring. Not only had they stolen my stash but, they'd robbed me of my hope; condemning me to a life of imprisonment.

But that was minor in the grand scheme of things. Lacey's permanence here made everything worse. It was unbearable to consider.

My scorn touched everyone.

I challenged Laquet in guard training and when he ordered me to run laps for insubordination, I walked off rather than comply. He edged close—but maintained enough distance to indicate there was nothing he would do.

Or could do.

Every tea cup I found, I threw against the wall—after drinking it, of course. I no longer adhered to the Unrests' guidelines. Screw them. Plague caught me mid-act, having already tossed one, taking relish in the shattering as it fell to the floor. I had a second in my hand.

"What do you think you're doing?" he asked.

At which, I replied by throwing the second at his head.

He ducked, avoiding the hit, but the glass shrapnel dusted him.

I walked in a linear, unyielding way so when people crossed my path, they were forced to dive out of it.

And then there was the door slamming.

Once, while exiting the Poison Quarters, I managed to shut the door with such a force that ripples traveled up the wall, dislodging a skull on display and sending it to its demise against the marble flooring.

Bits of bone, as well as my distaste, scattered everywhere. Pastel servants were quick to descend on the mess.

I glanced up to see if I recognized whose skull it was—but it was a nobody.

And as others attempted to sweep up my mess, containing as much damage as possible, the shadows in the corners whispered behind cupped hands. I made sure to pass the only intact piece—the jaw. I stepped on it—*hard*—and sent teeth in every direction.

I whistled as I slammed the door for the second time.

Only no skulls fell from the shelf.

A sore disappointment.

AN INTERVENTION WAS COMING. How could it not? I was out of control, and the one thing the leaders couldn't handle was someone not in control. I think control might've even been part of their behind-the-scenes mission statement.

So when Scream showed up in my room later that evening I

was ready. I had a book in my lap and had reread the last paragraph a whopping three times.

It was hard to focus when my vision kept blurring with anger. My thoughts never strayed far from my stash.

I'd meet the man in red, and I'd make him pay.

"Well, you've been making quite a mess lately," Scream said. She opened the door without knocking, something she'd done countless times, only now it became infinitely more grating.

"The door latches for a reason," I replied. "Next time knock."

"Excuse me?"

"I said ..." I made sure to spit out the word. "Knock."

"You don't talk to me like that. I give the orders around here, and this flare-up of behavior is to stop now—"

"Or what?" I set my book down and stood up. I felt everything in me liven. "What will you do, Scream? Kill me?" I held out my hands and threw my head back, letting out a certifiable laugh. "Then do it! What are you waiting for?" I snapped my fingers and pointed at her as if an idea just came to me. "Actually, let's go to Thorn and have her do it. She can use my skull to replace the one that shattered. I love this idea. Let's do it now."

She took a step away, her face as white as the underside of the moon. I'd never seen her pale before—she was always translucent—except now she was near see-through. "What is happening with you?"

"I'm over it, Scream."

"Over what?"

"This." I indicated the room. Her. "Everything. I'm done. Done caring, done trying. Done."

"Something happened, didn't it? Tell me."

I smirked. "Nothing happened. I simply woke up."

"You were fine a few days ago."

"Well, I'm not now." I picked up the book and fell back on the bed. "You can leave."

"I will not." She took a step forward. "I want to know what this defiance is about, and I want to know right now."

"Dammit, Scream, not everything has to be analyzed. This is gonna be me from here on out, so if you don't like it, send in Thorn and have her ravage me with her vines. I'm done caring."

"They know your cousin and grand-uncle are gone."

I slowly placed the book down, and carefully regarded her with contempt.

"And that's supposed to mean something to me?"

"Is that why you have this attitude? No one else to hurt?"

"Are you asking me if there's any more collateral you can use against me?" I stood up for a second time and moved with a deliberate glide toward her. "Is that really the stance you want to take right now?"

Scream took two steps back, and then another. I moved with her, as if we were doing a dance braced in the arms of darkness. She batted her eyes and for only a moment something was visible: vulnerability.

It bolstered me. To not have control, to feel like a puppet on a string, and then to suddenly realize you're not helpless. It's intoxicating.

"I'm just letting you know it's been noted, and if this behavior continues—"

"Then what? They'll kill my beloved aunt Marie and uncle Dean?" I threw my head back and laughed. I sounded like a jackal. "Oh, damn. Wait. You guys already did that."

"Daniel—"

"Death," I corrected her.

"Death," she hesitated over my name. I wondered if she

silently cursed Thorn for giving it to me. It had a source of power to it. An omen. "They will resort to other means."

"Like?"

"You have a Velore circle you care about ..."

I shrugged and folded my arms. I was taller than Scream, not by much, but at that moment it seemed lofty. "Well, I suppose if they try, we can test out how dangerous I really am."

She looked down. Time spread between us; it went on for eternity.

"And then what?" she asked.

"Oh, I'll do my damage I suppose, and then they can kill me in that lab they were piecing together back when I first turned. I'll have had my pound of flesh, they'll have theirs, and at the end of the day, those of us who are lost will get to finally rest. No more manipulation. Or cruelty. Or crimes against humanity."

Her breathing shallowed. She touched her collarbone while searching my face, tears of black pooling. Then she nodded, as if coming to some sort of internal solution.

"That lab is a lie. It was never made to kill you. It was restored to scare you, to show that Thorn still had power. That she could execute you if she chose."

"She had no intentions of killing me?" I scoffed. "I highly doubt Thorn would've mourned my loss or even batted an eye. She destroys on a whim."

"No, it wasn't that—" She remained grave. "May I?" she asked, indicating the bed. I nodded and she took a seat. "Come, sit next to me." She patted the spot next to her.

I eyed it suspiciously. "I won't bite," she said. "Now come, sit." I took the seat, but remained on edge. "I never told you how I died, did I? How the Poison came to be?"

I shook my head, and she twisted her hands in her lap.

"The whole point of the immortal cure is that it can't be

given to the living—it destroys the host. In order for it to work, a heartbeat must cease." She cleared her throat. "Thorn's father never wanted me. He wanted Frigid, he wanted Ember, but he didn't want me. And, above all else, he wanted Thorn under his thumb and in his control. To love him the most. I complicated matters since I was Thorn's closest friend, and being he was a man of manipulation, he understood any bonds outside his own weakened his hold. So, he had to destroy me, but in a way that seemed accidental, natural, without fault.

"He decided to give me the cure while I was still alive, knowing full well it would destroy me." Her lips twisted into a cruel smile. "He lied about it, of course, said he had no idea it would react in such a way, told me before I took it that it would be the kindest turning of them all."

Scream looked down and her fingers intertwined in her lap. "Thorn found me, dead, and lost her mind over it. She was the one to give me the cure for a second time. To save me." Scream looked up. "And because the cure wants to preserve the host by giving them strength over their method of death it became ... confused. It had killed me; it had given me life. I was both death and healing.

"Now Plague, he was a different story. He shot himself, as you well know, annihilated a complete section of his face. He was instantly brain dead, but they managed to get his heart back and working, even if it was weak and momentary—and then I touched him." She shrugged and took a deep inhale. "And killed what was left. But the cure was a bit of a waste on him. His resurrection had that same confused angle, but with very tragic aftershocks. Much worse than my own. At least I'm not rotting."

"Wait. That's not right. Plague told me—the very first time I met him—that he was brought back by mixing the cure with the toxin. That's how he was made. Not that they were one and the same."

She shook her head. "How would he know? He was dead."

"So, is that what you told him?"

She nodded, a bit sheepishly. "In case you haven't noticed, we're prone to lying here. Very few Velores know how the Poisons were truly made. Mainly the Brilliants, and those who lived through the creation of us. Plague is a talker—it served us well feeding him the lie. It's a secret we guard and one that I trust you'll keep safe."

I understood then. Why it was lied about. Why they *had* to lie about it. They didn't want someone hellbent on vengeance to create more of us. We would be the ultimate weapon. A bomb that didn't discriminate on who ended up in their blast field.

Velores.

Humans.

Animals and earth.

We would destroy and maim.

And depending on who was selected, it could be perpetual and endless. A terrifying thought.

She was safe telling me—I didn't even want this knowledge. It felt too risky. I nodded, indicating we were on the same page.

Scream scratched her brow and the large onyx ring she wore flashed in the low lighting of my room. "The only positive thing that came out of Plague's transformation was my pool of people—whom I could touch—more than doubled. Ember, Frigid, Ferno, Polar ... Plague." The last name came out reluctantly. "Tipper thinks it recognizes the DNA of my family and won't attack. And since I was both death and cure for Plague—albeit at a lesser level—it recognizes his DNA and those Velores related to him."

Scream placed her head in her palms before looking at me with strain.

"So, yeah ... I'm both life and death, as are you—and because of that, there is a speculation, and they're not sure, mind you—but ..." She bit her lip, and I leaned in, engrossed.

"That Plague and I ... and now you, are the only Velores in all of Narivous incapable of second death, because anything they use against us could, potentially, make us stronger."

"You mean if Thorn ravaged me with vines then..."

"There is a chance we could, in turn, master that ability."

"What if they just hacked us off at the neck?"

"The axe may not even break through the bone. We'd become a Stronghold."

"And Strongholds must be destroyed from the inside."

"Yes."

"That would mean vines," I said, *or poison*, which I didn't say. "And could backfire on us."

"Yes."

"Are you sure?"

"No. No Poison has ever been killed, nor has it been attempted, so there's no way of knowing, but it's a possibility that is rather frightening to consider. The only way for us to die is if you managed to make the suppression happen and they harvest the formula to strip our toxic touch. To, in a sense, take away the cure component that destroyed us in the beginning."

"But even that's a guess."

"Yes."

"But then they could kill you."

"Maybe. But there's freedom in that, too. Besides," she took a breath and glanced at some far-off thought, "there are fates worse than death."

"But they built the lab to destroy me. That's what I was told. Even Polar—"

Her smile was twisted. "Polar doesn't know any different. Everyone was told that story."

"And it was all a ruse?"

Scream shifted in her seat, and her eyes fluttered toward me. She shook her head. "It was built for people to think it was your killing room."

"And then what would they have done with me?"

She grabbed her forearm, holding herself together with a tight grip. "I don't know for sure...."

"You do too."

"I don't."

"You have an idea."

"It's only speculation."

"Tell me."

"I have no proof."

"Tell. Me."

"Oh, Daniel." She covered her face and let out a moan that crawled from the very pit of her stomach. "I think they would seal you in a soundproof, impenetrable coffin and bury you—just as you are. Whole. Alive. With no one to know the difference, because they'll have thought you were taken to the lab and destroyed. And even if we knew, how would we ever find you?" She opened her hands up, palms facing forward. "We don't need food. Water. We consume those things for enjoyment only, and the cure reacts in accordance because it's there for our survival. To keep us moving. You'd be there for forever. And, need I remind you, only Thorn can find what exists underground. And they would use the scent eraser so the Animals couldn't pick up your trace; and if she made the land grow over your grave, you'd be lost to us forever."

"But it's not like there wouldn't be people who would know though. You would have to craft the coffin, put me in it, take me there, that would require a team of help—"

"A team she would destroy afterwards to keep the secret."

"I could tell people now."

"If they believed you—"

"I'd make them believe."

"But you're forgetting ... we wouldn't be able to find you. What is our knowledge but a way to torture us over our inability to unearth your underground prison?"

Well one person would be able to find me, considering, of course, her forbidden talent of mind reading held out: Fantasia.

Unless she was buried along with me.

I swallowed loudly. It was too detailed, too well plotted, to be merely a speculation. This was orderly terror.

"Have you done this before?" I breathed.

She glanced away.

"Of course not," she whispered. "We've only just discussed it, in the past ... long before you."

It was a loaded lie. And despite the terror that lodged deep in my marrow, I understood two things. One, this was my new threat, and it didn't apply to only me, but to Velores I loved as well. Eternity lodged beneath the earth. No death. No life. And two, there was only one person hated enough to warrant such treatment.

I'd only ever heard whispers of him. His name acted as a curse.

A tyrant King. A father.

Urrel.

I FOUND Fantasia in my room the next day. She was sitting cross-legged on my bed, her cloak draped over her lap in lieu of a blanket, her damaged hand carefully placed beneath the fabric.

I froze in the doorway as my heart stilled and my lungs lost the ability to churn out air.

She was in my room.

Here.

I could see her, smell her, and if I so chose, step forward and touch her. The mere thought left me frozen in place.

It had been too long, and in the span of distance and time, I'd convinced myself that the feelings I felt were indeed magic, a sick sort of Stockholm syndrome. She'd rescued me, and I fell for her and her selfless act. The fact that she was glorious and gorgeous, made the falling that much easier.

And now, here she was, just like that.

Real.

Beautiful.

Completely in control of my heart, mind, wants.

If it were magic, I quickly shoved the thought somewhere I couldn't touch—because I didn't care and had no desire to turn it over and analyze it.

Nothing mattered but that she was in my room, waiting for me, looking shy and a little uncomfortable.

She unfolded herself from my bed. She stood feet away, both of us locked in some sort of beating stalemate, afraid to move, afraid to break the moment. She was quick to place her hands in her pockets, and when the intensity of my stare became too much, she looked down.

We'd become strangers.

It was horrible.

Strangers. The word was wrong.

It was wrong.

We'd shifted to wrong, and I had a hand in that shift. Shame, guilt, remorse—every negative connotation you could define within the bounds of the English language applied. I resisted the urge to go to her—to wrap her in my arms, to make the time and misunderstandings fall away. She was too silent and uncertain in front of me.

It was more than distance that stood between us. It was actions too.

All of them mine.

I broke the impasse; it was my responsibility to do so. “You’re here.” Far from impressive, but it was the best I could come up with.

“I have permission,” she stated flatly. “For some reason or another, they think you still hold affection for me and that my presence might do you some good—despite my arguments otherwise.”

“You don’t think I want you here?”

She flashed her eyes—actually flashed them—in an act of translucence challenge. “I *know* you don’t want me here. Would you like to know the reasons why?”

I crossed my arms. Her energy, and the thick force of it, was already cloaking me in defensiveness, even though I had no right to be. Pride is a powerful emotion to work around.

Whatever she was about to throw at me I deserved.

Still.

“I’m all ears. Please, tell me all the things I’ve done wrong. I’d love to hear them.”

She smiled. For once she didn’t look so pretty.

“You never came to see me.”

“Yes.”

“You never sent me word.”

“Yes.”

“You’ve been flirting with other girls because I’m that irreplaceable.”

“That’s not entirely true—”

"How is that not *entirely* true, Daniel? You've been here, distracted by everyone that isn't me. I've become your nothing. You've made me your nothing."

"Fantasia, it's not what you—"

"NOTHING!" she screamed, and then in a burst akin to her Animal prowess, she lunged and slammed her fist against my chest. "NOTHING! Nothing, nothing, nothing."

It hurt—but the emotional hit was by far more destructive than the physical blow.

She took a step away, and I could see it then. What I'd done. I'd reduced her.

Made her small and invisible.

Narivous had treated her in a similar fashion—forcing her to wear a mask so her face wouldn't offend, a patchwork cloak to mark the absence of a clan, the urge for silence whenever she was in the presence of a Seven.

She'd managed, because she detached; it was her way of self-preservation.

Only I had managed to make her transparent.

Because I was bigger in her eyes. I was supposed to care, to love her. I was held to a different set of standards.

Which I'd failed miserably at.

"I'm sorry," I said. Meaning it. Feeling every syllable. "I'm so sorry.

She turned her head, unable to look at me, and burrowed her broken hand deeper. It was a stark reminder of consequences. Words. Actions. The lack thereof. They all had an impact.

"You should hate me," I said.

"I do," she replied, but there was little conviction. Her lavender eyes finally raked over my face, reading my expression, locking gazes with me.

"But not entirely?" I asked.

She shrugged.

"I want you here," I said. "I've always wanted you here." I stepped forward. She didn't move away. And when I grabbed her waist, she moved with my touch. I pulled her into my arms, and was rewarded with a tight hold in return. "I've missed you," I said. "I've missed you so damn much."

I meant every word of it.

She grasped me even harder.

I put my hand behind her head and buried my face in her shoulder. Cinnamon, Fantasia's scent, infiltrated me. It was like coming home.

This was how obsession is made.

"I forgot," I whispered.

"You forgot what?"

"Your power."

"I have no power," she said. "But thank you for the boost in confidence." I felt her smile against my chest.

"How could you think I wouldn't want you?"

"Because of the others."

I sighed, my whole body dropping with the breath, and shook my head. Grateful her mind-reading abilities never worked well on me, I was able to speak words on the offense and not defense. "You've been listening to your sisters too much. There've been no others."

"Only because you can't touch anyone."

"Even if I could, I wouldn't want to touch anyone but you."

She pulled away to search my face. My heart lodged in my throat. "You have a funny way of showing it."

I placed my hand under her chin and ran my thumb over her lips. Her perfectly-shaped lips. She shuddered. "Fantasia, I can't think right when I'm around you ... I get in your hemisphere, and all of a sudden nothing else matters but you. Don't get me wrong ..." I smiled. There was nothing forced about it. "I like it, but it's not helpful. You are, without fail, my greatest distraction—both for better and worse."

She angled her head. "Tell me the better and tell me the worse."

"You really want to know?"

"I need to know."

"Better, because when I'm around you I'm no longer afraid. Worse, because when I'm around you I'm no longer afraid."

I grabbed her broken hand and lifted it to my lips, kissing the back of it ... and then trailing to her severed finger.

"I think about what has happened because I'm intoxicated by you, and it frightens me that I'll cause more hurt." I placed my head against hers; we shared breaths. "You know you're still perfect, right?"

She bit her lip.

"I'm serious. And I suffer so much guilt over this. You clouded my judgement in a way I found so ... freeing. You became this addiction. And then, well, when we got caught and lost so much." I checked the door. "Speaking of, did you get details on what's allowed?"

"I'm not sure—they didn't say."

And, almost on cue—or as if she were listening in the other room, which was a possibility since my door was open—Scream materialized in the threshold.

"Don't mind my intrusion," she said, "but I couldn't help but overhear. If you must know," she flashed all her teeth in a winning smile, "you two are no longer forbidden."

I dropped Fantasia's hand as she let out a gasp.

"What?" I asked.

"Are you serious?" Fantasia followed.

Scream grew brighter.

"Very serious."

"But I thought," Fantasia stepped in front of me, her whole

frame rigid and cutting. "I thought we were only allowed to talk."

Scream pretended to knock a fleck of dust off her dress. "When it comes to Death," Scream said, carefully using my name, indicating the perimeters of her freedom, "you two are allowed to do as little or as *much* as you wish."

"That's if she wants me," I interjected.

The look Fantasia shot me assured me she still did.

I let out a breath I wasn't even aware I was holding.

"Our only request," Scream said, "is that you practice discretion for some of our more … sensitive Velores." She stepped back and gave a slight dip of the head. "And with that, I'll get the door. Don't worry, dear." Scream turned and shot me a purposeful glance. "I'll make sure to knock first."

And like that, Fantasia was mine.

CHAPTER 10

WEDDING DISASTER

"It's an urban legend," Fantasia said, adjusting my tie and smoothing it along my chest. "I've heard of it for years, but there's never been any proof, and if it were real, there would be proof. Just a scary story to try and frighten us into compliance."

"And you're sure you've never read anything?" I looked at the closed door, but kept my voice to a hum.

"No. I doubt Urrel is buried alive; I think that's too extreme, even for Narivous."

"Because they're known for their mercy."

"Because that would require a lot of effort. And could you imagine what would happen if he got out?"

I smirked. "I think it would give new meaning to the phrase 'all hell would break loose.'"

"That's putting it lightly." She ran her hands along my sleeves.

"So you don't think they'll do it to me? To you?"

"No. For the umpteenth time, no. Someone would find out. It's too risky of a punishment."

"I wish I had your confidence."

Fantasia reached up and stroked my hair. In a week's time, she went from nerves to ease. From anger to forgiveness. It was more than I deserved.

"You'll get there," Fantasia said. "So can I please tell them?"

"No. Under no circumstances are you to tell them—not until the day we're set to leave."

"But they'll need time to think about it."

"They'll have to think fast."

She blew out an exasperated puff of air. "Tell me again," she said. "About your plan. Your stash. Do you think if you got it back, we could get out?"

"I think we can get out without it. Quite frankly, I'm tired of waiting."

"It would help."

"But it's not necessary, big difference. And you know what would help?"

"What's that?"

I tapped her head. "If you could use this to get into the minds of other Velores—tell me who's involved. I could muscle my way back to the stash."

"I told you, I haven't been able to see lately."

"Why is that? Your vision is spotty. Sometimes it feels like it's crystal clear, and other times it seems as if you never had the ability to begin with."

She nipped her lip, and dodged my gaze. "I think it's the honeysuckle."

"Honeysuckle?"

"Thorn's been growing a lot of it lately. It's hard to work past it."

I froze, feeling my face lose its color. "Like the lavender for your mom?" I tested.

"Yeah. An allergy."

"That seems convenient."

I put my hand on her neck, a gentle hold, but made her look at me full on. To her credit, she didn't pull away.

Was she aware Camille's allergy was a lie? If she were a true Velore mind reader—then yes.

If she wasn't, then no. Either way, there was dishonesty resting between us. And she wasn't ready to let it go.

"I guess I don't need the stash. I told you what I can do. If they come after us I'll kill them."

Fantasia winced.

"You scare me when you talk like that."

"Would you rather I lie?" *Like you?*

"I'd rather you not say it in such a way that makes me think you're capable of more."

"And I'd prefer honesty."

"Some truths should never be spoken aloud," she retorted, hidden meaning embedded deep. It told me she was holding onto her story.

For some reason, I liked that. It offered opportunity for future moral aperture. Because deep in the recesses, I knew I was barreling toward a life where I would need loopholes—perhaps depend on them.

Lies without guilt or recourse.

Yes. I liked that very much.

I stepped back and straightened my lapels. Dressed in Poison Formal attire, I felt stiff but polished. "Whatever happens, I'm not going to be sorry for it," I said. "If they want trouble, I'll bring it. It's as simple as that."

She swallowed.

"We'd have to convince my sisters to come with us."

"That makes it too big, Fantasia."

"I don't care. That's my caveat."

I cleared my throat and put my back toward her, before

slipping into the bathroom to grab cologne. I hadn't addressed it yet, but there was a chance, one I didn't want to face, that I'd leave without her. Taking her sisters would require too much effort. It would make hiding more difficult: Doppelgänger or not, the more of us to hide, the larger the footprint we'd leave.

I wanted a needle in a haystack scenario.

Fantasia had her arms folded, face cross, when I returned.

"I'm serious," she said. "We have to get them involved."

Fantasia stepped up to me and started to attach the spider cufflinks.

"Let's talk about something else."

"Agreed."

"And Caseao and Bronson?" I asked again.

She shook her head. "It was so long ago ..." That's how she started it the last time. "Caseao wanted to marry Bronson, but she was promised to Laquet, and being Caseao was Dolly's little sister—"

"That's the little girl from her statue carving?"

"Yeah."

I'd seen other pictures of Caseao, one of which was in Polar's hallway, locked in time and held together in a silver frame. Caseao couldn't have been more than six years old as she held on to Dolly's hand and stared down at a pair of sparkly shoes bedazzled in monochrome. Dolly's face was stoic, unsmiling; there was a desperation in her eyes, and she looked at the lens—or perhaps the person standing behind it—in challenge. Even in black and white, it was clear the grip she had on Caseao's small hand was far more forceful than necessary.

As was anything related to Dolly, it hurt to look too long.

You started to catch the atmosphere.

"And Bronson," Fantasia continued, "was the older brother to Laquet and Cougar, he had no say either. They both ran away, and a hunting party was dispersed. They found them and brought them back. But Caseao and Bronson refused to relent and chose to kill themselves over being pulled apart through a forced marriage. They stood near Thorn's fountain, and in a public display that was horrifying—and terribly romantic— drank the only poison extraction they'd ever retrieved from the Poison clan."

"So Scream and Plague had been tested on?"

"Just once, and I believe it was only Scream. It was too painful."

"Ah, what they want to do to me. Comforting."

She shrugged.

"Why wouldn't they just let them be together?"

"Control."

"That's exactly why we need to get out of here."

She was quiet, thinking of her sisters. I was quiet, thinking of what it would feel like to leave her. To shift the subject, I brought up the only thing I'd yet to bring up.

"I meant to ask ... " I cleared my throat. I'd been parceling out information since we got our reprieve, gauging her reaction. This last one, I think the selfish side of me was too afraid of the answer—so I held on to it for a solid week, because I was hellbent on not stopping. "Who makes the tea? The balm tea?" I eyed the empty cup on my nightstand.

"Tipper makes it. Why?"

I wasn't sure, but she seemed to go a little stiff.

"One of those letters told me to stop drinking it. I complied, but after they took my stash I decided they could go screw themselves. I like it and I'll drink it as I see fit."

Before Fantasia had finished securing my other cufflink, she abandoned the task and walked over to the chair to grab my jacket. Her long, elegant back moved with little fluidity.

It was a strange sequence.

The moment passed, however, and she was all smiles when she turned around.

"Do you think there's something wrong with it?" I asked. "The Seven drink it on a daily basis—surely it's okay," I reasoned.

She shrugged. "I think if it brings you comfort," her lips tugged at the corner, "you should, absolutely, keep drinking it."

"I like that answer."

"I'm glad." She smiled. "And, may I add, you cut a dashing figure." She kissed me on the cheek. "Well, I better go. This wedding is a big deal—so naturally, I'm not invited."

She left, practically bolting out of the room.

I couldn't place it, but I was fairly confident there were lies embedded in her answers. She moved as if she were holding on to something that didn't fit right.

It wasn't just my poison telling me.

It was observation.

WE CELEBRATED under tents of green, held up by trees, at the farthest corner of the city directly behind the castle. I was given a seat of honor and stationed next to Polar, Plague and Ferno. Their camaraderie and drunken cheers lifted Plague from his depression.

He acted like the man I met ages ago. He even engaged in casual conversation.

Big leap from broody Plague.

The bride, Cheetah, wore a pantsuit of gold sequins that glittered as she danced with her groom, a short Velore of new order. He was recently recruited, rebranded as Augur, and from the sour look on his face and Cheetah's, it was an easy study to see that this wasn't a happy commitment.

I wondered why this arranged pairing took place.

It was an awkward fit.

Amelia sat at the high table with the rest of the Seven. Servants flowed throughout, filling goblets, offering plates of food, removing utensils and soiled napkins. Guests cozied up to whichever leader could grant them the most favor.

Amelia spoke with few and tossed her gilded cup back like water. All the while, she'd rake her feline eyes over the crowd, until falling on me like a gravitational pull.

There was a frequency to her focus that didn't pass unnoticed.

Perhaps it was my imagination, but Cheetah, too, seemed interested in me. Shooting daggers when she wasn't glowering at her groom, who, at the first available opportunity, took to drowning his emotions under vats of booze.

He'd chase the hard stuff with a swig of beer—something only the most seasoned alcoholics could pull off.

This guy was no amateur.

Jaguar encouraged him. Placing steins and shots glasses under his nose, and laughing with every swig.

By the time the music started playing and everyone took to the dance floor, it was a slosh party.

Amelia slipped away for only a moment, materializing wearing a set of gloves, and approached our table. She slinked when she walked. A hybrid between a slither and a stride. Same as Cheetah, she chose not to wear a gown, but a pantsuit. Rubies gleamed on her belt, matching the razor heels she wore.

A rubbery smile stretched across her lips.

She held out a gloved hand and purred, "Death, darling, care to honor me with a dance?" It wasn't really a question, but an order.

Ferno, his breath like fire—not from his powers, but from the whiskey—breathed in close.

"She's a fun one to dance with," he said, clapping me on the back. He flashed his teeth and winked at Amelia. "But be warned, she likes to lead."

"You make it sound like that's a bad thing," Amelia replied coyly.

"Never," he shot out. "You're just a woman who knows how to handle a man."

"And how would you know that?"

Ferno's grin widened. He held up his drink. "It's practically a legend around here."

Amelia laughed, bright and real. It gathered a few curious looks, her lightness wholly foreign, but she paid them no attention. Instead, she turned toward me and motioned with her fingers to take her hand. "Come," she beckoned, and pulled me onto the dance floor.

"Do you know how to dance?" she asked.

I shook my head. My feet, back when I was human, didn't come in a proper pair.

"Oh, this will be fun." She placed one of my hands on her hip and gripped the other firmly in her grasp; the fabric between us wasn't enough to stop my palm from burning.

"Follow my lead, darling," she said, and within seconds she had us both moving to the tempo of the band, guiding my footsteps with only her strength and confidence.

She twisted and twirled, training my body to glide with hers, moving as if we'd been dancing together our whole lives. Her Animal reflexes orientating me in a matter of moments.

The process was seamless.

And, most surprisingly of all, enjoyable. Which seemed wrong.

I captured a glance at Ferno, who was rocking back in his

chair, motioning for another round of drinks. Meanwhile, Plague was dazed in a drunken stupor.

Polar's gaze followed. His eyes flashed over, as Amelia twisted me away. The beat mellowed. She rocked me into a slow dance, pulling me into an embrace, edging her head near my shoulder, letting her hands slide behind my back.

She had the grip of a tourniquet.

"I've been wanting to talk to you," she breathed. I felt her lips curl close to my ear. Not touching. Never touching, but near enough I experienced the shift. She kept our bodies rocking to the music, swaying as if we liked each other.

I swallowed and her fingers pressed into my back. "I realize, my darling, that we've gotten off on the wrong foot."

I smirked. "That's an understatement."

She pressed tighter. I became oxygen hungry. She funneled the air, tricking my body into thinking it had all dissipated.

"Oh, I know you hate me," she started, "and I honestly don't blame you. But, trust me, Death. She is bad news. I have heard she has become ... permissible with you, and that in itself will seal your fate."

"And what fate is that? Happiness? That sounds absolutely horrid—"

"Naïve boy. She brings the opposite—grief and sorrow. Bodies without heads. Keeping company with her will be your undoing. Take this moment as a kindness, a warning, and pay close attention. She will destroy you."

"Don't act like you care about me."

"I never said I did, but I'm astute enough to know that if you're destroyed, your death will destroy others. And those others I do happen to care about."

She nudged her head toward Polar, and the cord restraining my anger snapped.

Amelia was passing on the blame, as was the way in

Narivous: orchestrate others to their breaking point and then guilt them when they shatter.

I pressed my fingers deep into Amelia's back, the same hold she had on me. Both of us wanting to bring pain, but locked by decorum.

"Fantasia wouldn't hurt anyone," I hissed. "You don't see her for what she is; you're too blinded by your own hatred."

She laughed, as if my words hadn't phased her.

"You're the one who can't see her for what she is." Amelia twirled me around, so I had no allies in my sight. I was left staring at the band. "You have fallen under her spell, like the others before you."

Others. Plural.

The tension in my shoulders grew before her words finished pouring in. Amelia softened as I went rigid. "You heard me right," she said following my thoughts. "Others. More than one. Chugknot was the first to die from her dealings. And now Crusher is heavy with rot."

"Crusher?" I flinched and stumbled. She managed to catch me.

I hated that she caught me.

"You didn't know?" she asked, dipping her voice in innocence. "Why, it's common knowledge how much he liked her. What's the word I'm looking for? Oh, yes ..." I captured the glint in her eyes. "Pining. That's it. He was pining for her. He'd follow her around. She'd let him, encouraging him the way she's encouraged you."

"You're lying."

"Am I?" Her fingers started to knead. "I can see how much you want to believe that. Paint me as your villain. But it's true. Don't you recall the time you were pulled from your rooms? The day you turned an innocent Velore into bones and tar, leaving him to seep into the soil of our graveyard?"

She was breaking into my head through cracks of doubt.

"Didn't you wonder how they got her belongings? The ones she wears so very often? To trick you into leaving? Crusher took them. And how, Death, could he have possibly collected them if he and Fantasia weren't on such friendly terms?"

I shook my head, fighting the rush swelling inside my lungs, the powerful pull of translucency. It wasn't true.

"The mask wasn't hers; it was a replica." My argument was feeble, she leaned in closer.

"Oh, yes, but the cloak was. The cloak was very much hers. How do you suppose Crusher got it?"

The space began to blur.

Faces turned to one.

Heat thrummed through my limbs.

"You're trying to get into my head. That's all you're doing. I'm not buying your story."

"Whether you buy it or not doesn't take away its truth. I'm trying to save you. I'm trying to protect you. Fantasia looks for Velores of power, for those closest to the throne, and she uses them to serve her own motives. Why, I wouldn't be surprised if she put him up to steal from the birch trees. To take for her own agenda."

At least I knew that wasn't true. I put on a smile. It was as wicked as hers.

"Is that what you're doing? Using someone else's crimes to sink Fantasia? She had nothing to do with it. You want her dead because you can't stand the sight of her. She reminds you of the one time in your life you couldn't maintain control."

Amelia shrugged, as if my words held no value. "Something made him betray his Queen, a Queen he adored. What better incentive than a pretty face?"

Fear ravaged the particles brewing in my gut. Was this my doing? The Unrests had framed Crusher for my crimes, as a way to earn favor—had I inadvertently given Amelia leverage to attack Fantasia?

No.

I told myself it didn't matter. This was Amelia. She could take anyone's crimes, anyone's treason, and circle it back to Fantasia—she was that committed to her craft.

"I think you're insane," I said, meaning it. "You're grasping at straws to have her killed. We all know of your hatred for her. We've all seen it played out, and I know you'll stop at nothing until she's dead."

"Because she is a threat to the Crown. To this city."

"No, because she's a reminder of your husband's betrayal."

"Oh, how I pity you. So far under her spell. Or is it Scream's spell? She, too, isn't on your side. You're simply her pawn."

We were speaking in clipped tones, drowned out by the band, by the rotating tempo of music, the laughter. We kept our voices to a low hiss, speaking with venom and forked tongues.

"So, you expect me to believe that not only is Fantasia using me, but Scream is too?"

"Again, whether you believe or not doesn't take away its truth."

"You killed my aunt, you killed my uncle, you had Lacey's neck snapped in half—"

"Kitten"—she dug her nails in—"her name is Kitten."

"Fine." Gritted teeth. "Kitten. You had Kitten made into one of us, and you really think I'm gullible enough to believe—"

"I didn't kill your uncle. My *husband* did." She spat the word, as if claiming him left her dirty and ruined. "He was angry with you for getting his bastard princess in trouble. He wanted to prove a point. Cougar has fallen under Fantasia's illusion, too. It must be something in a male's blood that makes them stupid."

"And Marie? What about that?"

"They never expected you to kill her, you know that, right? The goal was to keep her human, to test your powers on her, to see if you could make the suppression work." She stroked a finger down my back. "Your family removal was not my doing. I don't have that kind of power. Besides," she went syrupy, "I would dare guess Scream had more to do with it than me. She's the one who wants to test you. To get her cure. She wants it more than Thorn. And she knew you would come through when it came to your family. They are your soft spot."

The fluidity of our moves disappeared as each layer of poison spilled. "If that were true, then why would she come to my defense in the Room of Reckoning? She was the one defending me against you. You were the one wanting blood. You were practically licking your lips at the thought of destroying me. *You*."

"Because I thought you were against the Crown. Of course I'd want you to die. I truly thought you were a conspirator. And to be honest, Marie's death was for her own good. They would've kept her here, human, a checking point for you to practice your powers on. Do you want to know the truth? The honest truth? Scream was the one who planted the thought in Thorn's head to bring your family to Narivous. Only she thinks she's being clever. That no one can see her real motives."

"Lies."

"I came to Thorn's Throne Room to report your scent at the charred remains of your grandmother's house. I was asked to investigate; I did as I was told. Scream was at Thorn's side when they dismissed me, and they talked—*privately*. They plotted together. It was her."

"And La—Kitten?" I was waiting for her to trip. I was starting to need it. To crave it.

"Collateral to keep you compliant. And again, not of my

doing. But I offered to take her under my wing. To protect her. I will make her strong. I will make her vicious. She will be safe under my watch simply because I will force the weakness out of her."

"You think breaking her will make her stronger?"

"No." She arched her neck to look me in the eyes. For once they weren't rings of black, but her natural color, amber fire. She steadied them on my face. "It won't make her stronger, it will make her invincible. You may hate me for what she'll become, but she will grow to be a fighter. A woman of steel and stone. A woman who will make backs stand tall the moment she enters a room."

Cheetah drew my gaze and Amelia followed it. The bride sat glowering at her husband, who was laughing with Jaguar.

"Cheetah is going to keep Narivous safe," Amelia whispered. "And she will protect you from Fantasia—soon she'll be lost anyhow."

I stopped moving, and even her force couldn't pull me back in. I dropped my hands and inched away.

"She's involved in this uprising," Amelia said, her neck stiff, her chin forward. "Make no doubt about it. They're not looking into it because they can't afford to lose her. Not without a cure to the Poison." She smiled, the feline sharpness screeching through my heart. She glanced at Cheetah, and I knew what she was going to say before she even said it. "But the replacement is coming, and it'll start in the womb of my own daughter."

That's what this union was. An attempt to recreate Fantasia and her healing powers—a child.

"Fantasia's powers can't be replicated."

"No? Tipper thinks we may have found the winning solution, for the groom is a descendent of that whore Camille—something we didn't think was available to us."

And before I even had a chance to digest the power of her words, the wooden dance floor beneath us rumbled. A blast, powerful enough to quake the earth, rattled the whole of Narivous.

It felt like a bomb.

And then came the screaming.

CHAPTER II
THE UNRESTS

The ground pitched like tectonic plates had suddenly slipped.

We ran in a flood toward the source of the violence while the dirt trembled beneath our feet, rippling in savage aftershocks, making placement of our steps a new challenge.

The sky opened up with glass rain.

Shards of tinkling destruction and fine ash wrapped around the cobblestone cottages, shrouding them with dank refuse.

Smoke filled the city; it hung like a heavy fog, except it crawled into our lungs and scorched us from the inside.

The heat. The debris. The ringing in our ears.

All our senses were hyperactive, filling us with confusion and shock.

A tether pulled us to one concentrated place: the greenhouse.

Only now it was a massive hole. We froze around it, stopping at an invisible line as if someone had roped off the perimeter with magic and will.

We were mixed in dress and aura color—the upper crust slamming into the prosaic civilians, making for an eclectic cluster of confusion. The commoners grew quiet while leaders grew loud, and in the divides of silence and chaos, it was only whispers that held the strength to question.

A plume rose above the city over the treetops and the Telekinetics instantly went to work, pulling it down, hiding it from humans within squinting range.

Tipper ran like a sea-breeze cutting through a storm, into the ash and fragmented remains of her work, screaming as she lost the rest of her mind.

Her remaining sanity unfurled into the wind in billowing shrieks.

Covered in soot, she began throwing plants from the epicenter of the carnage, inspecting what was left, howling at what she discovered. Most had surrendered to disintegration, a few still held the semblance of shape.

She stood alone in the wreckage.

A wailing soul.

The Seven, vibrant against the gray, stood motionless with rage and disbelief. Thorn, her eyes glowing, had cracks fragmenting her complexion into jagged pieces.

Her chest rose in short stabs as shallow breaths strained against her ribs.

She managed to remain stoic, unmoving, just a ball of light glowing from the core. She wouldn't look at anyone and kept her gaze forward, locked on the plume.

Tipper managed to find one broken planter, still mostly intact, black threads bleeding from sappy soil and held it to her chest while collapsing in a fresh fit of tears.

"My babies. My babies. My babies."

Thorn pivoted on her heel and walked away. Scream followed close behind. Not a word was spoken. Or shared.

It was far worse than Tipper's screams.

Her silence said more than words could ever manage.

Frigid had lost some of her clarity and was twirling in maddening circles. Polar acted quickly and grabbed her arm, urging her behind Scream and Thorn. Before he did, however, he met my gaze and I swore I detected the hint of a smile.

He seemed happy it was gone.

What was the greenhouse exactly?

Tipper proved to be a worthy distraction as the remaining Seven, one by one, left the scene in quiet discretion. Only Amelia and Ember remained, their heads bowed deep in conversation.

I went to Fantasia, who held the same expression of shock as everyone else. The murmurs were growing; we would add our own to the thick of it. I tugged her to a private alcove with an evergreen bower. The only bald spot was a deep scald from the sheer force of the blast.

"This was the boom," she whispered. I nodded. I'd already surmised as much.

"We have to leave," I said, my eyes fielding all the chaotic energy.

"We can't now, they'll think we had something to do with this."

"They'll think it no matter what." I gripped her arm. "Amelia is set on making you the scapegoat for anything that goes wrong; it's only a matter of time before something sticks. And this rebellion is the ideal setup. We need to leave, and we need to do it quickly. This could actually work as a decent distraction."

"Wait? You mean now? Today?"

"If we can find a way to manage it, yes. Eric's truck should still be waiting. We can take his rig once we make it to the valley."

"What about my sisters? My mother?"

"You can tell them right before we're set to leave—give them the option of going with us. If they choose to stay, then we'll honor that decision. But that's the best I can do."

"But they'll need time to think about it."

"Time we don't have."

"If only you'd let me talk to them before."

"We couldn't risk it."

"My family isn't a risk though." She searched the wreckage, and then she searched me.

"Fantasia, I'm already bending enough on this. I won't yield anymore. This is about Lacey and this is our chance. You either take it or you don't."

"But I can't leave them," Fantasia said.

The look I gave her made her shrink. She didn't make me say it, but we both knew.

I was going tonight, with or without her.

"What about your stash?"

I shook my head. "We'll have to let it go. My powers will have to do." I continued to use 'we,' in hopes she'd come along.

"They found Bronson and Caseao."

"Bronson and Caseao didn't have my powers."

"It won't be enough. They'll find us."

Us. I liked that.

"We'll hide, and hide well."

"Not with Lacey. She won't be able to control her powers, and when humans see, the trail of mind reading will be easy to follow. We might as well draw them a map."

"I don't want to meet the Unrests, Fantasia."

"But you *need* to meet them. You're so close to getting your stash back."

And then it happened, quite suddenly actually, so fluid and quick, it appeared seamless. The smoke had started to settle, and the Telekinetics relaxed their hold since it no longer hovered above the tree cover.

And then, for only a moment, the smoke billowed in a direction that was artificial. I wondered if they were watching me.

No doubt.

Because as soon as I honed in on it, the breeze stopped—and through the chaos around us—no one even registered it except for those who were looking for it.

The direction I was supposed to head come twilight was crystal clear. I even had a good inkling of where it would lead.

"Fantasia, we can't get involved."

But she wasn't watching me. She was watching Chanticlaim enter the wreckage. He approached his mother with careful caution. Tipper's sobs slowed and she looked to Chanticlaim as if he would save her. He held out his hand and she grabbed it, pulling her to her feet.

He leaned down and spoke into her ear.

Both Fantasia and a slew of others watched as he led her away, her skin stained by soot, her neck hanging in spirit, Chanticlaim's solid grip the only thing holding her upright. She kept the plant cradled in her arms, talking to it as if she could revive it with words. She wiped her face on her sleeve leaving a glistening trail of snot.

Amelia glanced at us and smirked before following behind them. Fantasia tugged on my sleeve and gave me a smile that was both soft and twisted. "We'll always be involved." She glanced at Amelia's back. "Just like you said—she will find ways to make me guilty. Even if I'm not. And if I'm already guilty," she arched her brow in defiance, "let me be worthy of that guilt."

"Fantasia—"

"Meet them. Since they'll never let us be innocents here, we might as well partake in the trouble."

Dammit. She had a point.

Fantasia managed to sway me.

She did it with a promise.

I would meet them that night, and then she'd leave with me as soon as we were able. That could mean a week. A day. An hour. Minutes.

She'd even come if her family chose to stay.

A heavy compromise I was willing to honor. And, besides, as much as I told myself I didn't need the stash—I knew it could carry us a long way if I got it back.

Help was help.

Fortunately, it was my regularly-scheduled guard duty, so I had every excuse to be in the forest, a pleasant circumstance that didn't seem coincidental. Whoever was orchestrating this nightmare knew how to make timing align with their needs.

The moon was high, bright, and strong enough to leak in through the strong overhead barrier. The farther I moved from the city, the more light there was to guide me.

It cut my path into lines of darkness, and split the scene into slats. Smoke clung, but it was low-hanging now, a drift of rolling tendrils that dampened the sound of my footsteps and masked the scent I most assuredly left behind.

Everything together knitted an eerie atmosphere with an edge of danger. Ember's proclamation, issued shortly after the Sevens retreated, echoed through my reverie.

She stood in the great hole, surrounded by char and destruction, her gown of red a slash of blood in an open wound, announcing that the culprits would suffer the greatest consequence afforded to such violent acts of treason: familial annihilation.

Meaning entire blood lines would be eradicated.

So every footstep I took was a challenge. I told myself it wouldn't matter.

I could leave.

And my human family was already gone. The Velore one at least had significant standing.

Would they really destroy Polar? Or Ferno? Lacey held my greatest concern, but Dolly cleaved to her—she'd do anything to preserve her life.

All I had left to lose was myself, and I was lost a long time ago.

That's the thought I hung on to as I broke through the trees and spotted the small clearing, with madrone trees covered in curtains of moss.

The graveyard, down in a loamy valley, would always bring heightened emotions. It was lofty in its sentiments.

In the memories existing there.

I went to it quickly and didn't linger on the headstones with ornate designs, clean and well-kept, or the plainer ones covered in a thick film of lichen separated by a hedge barrier.

Velore versus human.

Marie and Dean were here. I couldn't bear the sight of their markers.

I passed the monuments of Thorn's mother and father, both grand, life-size, but otherwise opposites. Urrel's was deep and dark, he was leaning on an axe that I now recognized as Lucky, the battered tool used to sever heads at public executions. Thorn's mother was the light, with wildflowers in her hands and a smile playing on her lips. I hesitated near Urrel's and let the poison thrum through me.

I could feel it rattle beneath my feet.

And although I had no evidence—I was confident his grave was empty. He was neither alive or dead in the soil below me.

So, if he wasn't here, where was he?

I wanted to inspect it more, but a figure at the back, a man, took all my attention.

This was who was waiting for me, I was fairly confident. Fairly.

I neared and recognized the frame. My shoulders dropped.

"Spark?"

He was wearing his guard vest, along with the cloak designated for formal occasions—it had a red lining.

Of course. Cheetah's wedding. All the guards in attendance wore them.

Spark stayed silent. I went to his side. He was near a tombstone of black granite, with a large panther playfully on its back. I followed his gaze, and recognized the inscription.

"Bronson. Son, Brother, Friend."

And next to his marker, there was another. Where his was dark, this one was light. Same as with Thorn's parents.

The paler tombstone had a cherub sitting atop it, using its wings as a cover, bumblebees saturating every parcel of it. "Caseao. Dolly's heart. The child of the Doppelgängers."

Spark was no doubt part of the Unrests. I'd found my connection. With this revelation came a host of questions.

Was this why he followed me?

How long?

The purpose?

"You know, these two were happy here," Spark said. "Or so I've heard. It was before my time. I guess they were in love, content, and this place ..." he pinched his mouth, "... this place ruined them and no one really talks about it. I once heard

Laquet call Jaguar Bronson though. And Caseao ... Dolly never really got over her."

"Dolly's sister."

"Most people guess daughter."

"Fantasia told me."

He nodded, expecting as much.

"I told her everything, by the way. Just in case you're wondering. And I plan on telling her everything afterwards too. So if you want to mind your words, I wouldn't blame you."

"They'll think she was involved."

"They'll think that no matter what. At least this way she'll have a fighting chance of what she's up against."

"It was better when she was on the Southside."

"Agreed. But she's here now."

"Torti and Dreams will be pissed. They didn't want her involved; that was part of their condition."

I think the color flushed from my face. I leaned in close. "Are you saying they're in this mess?"

A cold breeze swept through me. *Familial repercussions.* If they got caught, Fantasia would be right along with them.

No matter what. Fantasia would be guilty.

No matter what. Fantasia would be in danger.

No matter what. Fantasia would fall.

Nothing mattered.

"We're all in this mess," he breathed.

Truer words had never been spoken. I couldn't help but wonder if this was his way of self-preservation. Was this shared tidbit a deterrent to turning him in? Bind Fantasia's sisters to the resistance and assuring his protection in one fell swoop? It was unnecessary.

No matter what.

They would come for Fantasia ... eventually.

"Is this why you were following me? Keeping tabs? Pretending to be my friend?"

He blinked, blindsided.

"I am your friend," he stated. "This hasn't changed that." He shook his head and honed in on the tombstone. "I just had to make sure you wouldn't do anything stupid."

"Like this isn't stupid?"

I skimmed around, careful to search for spies.

"No one's here," Spark said, matter-of-factly. "There are sensors. We'll be notified if anyone comes close."

"How is that?"

Spark smiled, but it lacked mirth. "Because for once, their paranoia is warranted. There's a higher-up leading the Unrests. Narivous has met its match."

"Who?"

Spark shook his head. "First, I need to know where your head is. Your loyalty."

"I'm here, aren't I? Isn't that enough?"

"Nope." He made a popping noise with his lips. "It just shows you're curious."

"I wouldn't turn you in—"

"I'm not saying that." He turned to face me head-on, folding his arms across his chest. "I need to know if you're willing to fight. To help the cause."

"Look, Spark—"

"You're worried about Lacey, right? That's why you want to run?"

"Who says I was going to run?"

"The little horde you were collecting says so. That's why I was keeping close tabs on you. I didn't want you to bolt, because it wouldn't have worked."

"I don't need a babysitter." I clenched my jaw. "By the way,

I want it back. All of it. That's the only reason why I'm here. I'm not getting involved."

"Help us, we help you."

"And if I don't? You won't return it?"

"Your plan won't work, Death. I assure you, it won't." Spark swept his hand over the tombstones. "These two came the closest to getting out and it didn't work for them."

"They're not me. And besides, what makes you think your plan will work?" I sneered. "You're running a bigger risk than I am. This rebellion? What's the purpose? You're putting your neck out for nothing. Think about your sister, Spark. Ember just announced there will be familial deaths when they uncover who's responsible. Familial. That means it's not just your neck—but hers, too. You can't change them, so you might as well not even try."

"Are you sure?"

"That you can't change them?" I smirked. "Yeah, I'm pretty certain they're set in their ways."

"Mentally, maybe," Spark gave a low smile, "but not physically."

"What's that supposed to mean?"

He shrugged, feigning nonchalance. "What can be done can be undone."

"You can't undo what's been done." I indicated the graveyard. "We're undead. Abominations. There's no going back."

"But there's a better way to move forward," he said softly.

"Such as?"

He shook his head and allowed his gaze to roam the graveyard. Something in him softened; his muscles fell. He was a living sigh, losing the tension. "Did I tell you my mom had another baby?"

I groaned. "Dammit, Spark. I asked a direct question. I would like a direct answer. *Tell me.*"

"I am. In my own way. Just hold your shit together."

"You better get to it." I folded my arms and waited.

"For the longest time, I didn't care I was here. They took me when I was twelve and Volt was nine. They got me away from a shit dad and a shit situation. When we turned up missing, they actually pinned our disappearance on him. They planned it, you see." Spark glanced in the direction of the city. "They knew exactly how to take us and deflect the blame. A Doppelgänger got him drunk, slipped him amnesia pills, then cut up his hands. Put his blood on our sheets, the door handle, the car, even mixed our DNA with his. It was seamless. He didn't stand a chance and eventually hung himself in his cell." Spark smirked, to demonstrate his indifference. "The only thing that worried me was Mom. She was broken. Not over him, but over us. I didn't hear much, but from what I gathered, it was like she had to live through hell.

"But it was okay. It got to be okay. Mom was free from Dad, couldn't be beat anymore, and Volt was happy here. And then Mom remarried, and well, it seemed like everything was going to be okay. Only ..." He squinted, staring off into the inky distance, seeing something that existed only in his imagination. "But she got remarried and had a baby. A baby boy." The cold night wrapped us in silence as his voice faded away. He seemed to expect some sort of response from me.

I said nothing and waited.

"You don't see it, do you?" Spark asked.

"I don't know where you're going with this."

"He has our same aura." He spoke through clenched teeth. "I'd hoped that the aura was on Dad's side. That it ended with him. But it didn't.

"They're going to take the baby, Death. Maybe not this year, or the next, but they're going to take him. They can't *not* take him. And when they do, there will be nothing left of my mom. She'll have sacrificed us all to Narivous, and she won't even know it. Even worse, when they take the baby, suspicion will fall on her. Too many kids lost in her care."

"Maybe they'll find a way to make it look like someone—"

"Don't you get it?" Spark grabbed me by my shirt. "This is never going to stop. Never." He let go, but leaned in. "Someone has to stop it."

His shoulders fell a fraction, and he took a step away.

I understood then, why he was risking his rank. His elevated position. His life.

It was for the same reason I wanted to run.

To save and protect.

"You could come with us," I said. "When it's time to run, maybe we can tip them off. Get them out of state."

Spark laughed. It raised my hackles.

"You can't escape. You just can't."

"You don't know what I can do...."

The moment those words slipped out, I wanted to take them back.

"You can do stuff with your poison, can't you?" he asked. "Unexplainable stuff?"

Spark stepped close to me. We were only a flinch apart.

"I know." He tapped his head. "I know you can. It was too easy with Crusher. You've mastered it, and you've been keeping it secret because you think it'll keep you safe." Spark's smile twisted into something less friendly. "But it won't work. In a matter of time, there won't be a place to run or hide."

"You don't know that."

"The Art of Famine," he said, flatly. "They're practicing the Art of Famine and it will catch up with every living, breathing thing on this planet."

"What does that mean?"

"It means more Velores will be made, and the rest...." He made his fingers arc, miming an explosion.

"Again, what does that mean? I don't know what that means."

"The rest—the human race—is going to die. All that will be left will be evil." He pointed at me. "And we have a plan. We can stop it. But we need you to do it. You're the key to ending all of this because what is done can be undone."

And like that—he had me.

This is what roped in felt like.

CHAPTER 12
THE ART OF FAMINE

I made him tell me three times.

Over and over.

Until the weight of it sunk in.

Still, part of me didn't believe.

"Ask your aunt," Spark challenged, meaning Scream, "and once you do, await further instructions."

He smirked.

He had me. If she verified his tale—which I thought was tall—I'd have no choice but to stay.

To leave, to do nothing, would make me just as much of a villain.

The Poison Quarters were stone-silent. The only noise to be heard was the sound of my own breathing and the mice scuttling in the walls. I went to Scream's door and knocked, knowing all the while it was vacant. Plague's room was empty as well—they'd both taken to separate rooms long before my arrival—and even though it was peculiar for him to be absent, I was far beyond the point of caring.

Next, I went to the Ice Quarters. I knew the moment I

entered life was there. Polar and Camille were lodged in an embrace in the living room, Polar's arms tight, Camille's equally as hungry. She had her head resting on his chest as they supported one another, in both hold and emotion.

Even though nothing intimate was in play, it felt like an intrusion.

Polar wove his hand in her blonde, curly strands, taking in a handful, placing a kiss on the top of her head before looking over at me. The hardness in his eyes reflected the moment. He gave a subtle shake, indicating he was fielding all his energy to the one in his arms and had none to offer me.

"Scream," I said. "I need to see Scream."

Camille remained motionless, except, perhaps a deeper grip.

"She's out in her garden," she mumbled against Polar's chest. "Now go away."

I took no offense. I didn't want to be here, in this moment. Whatever was passing between them was too much to witness.

Nor was it my place.

Before I ducked out, Camille—her face so very much like her daughters', with a beauty that broke the bounds of perfection—glanced at me. She was normally a bastion in strength, but today she was shrouded in weakness. Black tears hung in her eyes, and she bit her lip to fight back the cry that wanted to bloom from it.

Whatever the trauma, I left them to their crises.

I had one of my own to flag down.

Scream's garden. Every Seven had one, each one drafted from their sovereign inspiration. They all held statues befitting their powers—most were dark and frightening, with a striking resemblance that nearly paralleled their true beauty.

The sizes of the gardens varied too. The two largest—aside from the royal gardens—belonged to Scream and Dolly. If I had to order them, Thorn's would come first with Scream's being a tight second. Dolly's would be right on their heels.

I never contemplated why that was, but being Scream was Thorn's oldest friend, it made sense.

Scream's gardens consisted of ponds, bridges, nymphs and honeysuckle. Lots of honeysuckle. It was here long before Thorn began growing it in hordes.

There was a menagerie of topiary animals, one of which was a bunny about the size of an overgrown dog, poised to jump atop a bench within Scream's pergola. It was an alcove of quiet and tranquility.

And that's where I found her.

Silent, sitting on the bench, her legs folded beneath her in a pose of innocence.

The formalness Scream normally displayed evaporated in this pocket of privacy. Her beautiful neck was bent and she massaged the knots that settled there. Her gown—vibrant at the wedding—was both wrinkled and ashen from the trauma of the explosion. She wasn't pristine and for the first time since I'd known her, she'd fallen into the disheveled category. She failed to acknowledge me as I approached.

She clearly wanted to be left alone. Instead, I sat next to her.

We were both still and silent. Off in the distance, an owl hooted.

I finally broke the stalemate.

"I'm surprised you're not with Thorn right now."

"She took a sleeping serum. Her nerves were on the fritz."

"Why didn't you take one?"

"Oh ..." Her shoulders dropped. "I needed the time to contemplate."

Remorse hung between us.

"I heard some rumors as we were cleaning up the glass."

"I imagine you did," she said softly. She glanced at me. Suddenly, she no longer looked like immortal perfection. She was tired. Old. I could see fragments of her true age shining through.

"The Art of Famine?"

"It's on everyone's lips now, there's no stopping it."

"So, it's true?"

"Depends. What exactly did you hear?"

"Awful stuff."

She smiled; it was broken. "Ah, well then that tells me it's probably true." She ran her hand along her folded knee, trying to work out a wrinkle that was beyond smoothing out.

"How could you? How could you know about it and not do anything to stop it?"

She shrugged, and looked away—her avoidance spoke of shame. "I've never pretended to be right. I've never even pretended to be good. More often than not, I'm neither. I'm fallible like any other creature. But I'm also strong." She turned her onyx eyes on me. The aging of only a moment earlier had dissipated. She was back to fierce. "The Art of Famine is a cruel, horrible necessity, one of which I hope never sees the light of day. But there is only so much I can do from my ... position."

She ran her tongue over her teeth, her expression turning angry and venomous. Her eyes flashed in a spot of heat. Whatever thought was flickering through her mind, it was full of malice.

"You're in a better position than most to stop it."

She nodded.

"Did you try to stop it?"

"It hasn't even started yet. I don't need you to come down on me for something that hasn't happened."

"But you're working toward it? The plants? The greenhouse? That's a plan in action."

"That is preparation. Nothing more. It's no different than keeping a weapon in your home. You prepare for the worst while hoping for the best." She nodded, agreeing with her logic. "This is a cautionary maneuver. To not do so may condemn us all."

"So it's condemn us or condemn them? Those are our only options? We can't coexist? Live in secrecy as we're doing now?"

"Because they're outgrowing us. Don't you see that?" She pointed at nothing but indicated everything. "There are too many of them, and they continue to multiply with no end in sight. And there is only so much earth."

"You realize though ..." I spoke slowly, selecting each word with care, "that if a choice should be made, they should survive. Not us. We're the unnatural ones. To destroy mankind so the monsters can live is an abomination."

Scream darkened to the point that she challenged the thick of night. She unfolded her legs, and propped her elbows on her thighs, twisting her arms in an elegant bend. Her hands came together as she leaned on them, looking at me in a pose that accentuated all that was lovely in her. A stark reminder that even vile actions could come from the most appealing sources. "We should just leave them be? To keep on their destructive course? They are destroying the planet. Ravaging it with their filth. Eating away our atmosphere—and we're to sit back and let it continue?"

"Oh, this is altruistic then? Not to save us, but to save the planet?"

"I don't appreciate your sarcasm."

"I'm not being sarcastic. I'm trying to gain a grasp on what you're hoping to achieve. If it comes out sarcastic it only shows how outlandish your words are. That's not on me, that's on you."

"Death, darling—"

I held up my hand. "No. Wait. I'm getting a hold on this. Pause a second while I organize my thoughts. So, you're going to kill the humans to save the earth? That includes children? The old? The young? The good. Animals. Plants. Life. You want to take it all away?"

"We're not going to kill *everything,* just most things."

"Oh, much better."

"Your sarcasm—"

"Your argument—"

"My argument is sound. Tough decisions are made by those who are strong. Being weak, failing to choose, serves no one."

"That's absurd."

"To save us, we will do most anything." She leaned into me. "Even the absurd." Her voice took on its magical siren quality—had she been using it this whole time? Is that how she mastered my rage? For aside from sarcasm, I found little challenge in my tone.

It didn't sit well.

"To save us from what? Thorn can make plants grow by merely thinking it. She doesn't need ideal conditions. She can force an orange tree to grow on the peak of a glacier and produce some of the best damn fruit ever tasted."

Scream smiled.

"I think I might pass that compliment on to her."

"I wasn't trying to compliment her. I'm saying we live in a forest, far removed from any real threats. She doesn't need to move forward with this. If anything, she can save people with her gift. That would make ..." What would it make it? Better?

Right? "It would make us even. If we chose to use it for good, it would negate our bad. If she can kill plants with a chain, she can grow them too."

"You heard about the chain?"

"Oh, yes. I heard it all. How Thorn plans to kill the vegetation through a root system, acting as a chain, taking down an entire continent with merely her powers and not even having to leave the forest to do it. Livestock will starve and death will follow. The only place green will be the forest, humans will flock here in droves for food, and then you'll have your pick of Velores."

She smiled and I wanted to wipe it away.

"The greenhouse was the second phase," I spat. "I know that now. How Tipper is planning on reaching even farther, by making new breeds of plants, plants that resemble fruits and vegetables, but are really toxic, so you can transfer your death to other continents. What kind of demented freak show comes up with this?"

"A brilliant survivalist is who," Scream said. She wasn't smiling anymore, but defiant. She kept her chin up and her jaw square. "Tipper is teaching Thorn how to tell the difference from the real seeds versus the fake. So that afterwards, when the earth has been purged of the parasites, she can kill them off and life will resume. The forests will house enough woodland creatures that repopulation should happen in good order."

"I don't get it, Scream. I never took you as a villain."

"Villain is such a subjective term." She shook her head, as if I couldn't really see what she was trying to show me. Her words were all black, no color, and she was using broad strokes. "What is good, really?" She tossed her head back, revealing the soft, fragile skin of her neck, the vulnerability that rested there. Her heartbeat, albeit slow, ticked against the flesh. When she pulled her focus back, her brows were knitted together.

"I know what you're doing," she whispered. "You're trying to do what's right—when you're conflicted about what right is. You asked me if we had only two options: them or us. You're forgetting the other option, the most dangerous option of all: neither. They continue on their path, and soon there won't be much of a planet left. And if they find us? Capture us and harness our secret? Use it for their own global gain? It could fall into the wrong hands and humanity would crumble."

"It's already in the wrong hands."

"No, it's not. Not even a little. We're trying to survive up here. We're not looking for world domination or to start a war. We want to be left alone. It's as simple as that. They—" she swept her hand in a flourishing fashion, "are all about greed and gain. We are about maintaining. Humans are the enemy. I know you like to think that's not the case. But they are."

"I still have family that's alive."

"Family that's fled." She arched her brow. "They betrayed us."

Scream was old enough that this train of thought was easier for her, since her human past felt like ancient history. It's easy to discard that of which you have no attachment to.

"We were all once human," I said.

"And we're not anymore. We've been rewarded with both death and resurrection. Count your blessings, darling. You are with us—you are safe. A chosen one. Celebrate that, and rejoice in your position." She stood up. "I'm tired, I think I'll go to bed. Tomorrow we'll discuss this rebellion, and then we have a list of those to interrogate—and possible heads to claim. As always, I will keep your name off the list."

I dug my fingers into the wood planks.

"This is, darling, *only* a just-in-case." She stressed the word only. "Don't put too much stock in it. As long as the humans keep their distance, they're safe. We're safe. You're safe. Even your traitor granduncle and cousin are safe." She glimmered a smile.

She left then, her cloak spiraling around her, creating a black halo bleaker than the night skies. I wasn't sure what was more somber. Her message. Or the part of me, a part I didn't want to acknowledge, that agreed with her.

Who was to say what was bad or good?

Those terms were becoming more open to interpretation by the day.

MIDWAY BACK TO THE CASTLE, Fred fluttered in front of me, stealing my attention and stopping me in my tracks.

Fantasia came rushing up behind me, Dreams a few paces back, looking sheepish and uncomfortable. She was donning purple hair, her blonde roots starting to show. Dreams had this unique characteristic for unusual hair growth.

It allowed her to change her style every few days.

Fantasia reached for my hand and searched my eyes.

"Those bastards," she lipped.

I held up my hand, letting Dreams know she was dismissed, and walked Fantasia back to my rooms. We went in through the back entrance and carefully removed most of our clothes. When we were nearly undressed, we curled into one another in the bed, pulling the blanket over our heads, letting our breath blend, our heartbeats sync. All I wanted was flesh on flesh. To feel alive.

This wasn't about lust.

This was about intimacy and connection, a greater form of

desire. It was about the grave danger we were rooted in. On how we wanted to move forward.

We spoke with barely a sound, just exaggerated lip movements.

"How did you find out?" I asked.

"Torti confessed."

"Did she tell you everything?"

"Everything."

"Do you know who's leading them?"

She shook her head. "Do you?"

"No."

She sighed, it rolled along my body.

"I should be mad at them," Fantasia lipped, meaning her sisters, "but for the fact they're finally doing the right thing—I can't possibly muster the anger. This can't be allowed to happen."

"The Art of Famine." I shook my head, disgusted. "It's terrible."

"I know. And if they follow through, there will never be a safe place to run."

"I'm starting to wonder if there ever was a safe place to run."

"I had my doubts."

"That you did. You can, at times, display remarkable wisdom." I tucked a black strand of hair behind her ear, and smiled against her lips. She matched it.

"Finally, some acknowledgment." She touched my face.

I took a breath. So much had shifted in a small span of time. The morning had started off with a wedding and had ended in a rebellion. There were Amelia's words, coiled around my confidence, shattering the image I held of Fantasia. How much could I really trust her?

"Fantasia?" I asked. "Did you have an affair with Crusher?"

Nothing in her expression gave away the answer, and then she nodded. "Not so much an affair, but we kissed once. He liked me. I wanted him to like me."

"Because he was in a position of power?"

She matched my eyes, her lavender strong and hard like small glimmering shards of amethyst. "Yes. Yes, I won't even deny it. I wanted him to want me because he had standing and power. And while we're at it, Chugknot was in a similar position, and I wanted him too." She held her fingertips to my lips. "I've wanted to be out of this retched spot for forever, and I won't lie or deny it. Not to you. And when it came to Chugknot, I grew to care about him. Even Crusher, a little. Not much, but a little."

"Did you let him continue his infatuation when I got here?"

"No. I think that's why he hated you." The events surrounding the situation were clicking into a painful picture.

"The night Jester died, how did he get your cloak?"

She shook her head, her expression open and earnest. "I have no idea. I have multiple."

"That's not much of answer."

"Daniel, how did they get your stash? How did they frame Crusher for your dealings? If *they* want something, they'll find a way to get it."

"Fair," I conceded. "And you discarded Crusher for me, because of affection, elevation, or...?" I left it open-ended. Her choice would be more telling than any answer I could've given her.

"Magic," she admitted. I tossed the blanket back and propped up on my elbow to stare down at her. She'd just confessed, admitted in a shameful way, that this wasn't me or her. This was power.

My power.

"You're with me because of my strengths?" I asked. My

tone came out in a low hiss, I could feel the rage unraveling in my core, creeping along the skin, ravaging the flesh.

She too propped up. "No. I said magic." She grabbed my arm. "Which is more than love. More than lust. More than power. We will never quit each other. Never. We can place distance between us, we can pretend we don't care, we can even keep up the ruse long enough to convince ourselves otherwise, but the moment we lay eyes on the other, all our resistance is gone. Nothing can beat the energy binding us. You are greater in my heart than Chugknot was. You are greater in your power than Crusher was. And you are greater in my soul than I am. We are intertwined by magic and will never be free of each other."

She paused, then continued, "You'll hate it sometimes. I will too. But we are bound by magic. You can't come back from that."

"The aura draw? All of this is the aura draw?"

"I think it's more than that. I think it's authentic. But with the aura draw, we'll never know the difference and that's greater than any love. I feel you in every morsel of my being. Just ask my mother and Polar." She looked down. "They won't quit each other until one of them dies. And to be honest, I'm looking forward to sharing that same, toxic, impossible bond."

"Why is that?"

She kissed me. I kissed her back, only harder. "Because it makes my heart beat better," she said. "It makes me better. Now that I know how it feels to have my magical match, I don't want to ever go without it again."

I concluded that her demented speech was fairly romantic.

She inched closer to me, pulling me down to intertwine with her. She wrapped her legs around my torso, my arms instinctively circled her waist. Cinnamon and warmth enshrouded me; it was enough to get drunk off of. "I forgive you for things I would normally grudge on, Daniel. Things I haven't even brought up because at the end of the day I don't care, as long as you come back to me."

"What things?"

"You know what things."

"Tell me."

"No, you tell me. I shouldn't have to bring up dishonesty."

"The same could be said for you. I've had to pry, it's only fair the same treatment is reciprocated."

She pulled in tighter. "I know about Sarah."

"I'm not sorry for it," I said, surprised by my own vehemence. "It was the least I could do to save her."

"And the kiss?"

"I thought the honeysuckle blocked your vision?"

She shrugged in lieu of an answer. So I was to spill my secrets and she could hold onto hers? It wasn't fair.

"It made the moment easier to deny," I said.

"Did you enjoy it?"

"It hurt, if that's what you're asking."

"Because you were thinking of me?"

"Yeah." And even though that wasn't entirely true, she accepted that answer.

Her hold became tighter, more frantic. "Don't ever do it again," she said.

"With you around, I'm blinded."

This is what we had come to: a truce bonded by a power that was beyond our ability.

"So, what now?" she asked, slowly removing the rest of my clothes, and inching out of hers. I unhooked her bra.

Nothing was separating us.

"I think you know." I cupped her face and kissed her mouth, her cheek, and when she closed her eyes, I placed two more on her lids. "We have to stay," I said. "We have to fight."

That's all she needed to hear. Perhaps she had more passion for the rebellion than for me.

Either way, we surrendered and finally became one. Body and soul.

Both of us unsure if it was love or magic.

Neither one of us caring.

CHAPTER 13
THE REBELLION

Our instructions were clear.

Be in the Poison Throne Room at noon.

The Seven and their husbands would be busy discussing the events of the blast in the Room of Reckoning—the same location where Marie was ended and Lacey was made.

Fantasia slipped in through the back and stood by my side near the thrones in the Poison Quarters.

After last night, our bond was stronger than before.

I wasn't even sure death could undo it.

She looked at me with a certain hesitancy, almost a shyness, as if our powers had bled together and she wasn't certain where hers began and mine started.

Convoluted and intertwined.

I smiled and her whole face brightened. And for reasons I would later ponder, I grabbed her hand and directed her to sit on Plague's throne. Not Scream's—which was the larger of the two, but the smaller, brisker one placed slightly behind it.

A major breach in decorum, but one I wanted to envision.

How she would look, framed by power, a height matching my affections for her.

"You look good there," I said, a deep desire holding me. "Stop fidgeting. You're ruining the view." Her cheeks flushed.

I sat in Scream's throne, and wondered, briefly, what it would feel like if these seats actually belonged to us. How that would shift things.

My poison liked it; it hummed a pleasant tune.

Fantasia continued to shift uneasily. "We shouldn't be sitting here," she murmured.

I grabbed her hand. "But I want to, so we will." I spoke in hushed tones. "If we're waiting on a rebellion to come fetch us, we might as well do it in comfort."

"I'm not comfortable."

My eyes must've flashed, because she blanched.

"There could be sensors, cameras," she clarified.

I tsked. "Scream had them removed after Lacey's transformation. I think she wanted me to grieve without an electronic eye."

"They could've put them back."

"I would know."

She opened her mouth and hesitated over her question. I answered for her, knowing full well what was on her mind. "The Poison tells me stuff," I replied simply. "And I've learned to trust it. You will too. Just follow my lead."

She sat back, but not with a crisp spine.

A flicker of anger rose up and an overwhelming sensation to snap at her bloomed in my blood. It filled me with an acidic warmth which I partially enjoyed.

While the other part of me was revolted.

Never had I experienced such drastic upheavals in my emotions than I did here.

One moment I'm fine.

The next I'm not.

Something was hardening inside of me, an insidious undertaking with powerful ramifications. And as much as I hated the severe influx, I also welcomed it, for it built a shell that would keep me safe.

And it gave me strength and courage.

Hell, even recklessness.

For if my morals could flex, so could my guilt. Was this the way the cure compensated for what was to come? Was this its way of protecting my conscience?

Maybe all the insanity in Narivous was simply a side effect to their deviant cure.

Maybe I was experiencing it firsthand.

Was this the start of losing one's mind?

I glanced around the rich parlor, sleek and handsome with its dark floors and even darker drapes. The room had a solitary yellow rosebush growing around the mantel—where a fire hadn't been lit since my time here began.

I noticed the plant looked a bit on the weak side, petals turning brown and inward.

The sound of stone on stone made Fantasia let go of my hand and jump out of her seat. I rose too, but with reluctance. We both looked in the general direction of the noise.

It had a softness about it, like a whispered kiss. I turned and peered at the far back. There was a dark tapestry embroidered with a spider and skull; it pulled away, as a veiled hand covered in a peculiar flesh-colored glove waved us forward.

A secret entrance I had no idea existed.

I grabbed Fantasia's hand and we moved inside the dark door. The wall sealed up instantly.

"And you wondered how they got my cloak," Fantasia muttered, still holding on to our foregone conversation.

Spark gave a curious tilt of the head and then brushed it off with a crooked grin. He wiggled his fingers indicating the glove. "Secret passageways all over this place. Just remember to be quiet—we can discuss later," he said.

We then slunk along, following Spark without making a sound.

We made our way through tight pockets, slipping right and left, channeling down steps until we reached the underbelly of the castle, stopping at ancient handprint stations along the way. Although old, someone had geared them into working order. Spark would put his peculiar glove against the reader and it would activate, revealing the identity of the key.

The name that flashed wasn't Spark's.

It was Urrel's.

Spark urged us forward. The only light we had was Spark's watch, which drove away some of the suppressing abilities of the dark—our eyes and their supernatural strength made up for the rest.

I kept thinking of our scent and what we were leaving behind. Of how many people traveled these corridors.

But I couldn't detect them, not through olfactory measures, or through the poison's reach. Fantasia must've picked up on the lack of trace too, for she sniffed a few times.

My poison was confused.

I pushed it toward Spark, but it didn't react the way it usually did. It didn't hum and fizzle. It was in a drowsy state of awareness, fogged up.

Almost like a coma.

We continued down flight after flight of steps, moving along walls that spanned the breadth of the castle, traveling in circles, and angling around corners.

We landed at what I guessed was the farthest level of underground. I could tell by how heavy the stones were. They seeped with cold and kept your breath, shrouding you in a chill. We settled on a patch of stone and Spark used the imprint for it to open.

The abrasive light assaulted us.

Fantasia gasped and threw up her arm to shield her eyes.

"Sorry," he muttered, as he tugged us out of the wall and into the open. "I should've warned you to watch your sight. It's a bit of a bitch going from black to bright." He peeled off the glove and flexed his hand.

When I managed to open my eyes, I was greeted by a stone corridor with one direction leading to white walls and the other to a staircase with multiple exit points.

"How did you get that glove?" Fantasia asked.

"Great alibi, right? If anyone wants to check the sensors—which they don't even know are up and operating—they'll be greeted by a dead man. They'll think the machines malfunctioned or something."

"I couldn't smell you either." Neither could my poison, but I kept that close to the vest.

"Same here," Fantasia echoed.

Spark reached into his pocket and held out a bottle. "This is what our executioner uses, so no one can peg his identity. It masks the smell. A few drops and our brains can't pick it up. The walls are strategically lined with it."

Fantasia grabbed the bottle. "This is Concealment Cologne. Only the Seven have access to this. Or the Brilliants. There's very little of it too." She looked at me, waving the small vial. Her eyes wide, I could see the whites. "Someone big is involved."

"Well, no shit. I told you before." He was looking at me. "We've got a larger player on our side."

Fantasia was still looking at the bottle, holding it tenderly, admiring it as if it were something she always wanted to have.

Which was probably true.

"This is incredible," she muttered.

"We've thought of everything." Spark laughed. "Well, wait. Not me. Someone far better than myself. Speaking of which, come on ..."

Spark ushered us toward the white section with a door. A camera lurked in the far corner. Spark winked.

"It's on a loop of old footage. No one's really here, if ya know what I mean." He went to the door and knocked in a pattern.

A second later we were beeped in and I was greeted by Torti, Dreams ... Fred flouncing along her shoulder.

Standing a bit farther back was the leader of the Unrests.

I should've known.

He was holding a smile that reached his eyes and motioned to the empty chairs. "Welcome," he said. "We've been expecting you."

Chanticlaim acted like this was no big deal.

"So, it's really quite simple," he said. "We have a pretty large problem at play and a solution that could work out in everybody's favor."

He commanded the small room, shrunk down to a morsel due to the number of people occupying it.

It reminded me of when he came to our rescue at Gram's. Stopping Romeo from reading my thoughts.

And then blamed it all on the lavender—a lie he had to have known.

Because he was a Brilliant. There was no way he couldn't have known.

The room was sterile, a galley-type setup, with two doors flanking each side. On the East wall, there was a glass partition, revealing another room, one even whiter than the one we were in. The walls practically glowed. We were clearly on the outside of a two-way mirror. The observation suite. One table, strategically placed so you could write and scrutinize any events in the lab room, was shoved to the far corner. It had a series of three monitors—all of which were in sleep mode. A star emblem bounced lazily along the screen and I wondered if that was the symbol for the Brilliant clan.

Nothing hung on the walls except for a clock, the slow tick filling in the silence of our loaded pauses.

On a tripod was a whiteboard.

Chanticlaim chose to prop himself on the corner of the desk. Fantasia took a seat beside me.

"I'm grateful you're all here," he started, clearing his throat. "I know this requires a great deal of risk, for which I don't only acknowledge, but express my deepest gratitude."

Torti remained standing, her hand to her mouth, chewing on a cuticle. I could sense she wanted to pace but, due to the tight confines of the space, was limited to shifting from foot to foot. She kept shooting glances at Fantasia. At me.

Chanticlaim honed in on her; his eyes were soft.

"It's going to be okay," he told her. "You can trust me. Why don't you all sit?" He indicated the chair for her.

She didn't move.

Torti's eyes shot to the monitor behind him. He rolled his eyes in a gentle, good-humored sort of way, and then bumped the mouse, bringing the screen to life. The Seven and their husbands were all in the Room of Reckoning sitting at a round table. They all flashed before our eyes. "See?" he said. "They're still in the meeting, and chances are they'll be in that meeting for the better part of the day."

"It's not definite," she said, her gaze flickering to Fantasia then to Dreams who was—impressively—sitting cross-legged in a plastic fold-up chair. Fred pattered along her legs, bouncing from knee to knee. Dreams seemed not to care about the danger we were all in.

We may not have been mind-readers, but we all knew what Torti was worried about.

Ramifications.

"Torti," Chanticlaim approached her. He gently put his hands on her arms and made her look at him. "I need you to trust me, okay? We'll have our discussion and then we will go about our day as if nothing happened. Everything is going to be fine. We have Death now. He was always the key to correcting our issue—and look," he waved his hand across the whole of me, "he's here. The hard part is done."

"I never wanted them involved." She nudged her head toward her sisters.

"I make my own choices," Dreams said lazily. Fred climbed to her fingertips and she kissed him on the beak. "You have no say over what I do, or what I don't do, so stop pretending you have that sort of hold on me."

Torti's eyes flashed in heat. "I could have you kicked out," she spat.

"No, you can't. I was recruited first."

"Because he went behind my back!" Torti stomped her foot and shoved Chanticlaim away.

Chanticlaim held up his hands. "Torti, we've gone over this. I needed help." He grabbed her hands. "The Art of Famine is dangerous business and we must stop it. You know that. We all know that, that's why we're here. You are all here to help me defeat this threat."

"They're making a list right now," Torti rebutted. "A list of heads to take for the explosion."

"Yes," he said, solemnly. "None of us will be on it though."

"How are you so certain?"

He gave a look of smug certainty that required no explanation.

"But others will be?" Fantasia asked.

"Yes, but so far they keep grabbing those with no involvement, aside from Ether. But that was a risk he knew before getting involved—and I slipped him a memory serum as well as one to dull his stress. He couldn't confess even if he wanted to."

"He blazed bright enough at his execution," I said.

"Ah, yes. The moment before death usually wields unpredictable outcomes. Our bodies and minds either block or expand. He clearly chose to heighten."

"But the others?" Fantasia asked.

"Unfortunate collateral in a very dangerous game," he admitted.

"So, innocents are dying—" Fantasia said.

"Innocents will die no matter what, and had I not blown up the greenhouse, think of how much quicker human annihilation could have actively taken place." He raised a brow in direct confrontation. "This buys us time—and time right now is exceptionally valuable. That, and if my theory proves correct, Mother will be distracted with the rebuilding and I'll be in charge of another project, one of which will be infinitely more fruitful." He nodded. "We must stop this madness and we must do it quickly."

Fantasia fidgeted.

Chanticlaim released her from his scrutiny. He smiled and finally managed to guide Torti to a chair. "Well, I think maybe I have an appropriate distraction to limit the sacrifices of the blast," he added kindly. His whole expression brightened. He was looking directly at me.

He went back to the desk and leaned against it, crossing his arms. "How much can you do with your powers, Death?"

Now it was my turn to fidget. I scanned the room. Everyone here I considered a friend—even Spark with his duplicitous motives. Since we were already in deep, I opted for candidness.

"I can suppress fully," I admitted. "It's not even hard anymore."

Chanticlaim nodded. That clearly wasn't the answer he was rooting for.

"And?" he prompted.

"It tells me stuff. It hums and forewarns me of things. It's like it can see things I can't. I know if someone is near while I'm out in the forest. It alerts me." I ran my tongue over my lips. To describe the full essence of the poison was almost impossible. It was too many things to round out with words. "I think it also picks up energies—especially if someone is particularly angry or nervous."

Everyone waited, the thickness of their stares made me feel sluggish. The information I was giving enraptured them.

"I can manipulate it a little too."

Chanticlaim dropped his arms and came to stand in front of me. I'd given him what he was looking for.

"How so?"

I thought back to the cabin. How I made Thorn's magic unfold, only to come back. I told them so, in as great of a detail as possible. It was nearly an indefinable task.

At one point, Chanticlaim looked at Torti, who gave a short head shake; the look was hard to place. Finally, after I had attempted my best description, Chanticlaim motioned for me and Spark.

He led us to the other side of the two-way mirror.

He walked over to the intercom and pushed the button. "Can you hear alright?" he asked.

Torti's response came back scratchy, but clear. "Yes."

"Good. I'm leaving it on." Chanticlaim rubbed his hands

together. "This, my friends, is the true test. I need you both to take off your gloves and stand three feet apart, facing one another."

A curious turn of events, but we obeyed. Chanticlaim took the gloves and nodded. There was a lot riding on whatever was about to happen.

Spark looked at the door and shoved his hands in his pockets.

"Don't worry," Chanticlaim assured him. "We have Fantasia now. She can heal you and she's only a few steps away."

"Don't mess me up, Death," Spark said. He took a deep breath and squared his shoulders.

"I don't understand."

"I need you to take his aura," Chanticlaim instructed. "I need you to suppress and steal his energy."

I glanced toward the mirror, where our unseen audience awaited. "I can't do that. I don't know what gave you the impression I could, but you're mistaken."

That wasn't in the Poison's capacity. Nothing I shared was even close to power theft.

"Only because you haven't tried."

"Chanticlaim, I can't steal someone's powers."

The look he gave me was forceful and full of confidence. "Try," he said. He grabbed Spark's shoulder and gave it a firm shake. "Don't worry, we'll fix any incidentals."

And with that he walked out, the door sealing behind him. It was like a vortex, all the air growing tighter in the compression chamber.

Neither of us moved. The intercom kicked on. "We don't have all day, ladies," Chanticlaim said.

"C'mon, man," Spark said. "Get it over with."

I looked helplessly to the mirror for some sort of guidance. I was sorely disappointed with only my reflection.

"I can't do it," I said. "I have no clue where to even start."

The intercom buzzed again. "You start with suppressing."

That I could manage. I took a breath, and in under a second my aura vanished. Spark inhaled deeply, shocked and impressed. "You did that fast."

I held it with ease.

"Touch his arm," Chanticlaim's fuzzy voice commanded.

If he was directing it at me, I made no move for it. Spark, anxious, reached out and did it for me. He latched onto my forearm and clenched with his incredible grip. The poison stayed put.

"Squeeze tighter until it hurts," Chanticlaim said.

I looked at Spark, the whites in his eyes were showing and his face pinched into a look of determination. Then he clenched—so tight—my bone cracked in distress.

It was enough pain that my hold on the suppression slipped. My flesh turned toxic—but for less than a moment. It infiltrated Spark, we winced in unison, but his might and determination held out. He didn't let go and only deepened his grasp.

"Spark, shoot a volt of electricity into him."

Spark's face had gone gray with pain, and whatever self-control he managed to hold on to, was starting to falter.

He shocked me then, and the hold on us evaporated. I lurched back, stunned by the pain. He fell to his knees, holding his hand where my touch had left its mark.

The door opened and the others spilled in. Fantasia was quick to kneel next to Spark, focusing her healing skills immediately upon the damage.

He moaned as she took the aftershocks of the toxin. I leaned against the wall, trying to steady my breath.

"It didn't work," Spark said.

Chanticlaim came up to me and searched my face. His disappointment was palpable.

He pulled out a knife he had hidden in his waistband and held it up. Then he unfurled his fingers, releasing it, only it stayed put, suspended in midair.

I'd never thought to ask what Chanticlaim's power was aside from his Brilliance. A Telekinetic, his aura color shifted ever so slightly.

"I'm going to send this knife into your leg unless you stop me," he said, cool and collected. "We are with you, and we will all suffer the consequences if this blade breaks your skin. Do you understand me?"

"Don't," Torti said. She was leaning over Spark, who was still on the ground. His chest rose in shallow bursts.

"I trust him," Chanticlaim said. And as if to prove a point, the door locked from the outside, his powers sealing us in. The click was sickeningly audible. "He works best when his heart is invested. He will stop it. I'll give you to the count of three." He held out his arm, his sleeves rolled up to his elbow.

"Chanticlaim, I can't—"

"One."

"C'mon, man, don't do it," Spark said.

"Two."

"Be reasonable," I said, but we were beyond that. There was no backing down, this was going to happen whether I wanted it to or not.

Just as he started on three, I whipped my hand out and clutched him, gripping his wrist deeply—only I didn't suppress, I flexed and made my energy flair. It was purely instinctual. I didn't command it, it commanded me. The toxin cut into his flesh, slashing his resolve, shattering the steel in his expression. Chanticlaim screamed in agony, a high-pitched ear-splitting cry echoing around us. I deepened my hold. I couldn't break the connection even if I wanted to.

The knife held midair—a feat I would later marvel at, what with his contorted face and deep level of torment.

Yet we remained tethered by touch. His wrist shackled by the vehemence of my grip.

But it was more than that.

There was a shift. I bit down hard, determined, and kept pushing forward.

And before he ripped his hand away, two things happened.

One, he lost his aura. It was quick, lasting less than a millisecond, and had I blinked I would've missed it.

Two, the knife plummeted, landing with a loud rippling clang against the white tile floor.

Chanticlaim curled over his arm, landing beside the knife and whimpering like a beaten puppy. Fantasia was quick to remove the pain.

We stood around him then, as he pulled it together in achingly long seconds. Eventually he sat up and let his head fall between his knees.

Fantasia edged over to me and grabbed my hand. Most likely for comfort. Maybe to solidify the moment.

"Are you okay?" I asked Chanticlaim.

There was no reply.

Torti crouched next to him and gingerly tugged on his sleeve. "Chanticlaim?"

He finally looked up. I think we were all expecting a visceral reaction, stemming from either pain or anger. Instead his face held a smile.

"Just as I expected," he said, in short, shallow breaths. "You took it from me."

I didn't have the heart to ask him if he was sure. It was a blip, an incidental.

Dreams spoke up. "I saw it," she whispered. "You really took it."

I looked around. They agreed. Chanticlaim laughed, his brown almond-shaped eyes upturned in joy.

Chanticlaim turned to Torti, his relief matching hers. "See?" He stood up, shaky on his feet. Torti steadied him. "I told you, my plan is going to work. My theory was right."

"What theory?" I asked.

"That you're the key to removing our powers. The entire point of our rebellion rests on you."

"Wait. What? Removing our powers? As in take them away?"

Chanticlaim's smile grew wider. "As in taking them *all* away."

CHAPTER 14

THORN'S TALE

This was it. The moment of truth.

I left Chanticlaim's lab—after our thorough discussion—and headed directly for the Seven, who were still lodged in their meeting, just as he'd predicted.

Now I stood in the corridor, beyond the doors to the Room of Reckoning, wrestling with how to move forward.

I understood the decision should've been easy—remove our powers and give us a chance at normalcy.

Or stay on our current, dangerous course.

To admit I wasn't sure, further fractured my sense of decency. The Poison had become an unexpected friend. I'd not only grown fond of it, but the shield it afforded me.

I had a place here, a place with potential, and I was being asked to surrender it.

I didn't want to.

It wasn't even the thought of Lacey that got me moving, it was the sick satisfaction I would experience seeing Amelia without claws. Thorn without vines. Locus without telekinesis.

Terrible reasons to push forward, but the reasons that stuck nonetheless.

A vindictive standpoint.

It made me happier.

I chose not to dissect the reasons why.

Chaze and Taze, the twin sentries—normally reserved for the city's gates—were manning the doors. They looked at me curiously as I approached. They were part of the Animal clan—but with personalities like Jaguar. Light and carefree.

"Well, if it isn't Deathly," one of them said. With their matching uniforms, coinciding with their matching faces, there was no way of telling them apart.

"I'd ask what's on your mind, but I don't really want to know," said the other.

"Eh, it's hard enough knowing my own thoughts," the other replied.

"That's because you're a barbarian."

"And I'm your exact match, you talking twit."

Chaze, or maybe Taze, shrugged, not really caring. "You can't go inside, mate," he said. "Private meeting."

"With horrible material," the other followed.

"I understand, but it's urgent," I said. Putting on a tight smile.

They, however, vehemently shook their heads.

"Can't let you in. Orders."

"Yeah, they're pissed enough as it is. Don't want to add to it."

"I like my head."

"At least someone does," the other said.

"Again, I'm your exact match, you blubbering dillhole."

I took a step toward them and held up my hands. I wasn't wearing my gloves.

"Gentlemen, I'll make this really simple." My words were

stern, without bend. "I'm going through those doors—in direct disobedience to those orders. That is how this is going to play out." I stuffed my hands in my pockets and swayed on my heels, a lowly attempt to break the tension. "I will take full responsibility for the ramifications that follow. I'll tell them I threatened you; they won't challenge that."

Which wasn't entirely a lie.

It was a threat. I simply veiled it as something kinder, a barter of sorts.

"And if any heads get collected in the process—I assure you, it shall be mine," I added for good measure.

They hesitated, exchanged a look, and shifted to the side to let me pass.

I slipped into the vast room.

The space was formatted for an audience—allowing equal visual opportunity. It was circular in shape, with benches lining the walls, everything focused on the center stage. A round table had been placed there and every Seven—and Sevens' spouse—turned toward me.

The looks I received were eclectic and varied, ranging from annoyance to anger.

I can attest, however, that no one was happy to see me.

"What is this?" Amelia boomed, speaking even before Thorn.

Thorn stood up; her purple gown had soft creases. The taxing toll of the topic at hand wore on all of them. Tension was on everyone's shoulders.

"Death, why are you here?" Thorn asked.

Scream, too, stood up, appearing panicked—as did Polar. Chaze and Taze weren't kidding about wanting to keep their heads.

"Death, now isn't the time," Scream said.

"You shouldn't be here," Polar followed.

I threw out a smirk and stopped midway. “This couldn’t wait—”

“Everything can wait,” Amelia shouted, cutting me off.

“Not this,” I argued. “I need a moment with our Queen. Oh, and by the way,” I nudged my head toward the door, “I threatened them—that’s how I got in.”

Scream sucked in her breath.

Amelia looked between me, Thorn and Scream. My aunt’s bleached complexion made hers glow all the more.

Thorn walked around the table, slowly, holding eye contact. “Well, it better be good,” she said.

I held up my arms as if encompassing time and space and did what she had always wanted me to do—what everyone wanted me to do.

I suppressed.

With ease.

One second my aura was bright, the next it was gone.

Thorn inhaled sharply. Murmurs gathered. Excitement saturated the distance between us.

The annoyance, panic, and anger of only a moment earlier was replaced with joy. Surprise. Hope.

I continued to hold it and fell to my knees in an act of total subservience. Thorn approached me, her eyes searching my skin, looking for a flaw, a defect, that would negate all her hopes.

She found none.

And then she fell to her knees in front of me. We were eye to eye, her aura so much brighter now that mine was gone. She took her hand and rested it on my forearm, holding it as I held the power away.

“I wanted to make sure I had it before telling you,” I said. “I figured you could use a spot of good news.”

Her hazel eyes glowed. The Poison, shoved to the back,

wanted to clamber forward. Not because it wanted to hurt, but because it liked her. It sang in her presence.

"This is amazing," she muttered.

She placed both hands on the sides of my face. "Amazing."

And then, in a move that surprised me, she leaned forward and gave me a chaste kiss on the cheek as her thumb grazed my lips. It was perfunctory, nothing romantic about it, as if she wanted to test the hold.

"For you, My Queen."

Thorn smiled and an influx of one wrenching emotion filled me. I wasn't expecting it. *Guilt.*

Her eyes filled with black tears.

"Thank you," she whispered. "Thank you."

THE SPOKES WERE in motion and the churning happened quickly.

I left the room in disarray. Scream transformed from worried to radiant. She hugged Ember, who wrapped her arms tightly around Scream's shoulders, cooing to her that "They may just have it."

Serpent, sitting next to her husband Croc, a disarmingly handsome man who had the same jovial demeanor as his wife, exchanged looks and eclipsing smiles.

Polar, Ferno and Dolly were all silent in satisfaction. Even Cougar, Amelia's husband and Fantasia's father, seemed pleased. He actually started to clap, until Amelia shot him down with a hard look.

He lowered his massive hands slowly and tucked them under the table.

The only two people who held on to their sourness were

Amelia—she could sense the power shift—and Plague, who wasn't much for happiness anyway.

I walked back to the Poison Quarters triumphant, passing Chanticlaim and Tipper as I did.

They'd already been summoned and studiously held clipboards. The pair spoke in low tones and were completely entrenched in conversation.

Chanticlaim didn't even acknowledge me as he passed.

A smart move or a slight, I didn't know.

Nor did I care.

I went to my rooms and fell into a deep sleep. The aftershocks of the day and the physical toll on my body—having pushed limits I'd never experienced before—depleted me to almost nothing.

I was grateful for the darkness.

I WOKE to Dolly hovering over my bed and Scream smiling, standing in the doorframe. It was early morning by the telling of the light. Somehow, I'd managed to coma through early evening and beyond the night.

"I know, I know," Scream said, with the flick of her hand. "We're supposed to knock. But you were too far gone to hear it."

Dolly had a puzzling look. Having her in my room was disorienting. She'd never once stepped foot in the Poison Quarters, much less my bedroom, so to have her here, now, was enough to knock the sleep out of me.

"You need to come with me," Dolly ordered. She turned and shouted as she walked away, "And hurry. I don't like to wait."

I sat up.

"Well, you heard the lady. Get up. Get moving. She doesn't like to wait." Scream winked—which was the only indication that what was awaiting me wasn't completely awful.

Dolly had left her door ajar and I stepped inside her quarters without knocking. Dolly's apartment and Throne Room always struck me as peculiar.

They were pink.

And childlike.

With dolls lining the walls. And stuffed animals shoved into corners. Two arcade games on the eastern wall. But none of those things compared to what the room really was made for. The ceiling vaulted to accommodate the beast of the impractical—a menagerie carousel.

Four horses, a giraffe, a bear with a grotesque grin, a miniature elephant, and a tiger.

It was a kid's dream come to life. Lacey loved it. Dolly's apartment helped with the transition from human child to doomed immortal.

She took her job very seriously.

Her throne was practically submerged and lost in the sea of toys and lace.

But that's where I found Lacey—in a major breach of decorum—curled into it, fast asleep. She had a thumb in her mouth, a doll in the crook of her arm, and Bonnie—Jaguar's pet raccoon—nestled in her lap.

A blanket had been wedged around her, a pile of books left near the leg of the chair.

Lacey didn't stir. Dolly went to stand beside her. She wasn't smiling but she was clearly happy.

"Thank you," she said.

"For what?"

"For this," she indicated Lacey.

"I need you to break this down. I have no idea what you're talking about."

This time Dolly smiled, an occurrence that was almost as out of place as seeing her in my rooms. If I had to describe it, it was stronger than a solar flare. "Thorn has put her under my care. I will raise her from here on out, and it's all thanks to you."

"No more Amelia?" I stepped closer; she in turn, moved nearer to me too. Before I knew it, her hand was on my chest, and she was looking at me. Her blue eyes bright. Hopeful.

I never realized what joy looked like on her.

I wished to witness it more often.

"No more Amelia. I will love her, Death. I will protect her. This is a gift that is beyond measure."

"This is because of the suppression?"

She nodded and dropped her hand.

"Please don't lose it," she said, her gaze lazily drifting toward Lacey. "My heart is too invested." She took a breath and indicated the door. "Thorn wants to see you, perhaps to bask in her generosity. Perhaps to bask in yours. Best foot forward, understand?"

She smiled. I smiled. We matched exactly.

I wasn't entirely sure, but I thought I heard one more wisp of a phrase as the door sealed behind me.

It was spoken like a caress. Desperate and warm.

"I won't fail this one."

Dolly was still running from ghosts.

THORN'S QUARTERS were different this time.

For starters, she was alone.

And dressed in comfort, looking well-rested and

completely at ease—a complete topsy-turvy from earlier. A fire roared in the hearth, flames tall and wickedly hot. It threw the room in shadows and light, lines that spliced the furniture and shredded expressions.

Upon my entrance—which occurred with little fanfare from the guards—Thorn stood with her back to me, arms latched behind her. Her crown was placed curiously on the table, next to a stack of cards and a tea kettle.

She turned when I entered and I took a knee, which she was quick to wave away.

"None of that, not now," she said, indicating the chair. She settled into the spare.

Her tapered fingernails trailed the armrest.

"I took Serpent's advice," she said.

"And what advice was that?"

She smirked. "I decided to deliver bad news to Amelia while she was already mad. To confirm that her crappy day is, indeed, crappy."

We both laughed; I think neither of us were expecting it.

"Was she angry about the suppression?"

"Among other things," Thorn replied.

"Why?" I glanced off toward the paintings and landed on Amelia's. "Why would she be against a cure to the Poison? You would think she'd want this. For my aunt to become weaker."

Thorn took a sip of tea, considering. "But would this really make her weaker? Or level the playing field? Everyone is free to touch, free to love, even free to lose a grip on their powers—for all can be undone with relative ease. Everyone, but your aunt and uncle."

She winked at me. "I'm purposefully leaving you out of that list, since you have that miraculous suppression of yours."

I leaned back and cupped my hands in my lap, engaged and interested. Perhaps a little spellbound.

"But it makes her more vulnerable. To death," I clarified.

I didn't say we were incapable of death; I was careful with that. Scream's confession, and whether Thorn knew, was a whole different gambit.

"That's not vulnerability, that's normalcy," she said. "Rest assured, Death, this is a mercy to Scream, my most beloved friend. My hope is that this brings joy."

"And that joy is what needles underneath Amelia's skin? Is she really that petty?"

Thorn clicked her tongue. "A strong choice of words coming from someone in your position," she gently reprimanded. "I ask that you're mindful while in my company."

I shrugged, demonstrating my indifference.

Because I really didn't care.

Thorn took it in good humor.

"Oh, you are going to be an insufferable Velore," she said, but with a smile. The Poison started to hum pleasantly. "As far as Amelia ..." Thorn took another sip. "She is a passionate woman. She feels with all that she is and will never hold back. It goes against her nature." She arched a brow. "But in the same stroke, it makes her an excellent leader of my most feral group. That passion comes with a price though. It can rub people the wrong way. Create rifts. And," Thorn blew out a puff of exasperated air, "both her and your aunt are terribly stubborn. Grudges were made, rifts developed, a subtle undertaking from years of festering resentment."

"Resentments over...?"

"Oh, the typical things. What every great rift usually stems from. Jealousy. Power. Privilege. All three. And now Scream is about to have her greatest desire bestowed upon her, and through that Amelia is simmering. Rest assured, darling, we are not taking something away, we are giving something back."

"So now that you're giving something back to Scream, you commemorate the event by taking more from Amelia?"

She narrowed her eyes. I hadn't said it to challenge, but to gather my bearings. I had this habit of speaking before thinking—I'd have to damper that.

"Are you not happy with my choice?"

"On the contrary. I'm ecstatic with your choice. I dare say it's the best thing that has happened to me since coming here."

"More so than Fantasia?"

"Much more."

She nodded and took a sip of tea.

"That takes me to my next question. Was it her?" she asked. "Fantasia? Was she how you became unblocked? Because if it was, I would've made you two permissible a long time ago."

"It was lots of things...." I said, allowing the words to fade.

She didn't ask.

I didn't tell.

She held her cup in both hands, allowing the warmth to seep through her skin and then wilted into her chair.

"Well, I'm grateful to reward you. Not only as a token of my appreciation, but in turn, to keep you compliant."

"You're my Queen, you can command me and I'd have to obey. You don't need to reward me to keep me compliant." There was something ugly about the word compliant. I didn't like how it sounded, how it felt. The unfortunate connotations attached to it.

"I sense bitterness."

"Not bitterness. Weariness," I corrected. "If this isn't a gift, but a tool to keep me in line with your agenda, it doesn't sit well."

"Why is that? You'll still be satisfied. I'll be satisfied. It seems like a mutually beneficial arrangement."

"What one can give, one can take away."

Which was the crux of my concern. Lacey would no doubt flourish under Dolly's care, but if my dealings with the Unrests came to light, or our mission was unsuccessful, or even if the moon was full and the orbits aligned and she just decided she no longer wanted to reward me, would she undo this gift, this tool, this extortion?

She took a sip and percolated on that.

"Fair enough," she agreed. "But, darling, I have every intention of keeping my promises. Of keeping you happy. As long as you pay my kindness in return, we will both have advantageous outcomes from this arrangement. And as for your original statement, that I could command it and you'd have to obey, it's not nearly so simple." She set her cup down and stared into the fire. "My father thought that. He thought all one needed was power to command an army, to keep citizens in line. But he was wrong and it backfired. It is much more valuable to have your citizens love you as much as they fear you."

"That can't happen in equal measure."

"Can't it though? That's how my father kept me in line for so long. I loved him. I was terrified of him. It seemed pretty close to equal. If he'd issued as much care into the manipulation of others as he did with me, he'd still be here, the King of the Undeads. I only woke up because the others shook the fog out of me. And as for this current arrangement, you'll need to be rewarded. You have no idea how utterly torturous this experience will be. You need to brace yourself."

I had heard it was painful—from Fantasia. Chanticlaim chose not to mention it at all, and it made me curious if he was purposefully skirting the topic.

"How painful?" I asked.

She rolled her head and gave me a weak smile. The room

chilled despite the roaring fire in the hearth; she traced her fingers along the arm of her chair.

"Terribly, my pet. Terribly. But manageable if one has the right incentive. To get the information we need, they're going to have to pull your blood during dormancy, translucency. All of it." I thought I saw her gaze flick to the underside of her wrist where her veins throbbed with the retelling. "It's like ripping your essence away while running coarse salt along open wounds. A mortal injury is one thing, to die is another, but to pull the life force from the undead, it's ..." She let out a slow sigh. "It's like acidic needles and treachery."

"I thought it was more like an injury—"

"Nothing like an injury." Thorn clicked her tongue. "Our bodies don't like it. It swims against the current of our modified DNA." She tossed her head back and closed her eyes. Her skin flickered with dancing light. "My father used to draw blood from me all the time. When I was very little, he would hit me until I turned, because that's the blood he needed at the time. Translucent blood. And after he got it, he would always coo to me, tell me I was a good girl, make me think the mark of pain was the path to love." She opened her eyes and rubbed her temples, as if a headache had surfaced. "He needed it, like a man needs air, a fish water. It was his life force. Despite the pain, I was happy to give it. I wanted him to love me. I even worried," she paused and gave a brisk laugh, "that when your aunts joined the fray, he'd have no more use for me and his love would fade. But that wasn't the case. Their blood wasn't as strong as my blood, the cure not as potent. I became invaluable to him simply because I was the root of the power he so desperately sought."

Thorn sat up and reached for her cup, scowling when she saw it empty. I grabbed the kettle and refilled her drink.

There was a connection between us that grew less frazzled with every moment we shared.

"So, as you can see from my own experience, you'll have to be a willing participant, and the pain will be very real. Chanticlaim shall be the one to test on you—since Tipper is busy with ... other projects—and he's informed me he'll require utmost cooperation, he'll need you to enter different stages, pulling from the various levels of power. You'll not only have to work through the torture but be able to withstand the effects." She tapped her head. "Long after the pain is gone, the memory still wreaks havoc. Of all things, I can attest to that. Are you up for it?"

"As long as Kitten stays put," I said.

"Of course. Dolly, in many ways, is more painful to disappoint than Amelia. I wouldn't think of taking her away."

"Then I think we understand each other completely."

She smiled. "I have a feeling you and I will come to love one other. Let this be our new beginning." She held out her hand. I grabbed it, her warmth bleeding through my glove.

The thread linking us seemed to thicken.

"You shall stand on my right, in Crusher's place, and become a part of my heart."

She squeezed and dropped her touch. She stood and I followed. As she led me to the door, and before it closed behind her, I captured a sight that transcended time.

She was no longer an evil queen.

Or a tyrannical ruler.

She was a young girl looking back with bright love.

And that love cloaked me in a way I wasn't expecting.

I wanted more of it.

CHAPTER 15

WHAT CAN BE UNDONE

JC held the frame closest to Spark and Volt as they worked their magic to meld the hinges together. Cheetoh propped up the farthest end and Jaguar made a pathetic attempt to carry the middle—which he clearly wasn't holding at all. You could see light where the bar should've met his shoulder. His face was slack and bored.

The heat blasted away the snow falling around them.

The greenhouse skeleton was taking shape.

"It's nice to see the snow. Last year we hardly got any," Splint muttered. He had let his hair grow out and his bulldog appearance now had a shaggy quality to it. He folded his arms and kicked a rock.

"Yeah, I remember," I said.

"I'm sure you would," Splint replied.

"Why is that?"

Splint gave a surprising tilt of the head. "You know what today is, don't you?"

"No."

"This was the day you were made. You're officially one year old."

"It's been a year?" It couldn't have been a year. Could it?

Splint blinked. "Yeah." He looked up at the flakes managing to wheedle their way beyond the canopy. "No snow then. It was a warm winter."

I said nothing.

"And you were white as a sheet—which is normal. We're all a little off-balance when we get here. But boy, were you bright. I could see why they were so fetched with you."

"Lucky me. It's really been a year?"

One year?

One year.

One. Year.

"They don't usually make a big deal out of the anniversaries. Aside from Thorn's. It tends to stir melancholy in some. So, they usually avoid it altogether."

The days moved together in a slow blend. I had nothing to keep track of since my only responsibility was standing sentry, next to Locus, outside Thorn's quarters. Occasionally I'd tend to Thorn's needs.

But that was the extent of my responsibilities.

I'd been released from all other guard duties as Chanticlaim prepared the lab. A task that was taking far longer than expected. We were nearing almost three weeks.

He was waiting on parts.

Ventilators mostly.

Lots of them.

And when I asked why he hadn't prepared beforehand, he snapped, claiming he had only two labs available to him—and he wasn't going to waste "valuable real estate" on the off-chance I never suppressed again.

The conversation grew uglier when I asked him two more whys.

About the pain.

About the tea.

He told me he didn't warn me of the pain because he was creating a balm to make the draws less painful.

He said he thought the tea was hindering my abilities to suppress.

Two answers, swiftly spoken, and neither of them felt right.

Meanwhile, I was stuck with idle time and forced to wait.

Splint nudged his head toward the castle. "And think of how much has changed in that span. Narivous never seems to change. And then you show up and suddenly nothing is the same."

He started ticking off points, none of which I found helpful. "You get made into a Champion. Big deal. We haven't had a Champion in a long time. Fancy gets released. Big deal. Thought that would never happen. A legit rebellion. Big deal. Not saying you have anything to do with that, mate. This weird, unsettling concoction gets created." He indicated the greenhouse. "Big deal. Hopefully it never gets used, though. Lots of things."

"Lots of things," I parroted dismally.

The greenhouse's rapid rebuild made me nervous. It had gone from an empty vat of deep grooves and piercing shrapnel to a solid foundation of smoothly formed concrete and now, unfortunately, almost a completed frame.

Thorn had managed to calm the bulk of Narivous—stating the Art of Famine was a contingency plan. And *only* a contingency plan.

It seemed most everyone was willing to accept her explanation.

Perhaps they believed her.

Perhaps it was easier to believe her.

The only positive thing that came shortly after her speech—although it had nothing to do with her message—was that Amelia fled to the Southside.

She was disgusted by Thorn's twisting of loyalty and had no desire to remain in the castle.

Amelia's absence made the days kinder.

Spark swept his forearm over his face, trying to knock some of the sweat back. This welding session had deepened his scowl, both from the intensity and the consequences.

Volt, with her newly-shorn head—a preemptive attempt to keep the static down—worked with equal vigor. She didn't seem conflicted with the task.

Spark was quicker with his electricity.

Volt had more consistency. She burned brighter.

"I heard Chanticlaim is set to start on you tomorrow," Splint said. "I suppose a congratulations and a 'poor sucker' are in order."

I grunted.

Splint, like everyone else, thought Chanticlaim was only removing my powers, or at least the toxic touch. He had no clue. No one did.

That this opportunity was a decoy.

And if Chanticlaim were right, soon he'd take everyone's magic.

Heavy thoughts.

The consequences would change everything. I wondered how much grief would come with it.

"I wanted your spot, ya know. As favorite?" Splint said. "A lot of us did."

I shoved my hands in my pockets. "So I've been told."

"You and Locus getting along?"

"I wouldn't know. I don't talk to him and he doesn't talk to me."

"How do you manage that? You just stand next to each other, hours on end, and say nothing?"

"Yup."

"Damn, Deadly. You're cold."

I smirked. "I can't speak for him, but I like it that way."

"It's gotta be awkward."

"It is," I conceded. "But I don't mind awkward. I think it's more awkward for him than for me—and I don't mind putting him in an uncomfortable spot."

"He's an arrogant ass," he murmured. "But not as bad as Crusher. Which, by the way, do you know where his head went?"

"It's probably still being consumed by flesh-eating beetles."

"No way. They don't take that long."

I shrugged, not caring.

Ahead of us, JC dropped one of the metal railings. The seam wasn't fully intact, and it completely severed the hold.

It looked intentional from my angle.

Cheetoh barked a surge of annoyance at him while Jaguar looked oblivious.

Although JC wasn't part of the Unrests, he was clearly in disagreement with the use of the greenhouse. Chanticlaim was adamant that none of Amelia's litter be involved. As for additional players, of who was—and wasn't—part of the rebellion, they were unknown.

Only Chanticlaim held that knowledge.

And as for who paid for the destruction of the greenhouse, it wasn't any of his people.

Three servants took the axe.

Three Undead collateral that Chanticlaim chalked up to a necessity.

"Yo, JC," Splint called out. "Since when did you become fumble fingers?"

JC responded by flipping Splint the bird. Splint nudged me, and in a voice loud enough everyone could hear, said, "I think he misses his mommy."

"You know," JC shouted back, "rather than heckle, you could help."

"I'm here to supervise," Splint said.

"The hell you are," Cheetoh retorted. "No one with half a brain would put you in charge."

"Whoa, those are strong words. You have no idea who gave me this task. You could be committing treason—insulting one of our betters."

Cheetoh rolled his eyes. "I'd bet my head it was a self-appointed task."

"Well, yeah."

"Yeah, what? That it's a self-appointed task?"

"No, that you're betting your head."

"*And*," Cheetoh threw it into emphasis, "that it's a self-appointed task. Gimme a name. Let's see if it lands me on a pike."

Splint's smile grew, in a you-got-me sort of way. "I volunteered," he admitted. "But for noble causes. I wanna make sure you guys don't screw things up, which, for the record, looks like you guys are screwing things up."

"That's big talk coming from a guy with soft hands. Now do us a favor, shut your trap and help."

"But who's going to keep Death company?"

"I think he's okay on his own. So, what says you, ass-wipe? Gonna contribute for once?"

Splint gave me a look. This good-natured ribbing of his had

surfaced about the time he let the shag take hold and my elevation had risen to a place of untouchability.

Splint continued the farce of whispering. His face split into a smile. "He misses his mommy too."

"The hell I do. I'm just sick of you standing around with your dick in your hand."

"Do you see a dick in my hand?" Splint purposely held his arms up, giving them an exaggerated look. "Nope. No dick. Just a guy watching a couple of massive behemoths turn into a pair of butterfingers."

"Hey, for the record, Splint," Jaguar said. "Cheetoh is sensitive when it comes to his incompetency."

"Who the hell are you calling incompetent?"

"Dude, if the shoe fits." Jaguar laughed.

"Hey, real quick, your brothers know you're not helping to hold that beam up, right?" Splint shot out. And before the words had actually fully formed, Cheetoh and JC, in uniform speed and tandem pairing—let go of their sides. Jaguar, his Animal reflexes just as quick, was able to dodge the falling bar.

Barely.

It landed with a large clang, sending shockwaves under our feet.

"You lazy prick!" Cheetoh said. "Are you saying all this time it's just been me and JC holding this thing up?"

Jaguar gave a sheepish grin, threw his hands in the air and walked off, yelling over his shoulder at Splint, "I'll remember this!"

Bonnie, the raccoon, came when Jaguar whistled. She must've been loitering in the recesses. She had on a sparkly collar with a bow attached to it—an addition by Lacey no doubt. Jaguar placed her on his shoulder and disappeared.

Cheetoh gave Splint an incredulous look. "You suck at even

supervising," he said, and then shifted to me. "Could you see it the whole time? Did you know he wasn't helping?"

"Keep me out of this. I wasn't supervising. I was watching."

"No wonder I dropped it," JC said. He pulled out a handkerchief from his pocket and wiped his brow. "I thought it felt heavier. You should've caught that Cheetoh. I was focusing on the corner."

"Well, excuse me ... I was trying to keep it steady."

"Bicker amongst yourselves, I'm taking a break," Spark said.

"Me too," Volt followed. "I'm freakin' hot."

"She kind of is," Splint whispered. "I like the shaved look."

They went to a nearby bench and wilted from their exhaustion. They were both soaked through with sweat, radiating heat, so much so, that the falling snowflakes melted a good six inches away from them. Spark lifted his wet t-shirt to wipe his face, only it smeared rather than dried.

Cheetoh and JC cut away too, but they didn't move far either. Unlike Jaguar, it was clear they were going in for a second go of it.

I watched them until Splint nudged me. "Your Fancy looks good on a horse."

I turned toward the arena. Fantasia was working Barney—one of the few horses in the whole of Narivous. They weren't much needed since we were able to travel at break-neck speeds without them. They were mainly for enjoyment.

And in Fantasia's case, love.

Barney was a beast of a horse, tall, black, and majestic. He was light under her instruction. He whinnied and tossed his head, the dark strands of mane fanning upwards in a rush of energy. A few snowflakes dusted them.

She did look good riding him. Happy too.

"You're one lucky bastard," Splint said. "Favorite and

Fantasia." He let out a low whistle. "Well, until tomorrow that is."

I nodded. "I'm trying not to think about it."

"Fair enough. I heard it is brut-al."

"Has anyone ever told you how unhelpful you are?"

"All the time."

Still watching Fantasia, I was surprised to see Cougar walk into the open.

Thing is with Cougar, he was almost never visible, nearly as reclusive as Plague.

Fantasia trotted up to him and dismounted Barney in one fluid movement. She landed softly, as if made of air.

Cougar smiled—an expression that was unpracticed. They spoke in Animal whispers—meaning their lips moved but no sound was emitted—and then Cougar pulled her into his embrace. She burrowed into him, tucking tight against his body, the longing in her hold evident even from the distance.

Cougar wrapped his hands tight around her shoulders and gave her a warm, fatherly kiss on the top of her head.

"I don't think they're sad Amelia's gone," Splint murmured. "He only ever displays affection toward Fantasia when she's left the area." He leaned in. "Doesn't it piss you off a little?"

Being this was the first time I'd seen it, I agreed: it did piss me off. Not a little.

But a lot.

Coward.

He let Fantasia go and her eager smile transformed what was already dark and twisted inside me into a more menacing crook of hatred.

She didn't deserve background character status—especially not with her father.

I gritted my teeth and shoved my balled fists into my pockets.

Cougar walked back toward the stable and Scream came out. How long she'd been there was beyond me. Her dark hair was woven in a braid, the hood of her cloak shielding her expressions. But from what Cougar displayed, she was on siren mode. He radiated.

Something transpired and he laughed, a sound that was even more disjointing than seeing his smile. Scream was wearing velvet and the texture made her ripple with every step.

Cougar held out his arm and Scream took it. They exited, leaving Fantasia to resume her course with Barney.

I shot Fantasia a wink—it earned me a salacious smile—before I turned back to the skeletal build of the greenhouse.

Spark had gone back to inspecting the broken joint.

Scream and Cougar made their way to us, both linked at the arm. Cougar's height shrinking Scream's frame—he was looming, while Scream remained imposing.

"Well, there's my most darling boy." Scream's voice was syrupy. Beside me, Splint dodged into a bow. Cougar grunted his acknowledgment, while Scream swiped her spare hand. "Oh, none of that," she said to Splint.

He righted himself and took a small, meticulous step back.

Scream unhooked her arm and came up to me. "You look well-rested and happy," she remarked, tugging at the front of my cloak. Her eyes skimming over me and then to the greenhouse. "Are you all ready for tomorrow?"

"As much as I'll ever be."

"Good." She patted my chest and took her place next to Cougar, who held out his arm for her to take once again. She moved in, well-practiced and comfortable. "Today is a big day, tomorrow will be bigger. There's a surprise waiting in your rooms—it's from Thorn and me." She ducked her head in farewell, the pair of them sauntering off.

Splint edged up to me.

We watched them walk away. Scream, comfortable in her fabric shield, made a show of leaning into him. Cougar said something in Narivous' unique language and she threw her head back and laughed, chiming the air with her melodic touch.

Cougar laughed too.

It boomed.

Many stopped to stare while they talked in low undertones.

When they were out of earshot, Splint turned to me and asked, "Do you think she's doing that on purpose?"

"What is that exactly?"

Splint nodded at them. "Nuzzling. I'd bet money she's trying to stir the pot. That will no doubt make it back to Amelia —and being that those two don't like each other ..." Splint hissed. "It's like salting the wound."

"Maybe ..." Something was off with the interaction. Scream seemed too eager. Too comfortable.

"Yeah, maybe," Splint waffled. "Maybe he's just grateful. I guess she advocated for Fantasia's release." He nudged me. "I think he's always wanted that but ..."

"But he's too much of a coward to go after it?"

Splint sucked air through his teeth. "You can't say stuff like that."

I smiled; it was mean. "You can't. I can. And besides, that's what you were implying, right?"

Splint shifted uncomfortably. "I would never say that."

"Because they'd take off your head if you did?"

He shifted away. I was getting short and hostile, flexing my placement, feeling the power of elevation. Splint had done nothing wrong. I felt a pang of remorse—but I couldn't bring myself to fully soften.

That, and this new behavior, this chumminess, edging close for ulterior motives annoyed the ever-loving-hell out of me. Splint barely talked to me before.

Not to say he was rude.

But he was far from friendly.

Now he was friendly. Overly so. The cynical side wanted to know why.

I trusted it had to do with my great ascension.

The exasperated side no longer cared.

Truth be told, I liked Splint; my edge dulled.

"I'm just toying with you, man. I know you meant it in a ... kinder way."

His shoulders dropped. "Yeah, I wasn't trying to create a shitstorm. You had me sweating bullets for a second."

"My mistake. Thanks for the Amelia commentary, it was helpful."

It came out sarcastic. I didn't mean it to.

I walked off and spotted Scream and Cougar one final time —before they slipped into the castle.

They looked like a connected unit, with a familiarity that was both inviting and warm.

Scream said something, and Cougar unhooked his arm and draped it over her back.

I could see his muscles seize up as he squeezed her in a domineering hug before releasing her. It was friendly and chaste. But still.

My power thrummed.

Was this a cruel tactic? A show of thanks? Either one plausible.

I went to my rooms to see the surprise Scream had left.

On my dresser was a skull.

I looked to the corner where I kept Jester's severed head. It was still there, waiting and watching, in the hallowed-out way they were known to do. The bone had gone a nice, milky white. Clean and crisp sitting on my own mantel.

Which was built, at first, as a necessity. When Thorn presented me with his head, there was no other option but to display it. To not would've been considered an insult.

The shelf was erected with heavy wrought iron brackets, and a thick, black-stained pine.

Over time, however, I began to enjoy the sight of it. Both pieces had their own unique quality. The mantel was designed in beauty—it made me appreciative of the craftsmanship. The skull was a reminder of lurid fragility—it made me appreciative of my powers.

I liked both for two very different reasons, surprised by my emotions, and upset that I was no longer upset.

And then there was the reward of holding it, how it completed my palm, better than a glove and stronger than my values.

I would run my fingers across the smooth bone, marveling at how it was both porous and silky. Enjoying the thrum my poison took from having the weight of it in my hands.

On nights I was restless, I would polish it.

Talk to it.

And now there was a new skull. One I didn't recognize. I'd become familiar with every edge and plane of Jester's remains. This one was bigger. Clunkier.

Next to it was an envelope and a small vanilla cupcake, laced with rainbow sprinkles and adorned with a solitary unlit candle.

I opened the card and found a simple message.

To our exceptional Velore, on the anniversary of your great resurrection.

Happy Birthday.

May Crusher take a place on your mantel, as you take his place by our side. To the future and to greatness.

With love,
Thorn & Scream

I'd seen the print enough to know it was done by Thorn's hand. Scream shared in the signing of her name.

I picked up Crusher's skull and gave it a slight toss in my hands, letting the heaviness crawl up my arm. Enjoying the hefty quality to it.

This was a gift I could appreciate.

I placed it on the mantel next to Jester—both of bone and emptiness, but very different in shape. Subtleties I would've never been able to pick up on before, became clear as day now.

My door was open; when a shadow moved into it, I turned, a smile still on my lips.

Plague scowled at the new addition; it only deepened when he saw the joy I derived from it.

"Well, it looks like I was wrong," he said.

"Wrong about what?"

"I told her you wouldn't like that gift. It was too depraved for you. It seems she found your sweet spot."

"Are you implying I'm depraved?"

He shrugged. It was maddening.

"So, what if I am? What if I enjoy seeing his head? Having it for my own? He did me no good while he was alive, maybe he can make up for it in death," I replied acerbically. "He was horrid, and I'm glad he's gone."

"This place is rotting you," he murmured. "It's turning you wicked."

"Your wicked is my *happy*." Plague was so steeped in depression, I doubted he even remembered what joy felt like. Like hell was he going to ruin mine. "I'm making the best of a poor situation. There's nothing wrong with that. It's commendable, really."

He snorted. "Commendable? That's what you're calling this?" He leaned in, his face shadowed and angry. I could smell the decay on his breath. "By accepting and embracing your existence, you will no doubt destroy others."

"And what's my alternative? Spend the rest of my time miserable? Angry? Refusing to accept what is beyond my control? That there is no choice?"

He grew wistful, remorseful. "Maybe your suppression will give us a bit of choice back."

I turned toward him. Understanding hit. "Is that what you're wanting out of this? To finally end it?"

"I didn't say that."

"You implied it."

He righted his shoulders and cracked his knuckles. His words were strong and with conviction. "Maybe," he replied honestly. "It would be nice to have the freedom to choose."

"That's what Scream said."

He darkened, and stepped back as if I'd hit him. "That's what she said?" he whispered, his words thick with emotion. "That she wants the suppression to choose?"

"Yeah."

"Did she say what she wanted to choose?"

I cocked my head. Everything in me was screaming, my

poison rattling. "I assumed to have freedom over her own sovereignty. To touch. To live. To die."

He smirked, looked down, and then rubbed the back of his neck. His eyes had a steely glint as he turned away.

"She always had a way with word play."

He left. Shutting the door behind him, sealing it too gently when I would've preferred he slammed it.

Something was there, in front of me. I just had to look. To see it.

And then it focused.

All of it.

Scream and Cougar.

CHAPTER 16
TESTING

That was the reason for the rift. For the hatred between the two Sevens.

Why Amelia hated Scream, why Scream hated Amelia.

Thorn wanted the cure to the Poison curse to make her the strongest, most deadly. The one who would be able to defeat all. Scream wanted it too, but she wanted freedom from her lack of touch.

Now it all made sense.

To allow someone—no, to encourage someone—to have the ability to vanquish you at a moment's notice never really rang true. Unless, there was something you wanted more than life. That would be love.

Always love.

Scream disliked Plague. Annoyance was a befitting word to describe their relationship. Cougar never seemed happy, and the mirror slashes on his face only reflected Amelia's level of love. So, it would make sense that Scream would risk her life—

give someone the tool to destroy her—if it meant freeing her to love who she wanted to love.

What if that was Cougar?

What if this was Scream's way of hurting Amelia? I thought Scream was going to have me kill her, pose it as an accident, but now that seemed baseless.

It would be much more torturous for Amelia to see Cougar happy—with her enemy no less.

I thought of Fantasia. What if we couldn't touch? Taste? Feel? Commit our bodies to memory like braille to the blind? Scream could only do that with Plague. Was that why he was starting to shift in personality? He went from investment to resentment. Especially in terms of me.

A scowl was always involved in our interactions.

The more I pivoted this question, the more it made sense.

Scream had advocated for Fantasia's release. Something Cougar wanted, but was too cowardly to go after.

Was that her way of showing love? Not towards me—but towards him? A two-fold move, hurting Amelia at multiple points.

I touched the skulls. There was a chance Scream leaving Plague would spiral him into utter madness.

I couldn't concern myself with that.

It was too heavy, too thick a burden.

He would make his choice and we would make ours.

Love really ruled all.

THE TABLE WAS WELL ORGANIZED, hinging on meticulous. Vials filled with colors and textures, papers piled in neat stacks, a leather-bound notebook with worn edges and a pen sitting atop it.

Chanticlaim stood in the corner next to a stainless steel cart, laden with even more pilings and a hazmat suit. He held a clipboard and a yellow folder. He checked off items, murmuring to himself.

I couldn't decide where to place my eyes.

On Chanticlaim?

The monitors?

The whiteboard?

They were all decidedly better than looking through the glass partition into the lab he'd quarantined off for testing.

It had heavy ventilators at all four corners, connected by tubes that funneled particles into a solitary contraption—a big beast of a box—meant to capture all the released toxins.

Much like the screaming room, only more sterile.

None of that bothered me.

It was the gurney in the center, with its leather straps and harsh promise, along with the cart beside it that held a series of needles, vials, and tools bordering on barbarity.

"I think we're about there," Chanticlaim muttered. He was squinting at his supplies, focused. He lifted some mesh gloves and clicked his tongue. "I don't want to forget anything once we get started."

"Uh-huh." I couldn't stop looking at the gurney.

At the straps.

At the needles.

Chanticlaim tutted and walked past me, flipping a switch and blackening out the room.

"Don't get in your head," he said, offering me his best version of a smile. He pointed to a chair and encouraged me to sit. I chose to stand. "It won't do either of us any good." He tapped his temple. "I need you in the game."

He went back to counting supplies, pulling the file out from under his arm. It was aged and wrinkled.

Weathered from constant thumbing.

I spotted my name neatly written on the tab. He opened it and started jotting notes down.

"What's that?" I asked.

"Hmmm...?" He blinked, momentarily confused. "Oh, this!" He gave another nervous smile. "We have one on every Velore in Narivous. Nothing big. Just data."

"What's written in it?"

"Oh ... everything really. It's your life in print." He blinked and then held it toward me. Even though the move was fluid, he was reluctant. "You're welcome to look through it if you want. There's nothing in there you don't already know."

He didn't want me to take it. Not even his calm demeanor could mask it.

All the reason why I grabbed it.

Worry flashed, and then he turned away, rifling with a bunch of vials and tools—all of which were already in practical placement.

I peeled the cover away and skimmed the papers. My hackles spasmed.

Subcategories, all labeled, severed into distinct sections.

~Aura Color

~Method of Death

~Return Method, Time, Power Source

~History

~Aura strength

~Skills

~Weaknesses

~Abnormalities

~Tests

I flipped to the section titled "History" and was filled with abhorrence to see photographs of my family. Mom, Dad, Lacey, Gram and Marie. Dean. Charlie, Eric. Lacey's image was stamped with the word “TURNED” in bold red ink, and across Marie, Dean, and Gram’s face was the word “DECEASED.” I snapped the file shut.

Chanticlaim turned back toward me and I handed it to him. I already wanted to forget it.

“We’re thorough,” he said, placing the file on the table, name down. He took a seat in the corner, leaning forward, loosely wrapping his hands together. “Everything we do here is methodical.”

“And cold.”

“Yes,” he agreed sadly. “Cold. I’m afraid our clinical approach strips away the compassionate warmth far too often. I’m going to do my best to not let my analytical side get away from me. Especially ... especially here. With you, I mean.” He cleared his throat and glanced at the naked whiteboard.

“So that leads me to what I’ve been meaning to talk to you about. You see,” he cleared his throat again and brushed off a piece of non-existent lint, “I wanted to ease you into it. But I realized, I need a base, so that means I need a draw straight off the bat.”

“Isn’t that what I’m here for? A draw? I expected that.”

“Well, yes. However, as you very well recall, I spoke of a balm to make the experience less eventful. In order to create that balm, I’ll need a baseline first. I thought I could create it without a specimen, and if I had more time, perhaps that would be manageable, but being we’re warring against the clock, this is the most sensible approach.”

“How much time are they giving you?”

“I’m not sure, but they’ve thrown out a few suggestions. The scariest was a month.”

I whistled. “That fast?”

“Yeah. Narivous—for having all the time in the world—can be rather impatient. I worry if I take too long, they will reassign the task to Mom, and she'll hit it hard. And," he placed his hands in his lap, "we both know she'll be searching for *other* solutions. It's a complex problem. I'll have to run down the roster of powers, find ways to eliminate them one by one. You, for the sake of security, need to be last."

"You have to cater the formulas? It's not a one size fits all?"

"Not for what I'm looking to do." He shook his head; you could already detect the gravity of the situation weighing on his shoulders. "I have to work against every method of death and every turning. So essentially all the clans—and then some."

He rubbed his face and looked down, regressing into something smaller. "Daniel ... I'm going to be honest with you." He cleared his throat. "I may have downplayed the pain infliction and how much I could manage it."

There was the compassion he'd been lacking earlier, when his methodical reasoning had overwhelmed his ability to see there was a breathing vessel at the core of his testing.

"Would it make you feel better to know I expected pain, even when you said you could manage it?"

"A little," Chanticlaim replied.

"Well, I've had time to prepare myself." I sat in my chair, and leaned forward. "It is what it is. Thorn hasn't minced words when it comes to the pain component—so I've been preparing myself."

"Truth of it, I'm mad that Thorn better prepared you than me. It should've been the other way around. I'm sorry."

"It's fine."

"Is it though?"

"At the end of the day, it's fine. But you're right, you should've warned me. I don't need pretty lies in place of ugly truths. I'm a big boy, playing big boy games; I don't need to be coddled to comply."

He gratefully smiled.

"Okay," he patted his legs, a swift hit, and went to the whiteboard. "Now that we know it's going to hurt, I need to break this down for you, so that my methods make sense."

"You don't need to explain it to me."

"Yes, I do. From here on out, I want transparency. Full disclosure. No more deception between the two of us."

He turned, and the poison in me sang. I shifted in my seat, and the moment passed.

Chanticlaim drew a circle and printed the word 'CURE' in tight, block lettering—matching the print on my file—inside it. "I have a theory," he started. He drew a long oval at the very top, and made long lines coming off the sides, writing out every clan ever made—except Poison and Earth—including the bonus groups of Telekinetics and Strongholds. He pointed to the circle with CURE and said, "This is the cause of us. This right here, it's reactive and changes according to method of death. Correct?"

He wasn't really asking, but affirming.

"Die by water, the cure mutates, and becomes reactive to all things liquid. When brought back, the vessel—i.e., Velores—will now command the cause of its original demise. Adaptation at its finest. The solution recognizes the threat, whatever that may be, and it starts to move on the defense. It has both a parasitic and an evolutionary effect. Even healing at times. Mom calls it the chameleon—and I agree with her."

He'd gone back to being a numbers man. Precise and methodical. I was grateful. For when he was lodged deep in thought, when his mind rotated on analytical cogs, he had no time for sadness. For weakness.

His vulnerability faded in the wake of his superpower: his brilliant mind.

"Now, we know it changes even within ourselves, becomes

stronger depending on circumstance. Meaning, our translucent phase. Many of us even lose our memories when we turn. That, too, is a mercy of the cure. It makes us more animal and saves our psyche from any damage of the crimes we commit in the name of self-preservation."

He pointed to the clans and started naming off the methods of death. He broke up every line and wrote the type of death to produce that type of Velore. Including the ones I was curious about.

Telekinetics died by blood loss.

Doppelgängers were made by suffocation.

Ember, and the others like her in the Fire clan, were placed in boiling boxes, to die by heatstroke and not by actual fire. Only Ferno was made by flame. They almost ruined his chances of resurrection because of it, for they can't turn what's not intact.

All Animals started at a neck snap. "These are a little trickier," he added. "We actually manipulate the cure, infuse it with animal DNA—usually mountain lion since we have plenty in the area. Plus, mountain lions have great physical prowess. We like to mimic their abilities. Mom came up with that."

"Now, as you can see, I haven't included Earth—I'll bring that up later—nor have I brought up Poison, and that's for good reason." He pointed at me, and then pointed at the cure circle for a second time. "Because, as you remember, this is what killed Scream—and in turn, killed you." He wrote Scream's name on the whiteboard and drew a line directly to it. "The cure can't be given to the living; it destroys the host. In order for it to take over, it can't compete with a beating heart. Scream," he tapped the board for emphasis, "was brought back by Thorn ..."

He touched the underside of the pen to his lip.

"Thing is," he said, "when Scream returned from the dead,

the serum—as is its nature—wanted to adapt, to protect its host... only it couldn't." He drew a line next to Scream's name and speared both ends, making southward and northward points. "Because that would mean battling itself—it would go against the very nature of its chromosomal makeup." He pointed to the top peak. "The cure wants to live, just like a parasite, but in the case of Scream, it's confused."

"Scream's exact words," I said.

"Scream's exact words," he reiterated, "are incredibly accurate. It's either aggravated or in slumber. It can't be in the middle, not without it trying to kill everything around it."

Chanticlaim wrote 'CONFUSION' on the board and underlined it.

"Let's pretend this line is Scream's translucent phase. The top is slumber, where it's her touch we fear. Down here," he tapped the bottom point, "is the red zone, where everything and everyone becomes collateral."

He then drew a line in the center. "And this, this point, is neutral, or," again he indicated me, "aura suppression. When you can balance both the life-force of the cure and the deadliness of it. When you can make it cower."

Chanticlaim pulled up a seat across from me and used the pen as a pointer. He sat and, unlike the times before, when he was both proper and a bit pompous, was relaxed. He leaned forward, his whole body alight with excitement. "Scream may have died by the cure, but I assure you, what is now pumping through her veins is far different. It's a mutated concoction of both life and death."

Chanticlaim leaned back and sighed. "And that sums it up. You are both Scream and Thorn. The root and the cause. That's why you're invaluable. And because you are the solution, I imagine you have a tie to every Velore here. You've unraveled your poison's confusion, giving it clarity. Speaking to it like it's a living thing, because all along, I surmised it was living. That's why dormancy exists."

"So, this taking of our powers, is this taking them away completely or placing them into a state of dormancy?"

"Does it matter? The results are the same."

"True." A strange quiet fell over us.

"We've stalled long enough." He waved toward the blacked-out lab.

I entered first and waited for Chanticlaim to suit up.

He came in fully gowned—save for his mask, which he had tucked in the crook of his arm. He set it on the stool sheathed in plastic.

He wore gloves much like my own.

He motioned me to get on the gurney. Upon closer inspection, I realized it was wrapped in thick gauze. I touched the film and Chanticlaim spoke up.

"I imagine you'll contaminate everything is this room," he replied. "This will help with cleanup. Are you wearing the undergarments I had delivered this morning?"

I nodded; suddenly my voice no longer worked.

"Good. They're disposable as well. You'll get a new set every time we test." He touched the tools on his right, his fingertips soft, caressing. "Please strip down and do your best to get comfortable."

I took off my shirt and pants, socks and shoes. Chanticlaim grabbed them and set them outside the door. I was left in a thin mesh tank top and boxer shorts.

A chill raked along my flesh. It wasn't from the temperature.

I laid down on the sterile platform and Chanticlaim went to work, his face as dark as the vibes weaving around us.

He started to talk, more to himself, simply to keep his mind from latching back into the humane side.

The side that made him small.

He couldn't afford to be small.

"We'll test your release," he muttered, "and we'll test your translucency. All points when your powers are in effect. It'll take practice when it comes to suppression draws. You're strong, the pain will be stronger. Our blood changes with each step, and I'll collect during those points. We're chromosomal creatures." Chanticlaim cinched the strap on my right arm.

I tried to push down the feeling of claustrophobia.

"Our DNA is different, our nerves altered." He cinched my right foot. "Senses more responsive, genetic make-up ..."—left foot, a bit tighter than the other two—"more pliable. We're churning wheels, and every spoke shall be examined." He finished my last arm, and then pulled out a torso strap, that I didn't realize was there. He put it in place and closed it in. "You're doing us a great service," he said, something minute pebbling its way into the back of his throat. He hesitated, and then reached for another strap I was unaware of. "And I'm sorry I have to place this on you ..." He hesitated above my forehead and had I not already been locked down, I would've froze. "I won't make it too tight, but I need you completely secured to avoid *mistakes.*"

And since it was the last movement I had left, and I wanted to feel it before it was taken away, I nodded.

I was cemented. And frightened. And the thought of what it would feel like to be buried alive came reeling into me.

This was worse than death. This was inescapable torment.

He cinched the strap over my forehead, immobilizing me entirely.

Chanticlaim put on his own mask. It was a gas one, with a ventilator.

Then he dimmed the lights.

Lastly, most terrifyingly of all, he placed a piece of leather in my mouth for me to bite down on.

His breathing came out rusty through the mask's respirator.

He sat down, and looking out of the corner of my eye, I saw Chanticlaim reach for a vial.

It was green, but in the dimmed lighting, it shone like swamp water.

He undid the stopper and hovered the container over my leg's bare flesh. He hesitated.

I wondered what this was about. Where was the needle? The vials to collect? Shouldn't they have been at the ready?

"I'm sorry," he said. "I wish there was another way. I need you at your highest stage of translucency."

And then he poured acid on me.

Acid.

And before the pain hit—in that strange, bloated moment hovering between shock and disbelief—I thought to myself, *was this Chanticlaim's version of no more deception*?

Then the pain hit. I dropped from Daniel and plunged into Death. My body went reactive with the translucent release. I bit down, screaming. My poison infiltrating the air.

Chanticlaim reached for the needle.

It broke my skin.

And I realized I never knew pain.

Never.

Death would be a mercy.

I willed it to come.

I screamed. Even with the leather in my mouth, I screamed beyond it. I thrashed. I bucked. My marrow melted.

My body descended into limitless, everlasting time. I was being carved from the inside, and the pillaged organs were set on fire.

I had gone underwater in dry air.

The whole gurney thrashed and lifted, and I realized even the bolts holding it in place were no match.

Chanticlaim became a blur as I let out a wail I didn't know I had. Somehow the leather had gotten dislodged.

The poison in me wasn't particles, but a storm, a tornado that blacked out the dim lighting, enshrouding us in painful shivers. They hurt on release.

Like I betrayed them.

Then he gave me a moment of mercy. He sprinkled eggplant dust in my face, the Purple Magic killing my mind.

I was glad to live in darkness.

CHAPTER 17
TWO SIDES

I woke up in my rooms.

If I had to place a guess on it, it was two days before I truly broke the barrier of pain and rest.

Consciousness was an agonizing vise, with aching muscles and raging cells. Even the soft padding of my bed was too abrasive. The room was mercifully dark, with heavy blackout curtains covering the windows.

A warm body curled around my torso, and from it, a salve extended.

It was the only part that didn't hurt.

She was mending me with her touch, healing properties on full throttle.

But it wasn't enough, all the places she couldn't touch cried for relief, and even the places she made contact with weren't completely sedated.

The wounds I bore were deep.

"You're awake," she murmured, and even her voice, calm as a whisper was too much. I winced, and she placed her arm underneath my chin, wrapping my ears with her skin, curling over me like a smoke tendril. She dropped her voice, so low it almost couldn't be counted, and said, "It was worse than you thought."

Part of me let go. I nodded.

She grew tighter, her leg squeezing my stomach, her other leg running the length of me, draping herself over my body and it dawned on me she wasn't wearing much for clothes.

Neither was I.

We laid like that, in the dark, our breathing matching.

"Daniel?" she breathed. "Are you okay?"

"Better," I replied, and pulled her closer. I wanted to fuse into her. "That was hell."

"Chanticlaim said it was worse than he expected."

"It was worse than I expected, and I was expecting the worst."

"I'm sorry."

"Me too."

Silent ticks.

"They had me waiting here for you," Fantasia said. "They knew you were going to be in bad shape. They wanted me to heal you, to keep you invested." She stroked my chest and part of her hummed. It reminded me of a purr. "I think they're afraid you'll quit on them."

I closed my eyes; my lids even ached. "They're right to be afraid. I don't know..." My earlier thoughts reared. I wanted this—but I didn't. Why was I doing this? Why was I committed to the task of removing powers, when I, in turn would have to suffer for it?

And I didn't want my powers to go away.

I didn't want the Art of Famine either.

Not even the thought of Amelia brought low was enough to balm my memory. It seemed petty at this moment. And asinine.

I could just remove those who were a threat. My own abilities would remain intact. The same outcome, different results.

My strength was strong enough to destroy; I wasn't sure it was strong enough to withstand.

The Poison Quarters were silent. I couldn't even feel Plague nearby.

"I don't know if I can do it."

She peeled herself away and looked at me. Her lavender eyes vibrant, even in the dark. "You're going to quit?"

"It's not a matter of quitting," I seared, spitting out the last word. "I'm not a quitter. But this might be impossible."

"You're not giving yourself enough credit—"

"Stop." I grabbed her hand, seized it. My force was stronger than I thought. Even in my weakened state, the desire to thrive was overwhelming. She winced in my grip, overtaken by it. "Fantasia, it's bigger than that. It's beyond your understanding."

"Make me understa—"

"They're going to draw while I'm in suppression." I sat up, bolstering my words. The room spun. I held my hand to my forehead. There was nothing gentle in my tone. "I don't think I can hold it."

The nightmare slammed into me.

"With practice—"

I grabbed her face. It shocked me as much as it shocked her. But I held it, her jaw weak in my hands. "Don't. Talk. About. Practice."

I let her go, flinging my hand away. For the first time, her touch was not something I sought.

Or wanted.

I left the bed—albeit slowly and with great care. My feet were unsteady, but strong enough to make it to the bathroom. I slammed the door.

I didn't have to look to see the confusion on Fantasia's face.

And something boiling inside me was too prideful to offer an apology.

When I came out, she was gone.

I WAS SUMMONED to Thorn's room and went with slow steps.

With hollows under my eyes and my pallor sickly and drawn, I resembled Plague more than Scream. Just carve out a side of my face and I'd nearly be his twin.

Polar, Scream, Serpent, even Dolly, had attempted to fuss over me. I brushed them all away, turned down every invitation.

But one doesn't turn down an order from their Queen, so I found myself standing at her doors, age having settled into my appearance with lines and brittleness.

Locus stood alone outside Thorn's chambers, and I wondered if Thorn felt too guilty to have anyone else stand in my stead.

Especially when I was out of commission.

"Dude, you okay?" he asked. He reached out his hand to steady me; I must've been swaying on my feet. I blinked a few times. He looked concerned, so far out of character, it made me wonder how tragic my appearance actually was. Since when did he care? "Do you want to sit down?"

Now he was being nice.

I must've been a mess.

I shook my head. "I don't want to keep her waiting."

"I don't think she'd mind if you needed a moment."

"I'm fine."

He hesitated and shifted a step away.

The scar on his face from my poisonous touch winked at me.

"Alright, good luck, man."

Thorn loved her fires. That was for certain. She was standing next to a robust hearth that held a crackling one. The flames snapped and spit, breaking up the silence that cloaked the air. She had her back to me, and I could make out the sharp ridges of her shoulder blades and the cutting bones of her shoulders. She was dressed in a thin gown, the material almost see-through. It was delicate and extravagant and flowed off her in streams. Her hair was loose, falling in waves down her back. No crown.

Simple.

She didn't turn, but chose to stare at the disintegrating logs.

"You can sit," she said.

My place had been set, an empty porcelain teacup next to a kettle and a deck of stacked playing cards.

"I heard how it went." Thorn's silky voice broke the room as she turned to face me. Her expression drawn, she seemed to wilt as she neared. She grabbed my gloved hands and brought them to her chest. "You look ..." she stopped and searched my face.

"Awful," I finished for her.

"Yes." She indicated the chair and I fell into it, my legs giving out. She reached for the teapot and poured me a cup, serving me as if born to a different station. "Drink this. You've earned it."

She took a seat, her eyes tracing me.

I was too tired to care.

I drank. And drank. Until my body liquified. "I had them make it stronger, just for you," Thorn said. Her voice had the lull of a soft siren, mesmerizing.

I nodded, grateful.

"I remember what it was like," Thorn said, her lips contorting into a grimace. "I worried for you."

Her sincerity made the Poison in my belly sleep.

"How did you manage it? It feels so hopeless. I don't know if I can do it—"

"You can," she said. "You can do it. I was able to, so you will be able to, too."

"It was so bad. A nightmare."

"Yes. It is bad. Very. But with each pull, your body will adapt. That's what we are. Adaptation." She poured herself a cup, filling it only halfway, and topped mine off, which I greedily threw back. "Careful," she cautioned, "you'll put yourself into a slumber."

"That wouldn't be the worst thing." I closed my eyes and let my head fall back. I wanted to sleep. Damn, did I want to. To put that whole kettle into my system and fall away from reality.

"But there's something that has been bothering me. Something I need to tell you." Her tone unnerved me, and it woke me up.

Thorn's hazel eyes sparked, as the waves of her brown hair danced around the heated light. She stood up, restless, and paced in front of the fire, her gown billowing with each ragged movement. Thorn rubbed her hands together and held them in front of her face. After a few seconds she let them fall and stopped to stand in front of me.

"I wanted to start with saying your cooperation has pleased me. *You*," she stressed the word, "have pleased me."

I nodded. Between her genuine concern for my welfare, and her gratefulness, the pendulum between hate and love continued to sway in her direction.

She gave me a tight smile.

"I've been dreading this conversation. It's one of those dreadful affairs. But the time has come."

Thorn started to pace again, then saw the chair and opted to place herself back in it.

She crossed her legs and cleared her throat.

"You haven't spoken to me about the injustices placed on your bloodline," she began, staring at the fire—her fingers plucking at the plush padding of her armrest. "I keep waiting for it to fall from your lips—for you are young and impulsive, as is most youth—yet you've kept it contained, and I must admit, I've found that restraint admirable."

Tony. Gram. Marie. Dean.

Everything within me shallowed. My heartbeat. My breathing. The slumbering poison.

"But the time has come. You need to know the truth."

"I know the truth. I saw it with my own eyes."

"Not all of it."

"Enough of it," I spat.

"True, you've seen some of it. In your eyes, it may be enough; in mine, it's not. You've seen the surface only." Thorn was selecting her words carefully, rolling them around in her mouth, tasting them before spilling them into the atmosphere. With each stilted pause, I grew more curious. She needn't mind her words.

She was our ruler.

And commanded all.

"All stories look different when it comes to the teller. I never told you my side. I feel like I should."

I looked away. Why was she bringing this up now? When I was weak and in a state of exhaustion?

An explanation wouldn't fix anything.

It wouldn't do anything.

The tea in my system evaporated from the heat of wrath.

Thorn sensed it. She stood and her faltering shadow loomed over me.

She waited for me to turn back and when I didn't, she spoke to my profile.

"Since you can't bear the sight of me over this tender topic, allow me to speak without your eyes."

Her shadow shifted away. Her pacing resumed.

"I'm going to start with the first and move to the last, a linear method. I like it when events are told in chronological order."

I wanted to stay removed, but she drew my gaze like a hypnotist. Her lip twitched. She held out a finger and let her other hand wrap around it. "One: Your grandmother. Who I didn't know was your grandmother until it was too late. I was in the forest, taking a stroll—something I don't often do, as you well know—and fell upon a woman screaming for one of my undead. For one of my undead *leaders*."

She stopped and turned toward me. Her gown eddied behind her in a great massive sweep.

"What was I to think? That this was a common occurrence? That my trust had been violated, by someone I love, no less? Polar ... Polar is part of my heart, and I felt a violent rearing of betrayal. To say I was enraged would be a gross understatement." A glow of heat crept up her neck and filled her cheeks. "I wanted to destroy the cause of my pain. To eradicate the betrayal I felt."

The crackling fire did little to soften the overall menacing effect.

My mind went to Gram. At how she must've looked when Thorn commanded her vines, briars with sharp points, to hold her in place.

It was Polar who ended her misery, by giving her his ice kiss and freezing her in place.

I clenched my jaw.

"Say it," she commanded. "Say what you're feeling. This is our moment for candidness."

"You pinned her with vines—"

"Yes."

"You hurt her."

"Yes."

"An old woman. A woman who posed no threat. You killed someone who was of no danger, in the vilest of ways."

"No."

"What do you mean no?"

"You're incorrect. First off, she was a danger. Not physically, but with knowledge—and that's the very worst type. It's insidious, creeping in and catching you unawares." Thorn clasped her hands behind her back and resumed the pacing. "Knowledge of our existence is perhaps our biggest threat. I've gone over this. Countless times. We must remain hidden. We must remain a lore in fantasy stories." She stopped and stared at the paintings of her Sevens on the wall. I wasn't able to trail her gaze, so I wasn't sure which one held her attention.

"She knew and that was a problem. That was why she was a threat. And as far as your killing assumption in ... how did you put it?" She cocked her head, and air quoted me, "'in the vilest of ways' is so erroneous, it breaks me to hear you thought me so evil. I was weighing her character. I was measuring her worth—not to destroy her, but to keep her. Alive and *human*."

At this, I leaned forward.

Something in me loosened.

"What?" I challenged. "Are you really trying to argue you weren't going to kill her?"

She turned, and her whole body acted on a sigh, her shoulders dropped, her elitism falling.

"That's exactly what I'm arguing—"

"Bullshit."

She flashed her eyes. I quieted on command. "I only used the vines to get information from her. She knew about Narivous, and I needed to know how. I asked her, over and over, and when she refused to answer me, I used the briars as a tool to frighten her." Thorn moved in. "Your grandmother was a brave woman. She showed remarkable courage and would've been an ideal Protector. I've been searching for more and would've loved to have added her to my repertoire. Not only was her temperament perfect—so was her physical appearance." She slipped into a smirk. A bitter, mournful smirk. "No one would suspect her, for she is an elder, a matriarch worthy of respect. *Perfect*," she spat. "But Polar destroyed her before I could stop him. I was not pleased with her loss."

Thorn's conviction didn't falter. She was making sense and I hated her for it.

"As for your friend, Sludge, was it?"

"Tony," I corrected.

"Very well," Thorn amended. "Tony." She cleared her throat and angled her back toward me. "He was an unfortunate casualty. Unfortunate but necessary." Thorn rocked on her heels. I wanted to see her face, to read her features, but she kept them from me.

"My people," she said, "own my heart. Leaders have a responsibility to watch over their kingdom, to protect it—through any measure necessary. Tony ..." She breathed his name as if those four letters were painful to speak. "Tony was a sacrifice for the greater good. I have created a powerful civilization with powerful citizens, many of whom don't want to sample grandeur, but to own it. They seek glory on the grandest scale, and there is only one way for them to achieve it." Thorn went back to her chair and melted into it. "They want my crown." Thorn touched her head, as if she could feel the spires, but her regalia was missing.

"My reign has been filled with whispers—and some of those whispers turn into conspiring—and if left to their own devices, grow into a rebellion. Hence why we're here now, with these wretched Unrests. This isn't a first, and it won't be the last. It's a dangerous place sitting on the throne, ruling all. But it's my place. It's my right. It's my destiny."

She gave me the saddest smile.

"I've worked on making my citizens love me—most do. But when that isn't strong enough to secure their loyalty, I'm forced to swing the pendulum to fear. I've told you, equal measure, love and fear. We must have both. I have—through trial and error—discovered public executions to be the most effective. They're never easy, but they work. They quiet the restless tongues and maintain order. In turn, for every life lost, we save countless others."

She paused to collect her breath. "And who," she continued, "do I sacrifice to instill fear when the whispers begin to ripple and have no bodies attached to them? No names to identify. Who?" She lifted her chin in righteous atonement. "I select the newest—the one I have no attachment to. The one who is a stranger to me.

"Those sacrifices never leave me—no matter how I clear it in my conscience." She sighed and tucked a strand of hair behind her ear. "The skulls on the mantel bring me no pleasure, but they keep further executions at bay. My beautiful citizens look at them and it keeps the fear alive. And in turn, keeps them alive."

Thorn stood up and walked to the far side of the mantel, and stood under Amelia's painting. She touched the frame with careful fingertips.

"Amelia was angry about you. About Fantasia. She told me

you were a traitor, and for a moment, I worried it to be true. She took torturous liberties with your uncle—I only learned about it afterwards." She dropped her hand.

"I had to rein Amelia back in. I had to rein you back in too. After you suppressed, I couldn't bear the thought of losing you. Even if you were guilty, I wanted to give you an opportunity to atone for your behavior. To right your wrong. That's why I elected to have your niece here. To appease Amelia, give her a morsel of power and redemption, and for you to have something to tempt you into obedience. And I thought ... I thought it would warm you to have her close."

"You were wrong." Even I was surprised with how forceful my words came out. "You destroyed Marie—"

"Yes. Your aunt unfortunately was collateral. But I did my best to make it painless."

"What do you mean?"

"I drugged her. I was the one who put her in a catatonic state so she wouldn't see. Wouldn't feel. She'd be free from the pain I was about to inflict."

"But ... you ordered Dolly to read her mind, to tell you who had done it. I was there. We all saw it."

"A show, my darling. Just a show. One to placate Amelia—Dolly is well versed in how we operate here. She understood.

"I'm not the enemy," she continued. "I want peace, but I'm a tragic realist. I've seen evil." Her eyes wandered off, as a film of onyx flashed over her eyes. "I have someone I want you to meet," she said. She walked off and went to the far side of her corridors, where, next to her bed, was a cabinet beyond my line of sight. Hinges creaked, and then she approached.

She held a skull in each hand.

She held out the larger of the two skulls, and in a tone of compassion said, "This is part of my heart." She sat down in front of me and placed the head on the table. She ran her hand over the smooth bone.

She naturally gravitated toward the smaller one, with the blunt injury to the back. She placed it on her lap and cradled it.

"This is my mother," she said, still massaging the bone. She nudged toward the head on the table. "And that's my father." Her face twisted. "Do you know the difference between love and hate?" She smiled sadly and said, "One act. That's all it takes. Love is the grandest emotion of them all. But when you love something fully, with all your heart, it takes only a single act of betrayal to corrode what was once good. Because we don't expect betrayal to come from those that hold our hearts. We expect it from our enemies. Betrayal ruins the lie. And when that lie is all you've ever known, well ..."

She picked up Urrel's skull. There was a detachment there. "Sometimes I want to go back to those lies. To give him back his kingdom and to live a life of falsehoods. But it's too late for that."

"May I?" I asked, and she nodded.

I took his skull and held it in my hands. And even though my poison was tired—perhaps even angry—it managed me a small favor.

It fled to my fingertips and hummed its search. I pushed it to expand and thrum beyond my gloves. It seeped, and toyed.

It told me what I'd already expected.

I looked around the room.

At how empty it was.

I could see where the walls had been taken down, reinforced, to make everything open. My first impression, back when I was playing cards with Scream and Serpent was correct: this was a room to ward off phobias.

For those afraid of small boxes.

“How did he die?” I asked, handing the head over. Thorn took it and placed it in her lap.

“I killed him,” she said. “And made myself queen.” Her eyes were soft and faraway.

She had indeed made herself Queen. That was truth.

But the skull in her hand was a lie.

That wasn’t Urrel.

My poison was certain.

CHAPTER 18
A SECRET

Days turned into weeks.

Weeks into months.

Spring was encroaching.

And then it was in full swing.

The world began to transform into a topsy-turvy. Thorn continued to shift my affections. She was kind and thoughtful.

She spoke in ways that eroded my resistance.

Even the silence between me and Locus couldn't remain intact.

I learned pieces that made him more human, more likable. And if not entirely likable, at least understandable.

Unlike other Velores, he'd been murdered by another human and rescued in the nick of time. Camille had found him bleeding out in a parking lot—she'd been following him—but the actual moment of violence was a consequence of a love gone wrong and a custody battle turned ugly.

His ex hired someone to stab a knife into his throat.

In turn, Locus was promised immortality for his daughter

—when the time was suited and if he followed orders with utmost obedience.

Which explained his decisions and actions.

Again, I understood him.

Started to like him.

Hated every bit of it. Because the vindictive, petty side of me wanted Locus to remain my enemy.

Because the less I cared about other Velores—the better. Especially considering what Chanticlaim and the Unrests were attempting to accomplish.

Chanticlaim failed on his timeline. He was able to stall, however, by claiming I was the sole problem.

He said it was a failsafe. If the issue were mine, they wouldn't be tempted to reassign the job to Tipper since the main component, i.e., me, was defunct. It wasn't the engineer. It was the parts.

I went along with it, mostly because I didn't care.

"Are you intentionally doing this?" Chanticlaim asked, on a particularly sore morning. He ripped off his ventilated mask and threw it against the wall. It landed with an unsatisfying plop. "I swear you're deliberately sabotaging."

"Excuse me?"

I didn't have to bite down on the leather strap anymore, so at least I was able to shoot back a response. My hold on the draws was indeed better.

"You heard me," he spat back. He grabbed a vial and flicked it with his fingers. The blood inside was purple—Narivous blood—laced with black. "I keep getting mixed results. If I draw from you in a translucent state, you need to stay in a translucent state until I'm done, got it?"

"That's what I've been doing this whole time. Despite the raging agony, I've been holding it."

"Have you really?" He snorted.

"Are you accusing me of something?"

He arched his brow, in that insufferable, pretentious way. Only he struggled to pull off the look, as drawn as he was.

"It seems awfully convenient that I can't get what I need from you."

"And what the hell is it you need exactly, Chanticlaim? I've done everything you've asked. Moved into every state of translucency possible. Held it while there, despite what you may think. And this is the thanks I get? It's not my job to be the brain behind the scenes. It's yours. If you can't do it, you can't do it, but don't put the blame on me."

He leaned in close, his breath hot on my face.

I was strapped to the gurney, confined by my ankles and wrists. Vulnerability and resentment heated along my core. I didn't like it and called on my powers—a subtle tug that in Chanticlaim's rage was overlooked. The poison wove over my flesh and, like biddable mites, began to eat away the leather shackles.

"I need suppression blood," he whispered. "I need you to hold it while I collect it."

"I've been giving you suppression blood," I whispered back, only my voice was huskier. Meaner. "But it's a bit hard when my veins are on fire."

"You need to try harder."

"Screw you. I'm doing all that I can."

Chanticlaim darkened. He jabbed my chest—not enough to hurt but to send a message. "And I'm telling you, your best isn't good enough. I need the suppression blood. Cleaner samples," he spat back. "You're holding out on me, and you damn well know it. I won't tolerate your deception, understand?"

His struggles were manifesting into madness. He was, without fail, losing his mind.

"You've taken vial after vial!"

"It's not enough!"

"What are you doing with it?"

"Trying to save the world," he snarled. "With little help from you."

His finger dug deeper into my chest. It was symbolic of sorts. The poison managed to gnaw off one shackle, freeing my right wrist. "Keep your dirty mitts off me," I spat, as my hand flew to his neck. And before I could process what was happening, I had him in a grip that was equally as debilitating as the gurney was for me. As a kindness, I made sure to call back the toxic touch. We stilled, in that bloated moment, both of us seeped in frustration and suppressed anger.

His complexion blackened. My fingers wrapped tighter. His throat felt nice in my grasp.

"Look at that," he said. His words hushed, revered. "Your poison can do all sorts of things." He pulled away; I let him.

My grip was strong enough to leave faint marks; it left a sick sort of satisfaction.

It was a snarl of a reaction.

Not a bite.

But enough of a warning.

He looked at the severed leather, just as the poison managed to work off the others. My three remaining restraints released in uniformed synchrony, a light pop as they let go of their hold.

"How long has it been able to do that?" he asked. He used one gloved finger to lift the fragment, his face slipping from anger to awe.

He always referred to my poison as an "it".

"This is remarkable," he mumbled. He'd done a personality shift in less than a heartbeat. "Remarkable. How long?" he repeated.

"This is a first," I replied. "It adapts, remember?"

He smiled.

It seemed genuine. And grotesque.

"And it just happened for the first time, right here, right now?"

"That's what I said."

He crouched low to inspect the damage. "It concentrated in tight pockets, liquidizing what was once solid. Linear, and rather clean too." He whistled, unaware I was staring at him. "I didn't even see it happen. It was so subtle."

"That's because you were too busy accusing me of sabotage."

He tsked, unfazed. "Can I draw on you while you do that?"

"Sure." I stood up then. "But not now. I'm calling it."

His face slackened. "But I haven't done a draw today."

"And you won't."

"But I have to do a draw. No is not an option."

"Oh, it's an option." I leaned in; he could feel my presence all over him. He shrunk, but only a fraction. "Consider it a consequence of your words. And, because I'm in a rather forgiving mood, I'll be back after only..." I made a show of contemplating, "three more days."

"Are you kidding?" He stood straighter. We went nose to nose. "Three days? We don't have three days to lose."

"I'm afraid we do."

"This is ludicrous. May I remind you the greenhouse is built and the plants are nearly ready?"

"Consequences."

"We are running out of time."

"And whose fault is that?" I arched my brow this time. It came off far superior to his own. "You're in charge of coming up with the solution. You. Not me. I've done my part. The painful, agonizing, gut-wrenching part. Over and over. Countless times. I won't stay and listen as accusations are flung at me. And why should I? What's in it for me?"

"To save the better part of the world."

"Oh, get off your high horse. That's bullshit—"

"Bullshit? The Art of Famine is very real."

"I'm not saying it isn't real, I'm saying it's not an immediate threat, so it doesn't need your help making it uglier than it is. Meanwhile, I'd appreciate it if you'd stop blaming me for your shortcomings. I provide you with the material, it's up to you—and you alone—to work with that material for the solution *you* want."

He narrowed his eyes. "What *we* want," he corrected. "Or is that no longer the case? Is it just my endeavor to be the good?"

I smirked.

"You're awfully defensive for someone who claims to be on our team," Chanticlaim's eyes flashed. "You say you're not holding back, but that doesn't eradicate the simple truth."

"And what's that?"

Chanticlaim stepped up close to me; he lifted his cheek in a sardonic smile. "You're becoming team Thorn."

I didn't even honor that with a reply.

I left his lab and would later contemplate, in the thick of the night, whether he was right.

Was I intentionally sabotaging? Had Thorn grown bigger than the Unrests?

I wasn't sure.

And I wasn't certain I cared.

I SPENT my hiatus doing reconnaissance work. The first two days I spent in the graveyard, walking pathways, breathing the air, allowing space and time to talk to me. Not even the rains deterred me.

I commanded a few of my particles to burrow and search. They abided my bidding with an eager spirit.

I think they were grateful to perform without pain.

The first day was bumpy. Fortunately, the heavy rains warded everyone away, and I could struggle in silence.

The second was marvelous.

I went over Jester's grave, and asked the poison to report back.

Their response was accurate.

I went over Crusher's grave, and asked the same.

Their response was accurate.

Come midday, when Fantasia showed up on that second afternoon, my confidence had hit a high and I was eager to test my new skill on the unknown.

She approached with a tentativeness, holding her patchwork cloak tight, as if to ward off bad words or emotions. Both of which I was becoming renowned for.

I wasn't selective with my cruelty. I acted hostile toward most everyone.

Aside from Thorn.

I smiled as soon as I laid eyes on her, my whole being brightened. "I was hoping you'd show up," I said. I held out my hand and moved my fingers, beckoning. "Come, stand with me."

She took my open palm, confusion knitting her brows.

It had been a long time since I had greeted her with such warmth. Disappointment and guilt stung somewhere deep. It sat in the sour spot of my compartmentalized feelings.

Feelings led to trouble.

I preferred not to have any.

"You're glad I'm here?" she tested.

I pulled her into an embrace, my arms draping over her shoulders. The magnetic hold she had on me hitched; I relished in it. I placed my hands tight against the nape of her neck, and burrowed my face in the angled spot of her collarbone.

She softened against me, our two bodies resting against each other. I breathed her in and was infiltrated by cinnamon.

It was sweet and warm.

"Yes," I said with a kiss below her ear. Her hands dug into my shoulders, kneading the flesh, almost painful—punishment and relief.

And I found her lips and kissed her hard.

Thankfully, she kissed me back.

When we came up for air, I gave her a smile, and brushed a strand of hair away.

"I know I haven't been fun to be around."

"Well to be fair, you actually have to be around in order for me to determine if you're fun or not."

"Fair." When was the last time I was at such ease? I honestly couldn't remember. It made me bitter. "I can't recall a day when I didn't have some sort of responsibility."

"And yet you're here. Been here all day."

"Ah, so the spies have reported."

"You're a popular subject." She pulled me tighter and let out a sigh. "I heard you pissed off Chanticlaim."

I snorted. "For the record, Chanticlaim is always pissed off."

"Pressure can do that," she said.

"Don't I know it."

It was an unspoken concession. Yes, I was absent. Yes, I was a dick. But it wasn't willful behavior. It was a side effect of force and time. It brought about the darkness.

I held out my arm and felt the tension between us evaporate. "Can I convince you to take a walk with me?" I said it all proper-like, and she responded in turn.

"Well, yes, that would be delightful."

Her hand nestled into the crook of my elbow, and I patted it as we started on the path.

"What are you doing out here?" she asked.

"Checking stuff."

"Checking stuff?"

"Yeah. I discovered a new trick."

"With the poison?"

"Yup." I pulled her tighter. She moved as if we were one. "That's why I'm glad you're here. You can be my quality control."

"Your quality control?"

"Yeah."

"I'm not sure what that entails." She squeezed my hand. "I was hoping you were just happy to have me around."

I leaned down and kissed her, long and deep. It took the better part of a minute. "Oh, I am," I said.

"I like that."

I cupped her jaw and stared at her in earnest. "Of course you do."

She squinted, not entirely pleased with my response. I knew Fantasia. She wanted me to say I liked it too. Which I did. Only I wasn't as agreeable anymore.

Another side effect.

"So, what's this quality control task you need?" she asked.

I pointed to a random tombstone. It was on the Velore side. "Did you know this one?"

She shook her head.

We went to the next.

This one her eyes shuttered on. She was familiar. The name read: Clogdin. I suspected it was male.

"Okay, so we have one you're familiar with. Good."

"Good?"

I shushed her with my fingers before holding her in place. I rested my forehead against hers, our eyes locking. "I want you to watch this," I whispered. And then I opened my mouth and a particle came out.

She trailed it with her eyes, and I allowed it to hover around the crown of her head like a halo. Then, I sent it reeling into the earth.

Her lips moved, but no sound came.

I told it what to do, and because it was a tether, it told me what I wanted to know.

"He was a little under six foot," I said. "Tan skin, long black hair—a little unkempt, really, should've probably kept it short."

"How do you—"

I held up my hand to silence her. "He was a Stronghold—but not a very good one. No. Wait. Not necessarily a Stronghold, although I think that's what he would've technically fallen under. He was particularly good at bending metals. A peculiar trait even here, where weird rules."

I looked at her. She was speechless and frozen.

The look on her face was all the answer I needed. "Good. I got it right." I grabbed her arm and pointed to another grave. "This one? You know this one?"

She nodded. I performed the trick again.

This one was a girl. She was another weak Velore, without much substance. Part of the Water clan who had a tendency to float because she carried more body fat than usual.

"It's a little tricky because their heads are gone." I smiled all lopsided, taking great pleasure in Fantasia's awe.

"The heads are where the real information lies, but the bones still hold pieces. Hair color and type is the hardest to figure out without the skull, but I'm pretty sure I'm getting it right." I winked at her. "And from the look on your face, I'm guessing you'd agree."

"Why are you doing this?" she asked.

"I'm on a treasure hunt."

She looked towards Urrel's monument. "You can't be serious. It's a legend, Daniel. A legend. Nothing more."

"I've already checked that grave. It's not him."

"This is dangerous dealings. If you're right, and you find him, you'll be putting yourself in danger."

I laughed. It was far too loud.

"When am I not in danger?" My eyes turned mean, as my poison particles returned to me, expended and satisfied, with their preliminary work. "This intrigues me; it's something to distract myself from the pain and disappointment I experience in Chanticlaim's lab."

"There's me," Fantasia said. "You could distract yourself with me."

I squeezed her. "I want both. Besides, a mystery like this is practically begging to be discovered. I need a little fun."

"Daniel, this isn't fun. This is scary."

"Same difference."

"But it's not."

"To me it is, so why don't we drop the argument because you're not going to convince me otherwise."

"And what will you do if you find him?"

"*When* I find him," I corrected. She waited, shifting from foot to foot. "And I dunno. Maybe nothing. Maybe something. Maybe I'll go in for a visit, see how the underground is treating him."

"A visit?"

"Yeah, I'm starting to believe," a lingering particle floated to my fingertip, I held it up for both of us to see, "that I can have a conversation through these guys." I made it move then, opening my jaw, allowing it to go back inside. A strange exchange I took a peculiar pride in.

"You'll talk to the old, dead king?"

"Not dead. Undead. He'd have to have a semblance of life to have a conversation. These guys," I swept my arm over a random tombstone, "are revealing imprints. I can't exchange with them. They just report the residue left over."

A spark of red swooped around us. In the heat of our exchange, we'd broken a fundamental rule: keep track of your surroundings. Dreams and Torti had managed to descend upon us, and we both failed to notice.

The looks on their faces told me they'd heard enough.

Dreams was back to blonde—looking very much like she did when I first met her—and Torti never changed, always pieced together.

Torti's face was white with shock. She ran her hand along the length of her hair, combing it with weighted nerves.

"That's lore," she said. "A scary story created to spook us into obedience."

"Yeah," Dreams parroted. Fred twittered on her shoulders. A united front. "There's no way that happened."

Dreams spoke with more conviction than Torti. That in itself gave credence that I was pulling on the right thread. The poison buzzed and told me Torti knew more. She was older. Wiser.

Keener.

I smiled at them. "Well then you have nothing to worry about. It'll be a treasure hunt with zero probability."

"You'll be wasting your time," Torti reiterated.

"So? What's it to you? It's my time to waste."

Torti shuffled; she matched Fantasia's look of worry.

I didn't like the exchange. It was an indicator of words

spoken behind my back. They were discussing me in private and they acknowledged that fact directly in front of me. The warmth I shared with Fantasia iced over.

I stepped up to Torti, removing myself from Fantasia's eclipse. Space between us was amplified. It indicated Fantasia's power and hold.

More importantly it highlighted how we could sever that bind.

"For someone who claims it's lore, you seem awfully nervous."

She shrugged, glanced around, and then cleared her throat. Her voice dropped an octave. "I just think it's dumb, in a time of turmoil, to expel energy on worthless tasks—not when we have bigger objectives at play. Speaking of which, you should be in the lab."

"You're right."

She flinched, caught off guard by agreement.

"It is dumb wasting energy on worthless tasks—like this conversation." I gave a mock bow. "Ladies, I'll be on my way. I have a fruitless treasure hunt to embark on."

"Daniel," Torti said. I froze. She was not one to use human names. I turned toward her, and her expression fractured. "Please don't look."

The quiver in her voice was almost enough to stop me.

Almost.

I WENT off campus on my third day.

To the path with the creek running through it. A story sung here, but it wasn't the one I was searching for.

Neither was the field.

It foretold of endless winter.

I kept pressing forward, to the one place that seemed the most certain: the cabin swallowed by briars.

Only I didn't make it there before Cheetoh came up on me, his breath heavy in his chest, his lanky form rigid with information.

"What the hell are you doing?" he barked. It was far too loud for an Animal. "You're way out of bounds."

"I'm going for a walk." I popped the word and shoved my hands in my pockets. "What's it to you?"

Just then, JC came running up, and the nonchalance I was faking quickly evaporated. Dealing with Cheetoh was one thing.

JC was another. The look on his face told me there was a problem. And it was big.

"What's going on?" I asked.

"We've been given specific instructions not to tell you," Cheetoh said.

JC nodded regretfully.

"Is it that bad?"

"Not to be dramatic, but very," JC said. He shot a look to Cheetoh—relaying he would've told me had we been alone.

"You're gonna wanna hurry. Thorn wants you in her rooms," Cheetoh said. "Don't worry, we won't report where we found you."

The fact Cheetoh was giving me a kindness worried me more than the expression JC wore.

We ran to the city—and the looks of those we passed made the sinking feeling deepen.

The earth was threatening to swallow me up; it nearly faltered beneath my feet. A rush of blood hammered my ears and muted the noises of the city.

I passed guards who held no features and entered Thorn's apartment—which had grown so familiar I could navigate them blindfolded. I stepped inside and my skin turned to ash. Damp and dead.

"Well, there you are," Thorn said. "Look who came for a visit."

And there, sitting across from Thorn's customary card table, was Sarah.

CHAPTER 19
A SPLINTERED HEART

Sarah and I had a favorite hobby. At the back of Gram's property, amongst the twenty acres she let go to seed, there was a pocket that dipped just right, and when the stalks were long and tall, we disappeared into a bed of our own making.

We'd bring a blanket and listen to the stillness, staring at the star-filled expanse—the only interruption our traveling hands.

It was an easy, cheap date.

Complete perfection.

"It makes you feel small, doesn't it?" she'd ask, as she always did.

It's like her thoughts snagged on how inconsequential things were the moment she recognized how luminously large everything else was. Our problems. Our mundane insecurities. Our existence. We were nothing but microbes in a petri dish.

There was comfort in knowing there were bigger forces at play. Our everyday decisions would be a memory of no merit come the day after.

It took the pressure off.

The last time we laid on the ground and stared at nothing was after we'd had a fight. One of our last, really, before Narivous got involved and severed us indefinitely.

When I really considered it, thought long and hard about that argument, it was the one that laid the pavers, guiding me onto a different path, so sleek and properly done I had no idea I'd even steered onto a new course.

The power behind subtlety.

"So, I feel like we should talk about it," Sarah said. She was nibbling her lip, worrying it into the red.

"We don't need to hash it out again. I had my say, you had yours, and now it's done. Let's forget it."

"But you're right."

A grin coiled my lips. "Wait." I squinted, focusing on a constellation above me. "I think I'm hearing things. Because surely you didn't admit ... defeat? I don't know if I've ever heard those words from you. *Right*? What's that mean exactly? Riiiiggght?" I rolled it around in my mouth.

She knocked me with her elbow. I didn't have to see her smile to know it was there.

"What?" I followed. "It's not every day I hear I'm right. Actually, now that I think about it, I think this may be a first. Here, lemme grab my phone so I can record it. Can you repeat it, same tone and everything? I'll set it as your ringtone."

Sarah laughed and snatched my phone away. "This is a cell free zone, no exceptions." She arched her spine and shoved it into her back pocket.

"I actually like where you put it; it'll be fun fishing it out later."

"Daniel, I'm serious." She laughed again, and her elbow jabbed into my ribs for a second time.

"Stop elbowing me!" I faked a groan. "You're gonna gimme

a bruise and then I'll have to report you, and Gram will start asking questions, concerned for my safety and well-being and all that."

"Would you stop for just one second?"

"Stop what?"

"Joking around. I need serious Daniel right now, not this." She indicated all of me while fighting a smile. I fought one too, until she took a weighted breath. Her happiness was replaced by sobriety. "Because I really wanna talk about this. I've been ... well ... thinking about it. And I've decided," she swallowed and kept her eyes on the stars, "I won't do it again. It was dumb, and kind of reckless."

The grass was sweet smelling, overripe, and I trailed one of the blades, plucking it and twisting it between my fingers.

Sarah's warmth ran the length of my arm, and I grabbed her hand.

Her body softened on a sigh and she melted into me, laying her head on my chest. I stroked her hair.

"I don't want to forbid you from doing anything. I'm not your dad. I just want you to be more careful. There are shit people in this world—and you're cute and sweet—and people take advantage of cute and sweet."

She propped herself on her elbow and stared down at me. Her blonde hair cropped against the black endless sky; it fit a picture of perfection.

"I know you're not forbidding me. I'm not going to do it—and that's *my* choice. It was stupid what I did. And, for the record, I didn't think Laura would ditch me. I thought I was being careful, but she had to whore off with Andy."

Her cheeks flushed.

"No, that was too harsh," she amended. "Forget I said that. She didn't do anything wrong. This is me. All me. No one else."

"You make it sound like you robbed a bank. You got drunk, that's it."

"I got drunk around a bunch of people I didn't know. It was unsafe."

I didn't say anything.

That's exactly how I felt.

I swung by the party after work and found her, close to passed out, on a couch with sketchy stains and cigarette burns. The aroma of ash and body odor hung in the air. Next to her, a guy with green hair and a glazed look in his eyes had his hand precariously close to her thigh, and I made sure to knock it back with enough force, he blinked into sobriety for half a second.

I saw to it she made it home safely and after the hangover wore off, we had a fight.

I screamed safety.

She cried.

We had six solid rounds.

And then we both settled for a date of cheeseburgers and fries, eaten in the cab of my truck, both of us miserable and deflated—but satiated in our exhaustive resolution.

"I promise I won't touch the stuff anymore," she nestled into me. "I know how much you hate it."

"It's not so much I hate it." I grabbed another blade and rolled it between my fingers. "I'm scared of it."

"You're scared of drinking?"

"What if it's hereditary?"

"You've never told me you worried about that."

"It's not a topic I like to think about." We both lay in silence, one of the few times the quiet was awkward between us and I asked softly, "Do you think it is?"

"Do I think what is?"

"Addiction and stuff, do you think it's genetic? Do you think that's what I'm destined for?"

"No." She spoke carefully, managing each word before speaking it. "I think some people make themselves believe it, like a security blanket or whatever. It takes away some of the guilt if they do fall, as if it's not their fault, as if their decisions are not their own, rather, they're simply incorporated into their DNA." She clutched my hand and squeezed. "But, no matter what, we're the ones responsible. We're in charge of our choices. That's why I'm making the choice not to drink. It's my choice and mine alone. There will be no one to blame but me." She kissed me then, softly on the lips, and before we were lost to the moment, she punctuated her message with a final abbreviation. "Our destiny, our future, is in our hands. We can make what we want of it." I kissed her harder then, and we melted under the stars.

The irony of it all was that Narivous had proved her wrong.

They had tricked her.

They had tricked me.

And here we were.

SARAH SAT STONED-FACED. She didn't flinch upon my arrival and it dawned on me she was sedated. Blinking operated at automated intervals.

"Oh, don't worry, pet," Thorn purred. "She won't remember ... this will all be just a dream. You know how that works, right?"

Clearly, I was caught. There was no mistaking it.

"Let her go," I said.

Thorn's smile was serene. One extra chair had been pulled up to the table and she indicated it. "Don't worry, I plan to."

I took a step forward. "You're going to release her?"

"Yes."

"As a human?"

"Yes."

"Are you going to make her a Protector?"

"No." She swept her hand at the chair. "Now, would you please sit? You've asked a fair amount of questions, it's my turn."

I sat gingerly, butt half off the chair, my eyes moving to Sarah. She wasn't much dressed for a hike, save for the boots and windbreaker—but Sarah was never one to dress appropriately. She was wearing leggings and a dress with her hair in a ponytail. I moved my hand in front of her face. She saw none of it. The stupor held.

"Trust me, darling, she won't recall this. She's nearly in a coma." Thorn picked up her tea cup and took a sip, regarding me carefully. "But we have bigger issues to discuss."

"How did she get here?" I asked, ignoring her. "Did you lure her here? Collect her?"

Thorn tsked. It was all in good humor.

She reached down and pulled out a slip of paper lodged between the arm rest and seat cushion of her chair. She tossed it toward me.

It was the original note with the map. The one Tony—correction: the one I thought Tony—had left me.

The wrinkles were deep, the red smudge stain was still there. If it were a replica, it was extraordinarily well done. How had she gotten it?

As if Thorn could read my thoughts, she shrugged. "I don't know how she got it. Nor do I care. She came here on her own accord, discovered and brought to me by Romeo—no requests were made on my behest."

I squinted at the sheet, running my finger over the printing. Thorn took it back, but in a tender way.

She regarded it with soft eyes.

"So, tell me, Death, why would Romeo report to me a peculiar memory she had? A dream—but so very real on so many different levels—it would seem nearly honest?"

"I wanted her gone," I said flatly. "I did what I could to make her leave."

"Good."

"Good?" Had I heard her correctly? Did she just praise my confession?

"Good," she reaffirmed. "You're being honest with me." She folded the paper. "I would've preferred I found out in a more forthcoming way. Had you simply come and told me, but being our relationship was strained, I understand. I'm assuming you had a hand in your uncle and cousin leaving too? It all happened about the same time."

"Yes." The lie was quick. Easy. I wasn't going to divulge more than that. Fortunately, it seemed to be enough.

She nodded, and touched Sarah softly on the arm. Sarah remained still, unseeing. Thorn let go and leaned her head back.

"Stupid boy," she said, her face teasing a smile, "you're going to make my hair go gray."

"We don't age," I shot her a wink, reading the mood, recognizing that there was no simmering animosity lingering. "So, I think your hair is safe."

She laughed. "Good for us, right?"

"Good for us," I agreed.

Thorn took a deep breath and stood up. She waved her hands for me to do the same.

Eye to eye, she stepped close and placed her hands on my shoulders. "From here on out, I expect honesty, got that? This is your one pass. Don't test my affection for you. I don't think my heart could manage it."

"Thank you," I said, something thick stuck in my throat.

"Chanticlaim says you are the reason for the delay."

"I know. He's blaming me for everything."

"He has no idea your level of sacrifice. The rawness of the draw. I understand it, I see it, and I appreciate it. You need to understand the breadth of my gratitude." She let me go and looked at Sarah. Something indecipherable played across her face. "So, we're in agreement then?" she asked. "We will be open and honest with each other?"

My knees buckled. Deception had never weighed so heavily. Fortunately, Thorn was staring at Sarah and not at me.

"I'll see to it that Sarah makes it home untouched," she said.

And as if to prove a point, she went to her intercom and called for Romeo. He materialized as if he'd been waiting outside the door.

"Take her home, keep her safe, see to it she remembers nothing."

Romeo bowed his head in compliance.

"I'd like to take her myself," I said.

"I know you would," Thorn replied, "But I need a Doppelgänger to do it."

"Then allow me to go with him."

She shook her head; it was not without regret. "Romeo, you have your orders. See to it you take video evidence of her safe arrival for Death's peace of mind. She'll be fine," Thorn assured me.

Romeo guided Sarah away; she moved like a suggestible whisper. I watched her go, part of me splintering inside. Romeo looked dogged and worn.

Thorn pulled my gaze away by curling herself around me.

The hug was genuine, warm, all the things a hug should be—and even though she took me off guard, my poison knew to retract. She had become an extension of my powers. To cause her harm would be to cause myself harm.

We were one and the same.

In the changing of the seasons, I had unthawed, the same as the winter chill relinquishes to the spring.

I wrapped my arms around her in earnest. Her grip tightened, my grip tightened, until we were two pieces fused together. Her head fell into the crook of my shoulder, and I buried my head in her hair.

We were no longer a queen and a subordinate.

We were just two people who cared.

And dammit, did I care.

"She'll make it home safely, Death. I promise you that."

"I believe you." And I did. As strange as it was, my poison was assured—so was my mind. Thorn was earnest with her words. Especially, as I was learning, when it came to me.

She smiled. I felt it.

"And what is my punishment?" I asked. This surprising pardon was worth any consequence delivered. I was okay with it too.

"None."

She pulled away. I was reluctant to let her go. She ran her hand along my cheek.

"None?" Had I heard her correctly? I was to get off scot-free?

"I see no need."

"But I went behind your back."

"You're in front of me now. What was done before our bond can be forgiven."

"And Charlie? Eric? The same goes for them?" Why was I doing this? Testing her goodwill? It's as if a part of me needed her words cemented—to look back and immortalize later. To reaffirm this moment. That it was real.

"You don't see it, do you?"

"See what?"

"You." Thorn grabbed the edges of my vest and gave it a gentle shake. "You," she repeated. "Your parents were fools. They didn't see what they had in front of them, and I'm grateful for it. It brought you to me. I've grown to love you, stupid boy." Her eyes held it—the true rawness of her words.

I swallowed. Something fervent welled inside me. I felt her words. This wasn't a romantic type of love, but something bigger, deeper, more profound. The type that didn't require sacrifices or requests. It was the infallible kind.

She loved me for me.

And then an inconvenient, secondary thought trickled along my flesh.

Because it dawned on me that I loved her too. And this one act—this great pardon—only drew me in deeper.

She handed me the map. "It's best we keep track of these things." I closed my fingers around it and nodded.

"Thorn, I ..."

She held her finger to my lips. "I only ask of you one thing from here on out."

"What's that?"

"No more hiatuses. I need you in that lab."

I wanted the floor to open up and devour me. Guilt was a terrible burden to be chained to.

If only I could convince myself that we were pushing her agenda and not our own. Deception and guilt crept in like an insidious cloud.

She had, without my approval, taken the edge off our relationship. I began to crave her presence more than anyone else's.

Even Fantasia couldn't stack up.

I was torn. I wanted Thorn to have her powers. I wanted to have my powers.

I told myself that the only solution for normalcy was to take them away.

For Lacey.

For Eric. For Charlie. For Sarah. The Art of Famine would always be a risk—as long as we were a risk. To save them, I would have to sacrifice.

I wanted to be done regretting.

Dread told me it was only the beginning.

I left feeling light and heavy.

No longer knowing who was wrong—wondering if it was me.

ROMEO FOUND ME AFTERWARDS. He was permitted into the Poison Throne Room, and stood nervously in the center of the sterile space.

"I've never been in here before," he said. "All this time, I've only ever seen slips of it when the door is open. It's really dark."

He gaped, taking in the thrones, the curtains, the mantel, and then looked at me and smiled. It was genuine.

He pulled out a phone, unlocked it, and a low light illuminated. He thumbed, and then he was holding it out for me.

I took it.

"As Thorn requested," he said. "You can see it's time stamped."

The image showed Sarah in bed, still wearing the dress from earlier, her ponytail looser—but other than that she was unscathed and completely whole.

I handed the phone back and he was quick to put it in his pocket.

"How did she get the map?" I asked. "Surely you must've seen how when you read her mind."

He shrugged. "She found it on her bed. Someone left it there."

"For her to find and come here."

"I would assume so." He rocked on his heels and continued to take in the room. His awe was on display. He whistled. "I'm always impressed how the flowers grow with no lighting. It's kind of like a tomb."

"Do you know why she was back in Oregon?"

"Back?"

"Yeah, she was supposed to leave for college—early enrollment. Did she not leave for college?"

He blinked, confused. "She never left."

I pinched the bridge of my nose. What the hell. I thought for certain she would've taken the opportunity to leave. Eric was supposed to encourage her too. How had she stayed? Why had she stayed?

"I thought she was leaving," I said.

"Well, she was going to, but then her dad got sick so her plans changed. And I can tell you this much—she has no intention of going away until he's better."

A swarm devoured and rattled, my eyes flashed on translucent instinct. Romeo must've taken it as a threat—or perhaps he was fearful with my proximity—because he held up his hands to ease me out of my transition.

"Easy, I'm not trying to rile you up."

I shook my head.

This was a warning—a siren flashing. Even had my poison been quiet, it would've been impossible to miss.

"What was the illness?" I asked. My voice had gone rusty.

"They're not sure. He's still in the diagnostic stage. They're running a battery of tests though."

"It's been months. Seasons have changed. How can they not know?"

Romeo narrowed his eyes. "I guess the symptoms come and go—the inconsistency is making it difficult to figure out what's wrong." He blinked. "This line of questioning is weird."

"Yeah, I know." I waved my hand, indicating the door. "Look, thanks for the photo. I appreciate it."

"No problem," he said like there was a problem.

He turned to leave, and then he shifted and came back.

"If you want to ask me something, ask me. You don't have to work around it."

"You make it sound like I can trust you."

"I'd like to think you can."

"Do you think Sarah's dad has been made ill intentionally?" I asked, spitting the question out before I even truly computed it.

Romeo folded his arms. "I didn't consider."

"Would you?"

His face cocked into a smile. "Are you asking me to spy?"

"Yeah, I'm asking you to spy."

"Do you suspect a human, or one of us?"

"One of us."

He nodded, weighing the words. "Well, I can tell you this much, if it is one of us, it's not Thorn."

"And why do you say that?"

"Because I'm her go-to—if she wanted him poisoned she would've asked me to do it."

"You're certain she would've asked you?"

"Fairly certain. I'm in charge of this area, remember?"

Oh, I remembered.

"I'll tell you what," he said. "I'll pay closer attention, and if anything sounds fishy, I'll let you know. It's good to have friends in high places. I could use your elevation." He scanned the quarters, indicating my position and power.

I believed him on that.

"One last thing," I said.

"What's that?" He had his hand on the door, ready to leave. Perhaps to process our conversation. Perhaps to report it.

"If it had been Thorn—would you really have told me?"

His smile grew wicked. "Nope," his lips popped. "I guess that's the catch, right? You gotta go with your gut."

Truer words had never been spoken.

CHAPTER 20
TRUTH BETWEEN LIES

I interrogated everyone. My plans to find Urrel were all but forgotten as I attempted to root out the creator of Sarah's sabotage.

Denial. Claims of ignorance. They only escalated my paranoia.

And enraged me.

I knew one thing, however. A Brilliant had to have been involved.

Tipper was a likely choice.

But so was Chanticlaim.

Had he kept Sarah here as a form of collateral? He who sabotaged Crusher and monitored cameras—knowing full well I'd left on the day of Crusher's execution?

It didn't feel like much of a stretch.

There was even the possibility he was punishing me for taking a hiatus from the lab.

But I told myself he wouldn't.

He couldn't.

Could he?

Romeo turned out to be my most valuable ally. He went out of his way to visit the house.

"Not even an inkling of anyone coming and going," he'd said, an apologetic twist angling his mouth. "I couldn't detect anyone through thought or scent. I can't smell as good as an Animal, but I should've gathered something, somewhere. Right?"

He shrugged and stowed his hands in his pockets.

"I suppose the lack of evidence is evidence unto itself, huh?" He followed up with, "Sorry I couldn't have been more help."

Only he was help. Lots of it. His efforts were sincere.

How was it my enemies were becoming my allies and those I thought were friends were slipping into suspicion?

Chanticlaim.

I kept coming back to Chanticlaim.

He was molding into a liar before my very eyes.

The map held only the scent of Thorn, Sarah, and me. No one else.

The Concealment Cologne was used.

An expensive product nearly impossible to obtain.

Unless you were a ruler.

Or the one making it.

Chanticlaim.

Instinct warned me.

THORN ENJOYED MY COMPANY, of this I was certain. I had my own seat in her quarters, across from her, a deck of cards piled neatly on the table. She kept looking toward the fireplace even though it was empty and cold.

The weather was too warm, but she seemed to miss the flames.

She had a teapot out and I helped myself to it. Thorn propped her elbows on the table and looked at it curiously. She picked up the cards and began to shuffle.

"Chanticlaim thinks that's hindering your ability for proper draws," she said.

"Of course, he would. It's one of the few things I love—naturally he'd want to take it away."

"Cynical," she said.

"The blame game is getting old. I think he's becoming unhinged."

"He doesn't look well, does he?"

"Far from it."

He was indeed starting to look the part. Wild hair to go with his wild thoughts. Tipper seemed more balanced in comparison.

Thorn began to bridge the cards to shuffle, making a soft fluttering sound.

"I must ask," she cleared her throat. "Is it you, darling?" she asked, sincerity bleeding through her voice. "Are you really the reason he can't come up with a solution? I wouldn't blame you if it was, I know how—"

"It's not," I interjected. I wouldn't even allow her to finish. The tenor of her voice, the vulnerability in her words—she felt like the only person who was actually being transparent with me.

That, and my Poison liked her.

She arched a brow.

And then she smirked. A look for which I would later contemplate. Was it rage at being the scapegoat or simply pent-up frustration? Had I grown weary of the lie?

Did I simply want her to know?

Regardless, I opened my mouth and allowed one lone particle to float out. Thorn froze, watching it dance between us. I held out a finger and it landed on my glove. She leaned in, studying it.

I'd yet to show her my magic. She was spellbound by it. And since she was at a loss for words, I spoke for her. "I'm getting pretty good with them, Thorn. The tea isn't hindering anything—they speak to me, they do as I ask, they are willing."

She sucked in air.

I'd hit some sort of chord, and her face reflected a moment of panic. The poison on my finger reflected it too—it quivered, almost in fear.

And then, as quickly as it came, the moment vanished. I had laid down my king in a chess match—I felt it as the Queen in front of me shuttered slightly. She wasn't as open as before.

Or so it seemed.

"I'm delivering what he needs—over performing in my opinion, so if anyone is holding up the process it's him. Maybe Tipper should lead the testing," I said. Forcing my poison back into my mouth, burying it deep within my lungs. I gave her a smile. It was full of nerves.

She took a sip. Her composure regained.

"Well, well, well," she purred. "You are quite the talent. I'm grateful you're on my side."

Words with hidden meaning?

"I'm over being blamed, Thorn."

She nodded, in full agreement. Although, truth of it, I was partially to blame. More so as of late.

What was once speculation on Chanticlaim's part—sabotage—had become reality. My certainty faltered.

I allowed the suppression to slip. And every time I did it, I felt good about it. I began to wonder what my own intentions were. Was this the poison begging to remain? Was it Thorn? Was it something else—perhaps more nefarious?

I was in a suspended state of uncertainty.

The only thing I was confident in was that I was no longer confident with the Unrests and their mission.

Or Chanticlaim.

"Tipper will be brutal," Thorn mused. Her smile was sad. Something had shifted between us. I ignored it. "I can't let her do that to you." She grabbed my hand and gave it a squeeze. "Besides, she's busy on other tasks." And as if that gave her a thought, she went to the intercom and ordered more tea. She was direct, requesting the batch with the green tags.

She stood next to me as she waited, her eyes hooded and drowsy.

Something was most certainly off.

"I think that's incredibly thoughtful," she said. "To offer your services to Tipper. Not just anyone would do that." She crouched so she could look me in the eyes. I was struck by how weighty her gaze was. "She's busy with the Art of Famine and I don't want to interrupt her."

The tea arrived and Thorn made a point of preparing it for both of us. She brought the cups to the table, handing me my own.

"This is the good stuff," she said with a wink. Indicating I should drink up. "Let's play a game, shall we? Jaguar showed me a trick the other day and I want to see if I can replicate it." Thorn made collapsible bridges, mixing the deck in practiced fashion. "I was rather impressed—which in itself is a miracle. Jaguar rarely impresses me; he goofs off too much to be of real value.

"So, let's try it out, shall we?" she asked. Her tapered fingers fanned the cards.

"Grab one," she ordered.

I did. She tapped the cup; I drank on command. Not caring much. Feeling more relaxed by the second.

"Now, commit your card to memory and make sure I don't see it. Then put it back in the deck. Only put it in a different place."

I looked at the card, and it got all funny around the edges. It was the three of clubs. But then it became the three of spades. Then it became the six of both, because it shifted into something it couldn't be, and I had to focus on focusing.

Three of clubs.

I think.

"This power of yours—it's a tricky thing, yes?" she asked casually.

I nodded and slid the card back into place.

Thorn started shuffling.

"Do you learn things about it on a consistent basis?"

"It's a process—it seems to shift every day."

She gave a non-committal hmmm. "I've always been told it was alive," Thorn said. "That was the theory all along. You know how the Poison came to be, right?"

"Your dad gave the cure to Scream while she was still alive."

She nodded, her face scrunched. "It was, without fail, the most horrific moment of my life. I was happy to bring her back, regardless of the outcome. It turned my father into a fury. My first true act of disobedience."

It was a disembodied experience, sitting across from her, as she plucked a card and held it up.

"Is this your card?"

Queen of Diamonds.

I shook my head.

At least, I think I shook my head. Her image transferred

from left to right, but I wasn't sure my neck made the swivel. I followed it up with a "no" and my tongue lolled like it was coated in molasses.

Thorn didn't seem to pick up on it.

"Can it tell you thoughts?" she asked. "Of humans? Of other Velores?"

I squinted. Lost in a thick fog. "No."

"To which one?" Why couldn't I think?

"Both?"

"No, of course not."

"Truth?" she pressed. "Are you telling the truth?" She leaned in and searched my face for an answer.

"Yeah. It's not a superpower." The last word fumbled. Why was it so hard to speak?

Danger bellowed at me.

She held up another card.

The five of Spades.

I tried to do my head shake again. It must've worked, because she placed it back in its place.

She was beginning to blot out, my vision winking in darkness, and then reanimating through light.

Thorn only grew more vigorous. Undeterred, she furrowed her brow and continued the cycle until she held up half a dozen cards, none of which were mine.

Fog filtered in through the room, fog that I was able to push back if I blinked hard enough. Even with the mist coming in, wrapping itself around my mind, I had pockets of terrible clarity.

My tongue tasted metallic. It wasn't the usual layer of film that the tea typically left.

Her voice faded in and out, and after her seventh failed attempt, she slammed the deck and leaned in, staring at me, searching for something in my face.

"Something's wrong with the tea," I said. It took a maximum amount of effort to get the words out. I was fairly certain they were slurred and lacked proper enunciation.

She gave me a smile, and through the film it looked gentle. She reached for my hand. "I think Jaguar used a marked deck," she said. Her thumb stroked in circles. "And there's nothing wrong with the tea—I just gave you the stronger stuff."

"It's wrong," I said. I wanted to slump, but my body reacted on a reflex. It remained upright.

"It's not wrong, dear. But it does have a bit of truth serum in it." Her fingers coiled tighter. "You passed."

"Why would you ..." I couldn't finish, my words sealed off by the weight of the drink.

"I needed to make sure you couldn't read minds." Again, her smile. It was gentle and wrong at the same time. "That's so very important to me. I worried—for a moment—that the special gift of yours had surpassed my comfort level. I can't have that. Not here. Not ever. It's far too dangerous of a feature."

She stood then, releasing me, and walked behind my back, placing her hands on my shoulders, kneading the muscles there. She leaned in close. "I take no pleasure in tricking you, and I beg your forgiveness," she whispered. "But I can sleep better knowing you had no choice but to be honest. Well, as honest as one can be; it's not foolproof." She laughed. Her breath was warm along my cheek. Numbed out as I was, I relished in the heat. My poison quieted. It wasn't angry, it was sleeping. "I sometimes wish it wasn't so expensive and difficult to obtain; I'd make it mandatory that every one consume it, but I suppose we're all limited in one way or another. I suspect you'll forgive me. I just needed to know."

She rang for a servant and a Pastel showed up. Taking in

the scene, even with a loss of sharp sight, I could tell he was nervous. "Please, take Death to his rooms. He's tired."

She cupped my face.

Even in my vulnerable state, I managed to make the poison suppress. As Thorn touched me, I held it back. As she betrayed me, I held it back. As the Pastel helped me to my feet, I held it back.

I'd gotten that strong.

And that weak.

"WHY AREN'T YOU MAD?" Fantasia asked. "She drugged you. *Drugged.*"

I shrugged.

"If I were in her shoes, I'd want to know the answer too."

"Oh, boy. She's worked hard on you. This is her way, you know." Fantasia was languidly sprawled across a blanket on her bed. I was right beside her, both of us in a state of undress. Fantasia propped up on her elbow. "She does this to anyone who gets close to her. Makes them think they're important. Trust me, Thorn is a master manipulator. She's twisting history to serve in her favor. Even the story about numbing Lacey and Marie's minds is crap."

"I asked Scream. I asked Dolly. They both said the same thing. That it was most likely her."

"Most likely, not definitely."

"What more do you want, Fantasia? Dolly, she was wishy-washy, but pretty much said yes. And Scream said she was certain."

"Of course Scream would say that."

"I can't win with you, can I?"

Fantasia touched my cheek and then let her fingertips run

beneath my eyes. They were hollow, growing dark, two shadowy half-moons that deepened with every session Chanticlaim subjected me to. "These look worse. I think you need to rest more." She kissed the fragile, wilting skin and then brushed my hair back with her fingertips. "I can see it. I can see what you can't and I want to stop it."

I grabbed her hand and ran my lips across it. "Stop what?"

"Your affection for them." She cleared her throat. "Chanticlaim knows you asked Tipper to take over."

"So maybe I did."

"But her agenda isn't our agenda."

"And you're sure our agenda is right?" I sat up, running my fingers through my hair. "Chanticlaim hasn't seemed trustworthy. He's hiding stuff from me."

"Well considering his work, I imagine he's hiding stuff from everyone."

"And doesn't that bother you?"

"It's Chanticlaim," she said simply, as if his name negated doubt.

"This is why I can't talk to you; you're not even marginally open to a different viewpoint. You get a thought into your head and you hold it there." I stood up and started putting my pants back on, and as I reached for my shirt, I said, "You're stubborn, you know that, right?"

"Chanticlaim isn't the bad guy."

"And Thorn is?"

Fantasia sprang from the bed and grabbed my arm to stop me from leaving. Her fingers twisted and she gave me a frustrated shake. Her Animal force was enough to remove my center and I stumbled back, reaching for the post to level gravity. Something faltered and, with a thunk, landed on the floor.

I followed the sound and discovered a baggie near my feet.

I grabbed it and then my eyes traveled to the bedpost—part of it had come undone.

Fantasia had burrowed her own secret compartment.

She'd been hoarding pills—not just any pills but Brain Blockers.

"Why do you have these?"

Fantasia looked away. Color rose to her cheeks and she bit her lip in defiance.

I tossed the baggie on the bed and stepped up to her. "You wonder why I'm starting to trust Thorn, Fantasia? This. This right here. You tell me nothing, meanwhile she tells me everything." I shook my head, catching sight of the bag. "You can't read minds, can you?"

Silence.

I stormed out of her room and their bunker of a house, taking the steps two at a time, removing myself from the thick of deception and the chill that radiated in Fantasia's home.

It was near impossible to retain warmth lodged deep beneath the earth.

When I surfaced, I felt a tug on my sleeve and turned to a contrite Fantasia staring up at me.

"Come with me," she said.

"No."

"I'll tell you everything," she said and she took off at a run.

Trusting I would follow.

I did.

I knew where we were going, too. It's where she told me her secrets. Her cave.

I followed her off the cliff using the same rope swing as all the times before, landing with grace and practice, never seeing the forest.

Her chairs were there, as were her blankets.

She sat in one and waited for me to take the other.

And then I waited. This was on her.

"You're right. I can't read minds. At least, not Velore minds. I never have and hopefully never will." She glanced at me under nervous brows, her whole body flinching on a tick. "I let you believe it because it was easier. If Thorn ever thought, even for a moment, that one of us was capable of such a task she'd massacre the Doppelgängers in an effort to root them out. Even if the mind-reader were gone, she'd constantly be on alert. Executions would happen with little more than a cross-eyed glance counting as evidence of their guilt. The safety we have—albeit small—would be gone. Eliminated through paranoia. It doesn't matter who ... it only matters that someone can. That's all it takes. A whisper of a rumor to make ripples. We'd be extinct."

I sat back. The logic was right. She'd drugged me out of desperation and fear. My bond with Thorn had grown strong—it was assuring and real. A steady hand amongst angry fists. For her to enact desperate measures spoke of her concern.

"I worry she thinks you may be capable—maybe not now, but later—and if that's the case, you'll have no safety."

"What is safety anyway?" I snorted. "So how many can read Velores' minds?"

"Just one that we know of."

"And you know who this person is?"

"Yes."

"Who is it?"

"I won't say. It's not my place."

"This person, are they part of the Unrests?"

She hesitated. I leaned forward. "They'll know no matter what. So, either they're privy to what we're doing and are on our side, or they're privy to what we're doing, and they're waiting for the axe to fall. That's it. Our only two options."

She worked on a hangnail. "They're part of the Unrests."

I nodded, piecing together as much. That was the trajectory that made the most sense. But if one could do it, there was a chance that others could do it too.

How safe were we really?

I was a bit with Thorn on this.

"Their vision is spotty, though," she added. "I know a lot of the stuff we consume ruins their ability to get into minds."

At this I narrowed. "What stuff?"

She hesitated. "The tea. The tea has brain blockers in it."

"Is Chanticlaim the mind-reader? Is that why he wanted me to stop?" She shook her head. I wasn't sure if it was in response to my question or that she wasn't going to answer.

"Tipper must know."

Fantasia rolled her eyes. "Tipper is paranoid by nature—and made the tea as a precaution. She also puts in mood stabilizers and sleeping meds. Those bags are brimming with ingredients to ease her worries and soften the tempers in the castle. She doesn't know, because if she did, she would've gone to Thorn and we'd be dead."

I rostered the Velores. Ticking off names, trying to mentally catalog who was who.

I wanted the name.

Damn, did I want the name.

"But I can tell ..." she took a breath, it syphoned all the air between us, "that you're growing to trust Thorn. To love her. And that's when people die."

"Fantasia—"

"No, listen. Chugknot was a telekinetic—one of the strongest we'd ever seen. Everyone loved him, Thorn especially—and still, she killed him."

"Oh, you mean the one person you refuse to talk about?"

She shifted. "I want to talk about him now."

I waited. It took effort to do it in silence.

“He was her champion. Her favorite. He was strong, could burst the hearts of animals with only his mind. He did that at the Dawning Rose Celebration—to showcase his strength—and the crowd went wild. Aside from Urrel, no other Velore has had that ability.”

“Quite the talent.”

“Thorn adored him. He was crazy about her too.”

“Until he fell for you?”

“Believe it or not, I don’t have the influence to pull affections away from Thorn. No,” Fantasia continued, “Thorn decided she wanted Chugknot’s nephew, Ben. He was six, and it fired up Chugknot like nothing else. We’d been talking—the crush was small, and there were slips of affection—but nothing more. It grew after the Ben bombshell.”

“Who came up with the idea to kill her?”

She looked down. “A bit of both.”

I folded my arms, defensive already. How had this happened? My urge to protect Thorn?

“Okay, how?” I asked.

“Poison. It’s the only thing she’s really afraid of—”

“It wouldn’t have worked. She can handle the poison touch.”

“Touch is one thing, ingestion is another.”

“Ingestion?”

“Tipper, back when she was almost as obsessed with a cure as Thorn, would scrape poison off the screaming room walls. We both know that Bronson and Caseao used up what very little they managed to extract from Scream.”

“Tipper thinks the same way Chanticlaim thinks. In order to kill a disease, you first have to create it. She made the poison into something different. Condensed it into flakes. He put it in her tea to weaken her.”

"And then what? A weakened Thorn would simply heal and become whole—only she'd be more pissed off."

"Chugknot would've destroyed her from the inside—bursting her heart—but she caught him mid-act. We still have no idea how she found out, but the ramifications were horrendous." Her chest lifted. "She summoned Crusher to collect Ben."

My thoughts bungeed to Lacey, same age, equally innocent. I said nothing, and the air grew stale around us.

"Underneath her rooms is a soundproof basement. She broke that little boy in an attempt to get answers from Chugknot—but she didn't think her rage through, or her punishment. Chugknot couldn't have spared his nephew—even in time to name me as a part of the plot—because she made that little boy drink the tea that was meant for her. Ben liquefied right in front of him. And then she made Chugknot follow suit. He never even made it to the scaffold."

"What she did went against Narivous law. You can transform a child, but no torturous events can take place unless it's imperative to their resurrection."

I waited.

She waited.

"So aside from her goons that pulled in Ben, no one knows about this. And no one can ever know. I obtained this knowledge through illegal means."

"The *actual* mind-reader?"

She nodded.

"And you can't slip up. Not even once. Because she drugged you, remember? Because she suspected you could read minds. That tells you her fear. You slip about this forbidden crime, it will only heighten her paranoia. That suppression of yours is keeping you safe, but it won't always, and soon you'll be in as much danger as the Doppelgängers." She kissed me then, speaking words down my throat. They mingled with the poison. “You must be careful.”

And then we became a toxic coil—of hands and mouths.

It was only Dreams who severed us.

She came down on the rope—as she’d done long ago—her face pale, alarm in her voice.

“You two need to hurry,” she said. “Plague is dead.”

CHAPTER 21

TWO COFFINS

They buried him in a simple pine box, his clan emblem painted on the top, his body wrapped in a blanket of silk.

Those of great ranking huddled around the hole—clad in black—chilled to the point that not even the spring warmth could breach them.

A Velore funeral was a sight for the ages. Because most burials occurred in a haphazard fashion, usually the result of treason, their bodies were discarded in a hole without a casket and planted like an unwanted weed.

This one was both beautiful and clumsy, uncertain and elegant. A quartet played a melody, and a simple sonnet was sung by a Pastel at the back of the cemetery—far enough removed they melded into background noise.

Lest the silence swallow us.

No one really spoke. That was the trend since his body was found, obliterated in the screaming room.

The shock hadn't worn off.

I wondered if it ever would. It seemed one Poison was

vulnerable to being destroyed. I wondered, selfishly, if that held true for both Scream and I.

Amelia returned from the Southside to lend her support. Strangely, her presence was comforting. Completing the united front amongst the tragedy.

Words became small and inconsequential. No one really knew what to say. Polar, upon learning of Plague's death, turned his apartment into a brick of ice. It took over twenty-four hours to pull him out of translucency. Not even the Dexitrol dust could yank him back. His quarters were still unthawing—a constant puddle under his doors spoke of his grief.

Ferno was smoldering. Literally.

Scream. Scream cracked and chose to hide her grief behind a veil. She clutched me as we stared down at the box, her full weight resting upon my shoulders. I held her, grateful to be of some use.

Albeit small.

I glanced around the faces, all pulled down, and noted the range.

Amelia's expression was twisted in anger. Ember was pale. Frigid was surprisingly lucid, gripping Polar's arm and whispering in his ear. Whenever she spoke—whatever she said—it made his shoulders soften. He would pat her arm and lean into her. They were the warmest even with ice in their veins. Thorn was without emotion. Blank and blinking.

The Brilliants were in attendance. The triplets: Delilah, Esther, and Ruth. Ruth, too, wore a veil to keep herself hidden.

I recalled how Jaguar had said she was half and half. Esther with her black hair and dark eyes, the opposite of Delilah's fair and blue. It made me wonder what Ruth looked like.

How an even split would play out.

Ruth managed to keep herself in the shadows. It was easy to forget she even existed.

Delilah held tightly to Jaguar's hand, making her appear more childlike with his height and size to dwarf her own. The smile Jaguar was notorious for was washed away. He seemed most upset. Perhaps only because it was in stark contrast to his natural demeanor.

The animated lacking animation.

Tipper wore arrogance and annoyance. Plague's death was an inconvenience—stripping her away from her plants and whatever tasks she deemed important. Time was ticking away.

Chanticlaim was both sad and frustrated. But there was something else hidden behind his distraught exterior. Something I had difficulty placing, but the poison alerted me to.

Chanticlaim's mood seemed less about Plague's death and more about the backward bend of headway. Plague had stolen his progress—the formulas that should have led to the cure were now buried beneath us, part of a corpse that no longer looked like a man as we pieced him into that box.

The fragments of what had actually happened were coming together.

"He was always haunted by his demons. Maybe he's found peace," Scream whispered. I wasn't sure she heard herself speak, because she wavered under the weight of it.

I counterbalanced her loss of footing and helped hold her up. She patted my hand, grateful.

"Maybe," I muttered.

She nodded and closed her fingers into a desperate grip.

Plague had gotten ahold of the serums Chanticlaim was actively working on and grabbed everything he could find.

He took them to the screaming room and swallowed them all in one sitting.

They had an effect. Not wholly, but enough. They managed to dull his powers enough for the shotgun to finish him off.

He died the same way he had upon coming here, through a muzzle carefully placed.

A poetic, sick circle of life, with his wedding ring clutched in his free hand.

Thorn grew black roses next to his gravesite; we all took turns tossing a bloom on the simple pine box that housed his broken and depleted body.

There was no sobbing. Only numbness.

Self-preservation told me to walk, and so I did. The funeral dispersed as quietly as it collected and I found myself at the one place I wanted to spend time, but never had the opportunity to do so.

The cabin covered by briars.

A low hum deep inside guided me there.

Was it the look on Chanticlaim's face?

Or the fact Plague could die?

Maybe it was that Thorn had liquified a six-year-old boy, followed by her favorite Velore?

Perhaps it was all three.

Either way, I found myself eclipsed within the molasses of time as I sat on the porch and took in the stillness.

I was putting off what I felt compelled to do—whereas earlier it seemed more like a recreational treasure hunt, now it spoke of importance and strategy.

The tranquility of the moment was too much to overlook. I wanted to absorb what peace felt like. Even if it was temporary and artificial.

There were small rocks at the base of the stairs, black,

round pebbles, and I carefully collected a few handfuls, stowing them in my pocket, bouncing them to measure the weight.

I arched my neck and got a full hit of the sky. It was far too bright for a funeral.

Far too bright for an unearthing.

I allowed a dozen particles out, and then I began to amble, knowing I would end up where I needed to end up. It seemed the more I fought it, the worse things got.

One would think that would stop me from fighting altogether.

Stubbornness was too greatly embedded within me.

They dove and webbed, searching deep underground, burrowing like mites. The tether remained strong, as was always the case when I allowed them to remain alive, encouraging their connection and embracing their strength.

It was only during death that they seemed volatile, condemning me for condemning them.

It took less than thirty minutes for the report to come back.

I went to the spot ... it was innocuous in placement, the briars dominating as I'd come to expect. Everything else here was overrun, why would this location be any different? I took careful consideration of the area. There was a madrone tree, thick and stocky, the branches building a bower. Toward the East and merely paces away was the first boiling box—the one used on Ember. The tinny metal container was scarred and stained with rust, the glass thick and opaque from grime. Naturally my eyes were drawn to it. If anything, I couldn't see beyond it. Was this, too, conscientious placement? A sight meant to distract?

The poison wouldn't allow me to linger too long—the benefit of my gift and the strength behind it. It told me to pay attention to the ground and at the secrets that lay beneath it.

Otherwise, I would've been content to explore Ember's death chamber, to listen to the story that the particles were poised to tell.

Instead—and I wasn't sure why—I sat on the moist mound, forcing the briars to peel away. Cross-legged, with hands on my knees, a low pitch clambered in my throat.

My lungs ached with the pressure of holding back.

The rocks sat heavy in my pocket and I pulled them out, placing them into a tight pile. All but one particle returned, it remained underground, mapping out what I couldn't see.

I welcomed the distraction, pushing back the thoughts of Plague, of time, and enjoying the rapture of the unknown.

What was beneath me, far beyond my sight, was heavy and cumbersome. The poison relayed that it was both compartmentalized and sealed, with thick walls, and a stretch that was seven feet long.

A coffin. The angle, the depth, the build.

All of it matched.

A smile played on my lips, only I couldn't hold it there. Too much tragedy surrounded the arc. It reminded me of the graveyard where history had come to rest—only there was no rest in this place. It was suspended minutes, hours, days, all painfully experienced.

Time had not been kind, and even the most well-built casket would hold points of fracture. This one was no different. Besides, it was holding a powerful Telekinetic. I could feel where he used his powers to weaken the corners. To compromise the seal.

The casket was in sore shape.

The weight of the earth or the weight of his rage? Either one was a possibility.

The poison quickly went inside via the cracks, only it grew weak and winked out. The loss of it traveled to my lungs where the other toxins rattled in complaint. I opened my jaw and allowed another to search. It too, followed the path, and died when it found the box.

What was killing them? Snuffing them out?

I shallowed my breathing.

The third one found its mark, but I was careful with it, making it move in slower motions and I realized that the other two had not died, but had gone to sleep.

Dexitrol Dust was in the coffin. Lots from the feel of it. However, dampness and years had removed its potency and had made it weaker, harder, less powerful.

My newest particle shied away from the edges. I could feel the tether losing its hold, we were lightly bound.

And then I made it look, not for what was inside the vessel, but for the other two asleep pieces.

It found one, and the magical connection between us flared —as the lone particle used the Poison to stir the other awake— albeit temporarily.

And then, they both snuffed out.

I spent the next hour repeating the process, moving the particles, sending larger clumps, and as I did, something unique happened. The poison adapted to the Dexitrol. Or maybe the coffin wasn't as full as I originally thought. Regardless, my powers grew—they expanded—not even with my direction, but as if guided by some internal compass. They roused the sleeping flakes, and soon, even the ones lost to dormancy woke up. The item below me, long out of my line of sight, was taking form from my own army.

I rested my ear along the loamy soil. It dampened my cheek and left a film of dirt, the rustling of the particles burrowing blended with the sounds of earthworms and beetles. All of which had become heightened.

That's when one landed on an arm. It told me it was an

arm, a very thin arm … it wasn't stinging for I told it not to. Something I'd learned in the long months of study, my poison destroyed on direction. What was once limited to touch, was now expanded to my very being.

I could release.

And it wouldn't harm.

There were times I wondered if it could heal. I was too afraid to try.

The sequence became methodical.

There was a torso. A leg. A neck. A head.

All of it intact.

I halted where the heartbeat should've thumped, waiting, and as time stood still, and the sun began to fall, I felt it move under my touch by proxy.

I waited for more. To be certain.

More came.

The poison whispered to me. I tapped the pile of rocks.

"Make them move," I said, feeling foolish, for if I was wrong, that merely meant I was slipping into madness and speaking to myself. I continued anyhow, enjoying the mystery. Perhaps even liking the insanity. "If you have any strength left, make them move."

The rocks remained still, stoic.

"Dammit, make them move." I slammed a closed fist on the ground. "Make them move."

I closed my eyes and spoke through the poison. It could communicate with me, could it communicate with others?

I wasn't even sure if I was doing it right, but I let my gut guide me. Screaming my message, demanding he perform.

The sky had gone purple and a few stars emerged. My mind was numb as mosquitos hummed around me, careful never to land since I was a natural repellent.

Stubbornness forced me into place as anger screamed through me.

So much rage—and where had it come from? Why was I feeling the burn of anger? This terrible crime felt personal. I wanted a fight. I just wasn't sure from who.

It was particularly lonely resting in that spot. I started to talk, telling myself I was losing my mind—not caring if it was true—my ramblings were only for me.

Only, were they?

And then ... a vibration. At least, it seemed like one. It was distinct, not of my own making. That's when the top pebble rolled off the peak and settled a few inches away.

Was it gravity that moved it? The wind? Or something else?

That was the catalyst. I stood up, brushed the dirt from my clothes, leaving faint mud streaks along the whole side of my body. "I'll be back," I said. Meaning it, just not sure when.

And as the poison returned, slipping into my mouth and settling deep inside my veins, an unsettling sensation twisted my stomach.

It was grief.

Rage.

Despair.

All things ruined.

And it hadn't come from me. He told me through our tether.

Urrel had served his sentence.

And I was fairly certain—in a clairvoyant sort of way—that I would be the one to set him free.

"You shouldn't be avoiding Thorn on account of me," Scream said. "I don't need you hovering over me." She was sitting in the dark living room, attempting to knit in the low light—a task I didn't know she was capable of. It seemed too banal for her to take an interest in. From the looks of her creation, snagged and lopsided, a confused cross between a scarf and a table runner, chances are this wasn't a favorite hobby.

She snarled at her work, her fingers threading the yarn. The only lamp lit was across the room, and when I offered to bring it over, she tsked and said it was of no value. Her Undead eyes were just as good as my Undead eyes and we didn't need to be coddled by excess sensory input.

A snooty response that made me feel an ounce better. She was out of sorts lately. Uppity Scream felt very much like a normal Scream.

"I'm not avoiding Thorn on account of you," I said. "And for the record, I don't think I'm hovering. I'm coexisting in the same space."

She lowered her needles, and her lip twitched. "But you are avoiding her?" she asked.

"I wouldn't say avoid. I just haven't had much to say."

"Hmmm ... Well, you're in here all the time, and that's not really your way."

"Neither is it yours."

She resumed knitting.

"Don't you need to be in the lab or something?" she snapped. "You bog down the space with your breathing."

"Well it seems I'm appreciated everywhere," I replied sarcastically.

She almost smiled.

Truth was, I was supposed to be in the lab, but Chanticlaim's aggressive draws had sucked the energy right out of me. He was volatile and reckless, uncaring. I had endured nearly a dozen angry pulls in the two weeks since the funeral.

And throughout it all, my loyalty continued to falter.

The same could be said for Thorn. The haunting image of a liquified boy and his uncle was far too heavy. It encumbered like a mist, thick and draping, bogging down the silence and muting all other distractions. It was hard to push it out.

It became one of my prevailing thoughts.

And when it was, I performed the suppression and the draw from Chanticlaim with a seamless stroke. However, others, I allowed the hold to falter, managing in a way that it spoiled the whole batch.

It only added to Chanticlaim's madness. Lack of consistency was one of his greatest banes.

"Everyone looks at me with pity," Scream said. She stabbed a loop and pulled abruptly. "I hate pity."

"I doubt anyone is looking at you with pity, it's sympathy. You're confusing the two."

"Same thing."

"Hardly." I smirked. "They're worlds apart. One is judgment on you, and the other is judgment on the situation. There's no reflection on your character when someone respects your loss. You're simply letting your mind get away from you."

"Well, it looks the same, and I can't stand it. I don't need anyone's stares."

"I thought you liked to be stared at."

"To be revered and admired, yes. But anything steeped in weakness irritates me beyond words." To prove a point, she stabbed her project again. "I am not weak. Unlike Plague, who seemed to wallow in it."

Scream was at the anger stage of loss. I nudged my head at her creation.

"Is that why you're holing up in here? Trying to make some mutant scarf?"

She paused and held it out for appraisal. It indeed was a deformed monstrosity.

"Maybe." She clicked her tongue. "How do you suppose he got it?" she asked.

"Plague?"

"Yes, Plague," she snapped. "That's who we're talking about, isn't it?"

I held up my hands. "Easy."

She narrowed her eyes and waited.

"I don't know. Didn't he just find it down there? He has access."

"It feels too convenient. I wonder if it was given to him."

"You think Chanticlaim handed it over? He's highly possessive of his formulas."

She shrugged. "He's making me unsettled. I think the boy is becoming mad like his mother."

I shuddered and she twisted her lips in contemplation.

"More likely than not, though, I wonder if Thorn ordered it," she mused. "Rarely does anything happen here that isn't on Thorn's orders. Perhaps she told him to assist in Plague's death? Chanticlaim is such a pleaser, he would've done it—even if it would set him back."

"Why are you saying this?"

"Because Tipper said he's been hiding his formulas—he doesn't want her interference. And he's been hiding them well too. How is it Plague found so many to end his life? And, Thorn..." She dropped her project in her lap. The needle slipped out. "Thorn has been acting peculiar, in a way that portends secrets."

"Perhaps you're mistaking her grief?"

"No." Scream said it with certainty, in that far away, I've-thought-of-it-for-a-while sort of voice. "There's nothing sorrowful there. This is different. This feels like guilt and deception. I know her well."

"When was the last time a Velore died without her hand in

it?" I asked. "Like you said, rarely does anything happen without her orchestrating it. If it caught her off guard, she's most likely reacting to that—not only over his loss, but the fact it was done without her knowledge."

She shook her head. "It can't be though. It was before Plague's death."

"Are you sure?"

"Oh yes. It was after that horrible truth serum fiasco she put you through. That's when she started acting different. I scolded her something fierce for that too."

"Maybe she felt bad?"

Scream shook her head vehemently. "She should've felt bad, but there was no contrition there which only infuriated me more—and has made me wonder—as I've had time to ruminate on it all.... Are you sure, darling," she asked, "that you told me everything?"

I snorted. "Pretty sure."

"But not certainly sure?"

"Scream, I was drugged. I feel like, considering the circumstances, I was able to provide a fairly decent retelling. But who knows." I placed my cup on the coffee table. "My memory could be faulty. It's not like I had a clear head at that time. She's the one you should be asking."

She let out a low hum, considering. This direction was odd, uncomfortable. My poison rattled.

"I've asked her."

"And?"

"She assured me all was well."

"Well, there you have it."

This time she rolled her eyes. "That is one of the most pathetic responses I've ever heard come out of your mouth. You know there is more behind the scenes. Words hold little value here. She's hiding something."

Images of Urrel locked underground flashed forward. How many minutes must've slugged on like ticks of torturous doings for him. I'd been back to his gravesite. Those rocks had begun to shift.

It looked like he was trying to spell out a word, but weakness and lack of visibility made it difficult. The only thing going for him was infinite time—and even that was a harsh metric.

It looked like he was trying to write: SOS.

Thorn's cruel capabilities were unbending.

Like Ben and Chugknot.

Scream tossed her yarn to the side and leaned forward, piercing me with a look that was all seeing. "Darling," she said. "I need you to be careful. I feel like something is very wrong, and I worry it's centering around us. Around you. Watch your back, pay attention, and above all else, mind your words."

Maybe her poison talked to her the same way mine did, maybe it was more subtle, less defined, a nuance hard to define.

Because her instincts told her similar tales.

Something was wrong, but damned if I knew exactly what it was.

CHAPTER 22
MOVIE NIGHT

They made the dome look like stars; dots so vibrant, so real, it made us feel as if we were floating in space. It had a dizzying effect.

Fantasia, curled up next to me, placed her hand on my chest and toyed with the front of my shirt.

I thought of the lab. Of the testing. Of the instability of Chanticlaim's mental health and his rapid decline.

A third vial this week had gone missing. Either Chanticlaim misplaced it—something not too farfetched with his degenerative state of mind—or Tipper stole it.

Equally viable.

Both scary.

I wrapped my arm tighter around Fantasia and she let out a sigh. We'd stopped fighting.

For now.

After she told me of Thorn, of Ben, it became easier to distance myself from the Queen. Thorn seemed all too eager to oblige.

A curiosity that laid credence to Scream's fears.

I didn't want to see Thorn and she no longer wanted to see me. If I hadn't been actively avoiding her, it would've bothered me.

Wait. Correction. It did bother me.

Because she was avoiding me for a reason.

Same as I had a reason for avoiding her.

I pulled Fantasia closer. As the distance between me and Thorn expanded, my relationship with Fantasia knitted tighter. Loving both in equal measure went against the rhythm. A curiosity that lended itself to magic.

"Where's Torti?" I asked.

"Trying to pull Chanticlaim out of the depths of his madness."

Dreams sat on the other side, knees pulled up, arms hugging them. Fred pranced along the width of her shoulders. She had her hair pulled into a ponytail, with the underside shaved, flowers etched into the shorn fuzz.

Next to her sat Spark followed by Jaguar, with Delilah nestled into him. They made for an odd couple, one extraordinarily tall, the other extraordinarily short, an awkward pairing that seemed selected on purpose.

JC was there too.

It was nice having two of Amelia's sons present. It relinquished the tension: meaning talk of the rebellion was strictly off limits.

We could simply exist.

Fantasia softened next to me. Her finger tapping in tandem to my heartbeat.

It was the soft slow thud of calm.

"It's about time they reinstated movie night. And look at our seats, best in the house." Jaguar nudged me and gave Bonnie—now wearing a purple bow—a piece of popcorn.

Servants transformed the observation booths of the auditorium, removing thrones and adding cushions on rolled out beds. We, being among the favorites, had the best seats—the open balcony box that housed Thorn and the other Seven during Guard Trials. It had a clear shot of the projector screen. All the "peasants," as Jaguar liked to call them, were on the stadium floor on blankets, while the other half took to the bleachers, softening the cold steel with pillows and wadded up capes.

If I had to guess, at least a quarter of Narivous had showed up.

I kept scanning the crowd, searching for Chanticlaim.

"It's been almost a year since we've had one of these," Jaguar said, stuffing popcorn into his mouth. The movie hadn't started and he was already halfway through his bucket.

He was a food inhaler.

"I kept slipping it into the suggestion box," he muttered. "Finally, someone took me seriously. I mean, this helps with morale. They should gimme some sort of bonus." He snapped his fingers and butter fragments scattered everywhere. "Do you think they'll give me extra days off guard duty?"

"There is no such thing as a suggestion box," Delilah said.

"Oh, yeah? Then what would you call that box at the Enlightenment Center?"

"What are you talking about?"

"The box beneath the podium in room 3B? The one where you teach sorcery."

"I don't teach sorcery. I teach talent management."

"Same thing."

"It really isn't."

"It kind of is." He started ticking off points. "You have magic. You have magic practice. You have tournaments to test our abilities against each other with only our minds." He tapped his head. "Magic and sorcery are the same thing."

"It's psychological abilities derived from an evolutionary process through the manufacture and application of our cure," Delilah specified. "It's cerebral and physical talents—not magic. Magic is fake. Magic is an illusion. It's card tricks and sleight of hand."

"Exactly." Jaguar beamed. "Sorcery. Just like I said."

"No, not just like you said."

Spark leaned across Dreams and Fantasia. He muttered, "They do this all the time." I swiped my hand, shutting him up. This banter actually interested me.

"Why you gotta fight with me?" Jaguar said. "You're getting me all sidetracked."

"Jaguar, you get yourself sidetracked. It's not like you need any help with that." Delilah flicked her hair and Bonnie made some sort of chittering noise at her.

Jaguar squinted, as if he'd really lost his place and then brightened.

"Anyway," he continued, "the podium with the teeny tiny slot in the front—that's the suggestion box."

Delilah laughed and craned her neck so she could look at Jaguar. "I knew that was you, I simply thought you were sending me weird love letters in that peculiar way of yours."

"I'm not peculiar."

"You're very peculiar."

Jaguar shifted, and Delilah cupped his chin and brought him toward her for a kiss. He pulled in like a magnet. "And that's why I love you. But I hate to break it to you, that's an empty tissue dispenser."

Spark let out a bark of a laugh and Delilah looked to the entrance.

Chanticlaim stumbled in, his eyes glossy from lack of sleep, with deep shadows hollowing out his face. He had a five o'clock shadow—which was definitely not his way. Torti followed right behind him and clutched his arm, guiding him to a spot toward the back.

They were nearly eclipsed by shadows.

"Are Chanticlaim and Torti not coming up here?" Jaguar asked. He held up his arms and waved, letting out a sharp whistle that pulled half the arena's attention.

It had no effect on Chanticlaim. He hunkered down, allowing Torti to drape both her cloak and her arms around him.

"I think Chanticlaim needs space," Fantasia said.

But she wasn't looking at him, she was looking at Delilah —who was staring without abandon, the type of lurk you see from the unhinged.

"Well, that doesn't look like space," Jaguar said. Torti was indeed, wedged against him, in a very uncustomary display of affection. Chanticlaim draped his arm around her shoulders and squeezed.

"He's up to something," Delilah said. She cocked her head to the side and continued to study him. She narrowed her blue eyes into slivers. "He doesn't want space; he just doesn't want questions."

"What makes you think that?" JC asked.

I could sense Spark leaning in. Fantasia, curled next to me, fought to maintain a normal breathing pattern. Dreams, impressively, was unflinching. Fred felt the shift and chirped, which drew Delilah's attention for a spit of a moment. I went still as stone.

"Oh, don't get her started," Jaguar intercepted. He nudged me with his elbow. It was enough I managed to give a befuddled smile. "She's been on this kick lately."

"It's not a kick, Jaguar," Delilah glanced at us. "It's intuition, the ability to sense what's wrong before catastrophe hits."

"Intuition my ass. It's a kick. You get on these benders all the time ... this is just the latest conspiracy theory." He curled one of her locks around his finger; it sprang like a polished coil. "You have them every other week."

"Which is smart. Tactical." Delilah pulled away and angled herself so she was looking at our group head-on. My skin prickled and the toxin in my gut livened. "We should always be on our toes around here. Watching. Listening. Feeling. Narivous is nothing but a great conspiracy. There's always something afoot."

"No offense, babe. But even this one's a stretch." He winked at her. "You're just a few paces behind tinfoil hats and Tipper."

"Tipper may come across as batshit crazy, but that woman sees. She knows things, the inner-workings, the deceptions, the truths. And I think she's getting a good, long look at Chanticlaim—and he's coming up ugly."

"Babe, you're mirroring yourself after Tipper. Tip-per. Think about that." He tapped his head. "She's a nutter, and quite frankly, you're starting to turn into a peanut too. She always thinks something is up, and nothing is ever up—*usually*."

"Usually," Delilah mimicked dryly.

"But, c'mon, how often does she come up with wild conspiracy theories that never pan out?"

Delilah twisted her mouth, her small hands clawing the blanket. "Well, for once, I think she's right. He's up to something, and mark my words, it isn't good."

"Babe—"

"Actually, I wanna hear more about this," Spark said, all suave and chill. Inside, he had to have been volts and currents. Below us, Chanticlaim seemed near catatonic. He looked ahead at nothing. Torti leaned in and spoke in his ear, twining her fingers through his own. "What makes you think Chanticlaim's up to no good?"

"You're opening a can of worms," Jaguar said.

"We have time," Spark reiterated. "Look, the movie hasn't started; not everyone is even here yet. Have at it. Entertain us."

He offset his approach with a smile.

Delilah lifted her chin. I had to give it to Spark. He made it sound like pure curiosity driving his questions, not guilt.

Or fear.

"He's working on the formula to remove the poison toxin, right?"

Spark nodded. "So we've heard."

"Well, on every project he's ever worked on, he's always—ALWAYS—asked for a new set of eyes when he's been stumped. But this. This is different. He won't even let us come close. Tipper's asked about it—multiple times—and he's shut her down. *Multiple times.* She even had a directive from Thorn, and he comes back with this vial that is most certainly not the fix he's been working on. Anyone with even half a trained eye—or brain—could see it was a concoction from earlier trials. Even Ruth asked. He always lets Ruth."

"And?"

"Same thing. He wouldn't let her near it. He's even gone as far as hiding the vials so we couldn't have them analyzed—" She laughed, but it was without mirth. "The irony of it all is he's lost some. He's forgetting where he's stashing his own stuff. Vials. Work. Hours and hours of painstaking research is tucked into hiding places he can't even remember. And for what? Why would he keep this so quiet? He needs help; I can see it. We can all see it, and he's hellbent on no one coming near it. He's edging toward a full mental breakdown, one of which, I'm not entirely certain he can recover from."

I could feel Fantasia plummet in temperature. Fear turned her veins to ice.

"That's really not that weird." Jaguar leaned back. "He wants all the glory on this one. Think of it, Delilah, if he manages the task that Thorn has wanted her whole life, he'll be a hero."

"It's not that." Delilah chewed her lip. "He keeps saying he's close, but I don't buy it. When he comes close to completing a project, he gets energetic, bright; it's like the pilot light inside of him is triggered and he blazes like an inferno." She nudged her head toward Chanticlaim. "That is not an inferno. That's cinder and ash—burnout if I've ever seen it. Keeps saying we would set him back. He doesn't want anyone to have it. Makes me wonder if he's not up to something else. I mean, just look at him. *Look*."

She pointed, and Jaguar was the only one who leaned forward to get a better glance.

Jaguar shrugged. "Bigger game, better stakes, less sleep," he argued.

For being in the dark, he made an excellent ally.

Delilah's shoulders stiffened.

She spoke softly, with precision, and let her eyes trail over us. "I think we need to take the task away, give it to Tipper. Let him reboot. I know Tipper wants the job—and I don't care what he says, moving the task won't be a setback."

"That's Thorn's decision," Jaguar said.

"We can convince her."

"It would destroy Chanticlaim," Spark said. "All his work, his lack of sleep, stolen right out from under him. You can't do that. Let this play out; he'll get it under control. If he says he's close, then he's close. I trust him."

"Trust is a word I'd use cautiously around here," she countered.

She said it in a way that indicated it went beyond the cure —or even Chanticlaim's stalling—to something far greater. Nefarious. I glanced back to Chanticlaim and the poison jolted.

"Let the guy finish the job," Spark said. He swiped at nonexistent lint on his sleeve. "He's wanted it for too long to take it away."

"Plus, what if you're wrong? What if he's really afraid you'll mess with his progress?" Jaguar said. "It doesn't sound all that farfetched, not to mention it would totally blow if you set him back to square one." He motioned toward me. "And you keep drawing magic blood—"

"Ability blood," Delilah corrected.

"'Sorry—*ability blood.* He'll be anemic in no time. And where will that get ya? You'll have a hell of a time getting anything useful if he's been drained clean."

"I don't think it's going to set Chanticlaim back if we take it away. I just don't. It makes no sense—"

"Hey, are Esther and Ruth coming?" Jaguar asked. He shoved another fistful of popcorn in his mouth. "I thought they were coming."

"Don't try and change the subject."

Jaguar shrugged. "I'm not *trying* to change the subject. I *am* changing the subject. I'm done talking about it; you're being a downer with all this conspiracy shit. This is a fun day. F-U-N." He spelled it out carefully. "This whole idea of mine would be wasted under your cloud of plots and theories—"

"Not your idea," JC said.

"You know what I mean. This whole idea is to get our minds off the sludge happening in this place. Morale boost, remember?" He kissed Delilah's pout. "So, tell me, are Ruth and Esther coming?"

"Maybe Esther, but never Ruth."

"How is it I have yet to meet her?" I asked. This sidetrack, we needed it. Ruth was an optical illusion, a girl I'd only encountered once while wearing a veil so thick I couldn't pierce it.

"Don't feel bad," Spark said. "I've been here for years, and I've only seen her twice."

Delilah let her blue eyes settle on me. "She doesn't like the stares."

"What is it about her appearance that makes her feel uncomfortable? Here of all places?" We were in the land of the bizarre, with peculiarities that stretched beyond death to mar what was left. Depending on our human demise, some of us were permanently disfigured.

Plague.

Jester and his lopsided skull.

"Dude, I told you," Jaguar chimed in. "She's half and half."

"You realize that makes no sense whatsoever."

"It would if you put on your listening ears." Jaguar pointed to Delilah, "You see how she's fair, like a perfect, angelic representation of a goddess in living form, equal to no other—"

"Move on Jaguar," Delilah said.

"So, she's light, right? With blonde hair and blue eyes, and Esther looks like her except she's kinda the opposite—her coloring is all dark. Well, Ruth is a perfect representation of both." He gave a smile. "She's in-between."

"She has both white and black hair," Delilah clarified, "and her eyes are mismatched too."

It took a second as I tried to pull up what that would look like, and then, when I came up empty, asked, "But she could always dye her hair, wear colored contacts."

Delilah shook her head. "You would think, but the dye works only a short amount of time. She's got a unique molecular structure. Things don't take to her."

"Plus, she likes how she looks. It gets her out of everything," Jaguar said.

"That too," Delilah agreed.

"You best watch, if Narivous ever goes to shit, the one who's gonna walk away will be Ruth. She's invisible here."

"She's not a coward," Delilah shot out.

"Baby, I'm not saying that. I'm just saying she's smart. Drama free."

I swallowed and kept my gaze steady. Fantasia tensed next to me and then quickly corrected, transforming into a melt.

Jaguar's comments felt too close.

It made me wonder how much he really saw. How much he really took in.

I slid my eyes to Delilah, who was watching me closely. Her blue eyes, wide and innocent, grew a bit bigger. She looked guileless, but was anything but.

It was part of her skit—the one she used back when she was a guard, before they upgraded her to a Brilliant. Delilah had worn many hats, all of which she excelled in. She would roam the forest, dressed like a doll, appearing childlike and fragile.

When she'd stumble across a human, she would lure them in with her innocence.

Ruth and Esther stayed in the trees, armed with knives and superlative strength that did not fit their form.

With their mind-reading capabilities and their strict sense of right and wrong, unyielding like steel, they would execute anyone with suspect morals.

The triplets didn't like Narivous' recruiting habits: selecting from the slums. Forgiveness, in their eyes, was for the weak.

They didn't care about aura color, potential, or the likelihood of forthcoming loyalty. If a human's mind showed an awful vibration, they would destroy.

Usually in some horrid way.

I heard they were fans of the eyes—plucking them so they could inflict pain at their leisure. Every crime played out across the flesh. Thorn—unable to lose such talent, despite their disobedience—pulled them from guard duty and opted to deploy their other greatest gift: their minds.

The only three to ever buck the rules and still keep their cherub heads attached to their frames.

"She's as invisible as she wants to be," Delilah said. I detected some bite. "But if push comes to shove, and our city ever has to take sides, mark my words, she'll shine brighter than neon."

"Of course she would," Jaguar said. His hand began to swirl in soft, complacent circles along her back.

"She'll pick the right side," she said, looking at me, her face unreadable.

"The winning one, no doubt," Jaguar added.

Spark cleared his throat and pointed to the screen. "The movie's starting."

We all made a show of settling in.

Except Delilah. She let her attention on me linger. It took effort to stay focused on the opening credits as the theater dimmed to blackout and the surround-sound kicked on.

The audience below us hipped and hollered.

Jaguar and JC reached for their ear plugs—and Spark managed to shoot a meaningful look at me.

Delilah's statement had a prophetic feel to it. I pulled Fantasia tighter and glanced down at Torti and Chanticlaim.

Torti was trying to garner some sort of response from him. Anything over his nothing.

When all else failed, she did something I'd yet to see her do—at least not when there were eyes around.

She leaned in and kissed him. Not a chaste kiss, but a real one, full of feeling and passion. Even from my vantage point up high, I could sense her urgency.

Breaking his catatonic state.

He blinked and the spell, albeit momentarily, was broken. He spoke into her ear and they both softened. For a moment, they were normal.

For a moment, Chanticlaim looked as he should: whole.

For. A. Moment.

As I watched, a shadow, dressed in all black and sleek as a leopard hunting on the Serengeti, wove through the crowd.

Those nearby ducked their heads in respect.

The shadow didn't acknowledge them.

Fantasia shallowed next to me. She tapped my arm, indicating she was watching too.

I blinked and found focus on her dark face. Amelia was predatory in her search, scanning with precision that was anything but accidental.

She stopped in her tracks when she landed on Torti curled into Chanticlaim, the pair having snuck another kiss. Her eyes flashed and a sharp smile followed. She prowled out of the arena as if she owned it. As if she found what she was looking for.

Fantasia clutched me and she allowed a breathless whisper into my ear.

"I don't like that," she said.

I nodded and replied, "I don't either."

My poison hummed.

It agreed.

CHAPTER 23
THE LAB OF RECKONING

The next morning, the world shifted from light to dark.

Scream threw open my bedroom door, her eyes blacker than a depthless tomb as screams from far beyond the walls leached into the space between us. She wasn't fully dressed yet, and wore a silk robe tied tightly around her waist. Her normally pristine hair was free flowing. It hung in bedraggled waves.

"Come quickly," she ordered, pivoting on her heel, vaporizing as quickly as she materialized.

I leapt from the bed and bolted to the corridor, where the sounds grew both in urgency and volume.

One booming voice rose above them all. Perhaps it stood out because it was one never known to yell. Perhaps it was because I loved him as a father.

Polar.

A cluster had gathered, Pastels and guards. The Seven stood in various states of shock and sleepwear.

Polar was amidst the center, holding a hysterical Camille

back—his translucency gleaming, casting a chill on everyone. Camille was nearly on her knees, her legs lacking the ability to hold her up, her arms outstretched, absolute fear on her face.

I followed her gaze and landed on Torti, who was tightly restrained by Cheetoh and Cheetah, their mirror smiles slick and sharp. She wasn't fighting against them, but they still bit their fingernails into her flesh. Cheetah drew blood.

Torti was wearing the clothes from the night before—wrinkled and limp—and the cloak she used as a blanket was torn along a seam.

A flash of red grazed my peripheral as Fred fluttered to the rafters above the skulls lining the upper shelves.

Dreams stood with all the other spectators, who remained frozen, shellshocked.

Fantasia was blissfully absent.

Chanticlaim was on his knees, hands clasped, pleading to Thorn. He too, wore the same clothes from the night before. Even from my place near the Poison apartment, I could smell the damp soil and pine sap emanating off him.

They had both put their guards down for one night.

And this is what came of it.

Thorn hovered over him, who—with Amelia pinned tightly to her side—had fire in her eyes.

"This is a mistake, Thorn, a mistake!" Chanticlaim pleaded.

"A mistake?" Thorn hissed. Her gown whispered along the stone as she shifted closer to him. Torti was going limp—both from fear and trauma. Cheetah snickered. "They find Unrest contraband in her apartment, under her bed, and you're telling me she is innocent?"

Chanticlaim's eyes slid to Amelia, who was only a pace behind Thorn. Her eyes glinted, and she ran her hands along her short dark hair. Not a strand was out of place. It was as neat as her dark pantsuit, which was pristine and pressed.

Of all those lingering, she was dressed for this moment. She'd come prepared.

Even Thorn appeared haphazardly thrown together.

Chanticlaim saw it. I could feel him taking it all in. How he managed to keep the furls of heat from flowing was a testament to his self-control. I coiled with rage and found myself stationed in place.

"Most surely!" Chanticlaim said. "Torti is the most loyal of all subjects. I have no doubt this is a mistake."

"How? How could this be a mistake? The items were in her possession, yes?"

Thorn's free-flowing locks shimmered as she moved in on him. Chanticlaim remained unflinching. "Not in her possession," he argued.

"They were found in her room."

"But not *on* her. Anyone could've put them there. Her apartments have never been the most secure, and she *was* gone all night," Chanticlaim said. "I know, because I was with her."

"For such a smart man, Chanticlaim, you're not using your brain," Thorn purred. "I don't think it's a bright idea to admit you're chummy with a traitor."

"Alleged," he corrected. "Besides, she's not a traitor. I'd stake my life on it."

Thorn bent down and looked him in the eye. "Well, darling, I believe you are doing just that. Staking your life on it. I'm fit to have her executed before the sun sets."

The shadows in the hallways rippled, a murmuring broke out. Torti was the only one who remained stoic. As if she expected as much.

As if she was ready.

Camille wailed and buried herself into the nook of Polar's shoulder. His eyes were desperate and tinged.

"Thorn, we need to accurately investigate this," Polar said.

He already sounded defeated.

She held up her hand to silence him. All her focus was on Chanticlaim. The answer, the voice, she wanted to hear wasn't Torti's, or that of anyone else, it was his.

There was an angle here. There always was.

Fred twittered frantically while Dreams, whitewashed, held her hands to her mouth, suppressing moans.

Chanticlaim steepled his fingers as if in prayer. "Please. She wouldn't have done such a thing. Launch an investigation. Check the contraband for fingerprints. Look into this. It wasn't her."

"And what if I find them? Her fingerprints? What do you suppose I do then?"

"You won't. I know you won't. But let's say, theoretically speaking of course, you do discover them; everyone deserves a second chance. A pardon. We could work at rehabilitation—"

"That's a heavy request coming from a man who hasn't been able to fulfill one of my greatest desires."

Chanticlaim jumped on it. His face lit up.

"Allow me an opportunity to make this right. To make you happy. Give me forty-eight hours. That's all I need and I'll have your poison cure. I will present it to you on bended knee."

"Forty-eight hours?" Thorn fought a smile. And I spotted it then, what this was. This was her version of a rush job, knocking him into a higher gear.

"Forty-eight hours," he confirmed. "It will be in your hands."

Thorn seemed to contemplate it, smiling at him before sliding over to Scream, who stood with her hands clasped in front her. Scream was looking at Amelia.

Amelia was looking back at her.

Their expressions unreadable.

"I shouldn't have to negotiate for a cure you should've provided long ago," Thorn said.

"You're right. And this isn't a negotiation. You were always going to get it—it's your right after all. I take my responsibilities seriously. But if I can provide it sooner, in exchange for your leniency, I would be forever in your debt."

"I don't much care for leniency—it has a weakening effect."

"On the contrary." Chanticlaim shuddered from his core. "Your magnanimity would only elevate our revere for you. Our love for you. For you are both just and merciful."

"I don't need your pandering," she spat.

"She's not treasonous, Thorn. She is loyal and I will gladly back up my words with my life." He got to his feet, his hands still pressed in his plea. "Allow me forty-eight hours to get you your cure, and then pardon her."

"A pardon indicates guilt."

His madness muted him.

Thorn notched her chin slightly, and she angled her head at me. "I'll consider it," she said. "Your time starts now."

Chanticlaim bowed as they hauled Torti to the tower. He grabbed my sleeve and led me underground where his lab awaited.

As we descended down the familiar dank deep stairwell, I was hit with how different it felt.

Despair ensconced me.

There wasn't much room for hope.

"Someone set us up," Chanticlaim hissed. "It reeks of Amelia. I should've known the movie night was a ruse."

Just saying the words aloud made Chanticlaim break into a run.

We took turns and twisted corridors at a breakneck speed, only to stop when we made it to the entrance.

His door was ajar.

Light pooled out.

And even from a distance we could see the destruction.

TIPPER SPARKLED in the wreckage of Chanticlaim's lab. Her breaths, angry bursts, rattled in stabs of exhaustion. Glass shards littered the floor amongst fragments of research. Papers in shreds, manilla file folders emptied and flat, stainless-steel tools warped into useless shapes, the partition glass had a hole the size of an angry fist, fissures spreading to the four corners.

She was bleeding from a gash on her arm, the blood pooling down her flesh and dripping into a neat puddle on what was once Chanticlaim's pristine floor.

It ran over her tight grasp, which clutched something hidden in the folds of her fingers.

Chanticlaim walked in slowly, carefully, as if sneaking up on a spooked animal. I stayed a few steps behind until he held up his hand to still me on the other side of the threshold.

She knew we were there but refused to look. It was like she'd left her body, becoming a husk. The animation she normally wore, usually shrouded in insanity, was gone. A very sober Tipper—a very sound Tipper—with empty eyes had replaced her.

"I never much thought of right and wrong," she breathed, staring at her clutched hand. "They were just words to me. Society likes to define it, as if you could split morality down the center, compartmentalize it into black and white. But there is so much more to it, isn't there?"

She took a breath. "Like killing, right, Chanticlaim? Like killing? If you destroy someone wicked, is the action really evil? Or is it considered good? One life in place of many?"

Chanticlaim's shoulders dropped. He ran his hand over his pocket. There was a vial there. His chest moved in short gasps.

I inched inside the doorframe.

"History," she continued. "History and its peculiar ability to repeat itself," she mumbled. "What says you, my beautiful boy? Should we remove a known threat or allow them to exist?"

Chanticlaim didn't answer. I inched closer. I wanted to be the partition between the two. The toxic layer so they couldn't gouge out each other's eyes.

"Don't you move, stupid boy," Tipper snapped at me. I froze, and she turned back to her son. "You brought this gullible boy into this, didn't you?"

"He knows nothing," Chanticlaim lied. "And if you want it to stay that way, I would keep your wild theories to yourself."

"Wild theories?" She unfurled her fingers; inside was a vial with some of Chanticlaim's most recent work. I knew from the way he stiffened, the way she held it. "Movie night proved to be very useful. It got you out of the lab, it got me in, and then there were these hidden treasures. Tell me about my wild theories—tell me what I hold isn't what I think it is. Tell me I'm wrong." She breathed the words, and angled closer. Something sinister filled her.

It touched all of us.

"TELL ME I'M WRONG!"

"I don't know what you mean."

And then something frightening flashed. It was worse than her anger. Worse than her lunacy. A film of black tears veiled her eyes. She blinked them back, but we both saw. It crawled through the room, the power of her sadness. I took another careful step closer.

Her sorrow was dark enough, it was as if she were saying goodbye.

It was enough to trigger Chanticlaim. He held up his hands.

"Mom, I need you to talk to me, and not in riddles or rhetoric. Really talk. This suppression process has been tricky, uncharted territory. I don't know what you think that is, but from the look on your face you have it all wrong."

"There's that word again: *wrong*. So many different connotations attached to it. What is it you think I have 'wrong'?"

Chanticlaim opened his mouth, only to shut it. She nodded and held up the vial between two fingers. "This is to remove all Ice Powers." Then, in a flash, she threw it at the floor. Slivers and shards spread like shrapnel. She fished into her right cloak pocket, where more glass clanked. Chanticlaim's pallor went to that of a sheet. She pulled out another. "And this is Doppelgänger."

She slammed it into the ground.

She kept plucking. She went through the lineup. Fire. Water. Animal. Stronghold. Telekinetic. She stopped short.

"It seems you have it all, but for three individuals, the last two very limited clans." Her eyes shifted to me. "And after you failed so terribly on ending Plague's life, my guess is you're being exceptionally careful to get it right this time."

Did she mean taking powers? Or taking lives?

She moved on before I had time to consider.

"Don't think I don't know how you assisted in his death."

"It was a mercy," Chanticlaim said. "Assisted suicide."

"To feed your agenda," she argued. "You're stuck though. He wasn't a strong specimen to test on. Your results were feeble and it's causing the hollows under your eyes to deepen." She shook her head; Chanticlaim hung his. "Don't think I don't know you. What this was all along ... You are a liar. You are the copy of your father."

"I AM NOT!" He grabbed Tipper by the throat and

slammed her against the wall. His whole body heaved with every labored breath. "I am nothing like him!"

Tipper arrogantly spoke through mean teeth. "My darling boy," her words came out stilted, as his fingers tightened. "You are him, through and through. Just like your father—"

Chanticlaim's hand shot into his pocket and he pulled out a small, slender vessel. I blinked and it turned into a blur. I thought it was a vial that held the cure, but it wasn't. It was something entirely different. A syringe. Tipper jumped away, and the pair struggled—arm to arm—almost as if in a dance.

Pieces of glass lifted from the ground.

We were suspended in chaos, as the fragments went airborne. Her eyes flashed in translucency. Her powers maxed.

Tipper was a telekinetic, too, and she was sending an arsenal at them both.

I should've helped.

But I didn't want to.

The sound of glass, one of the larger pieces, shredded through the room and shot into his side. It landed with such velocity, the sound was poignant as it ripped into flesh. He winced, but didn't let go. He worked the cap off the needle. Shrapnel flew. Each one cutting into his wracked frame. I dove for the floor, missing a stainless-steel tray before it clanged into the side of his head.

She was cascading the room with mind boggling power. The air syphoned, peppering Chanticlaim. "Don't. Do. It," she sputtered. "Don't."

But he wouldn't give up. It was clear as day.

He had every intention of piercing her with the syringe—and the moment she realized it, a flare burst off her. It was one final attempt at self-preservation.

It worked. She managed to dislodge the syringe from his grasp, sending it hard against the wall, where it shattered.

The contents splattered and hissed, eating away the tile floor. Whatever was inside was lethal. Fumes furled from it.

He stumbled back and the room collapsed. All the wreckage held midair by Tipper's powerful mind came crashing to the floor.

It boomed in a collective sigh. Only to be followed by an eerie silence.

He waited.

I waited.

Tipper gave an ugly smile.

"I can only guess what was in that," she said. There was a gash across her eyebrow and dark blooms building on her clavicle in the shape of Chanticlaim's fingerprints. "You were going to kill me." She smirked. "And I was prepared to spare you—but I see you're too far gone."

Chanticlaim looked to me with desperation. I stepped forward.

She held out her hand to still me.

"If you want to keep your head, I advise you to stay put," she ordered.

"Chanticlaim?" I asked.

"Oh, you take orders from him, now?" She tsked. "Be careful who you follow. Monsters don't make for good leaders."

"Says the woman working on the Art of Famine," I spat back.

She threw her head back and laughed. "Why don't you ask Chanticlaim where we got the idea in the first place? Who our master orchestrator was?"

I stumbled. Chanticlaim shook his head. "I can explain," he said.

There was no explaining this.

"It was your idea?" Blood whooshed in my ears; every cell

in my body shrieked. The room tilted, and I closed in on Chanticlaim. His face betrayed him. The kindness in his eyes, the warm brown I was used to seeing, it had gone to shit.

My gloved hand went straight for his throat.

He started the Unrests, he used me, to stop an idea he generated. He was the source of so much death. He was the root of it. Both the cause and the reaction.

The damn seed of this soured germination.

Dark orbs danced in my vision and I clutched him by the neck, allowing my visceral spark of anger to manage the squeeze. My grip tightened, his heartbeat fluttered beneath my imprint, the panic tethering him to me.

I clutched harder.

He should've been thankful for my gloves, because I wasn't suppressing.

I was reacting.

"You did this?" I shouted, again. "Everything! The Art of Famine was yours? The Unrests were built on stopping an idea that belonged to you! You son of a bitch. Why? Why would you do that?"

"Dea—"

He couldn't get the words out. I was turning black. My skin crawled with poison; it fissured along the veins, splitting at the seams. I was glowing with righteousness and burning with vexation.

"So, you were a part of the Unrests then, too, Death? Ah, yes. I can see it. My son, the clever leader, preying on your desire to help." She blinked. "How was I so blind? The timing fits. The moment you suppressed, Death, was the moment Chanticlaim came up with this clever idea."

Chanticlaim still fought against me. He clawed at my hands, kicked my shins. I could sense the room lifting as items began to drift off the ground. Soon, he would send them flying at my back, anything to get me to release him.

I clenched tighter.

"You are your father's son—he's plotted well," she said. Chanticlaim shuddered.

It snagged my attention.

Tipper was standing close and the trim of her cloak brushed against my leg. She was breathing into my ear. A dull thud against my canal as my heartbeat carried like a slow, rolling drum.

I loosened, allowing Chanticlaim a breath, and he took it in a thick wheeze. "Why do you mention his father?" I asked.

She laughed. It shattered mid-center as a sob cracked the surface.

"Mom, don't—" Chanticlaim gasped.

"He is Urrel's son," she said, and I dropped him then. I let him slide to the floor. The pieces he'd been holding with his mind fell to the ground along with his body. They all collapsed together.

I appraised them both.

Chanticlaim, if he wasn't broken before, was nothing more than slivers and dust. He put his head in his hands.

"I'm really dead," he mumbled.

"You were dead the moment you attempted to shoot that syringe into my neck," Tipper snapped at him.

"Chanticlaim is Urrel's son?" I asked. I couldn't decide who I wanted to look at. At Tipper, who stood wounded and bright. At Chanticlaim, who sat wilted and wounded.

"No one knows," Tipper said. "It's been our secret." She held her finger to her lips. "He's going after his birthright."

"You have it wrong," Chanticlaim said. He was looking at me. "She wanted to create a new plague. She wanted to wipe out the human race entirely."

Tipper tsked. "Oh how you twist things. It was only a suggestion—"

"You never just suggest!" Chanticlaim said. "You act. That is who you are."

"And, apparently, who you are too."

"Don't listen to her, Death. Don't. She's the one twisting things—the reasoning, the timeline. I suggested the Art of Famine only as a means to distract her. I knew my suggestion would take longer; I knew it would require more effort. It would buy us time. And we're close."

"Close to destroying the leaders and claiming the throne for yourself."

"It's not true!"

"No?" Tipper reached down and pulled out something from the folds of her cloak. She tossed it on the ground. Chanticlaim twisted to look at it. The familiar block lettering, so neat, so careful, wrote out one word: Triplets. "This is a formula to kill Delilah, Esther and Ruth. Why are there vials— " she pointed to the acidic erosion in the floor—"with every leader's name printed across them?" She glanced at me. "Including your loving grandfather. He's still trying to cook up a formula to kill you, since Plague's demise was so messy. I saw the equations myself—"

"They're planning on burying you," he said to me. His breathing hurried. "Mother is building the box. I saw it. They think you can read minds. That formula is nothing more than a contingency. I would take you out before they had a chance of burying you alive—not for power, but for mercy."

"And the others?" Tipper spat. I pivoted between the two, as her word spinning continued. "Tell me why you would create something so heinous if you weren't intending on taking the throne, Chanticlaim? Kill off all the Brilliants, take away the Leaders, steal the powers of those who could possibly oppose you, and you will be the only one left to rule. You would be both God and King, with all the answers, and no one to question them."

"Those formulas are not to kill them, but are specific to the strength of their powers," he addressed me. "I have to be careful upon removing their powers—especially the Dead-bloods—to ensure their survival."

"You're so good at lying, you probably don't remember what the truth feels like."

"You deserve everything you get," Tipper said. "You thought you would rule, and with her," referring to Torti, "by your side. That you two would take the throne and reign supreme. She encouraged this, didn't she?"

"It was you," Chanticlaim said.

She smirked.

"You planted those cards. You did this." He pointed to her and looked at me. "She did it. She put Torti in danger."

"No darling, you did." Tipper shook her head. "Now you will watch her die and then follow in her place, because there is no going back from what you are and what you've done."

She turned to march out of the room. Chanticlaim looked at me, his eyes wide, his face twisted.

I hated him. I hated her. I hated the deception.

A low hum filled the room. It may have been the ventilators.

Or maybe it was my fury.

The poison knew where to go. What to do.

I opened my mouth and sicced them on the threat. They turned flesh to rot in a matter of heartbeats, eroding from the inside. The scream that followed ricocheted off the walls. It bounced through the air. It cut to the core.

I forced the poison to grow, to dig, to slash away at lungs

and eat away at the heart, all in the name of destroying the threat.

I only hoped I'd picked the right one.

It was a coin flip at this point.

I was surrounded by evil.

CHAPTER 24
TWISTED

A year before Gram died, when life had reached the apex of comfortable banality, we had a stray cat show up.

No doubt dumped.

An occurrence that happened frequently enough we knew to keep cat food on hand.

And as was usually the case, this one was pregnant, and while she may have had a swollen stomach filled with kittens, the rest of her was angles and bones.

A breathing skeleton.

Gram took pity the moment she found her cowering beneath the porch and managed to coax her out.

"Poor thing looks starved," she said, ordering me to grab a can of tuna—since clearly dry cat food wouldn't do. With her bundled in an old towel, we stationed her in the driest part of the barn with clean water and a heaping bowl of food.

She then put me on kitten watch.

Something I agreed to not because I cared for the cat—as awful as that was to admit—but because of Gram.

I had a feeling this one wouldn't make it. It was too reedy.

Too slow. It moved to a death march, with its ninth and final life hanging by a thread.

If it were to die, I wanted to handle the situation. For her not to see.

Thinking back, it was about that time her cough had shown up. Intermittent and with vigor.

We were all moving towards death. Only none of us knew it.

The next night I found the cat, still and stiff. Only one kitten had managed its way out. It too was gone. The size of a field mouse, all twisted and unseeing.

It was one of those things that even when you expect it, it still takes a second too long to process it.

I snuck out to the shed and grabbed one of Grandpa's old shovels and started digging in the grove. I kept the barn light off and fumbled in the black, while the rain fell in big fat drops.

It was weird work. I remember thinking it was weird. And that thinking it was weird, was weird. A peculiar cycle that played over and over as I continued to scoop and dump, scoop and dump. The soil sucking at the blade.

I kept glancing over my shoulder, the house an outline against the dark backdrop, and holding my breath as if somehow Gram would wake up and trudge across the yard to find this wayward cat stiff, its belly loaded with corpse kittens, and that would be it. She would lose her strength.

The strength she strained to maintain as the months crawled on.

So I kept working in tandem with the darkness.

Facing irrational fears.

Replaying the weirdness of it all.

That's how it was now.

Standing over a new corpse and thinking of how strange it

was. How I held my breath, afraid it was going to wake up, even though there wasn't much left to stir.

Chanticlaim stood next to me, staring at what was left of Tipper.

His mouth moved, but didn't speak. At one point, he kneeled and then went back to standing stiffly.

Miming words.

No tears.

"We need to work fast," I said.

He nodded. Nothing about him was fast.

I went to his office and made sure the door was latched. I checked the monitors and didn't see anything alarming. People were milling about, pacing hallways, congregating in corners, gossiping, serving, standing sentry.

All everyday behaviors, only the tension was there; it bled beyond the screen.

There was a button that tripped a red light outside the door signaling the lab was in use. I pressed it. Then I coasted to the back entrance and saw that the lock was twisted.

I went to Chanticlaim and grabbed his shoulder, shaking it harder than necessary. "How much time do we have before they notice your mom is missing?"

He didn't say anything, just kept lip miming.

We didn't have time for a mental breakdown.

I punched him in the arm and he stumbled. It was enough to clear the fog. "How. Much. Time. Do. We. Have?" I asked.

"I-I dunno." He raked his hands through his hair. "She's dead." He said it like it was finally hitting him. "She's really dead."

"Yeah."

"You killed her."

"I had no choice."

"But she's dead." He shook his head, his eyes wide. "She's dead."

"And we'll be dead too if we don't move quickly."

Nothing. Chanticlaim gave me nothing.

"Chanticlaim, did you hear me?"

"What?" His eyes were blank.

"We will die for this if we don't act quickly."

Nothing.

"We"—I indicated both of us—"will both die. Do you understand?" I spoke slowly, afraid to spook him. He nodded, numbly. "How much time do we have before they notice she's missing?"

Chanticlaim blinked. Once. Twice. Three times. Before he finally brightened. He pivoted on his heel, and looked around, almost as if he expected someone else to materialize and save him. "Um, I don't know."

"Dammit, Chanticlaim! What do you know? Think, man. THINK!" I grabbed him by the collar and gave him a shake. "We have to buy time to get Torti out of the tower—and in order to do that, I need to know how much time we have, and if we need to make more. THINK!"

"Torti out of the tower?"

His slowness sent me into a fit. I threw my hand back, fingers closed into a tight fist and sent it flying at his face, cutting him right in the jaw. Something cracked, but it wasn't my knuckles. Chanticlaim split at the waist as a thin stream of blood trickled from the corner of his mouth and ran down his chin. "What the hell was that for?" he sputtered.

The smile I gave him was more a sneer. I took a step closer, and he inched away.

I could smell his fear. "Take your pick, asshole. Maybe for the lies? The Unrests? Corrupt motives? Death serums?" I spat at the ground. My poison hissed against the marble. "Or maybe it's because I wanted to. It doesn't matter. You deserved it and I'll do it again if I feel the need, but lucky for you, we have bigger shit to worry about or else I would be content to pulverize your face into nothing but mush." I pointed to Tipper, who was both the consistency and color of tar. "Now, focus, dammit! How much time do we have before they come looking for her?"

The clock to the jaw was enough to wake him. He straightened and I could see the cogs slipping back into gear. "She has a light like mine," he pointed to the switch near his office door. "I can turn it on in her lab."

"How long does that buy us?"

"I'd say twenty-four hours."

"That's a start."

He swallowed, swirling in his lab. "We can still do this," he said. "If I can take out the leaders—we can get the upper hand."

"Take out, as in kill or remove powers?"

"Remove powers, of course."

"Your mom—"

"Got a lot of stuff wrong," he cut in for me.

If I shifted my head a little, no matter the direction, Chanticlaim's features blurred into a weasel.

"And what about the vial?" I lifted my chin a margin. I was taller than Chanticlaim, but I wanted to be looming. "The one with Polar's name? What was that for?"

"Of course I have a formula with his name on it!" He moved in on me. "I was specifically working on cures for the Deadbloods, individually crafted, to see that I didn't destroy their lives by taking their powers. I didn't want to worry you with the risk, but truth of it, there was one—albeit small. I was confident I could succeed with the power stripping as long as I was patient in my methods. That wasn't a vial to kill Polar, it was as we set out to do: strip him of his strength."

I checked him, and he made his eyes wide. "She got. A. Lot. Wrong." He looked around. "We'll figure this out." He started to grab at tools around his lab. "I'll pull some suppression blood off you, as much as I can take, and I'll bridge the gaps. Stress makes me work harder. I swear it does. Pressure only adds to my productivity." He tried to smile again; it was even worse than before.

"We get Torti out first. No more testing."

"Death, we're close. We can't stop now. If we stop now, we are done for. They will win." He went to gather some of the broken pieces of his lab, carefully skirting the remains of his mother. A few vials hadn't fully shattered and there was liquid lingering. "We can't let them win."

And that's when I saw it. The truth behind Tipper's claims.

Chanticlaim was the snake in the grass.

He was going to destroy the leaders—and I was the resource to help him do it.

"We get her out now," I said. "And then—"

"And then what?" He turned on me. "Look at this." He waved toward his mother. "We can't undo this. We can't go back to the way it was. People will notice my mother is gone, and when they do, the upper heads are going to want blood. We will all be dead; that only leaves us with stopping them now, before they find out. That's the only chance we have."

"We can run." *But not with you.*

"No. Running isn't an option. Never an option. Just because Mother is gone, doesn't mean they won't continue to plot. To plan. The Art of Famine doesn't cease to exist because she's..." he faltered, "because she's gone."

"Are you seriously trying to villainize them over *your* idea?"

"Do you not get it? If it's not one thing, it's another. This is their way. Mom was proposing a plague, a super-bug that would've wiped out the planet. The Art of Famine was a brilliant distraction, one with much more control and far less ramifications. I only proposed it to counter their evil. And mark my words, this plot—or another plot—will always be simmering below the surface. Their lofty goals of human eradication have only just begun. It's up to us to stop them. Trust me."

Trust. An interesting word coming from Chanticlaim.

"I don't think giving them sinister ideas constitutes as heroic."

He closed his fist around one of his formulas and walked over to me, his face bright. "So the alternative was to allow her to create a biological weapon and unleash it?" He snorted. It was filled with disdain. "Besides, Mom is talented—she would've accomplished it in a month's time. I needed a lengthier project."

"Was."

"Excuse me?"

I cocked my head. "Was. Your mom *was* talented—and if you're not careful," I inched closer, just enough to be menacing, "you're gonna be past tense too."

His mouth dropped.

"That's low."

"Is it?" I pointed at his hand, where he was holding the remains of his work. "Because I'm not sure who you are anymore— you might be the worst of them all."

The situation was narrowing, becoming more focused. It was aligning the way it should. A plague would never have happened, they couldn't control who it attacked, who it saved.

One of the ways they managed to keep their humans safe on the outside—both Protectors and collateral—was the ability to dictate life and death.

And how would they grow? Through procreation alone? Unlikely. They couldn't trust the newborns. They wouldn't be able to read and pluck only the most compliant.

A plague would've never been the solution. It wouldn't care.

It would sneak in and take the strong, the weak, the young, the old. It would take a Velore's family that were deemed too important. It would snatch away Protectors.

It would've burned everything in its path.

I took another step closer, our breathing space intermingled. The overhead lights flickered. Chanticlaim winced.

"I don't think she was serious about a plague at all," I whispered. "I don't think you're the man you've let everyone believe. You've been wearing a mask all this time."

I hitched internally, as thoughts knitted tightly. I started to crack; Chanticlaim felt it.

"Daniel, please."

"Don't you dare use my real name," I growled. "Don't you fucking dare." I jabbed him in the chest and he stumbled back. Something behind me screeched, but I was too red to pay it attention.

Chanticlaim's translucency was starting to surface.

My deadly translucency was too.

"My mom got in your head. It's still me. It's always been me." He tapped his chest. "I'm one of the good guys. I've always been one of the good guys. Think of that time we first met, how I saved your mind from being read and from Fantasia being executed for helping you out of Narivous? Think of all I did back then, putting my neck on the line. I did it because it was right, and sometimes right has a murky path."

"What is right's murky path, Chanticlaim?"

His shoulders dropped, no doubt relieved I could still form words.

My translucent state would soon enough stop me.

The light in his eyes continued to gain muster. "Right is putting an end to this madness. It's putting a stop to a hierarchy with too much power. It's doing what's right even when the right thing is hard."

"And then what?"

Chanticlaim inched closer. He made sure to look me square on as if he could dissuade me through the power of eye contact. "And then we hope. We hope by stripping their powers, we remove their thirst for ultimate supremacy."

"And if that doesn't work? Then what?"

"I don't understand."

The subtle rattling from behind continued to grow. Focused on the storyline at hand, I pushed it from my thoughts.

"I think you do. I think you know exactly what I'm getting at." I increased the pressure, throwing out venomous words. I glanced down at the remains of Tipper and realized I had selected wrong. "You were planning on taking the city, weren't you?"

He hesitated, not even a full millisecond, but it was too long. He sputtered out an unconvincing, "No." There was nothing honest about it. I grabbed him by the collar and threw him. Metal went scattering, glass pulverized beneath my feet, and he let out a dense 'oof' as I pinned him to the wall.

He had the good sense not to fight me; he went limp, bones to gelatin.

"You've got to calm down," he said. "I can explain everything; Mom was good with manipulation."

"And the apple doesn't fall far from the tree. I'm done hearing your explanations. They remind me too much of bullshit."

"And what will you do then? C'mon, Daniel." He shook his

head. "Who else do you have to trust? Who do you have as an ally? Whether you like it or not, you have me. Only me. I'm the only one who can change this. And I'm telling you, we have to keep fighting—I'm not the enemy. They are."

"You want the city."

"No." He shook his head. "But I'm not going to say it hadn't crossed my mind. I won't lie to you like that. I have a power—a far reaching one—that would make managing a city like this possible. But that wasn't my intention. Never was it my intention."

"Simply a convenient side effect then?"

"Perhaps so, but again, that was not the mission nor my objective. I simply wanted to right our many wrongs, remove the need for omnipresent rule. Give people the chance at normalcy."

Even his tone was that of a snake, I could almost hear a hiss.

That's when I spotted the movement out of the corner of my eye, a flash of something that went straight for Chanticlaim.

He had gotten one of the back cabinets open and sent—with his telekinetic powers—a piece of his pharmaceutical arsenal. I recognized the purple contained in the glass vessel.

That's the noise I heard.

That's why he kept me talking—to distract me.

And then we were fighting over it.

He wanted to knock me out; I wasn't going to have him blind me. I tried to pry it from his hands and we both went crashing to the floor. Chanticlaim fell first and I landed on top of him. "Stop," he shouted.

"Fat chance." I grabbed his hair and slammed his head into the ground. His skull bounced, and with it a sickening echo of bone meeting tile. He bucked his head back and knocked my mouth into my teeth. Metallic tang covered my tongue and particles oozed out, reaching in their desperate attempt to destroy. They found Chanticlaim's flesh as my cheek, in the midst of our tussle, grazed his chin. The poison grew into a quick bloom.

He screamed out in pain, but he didn't let the vial go. If anything, he held on to it all the tighter, his body coiling over it, centering himself like a frightened centipede. My forehead landed on a piece of flesh on his upper arm and his scream turned into a howl.

I could feel the snaking toxin weave along the tapestry of his skin. It was enough for him to release his hold on the Purple Magic, and I made a quick grab for it.

He was breathing hard, panting, the poison pain overriding his ability to create coherent sentences.

He looked at me, desperate, and I hesitated, the stopper plucked from its holding place. My shadow loomed over him and I found the insight to halt the toxin.

It still answered to me. It still listened.

If I was going to derive any truth from him, now was the time. I would use my powers as a pseudo truth serum.

"Were you going to kill the triplets?"

He gasped and shook his head. "Not if I could help it," he answered. It felt honest. Bare. "I made it ..." he wheezed. I could see him starting to dim, the poison intercepting his receptors. "I made it just in case. So they wouldn't undo the p-power stripping. T-they could u-u-undo the ultimate suppression, and bring b-back—" He arched his back and let out a hollow yell. His eyes were fading. The pain was swallowing him.

"And my grandfather? The other Sevens? Were you making formulas meant to kill them?"

He shook his head.

“Tell me!” I ordered.

“I-I already did.” He nodded. “N-not to k-kill Polar or the g-good o-ones, but ...” His teeth chattered.

“But?”

“The b-bad ones, y-yes, like A-Amelia. I-I always i-intended t-t-o kill Amelia. I s-still do.”

“Where’s the glove?” I asked.

He blinked, too dull from the toxin tugging.

“Chanticlaim.” I repeated slowly, “Where is the glove? The one with Urrel’s fingerprints? The one used to access walls?”

He nodded, understanding gave him a rush of light. It brought him back. “It’s in the stool. T-the c-cushion comes off.” He swallowed; his whole neck buckled from it. He started to gasp in short stabs. “It w-won’t get you into the c-cell, t-though. You need ... need m-more.” He pointed to the cabinet. “M-master key.” He paused, his eyes closed, and breathed so deep a rattle spun in his esophagus. “I-I’m not b-bad, j-just a b-bit broken.”

I crouched down to look at him, and the toxin stirred. They weren’t moving on him, but they were still present. He was fading, his body selecting release over consciousness. He was going to black out, Purple Magic or not.

He was waiting for that moment, where he could have a reprieve.

No. He wasn’t bad. There was still good there, the infiltrating toxin thrummed with it. It weighed morality on a scale. I took off my glove and hovered it over the wounds and pulled some back. It wasn’t enough, not even close, but the tension running along his core lost a bit of its edge.

It was enough to give him more time, to show him that I wasn’t going to let him die. That he was right—I needed to have someone to trust and my options were coming up slim. I kept the vial ready, uncorked and poised, in my opposite hand. He looked at me with hunger and gratitude.

"We're all a bit broken."

He smiled then—the old smile—filled with compassion and truth.

I wanted that smile more than I cared to let on.

I didn't want this to be my last memory of Chanticlaim, withering, broken, begging for the end.

Because after today, I hoped he'd be nothing but a memory for the rest of time. I hoped he'd honor our motives—the pure ones—and help us stay away from Narivous, that he would work to keep us hidden, from the inside; if not for me, but for Torti who I was hellbent on getting out of the tower and far away from this awful place.

I was done being a puppet.

"Save her," Chanticlaim said, his words steadier now that some of the poison had been called back. "Save her, n-no matter what."

I nodded. "I will. Or I'll die trying."

"G-g-good."

"But you're going to have to do me a favor."

He arched a brow in question. He wanted to collapse.

"You need to make sure they don't find us. You need to be your sneaky self and see to it that once we're gone, we stay gone. Understand?"

He looked up then, as I went back to standing, my shadow looming over him like the reaper with lethal promise. He didn't have the strength though, and his head fell back while his chest hollowed. What was left of me, lingering, was starting to bite, just enough for him to know: this wasn't a threat.

But a promise.

"Understand?" I pressed. I sent the particles seeking. He winced, and then nodded.

"Say it."

"I u-under ..."

"Finish it."

A sheen of sweat built along his brow. "I ... u-under ... s-stand."

"And?"

"Please ..." he begged.

I made them dig farther.

"Finish it Chanticlaim, tell me you'll do everything possible to make sure they won't find us. And so help me, if the Art of Famine comes back, if I catch even a whiff of it, I'll be back in a heartbeat—and I'll see to it I end all of you. This will be my city. Not yours."

And so help me, part of me wanted that to happen.

"I'll do e-everything t-to s-stop t-t-them."

"Good." I poured the Purple Magic into my hand, and was about to throw the blackout dust at his face, when he muttered, faintly: "D-Don't tell anyone a-about U-Urrel. P-please ..."

I tossed the fistful of release straight at him and he collapsed like a dying star.

CHAPTER 25
RUTH

I worked fast. I called the poison back by placing my bare hand on the contaminated areas—they returned to me on a beckon, crawling forth with their needles and bite. However, where they stung and bit Chanticlaim, they soothed me. His face, scrunched up even in merciful sleep, slackened to relief as soon as they'd vacated.

The damage was still there though; their traces left behind on his skin. Scars from our scuffle, and I didn't have the healing powers to take them away—not that I would've even if I could.

I wanted him to keep them. A token. A memory of what I could do—of what I was capable of—if he didn't follow my directions. A scar seemed like a suitable reminder.

He could never beat me.

I scoured his lab and found the glove and the master keys, then I yanked the cord from his computer and used it to make a constrictor knot, binding him in place, hopeful for more time.

Time. Time. Time. It was a high-pitch hum that hurt on repeat.

I found all the intact vials and crushed them beneath my feet. They wouldn't have their cure and Chanticlaim wouldn't have any leverage.

I worried, however, that in his madness he had stashed some far beyond my ability to discover. They could be hidden anywhere. That knowledge chilled me to the marrow.

With one last final look at the shattered lab, taking in the two Brilliants laying in shambles, one destroyed beyond recognition, the other in scars and bruises, a terrifying sound screeched at the back door of Chanticlaim's lab.

The deadbolt was moving.

Someone had a key. And that someone didn't care that the privacy light was on.

Being I was in the actual laboratory part, and not in the office where the door was stationed, there was little I could do but watch it develop directly in front of me. The few free, floating particles I had humming about the room stilled.

We all waited.

I held my breath.

They held their vibrations.

The person behind the door was quick with their movements—the door flew open.

I blinked. My eyes were centered too high, when I should've held them lower.

A sprite of a Velore entered, short in stature but imposing in presence. It took me a moment to process her.

Half and half, I was staring at Ruth.

Her black eyes had a ring of white in the center, and her hair was split down the center. Half dark, half light. She saw me, quickly scanned the wreckage, and then calmly closed the door, locking it behind her.

She entered on slippered feet, wearing an off-white gown

that only exacerbated her child-like appearance. With careful placement, she skirted the glass, and entered the lab room. Her attention focused on Chanticlaim.

On what was left of Tipper.

And her lips formed a small "o".

Strangely enough, despite the minor give of her mouth, there was no other indicator that the scene took her by surprise. It was as if she expected it.

She cocked her head and gave it a gentle shake.

Time moved achingly slow, before she pulled her attention away and focused it on me.

A blazing spotlight.

"Oh, dear," she said, moving closer. "This is trouble."

Her voice was sweet sounding, soft. She didn't have the commanding presence as Delilah and Esther. It was more reserved. Timid. A bit more frightening.

There was also an undercurrent of something I couldn't place.

I thought of what Delilah had said—about her scruples. About taking sides.

She moved closer to Tipper and bent at the waist to inspect closer. Being she was so short, she didn't have to flex much.

Her small hand reached out and she plucked a strand of blond, murky hair. She held it between her fingers. A look of morbid curiosity sliding across her features. She let it go.

The thickened weight pulled it quickly to the ground.

I noticed the poison remnants didn't seem to phase her.

"This is a doozy," she said, shaking her head. "We need to think this through."

Why was she saying we?

"You want to help me?" I asked, tentatively.

"Of course, I want to help you. That's why I'm here."

"How did you know I needed help?" I glanced at the monitors through the partition; they were barely decipherable from my vantage point. Was there some sort of trigger that alerted to the trouble?

Her lips coiled into a smile, revealing neat white teeth. She shrugged, throwing out heavy nonchalance that would've otherwise seemed out of place—but fit on her shoulders with practiced ease. "Some things can't be explained, so we shouldn't even try." She bit her lip, and glanced down at Chanticlaim. She dipped her hand into a dress pocket, so foiled into the fabric it went unnoticed. She came out with one of Chanticlaim's formulas.

"He hid this in my room." She tossed it at me. I caught it midair. "I don't like how it feels. The vibrations are off."

A curious comment. "You've got that right," I muttered, and gave it a sharp, violent toss at the tile floor. The pieces pulverized. There was hiss and steam.

Her smile grew.

"I knew you were going to do that," she whispered, a soft reverie in her voice. As if seeing my response had fulfilled some deep-rooted expectation she had. Then she pointed to something above my head.

It was a poison particle. One still floating, gearing around the room, trying to sniff out any other cures Chanticlaim had worked up.

"Can I see it closer?" she asked.

"Not to be rude, but I'm kind of on a tight timeline."

"This will take all but a moment. Besides, you have me helping you. I'll speed things along." She rocked on her heels.

"Why do you want to see it?"

"Because."

"That's not much of answer."

"It's enough of an answer." And then, almost to prove a

point, she held up her hand. The poison, despite being under my control, glided toward her.

Sorcery.

It landed on her fingertip and she threw her head back, revealing the soft rivets of her neck.

"Oh, it likes me," she said, her face all peculiar eyes. Then she closed her eyelids, her lashes resting against her hued cheeks and swayed gently. It reminded me of someone listening to an adored song. Turning off the other senses to incorporate the tones more clearly. "Let me see some others," she rasped.

And damned if I didn't do just that.

I called a flurry and they swarmed her. Not with any effort on my part. They wanted to come. This was an invitation they were eager to accept.

Ruth was peculiar indeed.

She held up her other hand, and they danced around her. No bite or sting, but caress and softness. They were life with her.

No mention of death.

I knew then.

Ruth was most assuredly on my side. And that gave me a powerful edge.

We were standing amidst a corpse and a coma; she was not only unperturbed, but alight in joy and intrigue. My poison thrummed liked small insects, specks of darkness hovering in a halo of force and movement.

Whoever this girl was, she was a treasure.

I secretly hated myself for not encountering her sooner.

"Did you teach it to do that? To talk?" Her smile stretched. "It's rather wonderful. The way they speak—although I don't know what they're saying exactly. Different languages."

A second particle landed on her hand. Was it me, or did the first quake with jealousy?

She was a magnetic field. I could feel the pull coming from her, the power she emitted.

That's why she hid. I was becoming more certain of it with every passing moment.

She was a draw.

"How?" I asked.

"This?" She raised a brow.

I nodded.

"My sister thinks I have ESP abilities. But it's simpler than that. *Instinct.*" She spoke the word with sharp definition. Making each syllable count. "I feel stuff. People, mainly. Some make me happy, others ... don't. It's hard to define." I started to call the toxins back, but there was resistance. They swarmed around her, a hive of bees circling above her head.

"If you don't speak the same language," I asked, "how do you know what they're saying?"

She shrugged. "I don't. Not really. I can feel tone though. I can sense what they're trying to say." She blinked, and her face looked like it was about to fall. "But I can tell this is cutting you in half. You are split. Broken and uneasy, yet satiated with strength. Allow me to help. What can I do?"

I blinked a few times, and she moved closer, bridging the distance, until she was right next to me. She surprised me by grabbing my hand and something sparked between us. It moved beyond my gloves.

"I need to turn the light on in Tipper's lab, the one to mark she's busy," I said.

"Okay."

"I need to see if there is a morsel of truth spilled from Chanticlaim's lips."

"Okay." Her lips twisted in something sardonic. "Tall order."

"You're telling me." I slid my gaze from her; it was hard. I wanted to stare at her all day long. "He's full of lies."

"I sometimes wonder if he even knows his own truth."

"You see a lot."

"Yes."

"I need to buy time so I can get Torti out."

"You'll leave this city tonight." She didn't ask, she stated.

"There's no other option. I have to save them."

Them. Such a large word.

She squinted at me, as if my reflection was too blinding. "That shows integrity."

I snorted. "Integrity? Look at what I've done." The lab was a marker of poor choices, from start to finish. "I've liquified Tipper and left Chanticlaim in shambles. I wouldn't call that integrity."

"I call it a must."

"I killed."

"Yes."

"I don't regret it."

"Yes."

"Part of me wants to kill Chanticlaim."

She smirked and rolled her eyes. "I've had that feeling for years." Then she pulled me down and I collapsed, not necessarily through force, but through want. She pressed her cold hands against my face. I didn't have to suppress; the poison wouldn't harm her—much the same as it worked with Fantasia.

It kind of sang. Like it recognized her and wanted to bask in the essence of her calm.

"So, show me how you travel without notice," she said. "I know you're not using the traditional methods."

"How's that?"

She lifted her eyes to the hovering poisons. "They're becoming clearer by the moment."

I stood up and called the poison back. They came, but I think it's partly because Ruth allowed them to. Something told me she dismissed them.

One stayed. The original. It felt right.

"So the tunnels?" Ruth replied, staring at the particle as if it were revealing all my secrets.

"Looks like they're *much* clearer."

"Much," she agreed, pulling her focus back toward me.

I took her to an inside entrance.

"I should've known," she said as I used Urrel's glove to gain entry. "Why did I not know this?" she asked. She scrunched her nose, the thought of something slipping past her distasteful. "That dratted scent blocker ruins everything," she muttered.

"Have you traveled in the tunnels before?" I asked. "Do you know how to find Tipper's room this way?"

"No and no." She lifted her shoulders. There was that nonchalance again. "But it shouldn't be too difficult." And as if to prove a point, she wedged in past me, completely unafraid and comfortable near my skin, and started to weave with such practice it made me wonder how much she saw without having to actually see.

I followed her.

She led us through twists and turns and then stopped abruptly.

"Here we are." I used the scanner and the room slid into focus.

The first thing I noticed was the coffin.

It was sitting center stage, on a platform, displayed in all its macabre glory. Erected from stone—built to house the undead.

"The order's over there," she said, following me in. I pivoted on her, and she stood stoic. "Go on," she encouraged. "Read up on it. You want to know who demanded the design." She held up the solitary poison particle. "It told me."

"You are a fast study."

"Or maybe they're learning me."

I went to where she pointed and found the order sitting on a table next to my coffin.

The writing looked familiar. The signature even more so. It was etched over every parcel of official paperwork.

Thorn's name neatly scrawled. It almost appeared too tidy. There was no haste involved.

Deliberate with purpose.

And the date—directly after she drugged me and then stopped requesting my presence.

It taunted me. I ran my hand across the coffin.

Someone had gone through the extra effort to have my name engraved over the top. There was no mistaking this would be my box, to house me alive.

And Thorn had been the one to issue it.

I turned to Ruth, my hand still on stone, a soft heartbeat bleeding through it. "Did you know this was being built?" I asked.

"Yes, but it didn't matter," she said, in a rather uncaring, collected sort of way.

"How can this not matter?"

"Because it was never going to happen." She pursed her lips and continued to move her hand so the toxin was always in her sight. She smiled. It was toothy. "Relevance only counts when something will come to fruition. I don't bother myself with hopeless possibilities. That's not a good use of energy."

She went to my side and placed her hand on the coffin. Then she grazed over to a vial on the desk. She grabbed it and gave it a curious look. Of all things, what stood out was the purple label.

"Healing potion," she said, and then she coiled her fingers around it and stashed it into her pocket. She turned those guileless weird eyes on me. Her appearance was less jarring by the moment. I actually enjoyed the look of her.

"You need to send a message before you go," she said. Her voice came out husky. Was this the evil side or the good? Or were the lines too blurred, the consequences too severe, to take a side?

I stood in stilted silence.

"You need to show them that they can't do this to you." Ruth went to the back wall and collected a crowbar under the bench. The link between us expanded.

She put it near my feet and then bowed.

It had a different heft to it than all the other bows given to me from those beneath my station. Ruth was my equal. She was a Brilliant. It was as if she'd read a story that hadn't been written yet.

"The king can't be buried," she said. "You understand?"

"No." And I didn't understand. Was she referring to Urrel? Did she know he was buried, and I was aware?

Or was she referring to me?

Was she seeing me as king and was the crowbar a symbolic scepter?

It felt less like the former and more like the latter.

"You may not understand now," she said, "but you will."

"Tell me what you mean. I need you to tell me what you mean."

She shook her head, her mixed curls bouncing. "I can't. Forgive me ..." she opened my palm and placed a kiss into it, "...

for it's best we let things unfold the way they're meant to unfold. Too much interference could sever the path, and your path—as it's laid out—is as it should be."

"You do that."

"What?"

"Talk in circles."

"Only when I have to."

"This path, do you know it? Is that why you won't tell me? Because you want it to come true?"

She arched a brow. "I told you I have instinct; I know it's not my place to meddle."

"This is more than instinct. This is seeing something that hasn't happened yet. This is seeing the future."

She smiled; it was all coy. "What is a future, really? A possibility of what might happen through a string of simultaneous decisions. We waffle so very much, in our actions and choices, paths never stay the same. I know I don't want a part in any interruption."

"You don't want to alter my path?"

"Perhaps."

"Those circles again." I shifted. "I'd like it if you'd give me a solid answer."

"I'd like it if futures were a solid thing," she rebutted. "I can give you one solid thing though."

She paused to align her words. Then she gave me one of her heart-stopping smiles. "Stop hiding. It has done you no good. It has made those who discover your abilities question if you're hiding more." She nudged her head at the lead coffin. "It has bloomed paranoia. When you walk out of here, shine bright, like your aura promised you would. Blind them." She put the crowbar in my hand. "But for the sake of safety, do so only after you've been healed. Use the tunnels, go to Ice Quarters, your healer should be there. Maybe change your clothes too, you smell a bit like decay. But from that moment on, don't you dare shy away from who you are. Let them see, let everyone see, for you will frighten them and that will only suit you in the future."

"I thought you weren't going to meddle."

"This part doesn't matter, nothing changes if you do or don't. This will only make your life easier for it will most assuredly expand your opportunities. Whatever those opportunities may be."

She bowed again.

"I'm keeping your poison. He likes me." And then, too quick to almost catch, she popped the particle in her mouth.

A dull heat swelled in my chest.

The poison was alive and had found its way to her lungs, where, for reasons beyond my ability to understand, it would most certainly thrive.

I bounced the crowbar in my hand. I took off my cloak and laid it across the casket. I put my gloves there too.

Ruth nodded in approval.

They would find it after it was too late, and they would know that I know.

I took the order, signed by Thorn, and folded it into a tight square, shoving it in my pocket—a memento that would remind me of lessons learned.

"Thank you for all your help," I said. "And as much as I hate to ask, I need one more favor from you."

"I'm at your service, Your Grace," she bowed.

A flash of déjà vu hit me. I ignored it.

"See to it that you find all my vials and destroy them. Chanticlaim had wicked plans—and he needs no opportunities to grow them."

"Like killing me?"

I wasn't surprised she knew. Nothing would surprise me when it came to Ruth. "Perhaps."

"I'll do my best." She promised. "But I'm not all too worried about it."

Something hummed.

It was my toxin buried within her.

I was unexpectedly not worried either.

We shared a knowing glance.

"I'll also put glue in the locks so the doors are harder to open, although I don't really think it's necessary. You have all the time you need."

I felt that.

It seemed there was someone in our midst that could read futures. It would stand to reason that this person would be half and half.

Not one or the other—but somewhere right in the middle.

We hit Tipper's red light as we went out. Time had been bought.

I WENT through the walls and slipped into the Ice Quarters via the secret entrance into the neglected Throne Room. The apartment was buzzing with life. I knew they were all gathered before I'd even stepped foot on the cool, marble flooring.

And that all I had to do was enter their living room and I'd find a small assembly there.

I hung onto Ruth for a moment longer. Her memory and her powers.

Both sang through me.

There was a trade.

My toxin tethered her magic with my own. Fractional, but enough to build a bond.

She'd given me insight, strength, and certainty. And of those three, in a land where I had done nothing but question every action since the day I arrived, I'd become weightless with certitude.

Ruth.

And her peculiar powers—blended with my own—giving us an edge.

I traveled down the memory-laden hall and found them all there, aside from Frigid who was conveniently absent. Polar was pacing the living room, his hands neatly placed behind his back. He moved like a man on the brink.

Camille, Fantasia, and Dreams sat on the couch, a trio holding hands. Camille's face was resting on Dreams' shoulder, as mother and daughter reversed roles. I'd never seen Camille so despondent. Her face was puffy and full.

The rest of her was limp.

Fear tucked them into coils of anxiety. Everyone stopped to stare at me. Fantasia stood up. Her hand nervously fluttered to her hair, brushing loose strands away from her face. She scanned the length of me and scrunched her nose at the scent. Between the bruises and battery from my scuffle with Chanticlaim, and the blood from his mother, I was most certainly an objectionable vision.

No one spoke, only the soft tick of the clock broke the room.

They'd been plotting no doubt, to free Torti. It was written all over them.

They had devised a way. One of which I knew would work.

Oh, yes. Ruth had left her touch.

Finally, I found a smile; it surprised even me. For I felt it blaze across my lips, a maddening joy emanating from deep within my core. It took all my strength to stop the laughter from bubbling forward.

For I was eager to tell them what happened, a boastful tale that would truly only suit me.

Tipper was dead. Through me. And Chanticlaim was broken next to her. I wasn't afraid. Not even a little.

They were though.

And part of me liked it.

CHAPTER 26
LONG LIVE THE DEAD KING

They had a plan.

So did I.

And as luck would have it, there was enough time to deploy both.

Except I kept getting distracted by Dreams. Staring at her as we bolted through the forest, tripping over my feet as I parceled out the newest bout of information.

Why was I seeing it now?

Ruth.

It was probably Ruth.

We were moving at a clipped pace. Fantasia reluctantly moving behind us. She mumbled a few objections, all of which fell on deaf ears.

We cut through the field and onto the path.

The trees were softer here, less dense, and large swatches of sunshine split in front of us. It threw us into a kaleidoscope and chopped up the ground into light and dark.

Dreams shifted under my gaze and stopped by the boulder next to the creek. This was a sticky area. The moving water did nothing to cleanse the energy, if anything it made it worse. Fantasia halted a few feet behind us.

She'd been nervously avoiding my gaze ever since the pieces snapped together.

Good.

She should've told me. Someone should've told me.

"You have to stop staring, it's weird," Dreams said.

"Why didn't you say anything? Why didn't either of you say anything?"

"It wasn't really relevant." Dreams smirked and tossed her hair back. It was gratefully normal. Long, blonde. It would make disappearing in crowds easier.

"It feels relevant. And a little creepy."

Dreams' lips twisted into a sardonic smile and she lifted a brow at Fantasia. She was chewing pink gum and blew a small bubble. "That means he thinks I'm hot," Dreams said. She ran her hands along her cloak. "And it's wigging him out. Now stop staring and hurry up. This was your idea, remember? And last I checked, we have until sunset before the real plan begins."

One day and everything had shifted.

In the apartment, I had unloaded the travesty of all that had happened.

I told Camille and Polar about the Unrests.

Our involvement.

That Tipper planted the cards in Torti's rooms.

And how Chanticlaim was behind the Art of Famine.

That the plan was to take our powers away.

And then there was the finale, the part they were all waiting for since I not only looked like death—but smelled of it too. I had killed Tipper.

We had to leave tonight.

"We'll move our plans up," Polar had said, catching

Camille's eye. Polar was the one person she could bear to look at.

The rest of us had sorely disappointed her.

She was seething—which brought her back to life. I recalled how she, long ago, chose anger over sorrow. She could cope with anger. It was easier.

Sorrow brought her to a wilt.

She paced the room, her voice reduced to a simmer. Had we not been in the confines of the castle she would've been shouting.

"Irresponsible, incorrigible, appalling," she muttered. "To get involved with the rebellion!"

"We'll get her out tonight," Polar said.

"Well, we have no other choice," Camille snapped. "Rebellion," she snapped again. Repeating the word to make it cement.

He swooped her into his arms and held her. She tried to pull away, but with a futile strength. Her heart wasn't in it.

"We'll get her out," he said again. "I promise you, before midnight, you'll all be gone."

Camille went ashen. "You're coming with us," she said. "I'm not leaving you."

Polar took her hand and kissed her knuckles, his entire body falling in on itself.

"I can't," he said.

Camille ripped her hand away. "You can't or you won't?"

He shook his head, and Camille scoffed, crossing her arms and turning away.

Polar grabbed her shoulders and made her confront him. "I'll be more useful here, to keep you safe."

"You're staying for her."

"I'm staying for us!"

"NO! For her!" Camille slammed her closed fist into his chest.

"For you!" he bit back. "For her!" And this time, he brought Camille into his arms, and despite her anger, despite the ice misting from his core, she melted into him. When he pulled away, he looked at her and repeated softly, "It's for you, *and* it's for her."

Only his eyes drifted to Dreams.

Polar swallowed. The stillness hummed.

I don't know why it took me so long to see it.

To understand.

The truth that was carefully danced around. Never addressed, but never denied, omitted through careful phrases and thoughtful maneuvering.

It was in front of me all this time.

Polar cupped Camille's face and kissed her again. "It's because you *are* my family that I have to stay. I will die before I let anything happen to you. To any of you."

"Polar, please—"

Polar looked at me, his face chilly with resolve. "You're all getting out and, so help me, you're never coming back."

Fantasia moved to my side and brushed along the length of me.

"I should've told you," she said, reading my face.

"I should've guessed," I murmured back.

Dreams.

Dreams was Polar's child.

And Polar, the common thread linking us, was ready to let us all go.

And now here we were, outside the city, taking advantage of the last lull we had until it was time to put our plans into action.

How I managed to convince Dreams and Fantasia to tag

along was beyond me. Neither were happy about it—but neither could pass up the opportunity.

Fantasia didn't believe he was actually buried.

Dreams said she wanted to make sure I didn't mess it up.

We all chose to omit this detour from Polar and Camille.

They had enough to manage without worrying over this component. There was a lot to manage in the few short hours before sunset.

I would battle with them—fight with a fierce force to get Torti out of the tower—but we needed distractions.

Dreams would be one.

Perhaps Urrel could be another.

"So if you don't stop staring, we're going to have problems," Dreams prattled on. She placed her hands on her hips and challenged me with her gaze. The green hues of the forest threw a tint over her complexion. It made her look ill and uneven. "I don't have time for you to go all mouth-breather on me. You need to get over it, and get over it quickly because this isn't the time to not have your wits about you. Got it?"

She didn't wait for an answer, just moved along.

She pivoted on her heel and I trailed behind.

We leapt over the creek in unison.

She was right; it wasn't time to lose focus.

Because it was mere moments when the briars around the cabin came into focus; we stopped and stared.

"We're here," Fantasia breathed. She grabbed my hand and squeezed it. I squeezed back.

"You two ready?" I asked.

Dreams smacked her bubblegum.

I wasn't clean on our entrance. The briars wilted from my touch, peeling back and creating an easily accessible opening. One nice thing on having gone too far: you didn't worry about reversing course.

I took them around the back. The chill cut through us as the wind picked up. Fantasia shuddered.

I stopped confidently on the spot.

The rocks had since moved. An H, E and an L were sloppily spelled out. The start of the word "help." Or maybe it was "hell."

Both girls looked at the layout curiously—neither one spoke of it.

"How are you going to do it?" Dreams asked. She smacked her gum again and then blew a small bubble. "Do we have, like, shovels or anything?"

I shook my head. "We won't need them."

She tilted her head.

"I have to remove him with my powers, and my powers alone," I said. "I have to show them that they can't bury me and hope for me to stay there. This is as much a distraction as it is a message."

"You know the rumors, right?" Fantasia asked. She searched my eyes. Dreams edged closer, not because she felt left out, but because there was comfort in our huddle. "He was the most evil of men."

"I've heard."

"No sense of right and wrong," Dreams added.

"I've heard that too."

"Vile." Fantasia nipped her lip. "He's gonna be angry."

"Yeah, but he won't be angry at us," I said.

"How do you know?" Dreams asked.

"We didn't put him here. Others did. We'll be his saviors; that's gotta count for something, right? Besides, chances are he's too weak to even stand. It'll take days, months, hell, even years for him to recoup. What damage can he do in his weakened state?"

"Well from the stories, a lot," Fantasia said.

"And those are just stories. Neither one of you met the guy, and we all know how Narivous likes to spin its tales."

It was a sound argument. Neither argued.

"We're doing this." Fantasia and Dreams got shifty. "Fine. *I'm* doing this."

"Um," Dreams arched her neck to look at Fred. He came swooping down to land on her shoulder. "Should we be worried with your method of unearthing?"

I paused, and then indicated the cabin. "Go inside. I haven't done this before." The poison was chattery.

"Weird," Dreams said sarcastically. "I thought you unearthed buried immortals all the time."

"Weird," I agreed.

Dreams started for the cabin, and then stopped midway when Fantasia didn't follow. "Are you not coming?" she asked.

Fantasia angled her head toward me. "I'm gonna stay close, in case he needs a hand."

"He's going to erode stuff. I don't think he needs your help."

"Fine. I want to stay then."

"That's dumb."

"Then I'm dumb." Fantasia flicked her hair over her shoulder. "But I'm staying."

Dreams blew a big bubble in lieu of a response and went inside. The house groaned in protest. A plume of disrupted dust wafted and filtered the sunshine as she slammed the door behind her.

"You got this?" Fantasia asked.

I nodded—even though I wasn't sure.

The confidence of earlier, the confidence Ruth instilled, made my powers better. The sky went dark as my vision blotted out, power wrapping around my torso, moving in swift vibrant rings. I was the nucleus of a reactor; it coiled through me, off me, and then I sent it into the earth, and it flayed with such a force, Fantasia shifted back.

Not that I saw her move, it was simply the atmosphere altering. She was close and then she wasn't.

The ground beneath my feet quaked and roared. I discovered the land could scream.

My own feet rooted, a strange sort of grip. They held place as if they knew this is where I belonged.

The poison liquified, turning molten, and the soil—what was wet, dense, and intact—began to flow like water. It bubbled and popped, shifting away. The briars collapsed, losing their shape and their thorns, becoming nothing but a puddle as the dark hole of power claimed them.

Time stretched on. What was seconds, surely, felt like an afternoon. I became detached from my body, allowing my magic to behave as it wished.

I no longer controlled it; it controlled me.

And then, I was done.

As quickly as I called it out, it came right back. Hurtling into me, eager to rest and recoup.

The clouds lifted, only they weren't clouds, but my vision. It still had the same effect. Everything came into acute focus as the world around me cleared. Tree limbs, many now bare from the blast of power, were well defined. The cabin lost its fuzzy outline, the sky became blue. I glanced around me. Fantasia had moved back to the cabin, her hand resting on the dilapidated door. The scars on the soil stopped shy of it. Dreams poked her head out, neither seemed to be breathing.

They were afraid.

Their genetics mirrored. Although one was fair and the other dark, in that moment, you would've been hard pressed to tell them apart.

They were whitewashed with fear, perhaps a bit awestruck too.

They approached, stepping over the fissures in the ground. And settled on each side of me.

Dreams no longer smacked her gum. Fred wasn't on her shoulder.

"You melted the ground," Fantasia said. "And you did it quickly."

"It wasn't even hard," I admitted.

"Remind me to never piss you off," Dreams muttered.

I jumped into the hole. Dreams had the crowbar and spun it like a baton. I took it. "This place is a wreck now; there's really no going back."

"Like there ever was a choice," I said. "Tipper is dead."

"Was she like this, Daniel?" Fantasia asked, her eyes trailing my destruction. "Is that how you knew what to do?"

I shrugged, not caring.

"It's about right," I said objectively. "The effects are similar. There wasn't much left of Tipper and there's not much left here, which is gonna work well in the long run. I need them to be afraid of me."

"I don't think that's going to be a problem," Dreams said.

That brought pleasure.

"Well," Dreams said, "shall we continue with our bad decisions?"

They both leaned forward and peered into the hole. I took in the casket. The edges were visible, one of which was severely damaged but still intact.

I immersed myself in work. Clearing mud with my hands, grateful I had the foresight to bring a change of clothes.

The casket held together, demonstrating a remarkable ode to its craftsmanship. It matched the one that awaited me almost perfectly. Simply take away the filth and the toxin runoff.

They must've had blueprints tucked away, or someone with an amazing memory to create the replica.

I got on my knees and put my ear against the stone cover. I knocked; once, twice, three times. My knuckles not quite scraping, but solid enough to bruise later.

I stopped breathing.

The girls must've too; we were all stagnant.

A faint knock echoed. Fantasia gasped. She stepped back and gripped Dreams' hand. I arrogantly said, "Told ya," and grabbed the crowbar. I found purchase in a crevice and was about to leverage my body against it when Fantasia shouted, "Wait! Are you sure you want to do this?" she asked.

"We have no choice," I said. "I can't leave him—that's nearly as sadistic as putting him here in the first place. Besides, this sends a message. They won't be able to bury me and hope to keep me in place. They shouldn't be burying anyone for that matter. What's to stop them if we fail tonight? They could easily give this punishment to someone else. Me. Torti. You. My coffin is already built, orders placed."

She audibly swallowed and twisted her hands. "I'm not condoning the behavior."

"You're not condemning it either."

"Dammit, Daniel, all I'm saying is we could leave him here where he can't get us. You've already exposed the box, let him find his own way out. We have enough to contend with as it is. We don't need to battle an irate, deposed king with—from the sounds of it—decidedly psychotic tendencies."

"Psychotic tendencies? I daresay those who are psychotic are the ones who came up with such a demented plan. This isn't a normal response. This is the response of the unhinged, which happens to be the same leadership in charge of having your sister in the tower."

"But the stories about him—"

"He's not the boogie man."

"He's about as close as it comes," Dreams said in a soft paltry breath, as if she were afraid he'd overhear. Fred chittered in agreement. "Mother can barely stomach the sound of his name without going red."

"Your mother acts like that when she hears Frigid's name too. She's temperamental. And I'm proving a point." I rested against the crowbar and squinted at them.

Okay, it was more of a scowl.

"But your point is already proven. Look at what you've done. They're going to see all of this," Fantasia swept her arm over the destruction. "They're going to know you're strong. They'll know it when they find Tipper. They will know. You needn't do anything more. We can leave now, and get away."

"How much strength do you think he's going to have?" I spat. "He's been underground for decades, sealed in a box, without fresh air, nourishment, space to move. His muscles have probably atrophied. Think about it." I tapped the side of my head, my whole body going nuclear. I could feel my eyes heat up. "Are you gonna help heal him? Give him strength?"

She shook her head vigorously.

"Then drop it. He'll be as weak as a kitten."

"You don't know that."

I shot her a warning look and she turned away, a bright pink resting in her cheeks.

"I'm letting him out," I said with finality. "I can't *not* let him out."

They settled into acceptance, albeit reluctantly.

I maneuvered the crowbar tightly into its prying position, and yanked. Hard.

And then I did it again.

When I glanced up, I spotted a sparkle in Fantasia's eyes. She was hoping it would be unyielding. I snorted at her with derision and she had the decency to look away.

It made me stronger. Two more hard hits and it popped and hissed. The whole box quivered under the release as the lid unsealed.

One of the girls gasped. It was anticlimactic, we hadn't even begun to really experience a show. I glanced at Fantasia—I still hoped she'd heal him, perhaps she'd see a shell of a man and take pity—for the one thing I could rely on was her soft spirit. Her compassion could be a liability, but in this case, perhaps it was a vast benefit.

With any luck he could add to the chaos.

That's why I convinced her to come.

Dreams was merely a proxy of support.

But seeing Fantasia now, it was clear as day she wouldn't help. With an equal expression of fear and disdain, there would be no convincing. She grabbed the edge of her patchwork cloak and fiddled with the seam.

Dreams smacked her bubblegum.

Again.

I shoved the cover off to the side, it groaned and scraped. And then it was done.

What I found underneath was something of which horror stories are built on.

The man they swore was dead was in front of me.

He didn't look much alive. But he certainly wasn't a corpse. And his head, with gaunt cheeks, hollowed sockets, and a bushel of wildly grown hair, was clearly still attached to his neck.

His eyes were closed, clasped into a tight pinch, perhaps to level his sensations against the sudden onslaught of intense light and sounds.

I could sense traces of translucency. There was fight left.

But he was a dying ember.

The scent of body odor, neglect and other bodily functions floated to the surface. It took all I had not to gag.

He remained still as a statue.

But he was alive.

"He's knocked out, right?" Dreams said. She smacked her gum. "Cause he looks dead."

"He's alive. I can see it."

"Really? Because I can't see anything."

I turned toward her. "I can tell when someone's alive or not. It's not an overly complex observation."

"Are you saying I'm not capable of such observations?"

"If the shoe fits, who am I to argue?" I arched a brow. She turned hers in.

I continued to stand over him, straddling the coffin, one leg on each side waiting for him to do something. Anything.

But the guy was frozen.

I leaned over and snapped my fingers in front of his face—it was a dick move, but one that was strongly rewarding.

He winced, but held course.

His sensory overload was in full throttle.

Screw him and his sensitivities. I didn't have time to coddle his pain, not when the city was ready to blaze. I leaned down and grabbed the front of his shirt.

"Careful," Fantasia said.

"Shut up," I hissed back.

She scoffed.

I smiled.

Urrel flinched.

I shook him, hard, and when his eyes opened, locking on me, I was instantly bested for they weren't what I was expecting. I assumed I had the upper hand, bracing for a stranger succumbed to decades of neglect and rage. He was to be completely unfamiliar. Only I was wrong.

I recognized him.

It was his eyes. The color matched Thorn's and the shape matched Chanticlaim's.

Paternal heritage staring at me.

He took in a wheezy breath, his focus acute, and if I ever saw evil, this was it. I refused to show weakness and managed a smile—it rested in an unhinged manner. He scanned my face, trying to decipher me.

The cogs churning, his gaze raked over my pale hair, my eyes, the pallor of my complexion. Micro-nuances in his face hinted his interest and a token of understanding. He seemed to be on the hunt for my powers, to see where I was assigned.

And although I was only one-half of a very small clan, a marginal twitch indicated recognition. I may have been a stranger, but the tokens of my gift left traces.

Or maybe it was the light in my aura. Ruth had been right; to hide it was a waste.

And to hold back in the presence of Urrel could very well prove dangerous. He was the beginning of Narivous, selecting and recruiting the strongest. It would make sense he'd measure the mark of another through potential power.

Even if he didn't know my clan, that subtle tick was something.

It could very well have been respect.

Or gratitude.

He quickly moved on—taking stock of his surroundings.

He looked beyond me, to Dreams and Fantasia, and where he clearly did not recognize me, there was familiarity with them. His pale face blanched, in particular when he landed on Dreams. She looked like Camille, perhaps he was seeing her through her visage.

His hands flexed into fists—it was his first real movement aside from his eyes.

I put my face very close to his, we were only a breath apart, and then I spoke quietly into his ear.

"I've got shit to do," I said. "And you have two kids that need some serious straightening out."

He groaned, my whispered voice too much for his pained canals.

I climbed out of the hole.

He remained there, staring. Not moving. Too weakened to do more than breathe.

And then a spark lit.

Apparently, there was still fire in him.

"I think it's time for some revenge, wouldn't you agree?" I asked.

Urrel's teeth were surprisingly white. He slipped them into a smile. It must've taken a fair amount of force, because it was slow growing. But when it fully materialized, I realized I liked the cut of it.

It was markedly the most evil thing I'd ever seen.

Needless to say, he agreed.

Revenge would feel pretty damn nice.

Now it was time for our second step.

CHAPTER 27

ESCAPE PLAN

We left Urrel right where we found him. He was, as I expected, too weak to move. He barely flinched as we fled, that mad smile still plastered on his lips. Both Dreams and Fantasia were quick to get away and they ran at a fast clip until we made it back to the city.

Our party dissolved. Dreams went one way, Fantasia and I another. Using Fantasia's Animal instincts, we hustled into our waiting spot, avoiding detection.

Fred helped too.

He was our eyes.

I tried not to think about the last time this scenario played out.

How it didn't work in our favor.

"I don't much care for this plan," I whispered to Fantasia, who was tucked in next to me inside the hedge maze.

"Well, I didn't care for your plan, but I helped."

"Barely," I snorted. "You just stood there."

"And offered moral support. This is our plan and I expect the same cooperation."

"To just stand around and offer moral support?"

"You know what I mean." She hesitated. "Do you think we should tell someone about Urrel?"

I gave her an incredulous look. It warped my features. "Are you out of your mind? Who would we tell?"

"Mom? Polar?"

"We need them to focus on this. Besides, you saw him, he was damn near mummified. It'll take a long time for him to crawl out of that hole." I shot her a sideways glance. "No thanks to you."

"I wasn't going to heal him."

"Clearly." I shook my head. "You let rumors guide you. You of all people should know how misleading stories can be."

She cleared her throat.

"His energy was off," she said.

"It was stale. Different thing."

"No. Not stale. Off. Wrong and completely unbalanced."

"And we could've used that unbalance. Do you realize what a glorious distraction he could've been?" I asked. "He could walk in that gate and no one would even know we existed."

"He'd be a liability and you know it. The man is rumored as being one of the greatest Telekinetics this city has ever seen—and I heard he used his powers to snap humans backwards."

"Humans, maybe. But not Velores."

"But he could."

"I don't think anyone is that strong." Not even Chanticlaim. I conjured up the memory of him in the lab. Yes, he was strong—but he wasn't *that* capable. There was a marked difference between humans and the undead.

"Let's hope you're right," Fantasia murmured. Annoyed, I knocked her shoulder, and she met my gaze square on.

"You act like you're going to be here to see it play out—which you won't. So drop the subject."

"Polar will be here."

"And that's his choice."

"I was just expressing—"

"Drop it."

She bit her lip and we sat in silence.

The sun was in a state of kissing the horizon, fading to twilight. Bugs whizzed about our heads, and leaves fluttered. The smell of cool, damp soil and an impending thunderstorm hung thick.

"I hope this works," Fantasia said.

I smiled and bit back my reply. Hope was a word I didn't have much confidence in. I wasn't going to stake our lives on it. I was going to make it happen.

No matter the cost.

We would leave a scar on this city.

Polar may have not wanted more death, but I understood it was a necessity. Thorn was right about one thing: fear was a fantastic incentive for obedience.

I would serve as a warning.

"Your mom should be back by now."

"Patience," Fantasia murmured.

And then the sky exploded with a flock of birds, and the air shifted. From far away, a roll of thunder rumbled.

It's as if the atmosphere knew we were going to war and summoned the appropriate weather.

Above us, Fred waited patiently.

Polar had laid out the details of what was to come. "No more death," became his mantra. He spoke it over and over, looking at me with nearly every utterance.

Camille had left to get us a car. She'd have to park it far enough away from Narivous to not attract attention. It couldn't come from the garage, but would have to be stolen from somewhere local. She had her eyes on the surrounding camping spots.

My fear rested on Polar, who refused to leave.

Because after tonight, there were going to be consequences.

"Twilight seems like an odd hour to do this..." I wanted darkness to envelope us.

"Not really. They're on edge, and they know if anyone acts up, it'll be nighttime. This is early enough to catch them off guard, but late enough that we can have some cover. That, and we can't have it too late, otherwise our distraction will look odd."

I nodded, not necessarily because I felt comfortable, but to greet the silence.

That's when Fred chirped and swooped. We both stood and she reached for me. "This is it," I said.

"Yeah. This is it." We both hesitated, and then we let our emotions die away. She pressed the length of her body against my own. I wrapped my fingers into her hair and she pulled into me, urging me closer. We kissed and when we came up for air, she whispered, "No matter what happens, we regret nothing."

"They'll get what they deserve."

She smiled against my lips.

Camille came barreling into the maze, Dreams close on her heels. They both appeared breathless, exhausted. "The car is waiting," Camille said. She handed over a vial of Purple Magic. I quickly tucked it away. "I think we're all set."

"Did you find out who's on guard duty outside Thorn's room?"

Camille shifted.

"Who is it?"

"Cheetoh and Jaguar," she replied.

On standard occasions, hearing Jaguar on duty would've

been enough to make me sag with relief, but this was different.

Hurting him, even through accidental means, would break something deep and irreplaceable within myself.

"I know," Camille said. "Jaguar complicates things. As much as I hate that she-devil and her spawn, Jaguar is one I like. I want him knocked out." She turned to Fantasia. "And I want it done quick; otherwise ... he's going to have to make a horrible choice. Our heads or his."

Dreams called Fred to her fingertips and she stroked softly down his spine. He ruffled his feathers in soft contentment. Of all of us, he was the least nervous. "I'll help," she said. "I can keep him distracted—you just worry about Thorn."

"What about Lacey? You can get her out, right?" I looked directly at Camille. "I can't leave without Lacey."

Whereas Polar preached no more death, I preached not leaving Lacey behind.

Camille did a flippant swipe of her hand.

"Yes, yes," she muttered—without much conviction. "First Torti and then Lacey."

"You'll personally see to it?"

"Torti's life is in danger, not Lacey's. May I remind you of who we should be focusing our energy on."

"Lacey is equally important. You will get her out or you will not have my help."

Camille lifted her brow and arrogantly followed, "Or what? Hmmm? Tipper is dead. You can't remain here. Lacey is under the protection of Dolly, and therefore safe, regardless of your actions tonight. Torti, however, is in immediate danger."

"I'll get her out, Daniel. I promise you," Fantasia cut in. "We won't leave her."

Camille turned away and tugged on the hem of her cloak. "We need to go," she said. "Follow me." We darted into the grove flanking the castle and ran all the way towards the back.

There was nothing special about the area. No statues to look at, no pavers to follow, only a collection of bare dirt and leaves.

Fred continued to be our lookout. He flew as high as the low-hanging tree cover would allow. Dreams kept her eyes trained on him, only to catch me gazing at her.

"You should pick less colorful birds for this type of thing."

"I didn't know I'd be doing this type of thing," she shot back.

"Shut up and keep a proper lookout," Camille ordered. A few bats surfaced, weaving around Fred.

Dreams shimmered under the failing light. "Fred's scouting, Mom. He's got this." She reached her arms up as if she could touch him.

I suppose it wasn't just Fred who was relaxed. Dreams was starting to get comfortable too.

She was confident.

Perhaps in her abilities and her peculiar strength.

I wanted to ask her how she did it, how it felt, and then I realized I already knew.

It was much the same as my poison. It told me what to do —even more importantly—it made me want to do it. All I had to do was surrender to the call.

Camille got on her knees and started to search with her hands. It took a breath or two before her fingers hooked on a small metal clasp and lifted.

"They put this in, in case Thorn ever needed to make a quick getaway. It's a secret few know about."

It made me wonder how she knew about it. Beneath the camouflaged lid, there was a black steel door, with a reader. In case it was ever discovered, not just anyone could breach it.

She motioned with her hand, and I placed Urrel's fingerprint glove—something I was in charge of holding since it acted as a repellent—over the reader.

"Whatever we do, we can't lose this," she said, giving me a cross look, "and see to it, you don't ruin it either."

She shook her head, indicating the glove. "Figures Chanticlaim would come up with such an idea." Her lips twisted, and then she dropped down. We all followed suit, slithering into the darkness of a long, low-hanging tunnel. When I closed the door behind us, the light faded to nonexistent. Even my perceptive eyes struggled to make out the shapes in front of me. Fred's vibrancy reduced to a tinged shadow. The temperature dropped ten degrees as the stone capsule seeped moisture, neglect, and forgotten time.

Camille didn't hesitate.

"Come with me," she whispered, and started through the corridor as if she had it memorized.

We slashed gossamer spiderwebs and found slippery footholds as we moved like thieves in the night. I held up the back, my poison rising to a clambering thrum.

The tunnel splintered midway; three exits, all as dark and depthless as the one we were in. This is where we froze. Where we were supposed to wait. For nightfall to overcome the dying sun, to end twilight and bring in the evening.

For Thorn to retire—hopefully with a sleeping pill in hand.

Camille wrapped her arms around herself as the time ticked on. She pulled out a watch and checked the time.

This was the worst part.

Waiting.

Minutes. An hour. All of eternity. It passed slowly and painfully.

Meanwhile, we hoped our excuses would hold and our absences would pass unnoticed.

Camille and Dreams were on a supply run.

Fantasia had taken heavy sedatives to sleep away the

horror of Torti's confinement and was holing up in her rooms, or cave—it didn't matter where.

I was in the lab with Chanticlaim.

We continued to wait.

"Do you think that sleeping agent she requested is kicking in?" Dreams asked.

Camille shook her head, noted the time.

The silence felt all ugly.

Fred chittered—an extension of Dreams.

Camille checked the watch again and let out a deep sigh. She nodded and indicated we should all hold hands.

"I want you to be careful," Camille said. She made sure to look at all of us. When she landed on me, the thrum in my gut purred. "If you fall into trouble, get out. Run. Don't wait for the others. If you can't make it to the car, remember our designated meeting spot tomorrow at nine in the morning."

Mick's Grocery.

The memories of yesteryears and the melancholy of a simpler life struck. Write-ups, work schedules, banality. I missed it. Fantasia, as if she could really read my mind, squeezed tightly.

"Except for me," I said. "If anyone gets into trouble, call for me—"

"No," Camille said. "You too. I want you to run. You're our insurance out on the road."

"As your insurance, I want you to call for me. To scream." I looked at Dreams. At Fantasia. "Do whatever it takes. Send Fred. Anything. And I'll be there. No one," I locked onto Camille, "gets left behind." Camille didn't speak, but I could see her working up a fight. "They can't beat me," I told her.

"Anyone can fall, Daniel," she said. "You can't beat them all."

"I'll take out more than most," I answered.

She sighed.

"Hopefully it won't come to that." She let go, breaking the formation. "Follow the plan, and fight like your life depends on it."

"Because it does," Fantasia muttered.

Dreams lifted her hands and felt the air. For the distraction.

"They're getting closer," she murmured.

"Is Frigid walking the corridors?"

Camille bared her teeth without even realizing it. It was a tick of pure reflex. She quickly wiped it away, replacing it with something more presentable.

"She's walking the corridors," Camille said. "Polar has seen to it."

Because that's how they were going to work the distraction. Make it look like Frigid had lost control. Back in the Ice Quarters, when Polar went over the details, he outlined why it was necessary and not corrupt.

"We only need them to think it's her in the beginning," Polar had said, "so we can get Torti and not send the city up in arms. Afterwards, they'll know it was Dreams but until then, this is our way of causing a diversion and making it look innocent." He ran his hands through his hair. "It'll work. It will work," he repeated. "Tensions make Frigid act out, and she loves Torti. The guards won't sound the alarm, they'll try and make it go away before too much time has passed. Besides, she's done it before; people will believe she's done it again. Frigid would be honored to be a part of saving her, even if it's in name only."

Everyone nodded. No one in particular felt good about it.

But it was a plan. And there was promise.

And that's what we were riding on as we took the corridor snaking to the right, weaving along the ancient passageways, until we reached a door that opened to Thorn's massive closet.

I think we all took a collective breath.

It was time.

I handed the glove to Camille, who held it uglily between her two fingers as if contaminated. She passed it to Fantasia, who took the liberty of slipping it on and stepping up to the reader.

What would Camille say if she knew what we had done? That we'd released Urrel?

I was right to hide it from her.

I removed my cloak, shirt, and gloves, remembering to place the orders for my casket into my back pants pocket.

Camille had warned me seeds were planted all over her apartment. Just because I didn't see any vines, didn't mean they weren't there, ready to grow on command.

She nodded in approval—my skin would trump her plants. "Remember, if she wakes up before the sedation takes place, do whatever it takes to quiet her. I don't care what. We need time to get to the top of the tower and get Torti out."

"Is the area clear?" I asked. I glanced at the hidden door above us. What was directly over it? Furniture? Clothes? Shoes? The odds of it being bare seemed unlikely.

"We had a little help this afternoon, you should be fine," Camille said. "Be fast, we'll be waiting for you up top."

Dreams was holding her hands toward the ceiling, no doubt feeling for her distraction.

Fred danced with nerves, but he didn't squawk.

"Good luck," Fantasia said.

"You too," I replied.

Neither one of us said goodbye, for failure wasn't an option.

She kissed me and put her hand on the sensor. The door popped open with a slow hiss and I hopped up, moving with a silent stealth that would've impressed an Animal.

There were two pairs of shoes close to the entrance point, one teetered on the edge before slipping into the underbelly of the crawlspace.

Fantasia's reflexes caught it before it made impact. She handed it to me and we locked eyes one final time.

We were well beyond words; we couldn't share them even if we wanted to. She nodded and I carefully sealed the door behind me.

I kept low to the ground, crouched under silk and satin, and carefully counted to one-hundred.

Only then did I start to move.

Thorn's closet was opulent and lush, with high angled ceilings to accommodate gowns with long trains. It was chock full of grace and expense, artfully designed and carefully arranged.

I did not belong here.

On the far wall was a vault door where her jewels were kept.

She was more concerned of thieves than she was of assassins.

The scent of cedar and roses crept around the room; it had an intoxicating power.

I was breathing in her essence.

And found myself loving her—despite the betrayal and broken pieces—knowing my affection for her would destroy me.

She'd seen me and I scared her. Dammit if it didn't get my blood moving in a way I wasn't fully prepared for.

It was an honor for her to notice.

It didn't matter if her view was shadowed by corruption—eternity in her darkness was greater than the light in her absence.

She was my Queen and I would love her—right up until I took her decrepit heart.

I would be her last sight, and in a perverse sort of way, we'd be tied together.

My fingertips tingled.

I carefully walked to the door, padding over lush carpet and achingly turned the handle.

Thankfully, Thorn's rooms were carefully attended. Hinges oiled, doorknobs smooth, every fathomable comfort and accommodation considered and provided.

Nothing was too good for her. It made me smile.

Such contradiction: to hate someone and love them in equal measure.

I stilled as soon as the door slipped an inch, and took a grounding breath. My fingertips tapped along my pocket where the vial of Purple Magic sat. I closed my eyes and beckoned a lone poison particle.

It drifted into the room, reaching and reacting.

I could sense the silence, the lack of awareness.

It told me what I needed to know: Thorn was asleep.

The room was thick and dark, heavy curtains concealing most of the light. I moved swiftly to the side of her bed, and found myself split in half on what I was set to do.

Her chest rose and fell with contented breaths, as the sleeping agent she took kept her deep in sleep.

The Purple Magic would help her into a coma.

I called the poison back and it returned to its place, settling beneath my larynx.

Then I remembered the sitting room that acted as a partition. Was the door locked? It would stall the guards if they heard a struggle and tried to come in.

Seconds most likely, but even mere seconds would be of great help.

I stealthily went to the other side of the room and carefully turned the knob. I poked my head in. The sitting room was dark and—more importantly—still. I spotted the lock on the exit already in place.

I began to shut the door when a voice leaked in from the Throne Room. My hand froze.

"I think Thorn's up," Jaguar whispered. I stopped breathing. The Animals and their ears could pick up on the most subtle of nuances. It wasn't Thorn I was worried about, but them. I didn't flinch. I didn't breathe. I ceased to exist.

"Do you smell that?"

Shit.

The irony didn't skip past me it was Jaguar who picked up on the indistinct shift. The guy who could sleep in the middle of class and died of boredom during every session was sharper than he let on.

And then Jaguar and Cheetoh called out in surprise—but it wasn't at me.

Cheetoh said, "What's that—"

Jaguar said, "Weird—"

And then the soft, clouded steps of moving feet.

Dreams' distraction had arrived.

I closed the door, flipped the second lock and then returned to Thorn's bed.

The sedative she was on was strong. She didn't stir.

And then I pulled out the order. I unfolded it cleanly and glanced at the signature. It spurred a heaviness in me and I crumpled it into a ball. I had my directions, to make it quiet and clean—but that didn't fit right. They wanted her to sleep, unharmed, while we made our getaway.

I popped the cork on the sleeping vial and carefully hovered the powder over her face.

Outside Thorn's door, I collected fragments of Dreams' chaos. Jaguar laughed while Cheetoh swore a vocabulary that'd put a sailor to shame.

Above it all, climbing higher than the voices, was a beating noise. The tempo fast and panicked. A phenomenal distraction.

Their shouts were getting louder, the beating intensified, and the swearing gained volume. I started to pour the powder on her face—as instructed by Polar—one hand gripping the glass, the other still holding her traitorous order.

I was torn as I administered it.

I could pretend while she was asleep that I still loved her. I could manufacture excuses. I could argue she had no choice.

The commotion continued to grow.

And then the crash happened.

A loud shattering broke beyond the walls; it was either in the Throne Room or the Skull Hallway.

Then it happened again.

And again.

Each hit was loud, obnoxious, and alerting.

Thorn's eyes popped open and I was left staring down at her.

And my hate flashed. Every positive attribute of hers voided. She blinked at me, orientating herself to the moment, and then rage rippled off her.

If auras could burn, I'd be nothing but ash.

"How dare you—" she said, as she started to sit up.

I snapped. *How dare I? How. Dare. I?* I lunged and threw her violently back on the bed. I jumped on top of her and straddled her torso. She was quickly working up her anger, but she wasn't one to scream. Too much sovereign training got in the way. It was an unqueenly thing to do, and she'd be damned if she dropped her supremacy in front of me.

Shrieking like a peasant was never an option.

"How dare I?" I hissed, leaning down to match her black gaze. The whispering of vines slithered along the stone floor. She would try to pin me with them, and I would, in turn, erode them to dust. "You traitorous bitch. You think I don't know what you did?" And before she had a chance to spit out an answer, I reacted without even realizing the plan.

The one I had set all along.

I took her order for my casket, clenched it tight, and shoved it deep in her throat. She thrashed against me, any hold on decorum officially bucked by the violation.

"You were going to bury me alive," I spat. And with every word, I grew stronger. Angrier.

Skin to skin, I was stronger, more painful, all my flesh piercing points. I fought with keeping the Purple Magic upright.

I grabbed at her face and she winced, her face blackening around the perimeter of my fingertips. She beat at me, her fury translating into a burst of power.

"You can never bury me," I hissed, and then dumped what was remaining of the vial on her face, focusing it on her nose, pinching her mouth closed over the wadded-up paper.

It gagged her, and I stilled her.

But before she lost the light, her eyes broke a fraction of their translucency. I was left looking at the Thorn I recalled with fondness.

Part of me still loved her.

For as much as I hated her, I was beginning to understand her. Which was the most dangerous revelation of all.

Understanding can make the villains victims.

And vice versa. Not all victims grow into heroes.

Sometimes their trauma transforms them into darkness.

Which meant we were all capable of falling.

Not that I had long to contemplate.

The guards had heard and I could hear the door to the small entry room cave in.

They were coming for me.

CHAPTER 28
RUN

Thorn, knocked out cold and her body convulsing from ravaged nerve endings, withered in the darkness as rot bloomed around her mouth. It seeped over her skin—the powder was mercifully stronger than the poison's reach.

"My Queen!" Jaguar shouted and I winced at both the sincerity and volume.

I figured the war must've started with the huge ruckus in the skull corridor. Our cover had to have been blown.

At least, I assumed it was. The door to the small sitting room had been infiltrated, but not the actual apartment.

The latches still held, despite the assault of anxious fists. Maybe they didn't know it was Dreams and not Frigid.

"Is everything alright?" Jaguar shouted. "My Queen?" Jaguar called out again. "My Queen, please! I'm going to break down the door if you don't answer! Please answer!"

His voice grew to a pitch, feverish and full of panic.

"Why is everything happening right now?" he hissed under his breath.

Cheetoh obviously wasn't with him—otherwise he would've busted in on pure undiluted instinct—which made me nervous. That meant he was somewhere else, and somewhere else could be anywhere.

Even near Lacey. Fantasia. Dreams.

The knob continued to rattle, and I swept my head from door to closet, unsure which course I should take.

The door cracked around the frame as the beating intensified. Jaguar called out, "My Queen," for the umpteenth time, a scratched record, growing more ear piercing with every hiccup. Desperation had closed off the rest of his vocabulary.

He was holding out hope all was okay.

When things were certainly not okay.

Jaguar showed remarkable restraint, however, and stopped himself from causing unnecessary destruction.

Ever the optimist.

The sitting room was enough damage for one night.

Although this door was starting to fracture.

"Please!" Jaguar continued, and I saw his shadow flash in the shallow space from floor to door. It was Jaguar's irresoluteness that allowed my cogs to rotate. "Tell me it was a nightmare. Just one of your nightmares." I looked back at the sleeping Queen.

Thorn had Nightmares?

Her body clenched under my gaze, as an onset of pain rolled through her.

The door flexed. The casing splintered as the panel absorbed the full shock of an unrestrained punch. "I'm breaking down—"

A *thwap* stunted his sentence, followed by a *thud* as his heavy flesh crumpled to the floor. Light no longer leaked from the adjacent room—his body was now blocking it.

"Hurry, open up." Camille's voice was barely above a whisper, and I undid the latches on the door.

They had made quick progress. Torti stood in the empty Throne Room, while Camille crouched over Jaguar and the splintered remains of the door casing, a red welt bloomed along the crease of his hairline as she poured Purple Magic down his throat. Dreams stood with her back to us, facing the direction of the skull corridor, her arms up, her aura on flare.

I could see where they entered.

The fingerprint glove had gotten them into the Throne Room through the walls, the ancient passageways now our greatest cover.

How they managed to bridge the gap between the tower and the tunnels was beyond me. But it hadn't mattered. They were able to disappear when it counted.

And not having to wade through the chaos in the skull corridor was enough to divert blame.

Maybe that's why the commotion, the voices, weren't panicked.

Annoyed, yes. But far from panicked.

Whatever was happening still fell on Frigid's shoulders.

But the glove was nowhere to be found. Neither was Fantasia. I looked for her and Camille crossed her arms. She glared, making her brow so heavy, her face pinched from the weight of it.

"She's on your fool's errand," Camille snarled. "I had no time—"

"Fool's errand—" I snapped, cutting her off. "How can you call saving my innocent niece a fool's errand?"

"I told you not to worry. She's protected."

"Leaving her here was never an option and you damn well know it."

Torti, although in some deep dark place, broke our battle. "Please stop," she said, the words a bare utterance. "Please."

It took a moment to process Torti. To *really* see her.

She had a fresh cut across her chin, blood spotted around the edges. She looked like she'd aged eons since this morning, as if a lifetime had passed, not mere hours. She'd lost her confident sheen.

Everyone aside from Dreams had bags on their backs. Polar must've packed them. They looked damp, as if they'd been in a room with too much ice.

Two spares sat on the floor by Camille's feet. She tossed me one and I put it on.

I silently started counting in my head, desperate to grasp the time lapse.

Camille watched the door, her foot tapping with annoyance. "Stupid boy," she muttered. Torti did little but freeze in a stupor. I wondered, briefly, if she'd have it in her to run.

Had the time in the tower really disintegrated her that much? Or did something else happen?

She looked at me, blinking, but empty.

"C'mon, Fantasia," Camille said. Dreams continued her incredible force of power. Her aura blazed like nothing I'd seen before; it switched hues, transforming to tinted ice. It radiated off her.

Aside from the noise beating in the hallway, the occasional crash and shatter, we were enshrouded in screaming quiet, just the four of us, well, five, if you counted Jaguar beneath our feet.

"I'm going to get her," I stated, just as a patterned knock came through. Camille ran for the door, undid the lock, and Fantasia slipped in.

No glove. No Lacey.

My heart plummeted.

Camille latched the seals back in place, securing us for the time being.

A small whitish colored piece of stone came in with her; I recognized it as a sliver of bone.

I knew what the crashing noise was.

Skulls had slipped—and were continuing to slip—from their place on the high shelves. Thorn's collection in shambles.

Fantasia's whole body sagged with exhaustion.

"Where's Lacey?" I asked.

Her lavender eyes grew big. "I'm so sorry, Daniel. She's gone. She wasn't in her rooms."

"I can't leave her."

Fantasia's presence in the hallway was enough to tip our hand. I think our secret was out. The clambering in the hallway grew to a fever pitch. Voices joined the frantic cacophony.

Banging started to occur on the Rose Door.

"Dreams!" Camille called, and she turned, eyes ablaze. "We have to go now," she ordered.

We were to leave the same way we came in.

But I wasn't going anywhere. "You guys go without me," I said. I glanced at the door opposite us. Where it would lead me to skulls and mayhem. "I'll meet you at Mick's, but I'm not leaving her behind."

"You can't leave *us*," Fantasia said. "She's not here. She's gone. There's no trace of her." She tapped her nose, indicating how she searched.

"I'll find her."

"Dolly has her hidden," Camille snapped. "You won't find her."

"Why would Dolly have her hidden? Did you tell her about—"

"Of course I did! Don't be daft! She's the one who arranged

the furniture and gave Thorn an extra dose of sleeping medicine in her tea. It was an exchange."

"How could you—"

"She needs to stay out of this!" Camille said. "It's about to get a whole lot deadlier and you want us to bring a child into the mix?"

That twisted me.

The door to the Throne Room shook on its hinges. Everything about it was weakening. The frame. The panel. The knob. The lock.

"Our advantage is officially up," Camille said. "We have to go now."

I hesitated. Fantasia strapped the spare bag to her back, and then reached for my hand. "Dolly is the keeper of children. She's safe. We have to go!"

The door started to flex.

It was time, whether I liked it or not.

Fantasia tugged abruptly and I went with. Every part of me screeched. Raking my bones.

Camille led the way, all of us stepping over Jaguar's limp frame and into Thorn's room. Torti sealed the only remaining lock. We scurried past Thorn's bed, each chancing a solitary glance. No one was exempt from the shudders as we bolted for the closet. Camille lifted the trap door and ushered us below. Dreams, and Fantasia landed quickly, followed by Camille—who had to help Torti—and then I followed suit, slamming the door behind us.

I managed to grab my discarded shirt, finagling it on, and rearranging the pack.

All the while fleeing at a breakneck speed.

Dreams continued her hold. Working her powers in tight flexing motions. She was shining bright enough she lit the way as we sped through the cold corridors, our footsteps slapping stone. Hearts matching our hurried breaths.

We reached the exit and we all leapt up and out.

The air was cool. Crisp. And electric.

Not only from the incoming thunderstorm, it rolled with powerful waves, but from the state of the city. Narivous was slowly coming awake, despite our placement in nightfall.

I chanced a glance at the castle and went slack-jawed.

The noise in the castle was so much more. It was swirls and shifts. It was a tornado of feathers and beaks.

Dreams' distraction wasn't contained, it was out of bounds. It touched everything.

It was, essentially, pandemonium.

They weren't just in Thorn's Throne Room, or even the Skull Corridor.

They were everywhere. They encompassed the night sky.

They surrounded the walls.

They shrunk the trees, the plants, the foliage through their sheer volume.

A thumbnail moon, barely visible through the tree cover, gave off enough light to showcase owls and bats circling the castle. Then there were the spots of color—red, blue, and white. Robins, blue jays, doves joined the lot. Nocturnal and diurnal flocking the fortress, slapping their wings, anxious to make their way in.

It was astonishing.

This level of power, of hold, could only belong to a Seven. This felt like Frigid.

I wondered if maybe some of it was.

None of it mattered though.

I could spot winks of light from the castle, but with each passing tick, more windows lit up, more bodies stirred.

The girls scaled over the spiked top fence like practiced

javelin athletes. I was at their heels, avoiding the nick of sharpened pikes, leaping with an arch so not even the tips whispered against my skin. We landed on the other side. I followed the sight of trailing backs as we bolted through the forest.

Fantasia stayed in the lead, the quickest of the bunch, but the girls with their strong running legs gave excellent chase. Dreams released her hold on the birds, her aura went flat, the tint transforming from vibrant to calm.

We struggled to broaden our gap between us and the city, as branches and roots tried to claim us.

Fantasia would dart to the left and sprint a dozen yards, only to alter her trajectory and return to her previous course, and we—her obedient shadows—followed in her wake. She was sidestepping the statues and their all-telling eyes.

They had to have known now.

The door wouldn't have held for long.

But we wouldn't make it easy, our path. Our course. Under different circumstances, we would've made our run quieter, cleaner, but even the minuscule amount of time lost was an amount of time we weren't willing to waste.

I kept trailing back to Lacey. I should've stayed. What if Dolly couldn't keep her safe? What if I'd just handed Thorn leverage?

But that's when something sang to me. Certainty.

Was it the tether between Ruth and I? The thought bloomed, and overwhelmed.

Worry became an afterthought.

We continued at our unreasonable speed, turning, bowing, shifting.

We were arrows slicing through night.

Pattering—a tempo so faint it was easy to dismiss—gained volume. Fantasia, with her sharp ears, glanced over her shoulder and started to slow. Way back when, back before I'd become a Velore, I would've failed to notice the subtle shift in momentum at such a break-neck speed.

Camille, Torti and Dreams, in tune to Fantasia, pulled our formation tight.

The pattering transformed into the unmistakable beat of footsteps. They were gaining ground. We were nearing territorial bounds, the trees losing their fixed knit, and I could almost smell the roses which grew on the oaks flanking the clearing.

Darkness lightened. We were fixated on the sound of footsteps behind us; we were shocked by the shadow that flickered to the front. The red hair was unmistakable.

As were the claws.

Cheetah lunged for Torti, clipping her skin with the angled tips of talons. Torti let out a shallow welp, as she stumbled forward. Cheetah sidestepped, allowing her to hit the ground at full speed.

"Bitch," Cheetah sneered, her teeth flashing white.

I dove for the demonic ginger and she rolled away in an expert move—landing a high kick into the square of my back, knocking me off balance. I stumbled and she kicked my feet out from under me, sending me towards the dirt. A plume of ash popped up, as someone tossed a fistful of Dexitrol Dust at me. I didn't see where it came from; it simply appeared out of thin air. It hit me, perhaps more powerful than the kick sprung by Cheetah, and I inhaled through reflex and tragic timing, taking in a lungful. One moment the poison was alert and ready, and the next it was dozy and sluggish.

I landed near Torti. Her breathing was wispy, as if she were choking on her own fear. I scrambled to my feet.

And then another plume of Dexitrol Dust rose, like a phoenix from the ashes, only there wasn't any flame.

It hit me fast, and I understood a Telekinetic was nearby. They were assaulting me in an attempt to still my powers.

To prevent my scream.

I wondered who it was.

Two came to mind.

Locus.

Or worse, Chanticlaim.

He could shut me up with any of his pharmaceuticals, use me for his serum—he just needed me alive. Was this his way? To procure the solution, to take over the city, and then have me executed, his secret taken to my grave?

I tried to locate the source and thought about taking my shirt off, to cover my nose and mouth, but there wasn't enough time. And the damage was done anyhow. The toxin wasn't in fighting form.

Cheetah had become a one-woman army, slashing and darting, hitting and slicing. I started towards her, to use my flesh as a weapon, but Fantasia beat me to her and the two became blurs as they lashed out in brutal, immortal fashion. Bones unsheathed as claws spurted forward from tense, angry hands.

It took a moment to realize they weren't Cheetah's.

Fantasia had them too.

All those moments holding her hand, touching her, her touching me, I never even got a wisp of them.

And now they were exposed. Hooked, sharp, and built for tonight. For this battle.

The two moved like lethal dancers swaying to rehearsed choreography. And in the string of chaos, a body slammed into me, throwing me against a tree. Something in my shoulder popped, and the trunk shuddered from the blow. It knocked me hard to the ground.

I only caught the shadow of a woman with dark hair cutting through the night. I knew who it was though.

Her smell was one I would never forget.

Amelia.

The lull, that fall into a tree, absorbed all time—which really was a glimmer of a second—before she pounced.

But Amelia didn't go for me.

She went for the woman she hated most.

Everything happened fast—almost too quick to catalog. Amelia lunged for Camille with reaching claws. She covered meters in a single leap, landing on Camille's back and sending her forward. Somewhere in the fall, a bone snapped in Camille's body. Amelia landed on top of her, flattening Camille to the earth, using all her force to incapacitate her.

Every ounce of rage Amelia had kept bottled up uncorked in that moment. Her piston arms pumped like mad as she pummeled Camille's back, her fists clenched, her talons working as knives, stabbing Camille over every inch of her skin.

Thuck. Thuck. Thuck. Bits of tissue went flying.

Camille let out a haunting wail.

Purple blood spilled onto the soil, saturating the dirt, as Camille's clothing disintegrated to ribbons.

Torti was wrapped up trying to help Fantasia—who, during the attack on Camille—had started to lose ground as her attention turned toward her mother.

I staggered to my feet as Dreams pulled on her translucency, her head tilted towards the heavens, her eyes searching. Spots of birds swooped in, but it wasn't enough. There was too much distance. They were still hanging tight near the castle.

But the ones that came, they dived, pecked and clawed, while Fantasia and Cheetah continued to pummel each other. While Amelia tried to take the life from Camille.

My poison rallied.

I found my feet and lunged into the fight, landing on top of Amelia, and my hands somehow found themselves wrapping around her neck. I tightened and willed as much poison into my fingertips as I could.

Amelia screamed. It bounced off the trees. I held on and felt the rush infiltrate her blood.

And then I was yanked back.

Cheetah threw me—*hard*—and I slammed into a thick trunk. She sprang for me, only Fantasia knocked her off course. When Cheetah landed, it wasn't on her feet. She flopped to her side and her head—like a peculiar gift—was right near my hands.

A dark thought sprang.

It was near poetic, really. Considering how Amelia chose to hurt Camille through her own children, I could do the same.

I stuck one of my thumbs deep into Cheetah's eye socket—the right one to be exact—and felt the membrane give. My poison flooded her system.

I felt it.

All of it.

I tried to grasp her other eye, but she used her hand to cover it.

This wasn't like my time in Thorn's room, when I clamped my hand over her mouth and rotted her flesh as a result. This was different. I willed the poison to take route.

They quickly burned up the Dexitrol. They found their footing.

My toxin was creeping within her, weaving its way through her bloodstream; Cheetah became an extension.

Never had I encountered such a cry.

It was enough to rip Amelia off of Camille. Cheetah, half blinded and in burning agony, took off into the forest, tripping over roots, stumbling over what she could not see. Amelia gripped her own neck, her body flexing in pain as she ran after her.

Both women howled.

I could feel dual connections.

I willed it deeper.

Sound and smell—*everything*—vanished as I cocooned myself with the force of my energy. My poison, living as it was, was now on a wrathful path.

This wasn't like when I killed Tipper, when I destroyed her for preservation.

This was different.

This was revenge. And the poison reacted like acid. It listened to my hate. *It agreed with me.* If Velores were afraid of Thorn's vines, the mere promise of me would break them.

I stood on a precipice, wielding life, issuing death.

They kept moving away, as if the distance would stop the torture.

I laughed.

Laughed.

It came from nowhere, it landed everywhere—a hysteria that climbed and grew. It overshadowed everything in a feverish eclipse.

This was a taste of my ultimate greatness. I was commanding. Superior.

Above them all.

I nestled into my new skin.

It made my thoughts blur.

And the women I'd infiltrated were forced to my will. Each and every particle fed inside them. Parasitic death ready and eager to devour their host.

My skin grew numb as I zoned in on each of my toxins, flexing them, urging their hunger—to take chunks of their victims until it was nothing but remnants.

The only tragic part was distinguishing who was who.

I'd preferred to have focused all my energies on Amelia.

Cheetah was simply a bonus.

My mad laughter slipped into quiet elation as I continued to take my time in slow, cruel waves.

Their lives were almost mine.

With no urgency to my surroundings, time stilled.

I realized, if I wanted Narivous, I could claim it, and no one could stop me.

It was a warming thought, until I was knocked onto the cold ground.

I face-planted into mud that had grown sticky in my haze, and I realized it was from creeks of streaming blood, taken from numerous sources.

JC stood over me, his entire being wracked with emotional turmoil.

"What are you doing?" he asked. "Take it back, take it back." He grabbed me by the front of my T-shirt, and with one swift motion, had me back on my feet. He shook me hard. "You're killing them. You need to pull it back."

"Please," he begged. He let me go, standing over me. "Let them go."

Damn Amelia for having a few good ones.

I released the wrathful grip, all the while marveling that the tether was that clear, hoping it wasn't a one-off. It would create a wonderful lore once we were gone.

I gave a mock bow as the power shifted, hands held wide to indicate acquiescence. My ability to talk had been muted, and I realized the motion would come across as condescending.

There was no help for that.

JC took a step away, betrayal flickering across his features, and disappeared into the forest to tend to my damage.

My whole body was wracked with fatigue. And we still had to run.

And then, from those I could not see, I heard a distress call.

It fell somewhere between a coyote yip and a wolf howl. I'd experienced it before, during training. It would call Velores from every angle, its reach miles depending on desperation.

Our window was closing.

Camille couldn't stand. She was crawling, leaving a trail of blood and tissue.

Amelia had nicked her spinal-cord.

Dreams had earned razor marks across her face.

Torti was bruised and broken.

Fantasia—despite her healing powers—was moving as though her body had betrayed her. She crouched with a shudder and started to lift Camille over her shoulders. Dreams took her other side.

The unseen in the shadows were all but forgotten. They were waiting to ambush—perhaps hoping for greater numbers. It's not every day they see one of the Seven incapacitated.

"I'll fix you when we get out," Fantasia mumbled to Camille. "Just hold on."

I wanted to be the one to carry her, but I looked at my hands, still tingling, and knew there wasn't much I could do. The poison was fatigued and unresponsive.

If I somehow glitched on the suppression, it would most certainly finish her off.

We took off at a run—but our speed was lacking—and the forest began to close in around us.

The others caught up to us in record speed.

And then we were trapped.

CHAPTER 29

OUTCOME

The irony was we could see the break in the trees, where the meadow opened up and freed the sky. But we were too short.

Three men—all of which had a fair level of attachment to our group—emerged. I understood the strategy immediately.

This was their way of getting us in line without too much resistance.

Splint was my neutral, Romeo was Torti's, and Locus—he was power. When we'd sparred before, both of us were worse for wear. But through time, we'd come to respect each other.

And then a fourth joined the fold.

Spark.

He swallowed when he saw me, gave a short head shake. I wouldn't fight him—he wouldn't fight me—but we had to make it look good. Like he was still on Narivous' side and not on mine.

"We're your last lifeline," Romeo said. His voice wasn't strong, it wobbled. "There are others surrounding us and we have been asked to negotiate with you, to take you in peacefully."

He looked toward Torti, and something inside him clenched.

Fantasia gripped Camille, who softly groaned at the pressure shift.

The four fanned out, and with the weight of Camille's injuries, we had no other option but to let them come closer.

Spark stood farthest back. He was stationed behind them, and when he caught my eye, he gave a gentle head rock and lipped the words: that side.

A newly roused army was on one side of us. Only one side. *One*. It told me how to get out. And it put him in a precarious situation.

"They don't want any more blood," Romeo said. "It's best to give up now." He looked directly at me—the only threat left. That, and a hunch told me it was too painful to look at Torti. "Please," he said. "Come with us."

"There will always be blood," I said. I positioned myself so I was front and center. I looked at them all, each and every one shared eye contact.

No one flinched or shied away. That, if anything, was a testament to how far we'd come.

"If we go back, Romeo, they'll kill Torti. Do you want her to die?"

He blanched, and his hands balled into fists. "You don't know that."

"I know it. You know it. We all know it."

He shook his head, as if the action could reverse the truth. "If you keep on this path, you're guaranteed to die. All of you. This is your chance for a semblance of leniency."

"A semblance of leniency?" I laughed. It cut through them. "Surly you don't believe that? You and I both know what waits for us is far from leniency. I won't subject them," I indicated the girls behind me, "to their creative measures of justice."

"Listen, Death," Splint interjected. He ran his hands over his closely sheared hair. He'd gone back to being neat and tidy — all military and certitude. "We are the front men. There is an army in the shadows waiting to come at you. You're strong, but you can't withstand our sheer numbers. You can come with us, peacefully, and perhaps find mercy at the end of this road."

I scanned them. Spark made another lip gesture. It was either "not a lot," or "a lot," indicating numbers. It was too quick to fully grasp—and I cursed myself for not being quicker.

How many were beyond our sight?

I focused inward.

There weren't many.

But there was enough.

The surety of Ruth's gift was clear as day. I didn't need to see them to know. We were outnumbered, but with any luck, we weren't out-gifted.

"There will be no mercy. Stop acting like there will be mercy. I'm sick of that word—because it's a lie—and if you say it again, I won't be held accountable for how I react, understand?" I glanced at the forest behind him. "I'm to die. No matter what."

He shifted and glanced to Locus. Locus stepped closer and said, "I've seen them forgive many atrocities."

"They won't forgive mine—"

"You're useful to our cause; they can perhaps look past what has been done."

I smiled, no one liked how it looked.

"Did you not see Cheetah? Amelia?"

There was a collective intake of breath. They'd seen.

"Tipper is dead too," I added for proper measure. They grew waxen in the slivered moonlight. "There's no coming back from that," I said calmly. "We're leaving and you'd be wise to step away. Go back the direction you came."

They exchanged looks, and I captured Spark's gaze. He nodded. It was full of gloom and acceptance.

He knew what was coming.

I had his reluctant permission. It spoke of his goodness.

"Please," Locus pleaded. "We can't leave." He cleared his throat. "You know we can't leave. We have orders to follow."

"Orders or not, you're not taking us alive." Behind me, Camille groaned. She couldn't withstand more stalling. "If you don't step away," my voice rolled into a rusty growl, "I'm going to feed you some poison. Don't make me do it."

"You'll hit all of us," Romeo said. His eyes slid back to Torti, to Camille. "And we'll all die, including your little posse."

"Well, if we're dead anyway, why would the manner matter?"

The poison was growing in my belly, but it was still dull and expended. I could only manufacture so much. I'd wasted a great deal tormenting Amelia and Cheetah.

The cord that connected me to them was gone. Looking at Locus, I knew who was responsible for peppering me with Dexitrol Dust earlier. He slowly started to glow. There would be more of the suppressing powder to come. I could feel his energy collecting it.

What was beyond our line of sight?

An army?

A pharmaceutical?

An axe?

All of it?

Now I was trying—desperately—to build an army of my own. For there was only one way out, to carve a path—through poison and pain.

I just needed time.

"Why would someone select the most painful of deaths?" Splint said. He was speaking rapidly, the situation quickly unraveling before us. "Your method does matter. Do you really want to destroy us?"

"Do you really want to destroy them?" I pointed behind me, where the girls remained stilled and silent. "Because that's the alternative. We go back with you, they will have us at their leisure, to do as they wish, to torture us as they see fit."

"Executions are done quickly," Locus said. "You've seen for yourself, the axe is fast."

I flashed my teeth. "They won't have anything fast for me."

"You're not going to use your poison," Romeo said. He was inching away, trying to be discreet about it, but every movement in our standoff was embellished. That's what tension does. "You have too much integrity."

"You're right, I do have too much integrity." Romeo seemed to sag. "I have too much integrity to let them take us without a fight, for painful as it may be, there's pride in owning our demise."

"You wouldn't," Romeo said.

"I would."

The trees shook with frenetic energy. It swept along the wind, carried on a breeze. Spark looked behind him. The numbers were growing. The ambush would happen unless I stopped it.

The toxin rattled and clawed. It started up my lungs and churned at the base of my throat.

It was more feral. Untamed.

I didn't have time to break it.

My aura lengthened, and one of the four gasped. The girls collectively pulled in oxygen.

I did as Ruth instructed. I blazed, no longer hiding, and

blinded them with the flare. She had called it; it stalled them and made them shifty.

The others tucked away in the trees couldn't shy away from the vividness. I glowed like neon, and a subtle rustling crept out. There was movement away from us.

That's what my strength did.

That's what her advice got me.

Retreat.

I took a step closer and forced the light bolder.

Preservation had managed a final burst of power. The poison had grown. It felt like enough. Remarkable strength in an attempt to save me.

To save us.

Spark went white and I gave him an apologetic look. Behind me, Camille let out a choked breath.

"Don't do it," Locus said.

But it was too late.

I exploded. I opened my jaw and let the poison free in a scream that was wretched and soul-scraping. It was loud enough the leaves trembled.

It was everything.

It was grief.

Rage.

It was for who I once was.

For who I was becoming.

For all that I lost. Including myself.

Every piece of me went into the air. It hovered over everything. Thrashing resounded through the forest, as Fantasia bolted, Camille clutching desperately on her back, Torti and Dreams right at her heels. The four in front of me remained rooted—aside from Romeo—who was so enamored with his face that he couldn't stand the thought of it being ruined by me. The others were prepared to die for the cause. It was noble really. Spark, who truly had no desire to be a martyr, would fall like the others.

He was a good man.

I regretted what was about to happen.

A swarm of dancing death wove around us, billowing and compliant, thick and curly as smoke tendrils. And then I pushed them, hard. They were awake.

They answered to me.

They hit the three who refused to budge first. It drove enough pain that their wails were reflective of death itself. Then they ran.

Spark amongst them; whether he'd make it beyond my doings was up for debate. I hoped so.

From far away, deep towards Narivous, a small glow arched above the treetops. It carried the scent of ash and char, and it hazed the sky. It lit up the night.

Blocked out the stars.

The largest threat—bigger than escapees—had come to fruition.

Someone had started a fire—friends keeping us safe.

I wasn't going to waste their bravery.

I ran after the girls, forcing my swarms to span out into a veil of armor, drizzling death like an acidic shield. It was a clumsy effort, but it'd have to do.

Anyone going after us would have to go through them.

The girls had already reached the clearing when I realized they weren't moving. I cursed under my breath.

Don't wait for me!

I stumbled into the meadow. They were off to the far side, out of Narivous but close enough to be dragged back in. Their glistening wounds sparkled like glass under the moonlight—a sky that could touch them in a forest in which Thorn didn't control.

There was no car waiting for us either.

Of course not. To park it in the meadow would've been a clear indicator we were up to something. It must've been waiting for us father down the road.

And then my power snapped.

I no longer had hold on my particles.

It was too much. Too great to hold on to.

The effects of the fire were visible from the meadow. We could see the haze beating the sky, giving the forest its own halo. Between my deathly particles and the fire precariously close to their city, we might have a chance of making it out. No one bothered taking in the amber glaze.

Camille was fading on the ground, her aura reduced to a pastel, when she was accustomed to prime colors.

Fantasia's and Dreams' eyes were filmed in a sheen of black. Only Torti remained free of tears.

It was older sibling syndrome—protect the youngest from the truth. When I reached them, I checked my six. We were still in the clear. My death veil would give us time, but not much.

I looked to the girls and realized they weren't waiting for me. They were preparing to leave Camille.

"I can save you," Fantasia muttered, and Camille looked up at her, the light fading with every labored breath.

Camille shook her head, and winced with the movement. "Get out of here," She tried to pull on a smile, but it shaped into a scowl. "Hurry."

The girls didn't move and Fantasia's distraught face landed on my own. "We can't leave her," she said. A pang of fear hit me.

"There's a fire, Camille," I countered. "It looks like it's close to the city. We still have time. We can get you out."

Camille cringed. She looked to Torti and motioned for her to come near.

Torti leaned down and cupped Camille's face. For a moment, I forgot who was mother and who was daughter.

Camille looked at Torti and said, "Read it all and read it quick. I'll make it easy for you." Her smile was soft. "I didn't drink any tea, just in case."

Torti's eyes started to glow, and although her energy was weak, she managed to bristle into her powers. Cracks creeped, shattering her porcelain complexion. Their eyes locked, and the only sound was our breathing and the faint screams locked within the forest.

It clicked in a single instant.

Torti was the Velore mind-reader.

Fantasia did have inside information—it was simply selective to what Torti wanted to share. Chanticlaim was confident in his recruits, never doubtful, nearly braggart—because he had access to a mind telling him everything he needed to know.

And as for the tea—that's why they needed me to stop drinking it. It must've had brain blockers in it. That's how they found my stash. I'd listened just long enough for Torti to read my mind, and discover where my hiding place was.

"I forgave you a long time ago," Torti said, emotion breaking her voice. The whole scene seemed entirely too intimate. I wanted to look away, only I was enraptured.

Camille gave a grateful smile, one that wasn't filled with anguish, and laid her hands on top of Torti's. "I've repaid my debt." Her stilted breath labored with each word. "Go," Camille ordered with her last ounce of strength. "You're running out of time." She looked at Dreams and Fantasia, all fear fading, a warm cloak of peace drifting over us. "I love you," she said. "You're all worth dying for. Don't waste it."

Beyond us, in the forest, the soft tempo of chaos made its

way toward us. There was distance—my stalling strategy was working—but it wouldn't last much longer.

The girls hesitated but a loud snap from the forest brought their attention into focus. They each planted a kiss on Camille's forehead.

Torti was the first to start running, Dreams followed, then Fantasia. I gave one last look at Camille, she was watching the girls flee, a relieved expression flashing over her features. Her limp body softened on a sigh. She met my eyes and said, "Protect them with your life."

I placed my hand over my chest, an oath, and nodded. Her cheeks bloomed with a burst of unexpected life. She gave me a smile that only toyed with her lips and closed her eyes.

The immortal world had worn away its shine a long time ago—she was done.

The girls flew—despite their wounds—they flew. It was as if they didn't want to waste Camille's sacrifice, and their desire to live increased ten-fold. We ran parallel to the road, but not directly on it. Although that would've saved us time, it would've made us too vulnerable, running on a path with no trees to duck behind.

We barreled downward, the slope of the mountain aiding us with its natural descent. Fantasia would throw her head back over her shoulder, watching for movement, listening for noise. We remained grouped, the four of us covering great spans of distance in flickers of time.

When another distress call echoed, we shuddered as a unit. I did my part—feeling for the poison left behind, somehow still attached, although beyond control. Involuntary quakes rumbled along my spine and I wondered if each tremor was a touch that shielded us.

But it wasn't only time working against us. It was distance.

My connection was faltering.

And I was growing weak.

As it was, only pure adrenaline kept me moving.

A glint of green called for us. The car was there, an all-wheel drive station wagon—inconspicuous and benign—with the engine running.

Small miracles make for major wonders. It couldn't have come at a better time.

Dreams dove for the driver's seat and we piled in, not even bothering to remove the bags from our backs or attempting to land with any sort of grace.

Torti took the front passenger seat, Fantasia and I funneled into the back.

I sagged with relief when I spotted what was in the far rear.

Lacey was tucked in the cargo section, knocked out, breathing in shallow stints.

Someone had her cloaked in a blanket. There was a doll resting in the crook of her arm, along with an empty vial holding a rolled-up piece of paper.

Dreams slammed the car into drive and hit the gas pedal with far too much force. We lurched forward. She struggled to maintain control as we took corners at speeds threatening to topple us.

That's when Cheetoh jumped out, along with Amelia. She was at a stagger, but much like my toxic curtain in the forest—preservation, or perhaps pure undiluted rage—seemed to bring a second wind.

The fierceness in her blood, reflected in her face, was enough to sustain her, despite the injuries and black fractures in her neck.

She was out for revenge no matter the cost. They had with them reinforcements, a gaggle of guards, many of which were champions of their clans.

And then spike strips were flung out. Fantasia let out an audible moan.

We would have to stop and pull them. They'd somehow managed, despite the ravaging pace, to one up us. Dreams hit the brakes.

Blood pooled from Amelia's mouth, and the guards—six in total—centered. Cheetoh was the angriest.

Amelia wore a calm lethal expression. The flatness of her face was perhaps more terrifying than the snarl on Cheetoh's.

"Can you pull on your powers?" Fantasia asked.

So much of me was already depleted, I feared the answer.

Amelia stood center of the road, directly behind the spikes, and gave me a smile. Her mouth was all blood and teeth.

"Can you use the birds?" I asked Dreams as the car rolled to a stop.

"Not enough time."

And that's when it happened. A simultaneous string of events that would haunt me.

It started with a scream.

Amelia's scream.

First it came as a shriek of surprise, only to be followed by horror.

She was lifted midair, like a weightless apparition. One moment she was sure-footed, the next suspended feet from the ground. She went horizontal, a force we couldn't see commanding her.

And then she sharply snapped backwards—her spine splintering with an ear-crashing crack.

It rattled the car, or maybe it was the concurrent shudder we all shared at the sudden visible violence.

Her scream faded to a shriek and then stilled, as she crumpled onto the road.

Let go with sudden velocity.

Amelia was a broken heap, convulsing in angry shock waves. Blood pooling from her mouth.

Cheetoh and the other guards held the same state of shock and confusion as we did. They stood in a half-circle around the wounded remains of Amelia, and then, one by one, they too were flung with such force they snapped and splintered.

Cheetoh was first.

His scream matched that of his twin.

He was bent backwards, breaking in half—like his mother. The others were spared and merely dealt with the aftershocks of the violent trauma of being thrown at massive trees.

"Oh no," Dreams said.

We all knew what was happening.

Only one Velore was capable of snapping people in half.

Once the road was clear of guards, the spike strips lifted.

It was a gentle motion. Soft and light, the way a feather travels on a current, and then they glided, like a caress, to a placement behind us.

The entire gathering was gone. Amelia laid motionless in the center of the road.

And that's when our final reveal came.

Urrel.

He stumbled out. Weak and thin, but miraculously present. Rage had given him a burst of energy. His evil showcased in the remains of Amelia and the disbanding of her small battery of troops.

His power was far-reaching. Devastatingly so.

He could reclaim the city if he wanted it.

And there was no doubt he wanted it.

He grabbed Amelia by her arm and seemed to take great joy moving her with his muscles rather than his mind. Physical labor seemingly cemented something deep and wanting inside of him. He pulled her to the edge of the road and let her slump at his feet.

He gave us a bow and then swept his hand across the road, indicating our exit.

The smile he gave us was abhorrent.

We had an ally.

A horrible, effective ally.

Torti grabbed her throat. "What have you done?"

"What we needed to do," I said.

Dreams punched the gas pedal, and then we were gone.

EPILOGUE

The silence expanded with only the hum of the engine to break up the intervals. No one spoke for hours, perhaps too afraid of what would be said.

We stopped only to heal wounds, and even then no words were exchanged.

Camille, although gone, sat between us. Her absence a token of all that was lost.

I kept twisting in my seat, resting my hand on Lacey's shoulder, taking stock in the fact she was real and here. That we'd managed to escape.

Dreams guided the car north and we hit the interstate. Fred chittered along her shoulders and nestled into the sinewy crook underneath her earlobe. His feathers burrowed into her hair, a stain of red in a golden nest.

It wasn't until the sun crested over the mountains that I remembered what was stowed away in the crook of Lacey's arm. I looked behind me for the umpteenth time.

Lacey still hadn't stirred, her chest swelling with soft paced breaths, practiced in a way only a heavy sedation could elicit. I pushed the blanket back and found my stash hidden beneath it. I grabbed the bag and set it in my lap.

"Is that all of it?" Fantasia asked.

I shook my head. "It's more." And it was. Perhaps double.

I looked back at Lacey.

The blanket she'd been wrapped in was wool, scratchy, and lacked the frills of Dolly's room. That in itself was a curiosity.

The fact she was here was another.

I grabbed the doll, along with the small vial and paper.

Dreams watched me through the rearview mirror. "I recognize that," she said. "That's from the cabin. I didn't see you take it."

"Because I didn't." I flipped it over. The stains were still there, black marring half her face, the name Sally stitched across the foot. Aside from the scent of time and forgetfulness, a new trace lingered.

I recognized it and smiled.

I turned the vial over in my hand. It answered so many questions, even before I pulled the paper out.

"What's that?" Dreams asked.

"An empty healing potion."

"How do you know it had a healing potion in it?"

"Because the last time I saw it, it was in the hands of Ruth. She told me what it was. That's how Urrel gained his strength." I rolled it between my fingers, curiously contemplative.

Dreams sucked in her breath.

So did Fantasia.

"Ruth did this?" Fantasia asked, checking Lacey. A smile crept along her lips.

"That means we're safe," Dreams followed. "Ruth knows things."

"For now," Torti mumbled. "Ruth's visions only hold muster for so long."

"Releasing Urrel was mapped out too, then. You realize that. We didn't do anything wrong."

"Just because it's mapped out doesn't make it right," Torti said, curling herself into a tighter ball. Her hair tinted with light, it gave her a halo effect. Fred twittered and perched on her knee. She reluctantly held out her finger and he hopped along it.

From my angle, I couldn't see her smile, but knew it was there.

"You guys knew about Ruth?" I asked. "I kind of got the impression she was a bit of a secret."

Dreams shoved her glasses up the bridge of her nose. They were mirror avatars and they glinted. "Only through forbidden means." She nudged her head toward Torti, who continued to stare out the window. "And say what you will—but if she saw Urrel free, that meant it was supposed to happen."

"Let's hope the outcome is good," Torti said.

"Oh, I doubt she'd encourage a vision that wasn't good."

Torti twisted in her seat. Fred didn't like it and fluttered onto the dash. "Visions are visions. Do you honestly think all futures have positive outcomes?"

"No, but she wouldn't support one that was bad is all I'm saying."

"You make it sound like Ruth is wholly good."

"Are you saying she's not?" I asked carefully.

Torti turned to look at me and winced.

I understood then. She was avoiding me to avoid my thoughts.

Chanticlaim and Tipper were still screeching in my reverie.

"Ruth is a survivor," Torti said acerbically. "She will do whatever it takes to be on the winning side. Whether that side is good or bad is debatable." Her gaze slid to the vial. The paper was still tightly coiled inside of it. “What’s with the paper?” she asked.

I shrugged. “How should I know, I haven’t pulled it out yet.”

“Well then, get on it,” Torti bit out.

“Patience,” I muttered.

She rolled her eyes.

I unfurled it, and blinked. The paper only incorporated one word. It took an embarrassing long stretch of time to compute it.

Torti’s impatience went to my thoughts. She winced.

“What does it say?” Dreams asked.

Fantasia leaned over and spoke it aloud. “It just says ‘yes.’ What does that mean? Did you ask her something?”

“He asked her a lot of somethings,” Torti answered for me.

“I think we need to set up some boundaries,” I shot out. “Can you manage not to break into my head? Otherwise, we’re gonna have a serious problem.”

She tilted her chin in challenge. “Are you threatening me?”

“I value my privacy.”

She turned back around.

“Can you control it?” I asked, through gritted teeth.

“Yes, she can control it,” Fantasia cut in.

“Are you sure? Or are you taking her word for it?”

She bit her lip. She was most certainly taking her word for it.

“That’s gonna be a problem.”

Torti shuddered.

“I won’t be going back to Narivous, Daniel, so it won’t be a problem.”

“And what makes you think I will?”

She didn’t turn, simply pointed and assumed it was at the paper.

"What did you ask Ruth?" Dreams questioned, and when I didn't answer fast enough, she moved onto Torti. "Tell us."

Torti shook her head.

"Something spooked you."

"Lots of things have spooked me," Torti retorted. She twisted her hands in her lap. "Mother among them."

Fantasia swallowed and I put my arm around her shoulders, pulling her tight. She softened like malleable dough.

"We'll make it work on the outside," I said. "Her loss will not be for nothing."

"She was wracked with guilt," Torti said.

"She's been wracked with guilt for forever," Dreams replied. "You forgave her. And you meant it. That's all she ever wanted."

"Do you think she thought I harbored a grudge all this time?"

Dreams shook her head. "I think she was stuck on the past. It didn't matter that we were all okay; she couldn't get beyond how we became a part of Narivous. Well, Torti and Mom, that is. We," Dreams indicated herself and Fantasia, "came later, *obviously*."

"Were we okay?" Torti asked.

"I was happy enough."

"Me too," Fantasia said, even though she was careful to burrow her hand while saying it.

"What am I missing? How did you become a part of Narivous?" I asked. "No one ever told me."

Dreams looked over at Torti. "Tell me what you asked Ruth first."

"I asked her if she could read fortunes," I waved the paper. "Clearly that was a yes."

"That's all you asked?"

"No," Torti answered for me.

"What's the rest?"

"Nope." I folded my arms. "It's your turn. And you need to stay out of my head, Torti. At the very least pretend, even if you're unable to manage a semblance of self-control."

"For someone who melted Tipper, it's pretty bold of you to preach self-control."

"That was an act of self-preservation."

"And what do you think I've been doing?" She snorted. "My existence has always been a great coverup. I've been preserving my safety—and all those around me—practically from the moment I learned to talk."

"Well, not right when you learned to talk. It was all that blabbing that made people suspicious to begin with," Dreams said.

"You're not being helpful. Besides, I was learning to talk. Forgive me for not understanding etiquette while doing so."

"Oh, I don't think an apology is necessary," Dreams said.

"How you manage sarcasm so early in the morning is beyond me."

"I could say the same for you." Dreams flashed her smile and then quickly whipped it away. Fantasia squeezed my hand. Either it was remnants of Ruth or simply a strike of clairvoyance, it was clear—Dreams was partaking in the art of distraction.

To not think about Camille.

And all that was left behind.

The façade could only hold for so long before harsh reality came crashing down. It hit like an iron curtain.

"How many others knew?" I asked to break the awkward silence settling between us.

Torti shrugged. "It's hard to say. I was so little, and despite what Dreams has let on, I learned to curtail it quite quickly.

Either they forgot or they got really good at hiding their truths."

"And then there was the tea," Dreams added.

"Thank the stars for the tea," Torti said. "It made hiding my secret even easier."

"When Tipper made it, did she know?"

"I honestly can't say. I think it was an equal mix of paranoia and insurance. Urrel started to suspect someone could read minds. He often hinted he thought it was me, but no one wanted to side with him because to do so would be to open Pandora's box. He would've unraveled Narivous on his quest to root out a talent he wasn't even sure existed—and being I was a child, I garnered a certain level of compassion. But then he was gone, and it didn't matter anymore."

"And Tipper, either through knowledge, worry, or preemptive strategy, made the tea. I couldn't see into them, and with Mom acting as a partition—I almost forgot I could do it too."

She picked at a hangnail. "Until she began to give me more freedom, and then I remembered."

"How does it work? Can you shut it off?"

"Can you shut off your powers?" she snapped. I could. Sort of. They were a low-level power draw, always on, but not necessarily in operation. Yes, I could shut them off.

Mostly.

I chose to steer the conversation away. "So why did your mom seek your forgiveness? What did she do?"

Torti stilled, and then Dreams, with Fred's twitter of approval, piped up. "I'm going to tell him, okay?"

She shrugged.

"Mom suffered from postpartum depression after Torti was born. When her husband didn't come home one day from work, she assumed she was abandoned."

"But that's not why he didn't come home," Fantasia clarified.

"Yeah. It wasn't until later she learned it was Urrel. He killed Torti's dad and let Mom think she'd been abandoned."

Torti ground her teeth.

"I'd actually forgotten that part," Dreams said, sheepishly. "Maybe we shouldn't have let him out."

"Ya think?" Torti asked.

"Not helpful."

"If it helps, I forgot about it too," Fantasia said.

"That does help," Dreams said.

"No, it does not." Torti flicked her hair with annoyance.

"We were under a lot of stress," Fantasia countered. "What with you being in the tower."

"Stay on topic," I cut in. "So your father didn't come home. Then what?"

Torti turned and shot me a piercing glare.

"Mother, who was on the cusp of heartbreak before he went missing, lost it. She took a pillow and put it over my head —suffocating me in the crib."

"Mother said it was all the screaming," Fantasia murmured.

"Well, Torti is known for never shutting up," Dreams replied.

"Is that supposed to be funny?" Torti asked.

"It wasn't supposed to not be funny." Fred chittered. "Thank you, Fred. I knew you would side with me."

"That's because you're controlling him."

"Even still."

"Would you *please* stay on topic?" I asked.

Torti looked at Dreams sideways. It was a serpentine study, and then she took in a steadying breath. "Mother then hung herself from the rafters. That's how they found her. Swinging like a leadened sack. The only reason they revived me along with her was to keep her in compliance."

She hesitated a moment and then added, "Urrel had seen my mom and had wanted to claim her for his own. He was that taken with her beauty. First, he broke her—and then he used me to shatter her self-worth into nonrecognition. The fact he's loose right now." She shuddered.

"He's loose, and we're not in Narivous—he's not our problem," I said.

She reluctantly nodded.

"I won't go back," she said again.

"Why do you keep saying that? I have no plans on going back either."

"The letter," she replied stiffly.

There was only one other question I'd asked. At least, only one that stood out. To think on it for too long felt like a dangerous rabbit-hole of what ifs.

"Perhaps this 'yes' is only answering the one question. The one about future telling."

Torti snorted.

"It was the main question I was stuck on while down there," I argued defensively. "She knew to come to my rescue, for which we should all be grateful. I asked, on more than one front, if she could tell futures. This note is simply a direct answer to that."

"It's not. No matter your bonding moment down there, I'm still much more familiar with her. That response is too tightly packed to your second question."

"What was your second question?" Dreams asked.

"Daniel?" Fantasia added.

I looked at the block lettering. It was stiff and without pretense. Masculine almost. I rolled the letter up and placed it back in the vial, putting it under the seat so I wouldn't have to look at it.

"If we speak it, we could possibly ruin it," I said. "Ruth said meddling can alter paths."

"Does that mean you want it?" Torti asked.

"Want what?" Dreams followed.

"Tell us," Fantasia said.

I glanced out the window, at the cars breezing past us on the freeway, glints of colors with complete stories packed within them.

"Ruth saw him as king," Torti answered for me. "And I think he might just want it to happen."

She was right.

I did.

But Ruth had told me this for a reason—she *was* meddling—so I could shift the path and take my own. This was her gift. Allowing me to undo her vision.

Allowing me to choose.

Being King was tempting.

Right now I wanted freedom.

Only time could change my mind.

THE LEGEND

Her life started with promise.

She was born into a family of privilege. Her father a mayor, her mother an heiress. They had money, opportunity, and power.

Both her parents were kind.

Thoughtful.

Loving.

And she was beautiful, classically so, with blue eyes and golden hair.

Her future was carved with light and opportunity, every advantage laid out with care.

Only three moments unraveled her journey.

It cast her in the shadows and blocked out the brightness that should've belonged to her.

The first occurred when she was only ten years old.

Her mother died giving birth to twins—one boy, one girl, both healthy, one life sacrificed for two.

Sorrow eclipsed her father after her mother's death. He

gave up his position in the community and became a wisp of a soul.

In a sense, she lost both parents.

It made her love the twins twice as much. For she discovered that, above all else, she loved children. They made her soul magical.

And then the second moment came. It arrived three years later and shattered her into fragments.

Oscar, her darling, bright, happy brother, was playing in the garden. One minute he was toddling around, overjoyed to explore and laugh, grabbing at flowers, weaving through stems and petals, and the next he ceased to exist.

It was a bee.

A single sting.

A. Bee.

The doctor forewarned that the others could be susceptible to the same fate. That meant Cassandra.

It was a crippling fear.

The girl ripped out the gardens, closed up the house, and banished fresh air from spring to fall, all in an attempt to save her sister who had, in time, become one half of her heart. Oscar was the other. She'd forever be a partial person.

Their home grew dark and stale.

Her father lacked the stamina to contradict her.

And life held steady for three more fragile years.

And then the third moment—which was the most innocent of them all—would make the horrors afterward fall into neat order.

And it started at the market.

THE LOCAL MARKET was her only venture into the outside world. Every Saturday, between the hours of dawn and ten, Sally would travel to town and collect fresh produce.

The townsfolk looked for her. She'd become a sense of warmth—picking up her father's legacy the same way one would collect a small pebble.

Without effort.

On that particular morning, Mr. Ramsey gave her a bag of apples at a fraction of the price, and it was after Sally paid him with a grateful smile that she saw *her*.

In a town the size of Crow, everybody knew everybody. So anyone new was worth noticing.

And there was something about the newcomer's appearance that made Sally freeze.

The girl's heart-shaped face held a splattering of freckles and her brown hair fell in unruly waves down her back, matted and tangled, unkempt in a neglected sort of way.

She was wild, dirty, and strikingly beautiful.

In her hands, she held a potato.

She was tracing it with her fingers, her features scrunched in deep concentration. Mrs. Miller stood silently behind her table, a false smile plastered on her face, directly contradicting the frown creasing her brow. She kept glancing at the knapsack slung across the girl's slight frame.

Suspecting a thief, no doubt.

The girl didn't speak, but her lips were moving. Almost as if she were talking to herself but had forgotten to use volume. She rolled the potato between her hands.

Meanwhile, Mrs. Miller darkened, the way she was known to do. A widow for the past decade, she was a shrew through necessity, and cold through life experiences.

"You don't need to be handling all my produce, child. Pick one and move on. I got customers to attend to."

Sally expected the girl to obey. She had a brow-beaten way to her. Only the girl surprised her, growing in height, a slight haughtiness amongst the shambles.

"I see no one else," she made a show of looking around, pausing when she raked her gaze on Sally, before matching Mrs. Miller's scrutiny. "Besides, I plan on paying for the potato —once I've found the right one—so that would make me a customer, as well."

Sally would've placed her around nine or ten, but she spoke like an adult.

Mrs. Miller's chest swelled and she put her spindly hand on her non-existent hip. She was the shape of a cattail, her head making up most of her body. Pride was her most revered possession and she yanked the potato out of the girl's hand. "I don't appreciate a smart mouth. You weren't gonna pay for it anyhow. Know how I know?" She leaned in and bared her yellow teeth. "You look like a swindler. Now go on and get out of here. I don't need your business."

The girl didn't wilt.

She stood straighter.

But she did obey. Wordlessly.

She walked off, her worn shoes making a soft slapping noise against the pavement, her spine ramrod stiff.

Sally found herself running after her, catching her by her tattered sleeve as they turned the corner.

The girl turned and the air around Sally shifted. It grew fuzzy. The defiant girl threw her chin out and let her eyes blaze with rage.

"I'm sorry, Miss," Sally started. "I don't mean to intrude —"

"Then don't."

Sally tried on a smile. The girl took a step away.

"You're angry, but it's not at me," Sally said. "So, I'll forgive you for your rudeness, and in turn, explain that Mrs. Miller is rather rude too—to everyone. It's not just you."

"And that's supposed to make me feel better?"

"It's not supposed to make you feel worse."

The girl chewed on that, and then nodded. "Fair enough." She kicked a rock near her feet. "I wasn't going to steal from her," she muttered. "In case you were wondering."

"I wasn't. You don't seem like a thief."

"Ha!" She snorted. "I'm the picture of a thief. You couldn't paint a more realistic one if you tried."

"That seems a bit harsh."

"It's the truth." She shrugged. "I have an untrustworthy way about me."

"Why would you say that?"

She blinked blankly. "Because it's the truth."

"So, you're saying you're a thief?"

"No. I don't steal."

"Then you're dishonest?"

She shook her head so vehemently that her dirty hair fanned around her face.

"Then why on earth would you say you have an untrustworthy way about you?"

"Just ... because." Her words remained incomplete. Sally had the impression someone unkind was influencing her.

"It's rather simple," Sally started, "either you're a liar or a crook, and if you're neither of those things, that would, indeed, place you in the honest camp. Untrustworthy doesn't have an appearance, it is an action. And for someone to go against that logic—why, it's a reflection on them, not on you. I assure you, you do not have an untrustworthy way about you. I'm good at reading people."

She scrunched her brow. "That sounds reasonable," she conceded. "I believe that."

"I'm glad, because it's true."

There was a subtle unthawing that took place as the girl lost her hostility. Sally knew that she'd taken a liking to her.

As was usually the way.

Everyone liked Sally.

"Are you from around here?" Sally asked, eager to keep talking to this girl. It's like she wanted to hold her together, and attempted to through words. "My name is Sally, by the way."

"Um, hi." She clicked her tongue, almost like a nervous tick. "You're very bright."

Bright? That was a peculiar adjective.

"I'm good with my studies," Sally said modestly.

"Oh, um, that's not ..." the girl cut herself off, a blush followed by an awkward silence.

"And what is your name?" Sally pressed, eager to fill in the blanks.

She shook her head. "I'm not supposed to be talking to anyone," she said. And as if she forgot herself, did a quick check over her shoulder. "And I'm most certainly not to say my name."

"It's only a name. Surely there's no harm in that."

"I was told not to talk to anyone," she reiterated.

"You were talking to Mrs. Miller," Sally reminded her.

"But I didn't tell her my name." And then her whole demeanor wilted. "I needed that potato," she added bitterly.

"Well, perhaps I can collect it for you?"

She narrowed her eyes and ran her hands along her dirty dress, taking a timid step back. "Why are you being nice? You don't even know me."

"People are mean for absolutely no reason other than the push of a bad day, wouldn't you say so?"

She nodded.

"Then why can't I be nice for similar reasons? Simply because I want to?"

There was a pregnant pause. The girl looked back from where she came to the booth that lay hidden behind the corner.

"I'm not supposed to accept any help," she finally said.

"Who says we'll tell anyone?"

The girl fought a smile.

"So, it's settled then. I'll go back and buy you a potato."

"No," she shook her head. "Not any potato, but *that* potato."

"Like, specifically so?"

"Yes."

"I don't—"

"That one was perfect. I studied it, I know. It was my pride that stopped me from kowtowing to that bitter keeper of spuds," she spat.

She must've been nine or ten going on fifty-six, Sally decided.

"But potatoes don't need to be perfect."

"For me they do. I need *that* potato. It has five eyes on it, no more, no less, and the skin is of dirt that clings to a shoe but doesn't cause it to stick. And its shape, it's...." she started to motion with her hands, as if she committed the potato's lines to memories. "It needs to be completely oval, and fit comfortably between my two hands."

This peculiar request seemed to match this peculiar girl.

"I always thought six eyes made for the perfect potato," Sally kidded.

"That's what I thought too! But Father says it must be five. Even though it seems to go against the nature of the potato to grow only five."

"Um, well." Sally shifted on her feet. She'd attempted to be funny, and this serious girl had taken her very seriously. "Why does your dad care?"

"He expects perfection. Something I can never seem to do," she added bitterly. "He told me to come back with a proper specimen to study. What I make isn't good enough and that potato is exactly what he wants."

It should've been funny, this exchange Sally thought, except for the desperate pull around the girl's eyes.

"Vegetables are wild creatures," Sally said. "Perfection doesn't exist. All that matters is that they are hearty and edible. The earth shapes them—not the gardener."

"It's what he says." She shrugged. "This is my lesson."

Sally wanted to say her father was being unreasonable, but the strain in the child's posture made her hold her tongue. "Okay, I'll do my best. Do you remember where you set it down?"

"It's on the bottom right, maybe one or two up?"

"And it has five eyes?"

She brightened. "Yes."

"No more, no less," Sally confirmed.

She was rewarded with a brilliant smile of neat, perfectly white teeth.

"Will you hold these for me?"

The girl took the sack of apples.

"Feel free to take one if you want. I might've even picked out a perfect one." Sally winked, but the girl was stoic in her seriousness.

Sally moved swiftly away, eager to be near and far, a polarized reaction.

She made a quick inspection of Mrs. Miller's booth and landed on what she thought was the potato in question. She paid and returned with the prized possession in hand.

The girl was bouncing from foot to foot and eagerly

grabbed it from Sally's hand. She moved her lips as she silently counted the eyes.

She'd already set Sally's bag down, the top of which was folded over. Her expression was determined. "Thank you," she said in a clipped tone, and then turned and took off at a fast walk.

Sally would've called for her but she recognized the child's urgency.

Whatever was waiting couldn't wait any longer.

It wasn't until later, when Sally had made it home, that she realized that the girl had left behind more than a sack full of apples.

She left behind questions.

And three potatoes in exchange for the perfect one.

She noticed they all had six eyes.

And in Sally's opinion, they were far superior.

SALLY WENT to the market the following Saturday. With her, she carried a pair of shoes in her bag.

They were too small for her and Cassandra always insisted on new pairs. She was a picky child who loved frills and lace—and being she was practically banished to the indoors come spring when bees were busy doing all the things bees do, spoiling was not only accepted, but a necessity.

So these shoes should, for all intents and purposes, go to someone who could use them. And if anyone could use them, it was the girl.

Sure enough, Sally spotted her lingering along the fringes after a few hours of idle wait.

"I was hoping you'd be here," Sally said on approach.

"Me too," the girl admitted. "I realized I didn't properly thank you."

"You said thank you."

She shook her head. "I didn't thank you well enough."

"It was well enough for me and, besides, you gave me three perfect potatoes."

"Those potatoes had six eyes, not five, so they're not perfect."

"Says you."

"Says my father. But that's not why I'm here." She nipped her lip and rooted around in her bag. "I can't stay but a moment—"

"Why is that?"

She checked over her shoulder. "I worry the others might check on me—and that they'll see you."

"Is that a bad thing?"

She cleared her throat. "It could be. You're very bright. But that's not to concern you—I wanted to give you these, as a proper thanks." She produced, not one, but two, oranges. Sally gasped.

"Is something wrong? Do you not like oranges?"

"No. I love citrus. It's my favorite. But I can't possibly accept these," Sally said. She skimmed over the girl, her clothes, her unkemptness. "These are difficult to find and are very expensive." She took a step away. Perhaps this girl was a thief?

As if she understood Sally's trajectory, she went on the defense. "I grew these," she said. "I didn't take them, if that's what you're wondering."

"You can't grow these in Oregon."

Her face split in half, and Sally swore her eyes glinted. "I can." She put such a heavy stress on I, it nearly came with its own punctuation. "I can grow anything, anything at all. It doesn't matter the climate or the conditions, if it's a plant, I can manage it."

"An impressive talent."

The girl shrugged.

"This is an incredible gift," Sally said, taking the oranges, "and reminds me, I have something for you too."

The girl cocked her head, surprised. Sally produced the shoes, and if she ever needed an image of joy—it flashed on this girl's face with clear abandon.

"Tuesday, at noon? Can you come back?" she asked.

Sally nodded, already looking forward to it. Still not knowing her name, and realizing it didn't matter.

SHE WASN'T WEARING the shoes. That's the first thing Sally noticed. The second, she was lighter in spirit.

Happy.

And although she wore the same clothing as before, only dirtier and more dismayed, her joy was transformative.

Not even the smudges on her freckled face could pull away from it. She lit up from the inside.

And it looked in direct correlation to Sally, as if she'd found a reason for happiness and it was solely orbiting around her.

She nearly skipped over to Sally, who stood on the sidewalk under a big leaf maple in full foliage. It was then she noticed how swiftly she moved, the jaunt of her step, like an exuberant fawn.

There were less people around, the market was never busy on Tuesdays.

"Hey," she said. "Those shoes were a big hit."

Sally looked at her feet, and the girl smiled sheepishly.

"I gave them to my friend," she confessed. "She needed

them more than me. She can go outside now. She couldn't before. It was too dangerous since her skin is ..." she seemed to catch herself. "Her skin is sensitive. I've never seen her so happy."

"Well, I'm glad the shoes went to a good person. Does this friend live near you?"

"With me," she clarified. "Along with her two sisters."

"And her parents?"

She shook her head. "Dead," she clarified.

"Oh ... I'm so sorry. I lost my mother too."

"Me too."

Sally swallowed. It was suddenly very hard to do. Their joy quickly turned to sorrow. Sally wanted to undo it. "Well," she wiped her hands on her dress and reached for the bag she had set near her feet. Inside, there were clothes and bonnets, another set of shoes, even a doll—something she grabbed only as an afterthought.

"I packed up a bunch of stuff we were no longer using and thought maybe you'd like to have it."

The girl tentatively peered inside, and then kneeled to get a closer look. The first thing she pulled out was the doll.

It was a rag doll. Nothing fancy, but endearing to Sally. Truth of it, it had been one of her favorites—but she was happy to let it go.

The girl rolled it over in her hands, taking it in. She held it much the same as she held the potato, with careful regard, running her fingers over the plains of her face, the button eyes, the red woven hair.

"My nursemaid stitched my name into the bottom of the foot, but I figured you could undo it if you wanted to."

"This is wonderful."

"Really?" Sally let out a hefty breath. "I was worried you

wouldn't like it, but figured it couldn't hurt. And if there are others in your home ... perhaps they'd enjoy it too?"

"Fridge will love this."

"Fridge? Is that the name of one of your friends? It's very unique."

"Kind of. It's a nickname."

"Ah, I see." Sally waited, and then asked, "Will you tell me your name?"

"I can't."

"Well, we must find something to call you. The girl from the market doesn't seem right when addressing a friend."

"I'm a friend?"

"Well, yes. I'd like to think so."

She pinched her lip. "But you barely know me."

"I'm getting to know you. And so far, I like you. You have good energy."

The girl stood and shuffled her feet.

"Thorn," she finally said. "My name is Thorn, but don't tell anyone I told you." And that's when she handed over her knapsack. "This is for you. For the shoes."

Inside the bag was a marvel of treasures. Bananas, limes, oranges, even a pineapple. A fresh pineapple. *A pineapple*! And then there were others, she had no idea their names. They looked exotic and marvelous. She grabbed one and held it out in an evaluating position.

"That's a pomegranate," Thorn explained. "And there are mangos and kiwis too. I grew them all. I can grow anything."

Sally was speechless.

Thorn didn't show up the next week. Or the one thereafter. Desperation to see her again overtook Sally and she began to travel to the market every day in an attempt to locate her.

It wasn't until she arrived on a sleepy Thursday morning, that she finally caught sight of her.

She wasn't alone however.

A woman with wild blonde hair, frazzled and unruly, stood next to her.

Sally began to wave, but stopped mid-way, her hand suspended, when Thorn locked eyes with her. She gave a quick shake of the head in warning, and Sally lowered her hand—although she didn't act quick enough.

The blonde caught the movement, and her wild crazy face with eyes so blue they made Sally's look dark, alighted. They were matched, look for look.

She said something, Sally saw her lips move, but her message was a mystery.

And then Thorn kicked that woman's foot, and she glanced down.

Thorn took that moment to lip the words "run," and had it not been for the darkness embedded in her face, Sally would've disobeyed.

But in that moment she was afraid.

So she did as she was told.

She fled.

By the time she made it to her house, however, she realized that she may have made a misstep.

For although she couldn't see them, she was under the impression they saw her.

And perhaps had even followed her home.

It was six in the morning when Sally woke.

A soft buzzing broke the stillness; it cut the film of night. She looked at her window, and her lungs froze when the curtains billowed.

She never opened windows.

It was a steadfast rule of hers. Windows were a barrier between safe and unsafe.

She blinked, circling her thoughts in slow gears, when the softest of touches tickled near the base of her thumb. It took an achingly long time to look down as dread called. When she did, her whole body screamed—although her mouth remained silent.

A bee was tracing a path.

A bee.

A. Bee.

But it was nightfall. Bees weren't active at night.

But it was there, moving in short, stubby jaunts—awkward and non-fluid.

"I have a proposition for you," a woman's voice said. It seemed to transcend the thickness coating her ears—the blood swooshing in her head slugging down time and making the seconds achingly long.

Sally turned her head and saw a woman standing in her room. Although she was eclipsed by darkness, the unruliness of her hair revealed who she was: the wild woman from the market—the one with Thorn. As her eyes adjusted, she spotted something familiar in her hands.

"Your lore," she said, waving the doll. "And it was very helpful for you to have your name written on the bottom of her foot. It made finding you, finding your story, just a bit easier."

She smiled, no teeth were showing.

"You're beloved here—the tragic story of a mother lost too soon, a fallen mayor, a bee sting with the most horrific consequences." She sighed and leaned against the wall. "I'm guessing that's why the yard looks as it does, barren, dead. You don't want any of those around you and your remaining sibling."

Sally kept still—the weight of the bee holding her stationary.

"And I'm guessing from your generous gifts, that you may care for your younger sibling more than you care for yourself? Am I right?" Her eyes went white and black at the same time. Light and shadow.

The blankets pulled away on their own accord, and Sally fought the urge to grab them, to use them as a shield.

The bee from Sally's hand lifted and flew violently against the wall.

It was unnatural.

"I'm a telekinetic, pet," she purred. "It was the way of my brightness, of my coloring, of my death. Oh, but you. You are dazzling to the eyes. Your light is strong. Perhaps we can give you even greater gifts."

Sally held no words. She was lodged in her nightmare. Lodged. This wasn't real.

No. Not real.

She started to shake her head, when the window slammed shut. A pressure pushed hard against her back.

It was moments before she realized she was being held in place, her spine pressed tightly to the headboard.

Maybe this wasn't a nightmare.

Because nightmares didn't tamper with other senses.

And she could smell her own fear.

A man approached from the depths of the hallway. Although he was wholly foreign, there was something familiar in his presence.

"This is the one?" he asked.

"Yes, Urrel. This is the one."

He looked at her. He who absorbed the darkness, it's as if it sank into him.

Part devil, part man, fully shadowed.

He gave a noncommittal, "Humph."

"It's amazing how we stumble across marvelous light, isn't it?" she asked.

"It's only marvelous if she turns out as expected."

He smirked. His features were slowly coming into focus. "Regardless of her magic, perhaps she can look after the others. I don't have time for them and since you failed to mother them properly, we could use a better resource."

She threw her head back with a laugh. "And what on earth made you think I was a proper parental figure? Did I ever support that inane idea? No. I told you the opposite. Showed you the opposite. I was never going to be a qualified mother to your children."

"Child," he corrected. "The other three are orphans I kindly took in."

"So you say."

"Are you implying something, Tipper?"

"I'm always implying," she bit back, her lips curled into a snarl. "Always thinking, planning, plotting. That's why you chose me. For my conniving ability and my analytical brain—so I could help undo the mess you made with that poison girl."

"The mess I made?" He leaned in, breath to breath, their noses practically touched. "I was experimenting as a good scientist does. I had no idea it would do what it did."

"Keep telling yourself that, Urrel."

They continued to speak around Sally.

Revealing history that had no context. She was as much in the dark as she was in the nightfall.

"You are an ungrateful bitch. I saved you from the gallows.

You were on the cusp of being lynched and hanged, and what did I do? I gave you a new start, and this is how you talk to me?"

"Ungrateful? Don't insult my intellect by pretending it was a selfless act. You help me, I help you. You collected me for my mind."

"A mind most men are quick to overlook considering you're nothing but a female."

"Am I to commend you for overlooking my gender? Does that make you feel superior? Do you need the praise, poppet?"

He growled.

"Female or not, you need me." She jabbed his chest, and he reluctantly took it. He radiated a wrath, wanting to bite at her—but something inside him froze. "And after tonight, you will never question my abilities again, for this girl," she pointed at Sally without taking her eyes away from Urrel, "will be a crown jewel in your arsenal. She will break into the minds of humans, remove our poverty, and put us on a path of total dominance."

"You better be right on this."

"I dare say, I'll be more right than you were on that poison child you spoiled."

A thick shadow bloomed over him, and Sally—whose focus pivoted between the two—centered on him. Always intuitive, she saw a flicker of something she recognized.

It looked like fear.

Perhaps a slipping of control.

Tipper was to follow his lead, only she wasn't entirely right in the head to make for a proper sheep.

"Enough of that. Bring her downstairs and see to it she's dressed decently." He pivoted on his heel and began to stalk away, his heavy boots rattling the walls and making the doorknob shake. It seemed to ricochet through her bones, and she wondered where her own father was, why he couldn't hear what was happening in their own home.

She was afraid.

For her father.

For her sister.

For herself.

Urrel returned on a second thought, his stride just as powerful—perhaps even more so. He wagged his finger, like a man disciplining a child. "And be warned, Tipper, if this doesn't work, you will suffer the consequences."

"Which are?" She raised her brow.

"Let's leave it unsaid." He stroked her cheek and she withered from his touch. For once she showed a crack in her armor —one built on insanity and lack of regard. "Oh, and so we're clear, only human minds?"

"As I said before, yes. My answer hasn't changed."

He grunted.

"But the more you ask, the more I suspect you're hiding something. Something big." She tried to play it off innocently.

There was nothing innocent about it.

He narrowed his gaze. "Stop. Testing. Me. You. Infuriating. Woman. My thoughts are my own—and I damn well expect them to remain that way."

She threw up her hands. "Yes, Of course. Only human minds, you daft man! I wouldn't want someone poking around in my head either."

As soon as he left, Tipper released her telekinetic hold. "No matter the results," she whispered in Sally's ear. "No matter your abilities, if you can get into our minds—always pretend otherwise. This is your one warning."

Tipper walked off, the dark shapes of the hallway drinking in her inky frame.

Sally dressed and went downstairs, where a collection of bodies waited for her.

Thorn and three other girls. One with red hair, another

with black, and one with white stood huddled toward the back of the sitting room.

They were all peculiar.

In different ways.

Thorn refused to look at Sally.

They were so small compared to Urrel, who swallowed up the entire couch, spanning his arms along the length of it, making certain no one was comfortable alongside him.

Sally's eyes drifted to her father's high-back chair and her breath caught in her throat.

Cassandra was sitting there, silent as a mouse, eyes as big as fear itself. A bee ran the length of her arm. Sally had warned her enough, she was properly afraid.

The room spun.

"You're both coming with us," Tipper said. "You have no option, so don't try to challenge us."

"My father...?" Sally started.

"Can't help you now," Urrel snapped.

She was too petrified to ask why.

"We will take the fear away," Tipper said. "We will make her invincible. Immortalize her. Immortalize you. We will give you the greatest gift." She breathed into her ear, "Freedom from death."

"You carry the girl," Urrel ordered Sally, standing with authority, the children falling in place behind him.

He walked out of the room.

Sally grabbed Cassandra and followed.

For was there even really a choice?

ACKNOWLEDGMENTS

It always marvels me when I finish a book.

I don't know why, but it almost comes as a surprise. Here's this wondrous thing I managed to put together, word by painstaking word, and somehow it (hopefully) creates a story that is both immersible and enjoyable.

So much energy, heart, and time goes into a project like this. It's daunting, until all of a sudden it isn't.

And most of the time it's lonesome work, but not always. Not towards the end. Not when you need feedback and encouragement.

I've been blessed with lots of encouragement.

And in this world, you can never have enough gratitude.

That's why I love this section.

I not only get to reflect that I did it again (always a wow), but I get to talk about the people who helped me—either by reading my words (and giving their honest, raw feedback) or simply by loving me when I've had a hard time loving myself.

So let me begin.

Chris. I know this process frustrates you. I'm reclusive. I'm moody. I hide for hours on end in my office. Yet you tolerate it and still manage to love me. How I appreciate you. Thank you for supporting this dream of mine. For making me feel talented. For uplifting me when I'm down.

JD, you wouldn't let me give up, even when I wanted to. You stepped in, read this book and gave me the feedback I desperately needed. You encouraged me to keep going when I didn't think I had it in me.

You wouldn't let me quit.

You're a treasure in my life, and I hope you know just how much you mean to me. You make this world a better place simply by being in it.

To Stephanie, my beta. Girl, I love your brain. I've said it before—and I'll say it again—the idea of releasing a book without your eyes on it terrifies me. Thank you for carving time out of your busy schedule to work on this project. You've got a lot on your plate, and the fact you made room for Shadows only amplifies my gratitude. I value you. Appreciate you. All the things.

Lisa Lee, my fabulous editor, your mind is another one I'm grateful for. You were an unexpected find on this journey, and it makes me marvel at how wonderful things (and people!) often come about. Thank you for editing this book, answering my questions, and being so fantastic on this project. You were responsive and quick to help me with my anxieties, and always had a kind word to say. I feel lucky to have found you.

JV Cover Arts. What can I say? Your work is incredible. From the interior embellishments to the glorious covers, I look at your designs and I'm struck by your talent. Thank you for all your help on this project.

Rachel, Sonja, Brittany and Todd. You guys are shining examples of the best this world has to offer. Thank you for being wonderful friends. For standing up for me. For supporting me. For loving the parts of me I've struggled to love myself.

And to all my readers.

Thank you for staying with me on this story.

About the Author

J.M. Muller is the author of the *Colors of Immortality* series. When she's not writing, she's tending to all the heartbeats that fill her with joy.

www.jmmuller.com

Milton Keynes UK
Ingram Content Group UK Ltd.
UKHW011047240124
436611UK00001B/41

9 798989 581528